MW00749449

The Muse

of

Fire

Carol M. Cram

New Arcadia Publishing

Paperback edition is published by New Arcadia Publishing, Bowen Island

e-book edition is published by Kindle Press

www.newarcadiapublishing.com

ISBN-13: 978-0-9810241-4-1
ISBN-10: 0-9810241-4-1

Printed in Canada

For my mother, who first introduced me
to Shakespeare and the delights of language

O for a Muse of fire, that would ascend
The brightest heaven of invention,
A kingdom for a stage, princes to act
And monarchs to behold the swelling scene!

Henry V (Prologue, 1–4)

Chapter One

London, March 1808

For beauty lives with kindness.
Love doth to her eyes repair,
To help him of his blindness,
And, being help'd, inhabits there.

The Two Gentlemen of Verona (4.2.44–47)

Grace's mother used to say that London was the center of the world — sanctuary for the very best and worst of humanity. Grace grew up imagining the city as the place where dreams happened.

How wrong she'd been.

In the overheated sitting room, a roaring fire slicked her forehead with sweat, making her long for the fresh sea air of home. Her father loathed the cold. If he came back to find the fire burning low, he'd rail at her, remind her of her duty, accuse her of ingratitude. A log fell with sparks crackling; the clock ticked too slowly toward bedtime, another dreary day winding down. Grace read a few more pages of her book and then slipped it behind a sofa cushion and stood.

She might as well go upstairs. He'd not be home for at least another hour, and it wasn't as if they had anything to say to each other.

She was just about to open the sitting room door that led to the vestibule and the stairs when she heard her father's walking stick clatter against the iron railing bordering the pavement outside. He'd never come home this early. Grace stared at the closed door—her barrier between blessed silence and her father's peevish noise. Seconds later, she heard the front door swing open and bounce back against the coatrack before slamming shut. An umbrella banged to the floor.

"Damn me! Must I call for a candle in my own home?"

Sighing, Grace opened the door. Her father filled the vestibule with brandy fumes and malice. When she tried to duck around him to reach the stairs, he flung out one arm with drunken strength and barred her way.

"I'm going to bed," she said. "Please, let me pass."

He swayed backward, clutching at the doorframe to steady himself. "Why were *you* the one to live?" he asked. In the flickering candlelight spilling out from the sitting room, Grace saw rage chase grief across his swollen face.

"It was an accident, Father. You know that."

"All I know is that you're here and she's not."

Grace was almost past him when he drove his fist into her ribs and then let go of the doorframe and swung at her head, catching the skin at her hairline with the sharp edge of a heavy gold ring. For a few seconds, Grace stopped dead, too shocked to move. He'd never laid hands on her before. When his third punch went wide and he crashed to the floor, she wrenched open the front door and bolted into the night.

Within minutes, the frigid air dried the blood on her face and seeped through her gown, sucking at the pain left by his blows. Clouds layered like dough filled the dark sky, blotting out the stars. In the three months since coming up from the country, Grace had yet to see stars in London.

She ran for many minutes through silent streets, then busy streets, most dark, a few lit with sputtering gas lamps. The crowds grew thicker the farther she ran—south toward the river, she thought, but she couldn't be sure. No one looked at her, not even the gentlemen strolling past, top hats gleaming in the flare of passing torches. She ran through mud from rain stopped an hour since and likely to start again before she found shelter. The first day of spring had just passed, yet the air felt more December than March. She should have taken her cloak from the rack by the door after her father tripped over his own feet and sprawled across the floor—knocked out, passed out, dead? That last possibility was too wicked to consider and too much to hope for.

A man reeled out of an alleyway and planted himself directly in her path. He stank of gin and the privy.

"Yer out late."

Grace suddenly realized the enormity of what she'd done. London at night was not the bustling, cosmopolitan, clanking place she glimpsed from carriage windows in full daylight. At night, the streets came alive again but with people Grace knew nothing about—what they did, where they went, how they lived.

"Excuse me, sir. I wish to pass."

"Ooh, a lady, are ye? A toffer, I expect. Ain't the normal course of things to see your sort out alone, but it takes all kinds. What's yer price?"

"I don't know what you refer to, sir." Why would he not let her pass? What did he want? The stench of him closed her throat in a gag.

"Lost yer cock-bawd, have ye?"

Grace had never heard such words, but she guessed their meaning and blushed in the darkness. "Please, let me pass."

"Ah, no, I don't think I be inclined to do that." He seized her bare arm just above the elbow, grinding his fingers into her flesh, marking her with new bruises. She tried to wrench herself free, then gasped at the sharp pain in her ribs. He pulled her closer, his mouth now inches from hers.

"Give us a kiss, dearie. There's a girl."

She twisted her head away, but he was strong, his hands like steel talons. As he started pushing her back toward the alleyway, her gown tangled around her legs, throwing her off balance. Was this the worst of humanity that her mother had spoken of? First her father, and now this brute?

Enough.

The word grabbed hold of her thoughts and snapped at her fear. She was taller than the filthy man, who held her as though she were a helpless animal trembling at an unknown fate. How dare he?

To take arms against a sea of trouble . . .

How many hours had she spent with her mother reading and rereading that play, studying it and breathing life into Shakespeare's lines? Her mother once told her how the great Mrs. Siddons herself had sometimes donned a long black cloak and played Hamlet. Grace had been captivated and wanted her mother to tell her more. But as usual, when Grace pushed too hard about the past, her mother turned away and would not speak further. For weeks after, she refused to open the worn volume of Shakespeare, demanding that Grace concentrate on her needlework and learn to be a wife.

Grief for her mother and hatred for the new life she found herself in flooded Grace with strength. While the man was still laughing at having secured his prey, she raised her free elbow and jammed it full into his face. Teeth snapped against bone, and a howl of pain shredded the night. He let go of her so suddenly that she staggered backward, then turned and darted across the street, just missing an oncoming carriage. She veered into another street — this one empty of people. She had to get back to a more crowded area, perhaps find the constables. And tell them what? All they could do was return her to her father's house, bedraggled and cold. Her word would count as nothing against the testimony of Mr. Tobias Johnson, a respected man of property from the West Country.

Lights glowed up ahead. How could there be so many people in London but no one to help her? A knife-blade agony sliced across her chest, and her knees buckled, hitting the slick cobblestones with a smack. More bruises, but what did that signify now? She gave in to the shivering, the clattering of her teeth sounding as loud in her head as the carriage rattling past the cross street up ahead. She rested her hot, wet cheek against her arm. *Foolish girl.* That's what her father would say, and he'd be right. Where did she expect to go — a woman of her class alone in London at night? The street was silent now, plunged into comforting darkness, her assailant long gone. Even if he stumbled within a yard of her, he'd not see her.

She would have to go back to her father's house eventually. But for just a little while longer, it felt good to stay still and alone.

ဆဝ

Ned made one last circuit backstage at the Theatre Royal, Covent Garden. The prompter, the callboys, and the scene changers had all gone home, and he'd already checked the dressing rooms and made sure the props were put back in the property room and the painted flies were stored upright. Ned loved the theater best late at night. Like an exhausted dowager, the massive building settled itself for quiet after the noisy delights of the evening performance. Snuffed candles nestled in their metal flashings, machinery stopped clanking and creaking, and all the performers tottered off to drink and bed.

Mr. John Philip Kemble himself had promoted Ned from scene changer to stage manager at the beginning of the season, and Ned was determined to prove his worth. Before getting taken on at the theater, Ned had toiled in one dirty job after another—shoveling coal, stacking wood, and even for a few terrible months scraping out and carting away night soil. At the theater, Ned spent every evening from September to May in a blaze of light and heat. He liked to think of himself as the linchpin around which every performance at the theater revolved—actors and actresses, stage machinists and scene changers, callboys, dancers, musicians, even animals when they had them, which thank God wasn't every night.

Tonight, he'd his hands full when Thomas Renfrew had drowned his nerves with so much gin he'd barely made it through his first scene as Horatio before lurching into the wings and splashing vomit all over Ned's new boots. Fortunately, this time, Mr. Kemble had been too preoccupied playing Hamlet to an adoring audience to notice Renfrew's shaking hands and stinking breath. Kemble had warned Ned before about keeping Renfrew sober, and Ned didn't relish another dressing-down from the great man.

He felt his way down the long corridor that led from the wings to the small room next to the stage door.

"Cold as a whore's backside out there," said Mr. Harrison, the stage-door keeper. He nodded toward the door from his overstuffed chair. The chair was covered in thick brocade streaked green with mildew and set as close to a brazier of hot coals as it could get without catching fire. The company joke was that Mr. Harrison would need to be buried with his chair because no one had seen him rise from it in ten years.

"I'd have thought whores had warm backsides," Ned said. He cracked open the door leading out of the theater onto Bow Street. A swirl of damp air tossed bits of rubbish across the wooden floorboards.

"What do you know about it? The talk round here is that you keep away from the women."

"I'm dead on me feet after a night's work. Got no time for 'em."

"Fine lad like you? When I was your age . . ."

"Good night, Mr. H."

Ned stepped into the street and shut the door behind him. He'd heard Mr. Harrison's stories many times — of how in his day he'd had ladies clamoring for a glimpse of him leaving this very stage door. And it didn't do to get him started on all the actresses he'd had his way with. Ned had no desire to be like Mr. Harrison, but if Olympia ever showed any inclination . . .

But that thought was best put out of its misery. Beautiful, sparkling Olympia, who lit up the stage every night in comic roles and breeches parts, wasn't for the likes of him. Besides, she was too busy being taken in by Renfrew, the poncy bugger.

Out on the street, a carriage rumbled past, splashing Ned with cold mud. He had no illusions about the swells. For every carriage carrying a respectable couple away from the theater, another passed with men stuck on ladies who'd never be wives. Some of the women who traded flesh for guineas maintained expensive homes in Mayfair and commanded their own stable of servants, but most plied their wares in foul alleyways, in the boxes at the theater, and behind bushes in the parks. Ned knew all about them. They had his pity but rarely his custom. He wasn't like his friend Alec.

Ned headed toward his lodgings on Hart Street. No one at the Foundling Hospital where Ned and Alec spent six years of their short childhoods had held out much hope for the royally christened Edward Plantagenet. Ned would have liked a commoner name — Parker or Brown or Bishop, like Alec Bishop. He knew of one boy they'd christened William Shakespeare and another Julius Caesar. The girls had gotten off easier, although Ned remembered a girl named Prudence Cock. She'd died a few days shy of her fifth birthday, which was perhaps a blessing.

Halfway along Bow Street, Ned tripped over something soft lying in his path. He exhaled a curse. There had been talk of installing gas lamps to light up London's murky streets, but apart from some of the broadest thoroughfares, most of London was blacker than a whore's despair — never mind her backside. Nothing was visible in front of him, but he sensed movement. A child perhaps. How many children had he seen die? Too many to remember — and it was a big reason he steered clear of the whores.

He dropped to his knees.

"Are you hurt?"

The voice that answered was female and not a child.

"Leave me alone."

In the darkness, Ned was just able to make out a long body stretched across the narrow strip of pavement. It — she — seemed to be dressed only in a dark gown — the fair skin of one bare arm faintly glimmering. He reached out and touched it, felt it tremble in the bone-damp chill.

"You're freezing," he said.

"Please, go away." Her accent sounded posh, not rough like his. What kind of a lady lay bare armed in the middle of the street? Well, he wasn't the kind of man to just leave her there.

"'Ere, let's get you up." Ned tried hooking his arm around her waist. She pulled away, but when he did not increase the pressure, letting her understand with the lightness of his touch that he meant her no harm, her muscles relaxed a fraction.

"What do you want with me?"

"Come on. I'll get you somewhere warm."

"I'm not what you think."

"What? Oh!" Ned dropped her arm, thankful for the darkness. "I didn't mean that," he said. "I don't need, I mean, I weren't looking for . . ."

He heard a soft, wet sound different from the ones she'd made before. He leaned closer, smelled blood and dirt but no gin, and realized she was laughing.

9

"I don't suppose I could go much lower," she said, "but I assure you I am respectable." Her laughter stopped, and Ned sensed fear. "You will not harm me?"

"I'll get you someplace warm and fix you up. I ain't one to leave a helpless female in the gutter."

"Helpless?" She shifted her body away from him again, wriggling to loosen his grasp on her arm. "I'm not helpless."

"Maybe not, but it ain't weak to take help when it's offered, like."

To his relief, she stopped moving. "I suppose you are right. I am very cold. Do you know of a place where I may go to get warm?" She sounded remarkably matter-of-fact, like it was the most natural thing in the world for her to be lying in a tangled heap in the mud. Ned held her arm as she clambered to her feet. A groan, quickly suppressed, made him shudder. Someone had hurt her badly. He peered around the dark street. Whoever had done it might not be far off, and Ned had no wish to get between an enraged cock-bawd and his whore. She said she was respectable, but she would say that, wouldn't she? He wasn't worried about taking on most any man, but he didn't want to make things worse for the girl.

She seemed to sense his nervousness. "Thank you for helping me up. I can make my own way now."

Ned wrapped one arm around her shoulders, taking care to avoid touching her ribs, which he suspected were bruised, maybe even broken. "Don't be daft. I ain't leaving you out 'ere." He'd take her back to his lodgings and stay close to her side. Alec would laugh at him—fancy hardworking, pure-hearted Ned bringing a woman back to their room! But Ned wasn't going to let Alec stop him from doing what was right.

Together they shuffled forward. For a moment, the girl leaned against him, the top of her head even with his chin, making her tall for a female. He tightened his hold. She took another few steps, and then her knees gave way. He swept her into his arms, marveling at how light she was—like a bundle of dry sticks but with hard angles. One of her elbows poked his stomach. She winced when he adjusted his grip.

The moon broke free of the clouds, and he saw her face for the first time. Dried blood streaked her forehead, the cut near her forehead jagged. "Who did this to you?"

"Does it matter?"

Ned carried her as quickly as he could without jostling her toward a larger street, where gas lamps pierced the gloom. He realized now that she was not a girl, but not yet much of a woman—maybe nineteen or twenty years old. She wore a lady's gown with shiny patches of satin, smooth under his hands. He sometimes helped Mrs. Beecham, the costume mistress at the theater, and knew something about fabrics.

"Where are you taking me?"

"Home."

"And where, may I ask, is home?" She asked the question as if it were the most natural thing in the world that she was a young woman of obvious status, alone in London, dressed in a gown made for the drawing room, her face webbed with blood.

"My lodgings. Hart Street." He was starting to puff with the effort of keeping her still while he walked. "Or have you got somewhere you go at night? Mrs. Gellie's maybe?" He threw out the name of one of Covent Garden's more prosperous madams.

"I am not acquainted with that lady."

Ned almost laughed out loud. Fancy Mrs. Gellie being described as a lady. "Ah well, you did say you're not that sort."

She did not reply, and Ned didn't press her further. If she didn't have a madam, then she must work for a man, which meant he'd best get her out of sight as soon as possible. At least he'd be able to keep her safe until she healed. The next day was Sunday. With the theater closed, he'd have time to get her settled and patched up.

ℬ◯ℭ

Grace had never been carried in a man's arms, or at least not since she was a child. This man was large and broad shouldered—she could tell that much even in the dark. The coat fabric scratching her cheek was wool, thick, but not as fine as what her father wore. She smelled sawdust—he had to be a working man. On his way home from the tavern? Drunk? No. His breath did not stink of spirits—she knew *that* odor better than most. He was definitely not a gentleman. His accent was rough, but he didn't sound mean—not like the first man. His voice had a gentle tone to it, as welcome as silk on her torn nerves.

The man shifted her weight, and she clenched her teeth against pain so new she didn't know what to make of it. A smashing fist—the shock of it connecting with her flesh. Why had her father hit her now, after so many months? She closed her eyes, but that was worse than the darkness of the street. Just above her head, she sensed the man's breath coming fast—blooms of vapor in the darkness. Pain and anger rippled and swelled with equal measure.

They walked for a few more minutes. The man's arms shook with the effort of holding her steady, but he did not falter. Grace had no idea where or how far she'd run before collapsing, but she thought she might have come south toward the Piazza at Covent Garden. A church bell close by tolled one—Saint Paul's, Covent Garden. She knew it was called the Actors' Church because so many actors worshipped there, and many found their final resting place in its quiet churchyard. The man set her down in front of a skinny, tall house abutted on either side with other houses, rough looking, seedy even. A brothel? She knew of such places, although she was not wholly clear about what was done in them. The man held her steady with one thick arm around her shoulders while he unlocked a wooden door.

"Can you manage the stairs, miss?"

She nodded and stepped into total darkness, her only guide his hand on the small of her back. She shuffled forward.

"Bannister's on your left."

She nodded, reached out, gripped the bannister, and then bumped her toes into the lowest step. He followed close behind, his bulk comforting.

"How many floors?" she gasped.

"Three," he said. "Sorry, miss."

She gritted her teeth and continued upward, trusting her feet to find each step. Her thin evening slippers would be ruined after her run through the muddy streets. She almost smiled. Fancy thinking of footwear when here she was climbing stairs in a dark lodging house in front of a man whose face she had not yet seen. As each step brought her closer to an unknown fate, she had to trust that it could not be worse than what she'd left behind in her father's house.

The man reached around her waist to steady her as together they stepped onto a landing. She smelled sawdust again and candle smoke and another sharp smell that reminded her, incongruously, of paint.

"Here we are, miss. I reckon Alec's still out, so we got plenty of room."

They entered a small room and she waited in the darkness while the man fumbled for several minutes with a flint and tinder to coax a flame from the stub of a tallow candle. He held it aloft to reveal two narrow beds — one made, the other a tangle of dirty blankets. A table under the only window held two plates filmed white with grease — the reek of stale bacon still thick. An empty grate crusted black with coal dust nestled inside a small brick fireplace. Plaster walls striped with damp were bare of pictures; pegs held some clothes. Grace saw poverty in the bareness of the room, but not squalor. The men who lived there were employed. She was sure of it and felt less afraid.

"You can have my bed," the man said. "If Alec don't come in, I'll take his."

"And if he does?"

"Then I'll kip on the floor." The man smiled. "Don't worry about me, miss. Best get you settled and warm."

Grace could not say why, but she knew this man would not harm her. His face in the flickering candlelight had an honest, open look, like he'd found satisfaction with who he was and didn't need to hit a woman to be a man. She turned quickly and bumped her thigh against the bedstead. Her gown cushioned the blow, and she felt only a dull thud. She'd had enough of pain for one night.

"Careful, miss." He motioned to the bed that was made up — the brown cover threadbare in places but clean enough, the pillow striped and uncovered. A darkened halo showed where he lay his head every night.

She sat down on the bed; the mattress was hard and thin—nothing like the thick mattress she slept on in her father's house. "You're very kind to have me to your home," she said formally as if she was visiting a new acquaintance in Mayfair.

"Ain't no trouble," he said. "Why don't you lie down and get a bit of sleep? In the morning, I'll bring up water and do somethin' about yer injuries."

"Thank you, Mr. — "

"Ned will do just fine, miss. And I ain't doing nothing more than anyone would."

Grace lay back and lifted her feet with a groan. She knew she should pull off her muddy slippers but could not summon the strength. Instead, she let the man cover her gently with another blanket—this one smelling strongly of sweat. He sat down on the bed opposite and began pulling off his boots, his expression calm in the candlelight. A terrible exhaustion settled over her. She closed her eyes and saw her father's enraged face loom and then recede.

Grace knew she would have to go back to Russell Street. But for now, it was good . . . yes, good . . . to feel safe.

Chapter Two

Thou know'st 'tis common; all that lives must die,
Passing through nature to eternity.

Hamlet (1.2.72–73)

She told Ned that her name was Grace, but not much else, not even her last name. He guessed that she didn't want him to know where she'd come from, and he didn't pry. It wasn't unusual at the theater to work with people who had thrown off a past that no longer served them. The girl was not as young as he first guessed, perhaps two or three and twenty, a good eight years younger than he was.

She let him dab at her wounds with a cloth dipped into a pail of cold water that he brought up first thing in the morning from the pump on the street. Fortunately for her, the cuts on her face were up near her hairline and not deep. Her hair would hide any scars. The cloth Ned used on her was none too clean, certainly not what she was used to, but she didn't recoil or play the lady with him. She thanked him and smiled, revealing white, straight teeth.

"You ought to see a doctor," he said.

"Thank you for your concern, but I do not at present have sufficient funds for a physician."

Ned thought that might be an understatement. So far as he could tell, she didn't have sufficient funds for anything unless she had coins sewn into her underthings, which he thought unlikely. "I got some money put by," he said. "Yer welcome to it." After so many years living hand to mouth, Ned couldn't believe he now had money to spare.

"Thank you, but I do not have need of your money." Grace pushed herself up so she leaned against the wall. "I don't believe any of my bones are broken, if that is what worries you. My ribs have been bruised quite badly, but they are still whole. You have been very kind."

"Ain't no trouble, miss. And being as it's Sunday, I got all day to see to it that you're comfortable."

"What is your work? I surmise that you are gainfully employed."

Ned grinned. "You talk as fancy as a lady."

"I assure you I am not."

"I am gainfully employed," he said, mimicking her accent.

"You are making fun of me."

"Maybe." She was not at all pretty — not like Olympia at the theater. Her face had too many strong angles — cheekbones and chin sharp, eyes intense and wide spaced. She looked not frightened exactly but sort of yearning — like she saw something just out of reach that she wanted and couldn't ever have. He regretted teasing her. Someone had hurt her badly, and it wasn't right for him to make light of it. He opened his mouth to apologize and then closed it when the lines of pain and anger scoring her face relaxed into a smile.

17

"I suppose I deserved that."

"No, miss. I shouldn't have teased you. I'm the one what's sorry."

"You may as well call me Grace. We've just spent the night together, after all." She laughed. "Forgive me, but I believe I may have shocked you. I didn't mean to suggest that you've been anything other than honorable."

"I ain't got no intentions, if that's what you mean, miss. I know my place and all."

The watery light streaming through the one small window played across her hair. It was blonde, like his, but a fair bit cleaner, with curls and braids that must have been arranged by a maid. Some of the hair had escaped in tangled wisps from its pins, giving her a tousled look, like she'd been standing in a wind. She smoothed the blanket over her knees. "Are you going to tell me what you do the other six days of the week?"

Before he could answer, she raised her hand. "No, let me guess." She grimaced as she shifted her position and then fixed him with a steady stare that tracked the length of him from head to feet. Ned sat down hard on Alec's bed, his face flushed. "Your clothes are relatively clean, so you are not engaged in laboring work, and I detect a gentleness in your speech, which leads me to believe that you often speak with women, even ladies. I shall guess that you are some kind of clerk, perhaps at a bank where you have contact with customers? Mind you, I have to say that you don't look like someone who enjoys laboring over columns of numbers."

Ned laughed. "I'd sooner kill meself than be one of them pasty-faced pillocks. Plenty of 'em come to the theater of an evening, and some get rowdy in the pit. Just cuz they paid their shilling, they think they got a right to do what they please — even yellin' at the actors if they don't like how they play their roles."

"The theater?"

"That's where I work," he said. "I'm backstage at the Theatre Royal in Covent Garden, keeping everyone organized, like. Do you know it?"

"You're at the theater?" Her eyes were shining. "I've only been once to the theater, in Bath, when I was much younger, but I long to go again. My mother — " She stopped talking suddenly and sucked in her breath and then flinched at the pain in her ribs.

"Careful, miss — I mean Grace. Those ribs are going to ache somethin' fierce for a while yet."

Grace waved one hand dismissively and then sat forward. "Do you know Mrs. Siddons?"

Ned smiled. Everyone always wanted to know about Mrs. Siddons — and sometimes Mr. Kemble too, although not as much. Ned had often pushed past ladies and gentlemen clustered in front of the stage door waiting for a glimpse of the great actress. "I wouldn't say I know her, but I work with her now and again. She's real popular, like."

"I would like nothing better than to see her act. I've read about how she can make people swoon!"

"Ain't no one comes close to Mrs. Siddons for tragedy, except maybe her brother."

"You also know Mr. Kemble?" Her eyes were intense, staring at him as if he was the most important person in the world. Ned wished Olympia would look at him like that. "Mr. John Philip Kemble?"

"'Course I know him. I told you I work at the theater, and Mr. Kemble's one of the managers. He's as fine an actor as ever walked onstage, in my opinion, though he rants something fierce." Ned grinned. "You know the gentleman?"

"Good heavens, no! I've never even seen him act. But I'd give a great deal to — and his sister." Grace sighed heavily. "You will think me foolish, but I envy you working in the theater."

"Mostly it's a lot of hard slogging. You'd be surprised at what we got to do backstage so's people go away satisfied at the end of an evening."

"I'd like to be onstage."

"You might change your mind about that if you knew what it was like for most of the girls. Not everyone can be Mrs. Siddons. Mind you, she's had more than her fair share of troubles."

"Everyone has troubles, Ned." Her smile faded.

"Aye, well, you're welcome to stay here as long as you like. I'll tell Alec to stop over at Mrs. Gellie's, or he can kip at the theater, so long as Mr. Kemble don't find out, and I can make sure of that. Do you have someone I could fetch?" She had to know people in London who cared for her. Now that he'd had a chance to talk with her and get a good long look, he'd swear on a stack of Bibles that she wasn't a whore, or even a housemaid. She was a lady — or at least genteel enough to know nothing about hard work.

"I suppose you must be curious about me," she said, looking up. "I present rather a pitiful sight."

Ned saw nothing pitiful about her. Innocent she was — and a bit unworldly. She seemed more interested in the actors at the theater than her bruised ribs and cut brow.

"If you will be so kind," she said, "I'd appreciate trespassing a little longer on your hospitality. May I also ask that you not press me for information?"

"I ain't inclined to press you. I just want to know what I can do to help. You can't want to stay here, not if there's folks in London you can call on."

"I assure you there is no one in London whom I wish to call upon." She sat back against the pillow, her lips twisting into another wince.

"You must be hungry. I'll go fetch a couple of pies from the market."

"On a Sunday?"

"Ah, well, I knows where to go. Will you be all right until I get back?"

"Yes, Ned. Thank you."

As he left her to walk down the stairs to the street, Ned reflected how quickly life could change. Yesterday, his biggest worry was keeping Mr. Renfrew's drunkenness out of sight of Mr. Kemble and hoping for a kind word from Olympia. Now, he had a lady sleeping in his bed, who wasn't like any lady he'd ever met. Mr. Harrison was right about Ned — he wouldn't let himself get too close to women — even the whores. A few times, Alec got him out to the stews around Covent Garden to take a turn or two, but Ned never really enjoyed himself. He hated the misery he saw in the eyes of the girls who serviced him, and suspected they despised him as much as they needed his money.

He wondered what Olympia would think if she knew that he was letting a woman stay in his room. Glumly, he acknowledged to himself that she probably wouldn't think anything at all.

ଫ୦ୠ

As far as Grace could tell from the way the watery spring sun slanted through the one window in Ned's room, the morning was not yet far advanced. Her father never rose before noon when he'd been drinking—and he'd been drinking more than usual the night before. Once he did rise, he'd spend most of the afternoon alone in his study and then go out for the evening. If he was in a foul mood and not inclined to inquire after her, she'd not be missed until the next morning unless Betsy alerted him, and *that* was not likely. Three months earlier, when she and her father had arrived from Clevedon in Somerset, Mr. Johnson had brought with him Grace's maid, Betsy, and then hired a housekeeper who came by every day to cook the evening meal. Betsy was scared of her own shadow and wouldn't dare tell the master that Grace was gone, even if she'd heard all the commotion the night before—or maybe *because* she heard it.

Kind as Ned was, he could not keep her in his lodgings for more than a few days. The elusive Alec would surely want his bed back. Her bruised ribs would heal soon enough, and the scratches at her hairline fade to nothing. Thank God her father's rings had not done any lasting damage to her face.

At the sound of heavy footsteps on the stairs, Grace sat up and drew the blanket around her bare arms. She needed a plan.

ଚ୦ଓଃ

"I found hot pies," Ned said as he pushed open the door. He glanced at the tiny coal grate—empty as usual. He and Alec rarely bothered getting coal for a fire since they spent most of their time at the theater. But it wasn't right to keep a girl like Grace in a place with no heat. He handed her one of the pies and then sat on Alec's bed.

"I'll get coal for the fire soon as I've eaten," he said. "You're cold."

One slender white hand emerged from under the blanket and reached for the pie. She nibbled delicately at the flaky crust, careful not to drop crumbs on the blanket. "This is very good," she said. "Thank you."

He acknowledged her with a wave of one hand. She was a great one for thanking him, which he didn't mind. At the theater, people rarely remembered to thank him.

"What exactly do you do backstage?" Grace asked.

"I make sure that the actors and actresses get where they're supposed to go onstage and that the prompter's got the scripts he needs to keep everyone on track in the plays. I also help with the bits of machinery we use to create the big effects, and with getting the scenery up. Covent Garden's Theatre Royal's got the best scenery of any theater in London."

She finished her pie and sat forward. Some of the shiny bits on the parts of her dress that Ned could see were striped brown with dried blood. Ned didn't have any idea what dresses cost, but maybe he had enough money put by to get her a new one. Nothing so fancy as she was used to, but at least warmer. And a shawl. She couldn't go back outside dressed the way she was. Maybe Mrs. Beecham at the theater would help.

"Tell me about the scenery."

"We call them flies on account of some of 'em drop down from high up and go into these slots we got built into the stage. They're huge slabs of painted wood. The man Mr.

Kemble got to do the painting is famous, like. Names his own price, he does."

"What kind of scenes does he paint?"

"Mountains, lakes, castles, deserts—pretty much anything you can imagine. He's just done one set that looks all the world like a village from olden times—way back, you know? Medieval, I guess you'd call it. You wouldn't know it weren't real if you didn't walk right up and touch the boards. He's a wonder, is Mr. Capon. One night I overheard someone comin' out of the theater sayin' he didn't need to travel out of London to see everywhere in the world."

"Could you show me?"

"What? You mean take you to the theater? Backstage?" Ned frowned, not sure what to say. Mr. Kemble would have his head if he brought in an outsider. But backstage was dark as Hades most of the time, and he'd take care to keep her far away from where Mr. Kemble made his entrances. What was the harm?

"Please, Ned. I know it's a great deal to ask."

"Naw, I can do it. But you got to get better first. I can't be takin' no invalid to the theater."

"I told you. I am not helpless."

Ned wasn't so sure about that, but something pulled at him when he looked at Grace—her eyes blue as a clear sky on a raw winter day. He'd never had anyone depend on him before, not really. At the theater, everyone called for him all the time—*Ned, where's my dagger? Ned, the thunder box ain't working right. Ned, the dogs are fighting again!* But they didn't *need* him, not like Grace did.

He smiled. "I know, Grace, and I promise I won't never think of you as helpless."

Chapter Three

O brave new world,
That has such people in't!

The Tempest (5.1.188-89)

"Yer got a dolly in our room? Did you think of askin' me first? I pay half the rent." Alec Bishop leaned against the prop table backstage, arms crossed over his bony chest.

"She ain't no dolly, and she won't be in our room for much longer. And you're almost never there as it is. Ain't Daisy keepin' you busy?"

Alec loosened his arms, then picked up a stage dagger and ran it between his fingers as if testing the dull wood for sharpness. "When she can. But stop changin' the subject. Who is she?"

"A lady, or leastways proper, like." Ned grinned as Alec flung down the dagger and then clapped his hands to his mouth, black eyes bulging in imitation of an actor pretending to be surprised.

"A lady?"

"She had an accident—fell down in the street. I brought her home and got her warmed up."

Alec recrossed his arms, thin as strips of soiled leather. "She's stopping with the likes of you? Don't she have no family?"

"Her name's Grace, and if she's got a family, she ain't telling me. And I ain't asking. There's something wrong about her."

"What do you mean *wrong* about her?" Alec followed Ned around the back of the stage.

"Help me here, would you?" Ned grabbed hold of a pulley and then nodded at Alec to steady the fly attached to it. During the performance, one of the callboys would crank the pulley and make the fly shake in imitation of an earthquake. The evening's afterpiece—usually a farce or some kind of spectacle put on after the main play—featured a trio of natural disasters—earthquake, fire, flood. "Don't know," Ned said. "There's just something not right about her." Ned would have his hands full making sure all the stagehands got where they needed to be. He particularly hated doing the fire effects. Any carelessness would result in disaster. The theater was stuffed to the gills with props and costumes and flies, with paints and pots and scripts, benches and plush seats. A voluminous curtain was looped across the top of the proscenium, and most of the columns that were painted to look like marble were made of solid wood.

"Like what? Not right in the head? Should you be takin' her out to Bedlam?"

"Don't be daft. She's just different, is all."

"What are you planning to do with her?"

"I dunno. She'll go her own way as soon as she's better." Ned thought it best not to tell Alec about his plan to bring Grace backstage to watch a performance. Alec might be Ned's oldest friend, but that didn't mean Ned trusted his friend's big mouth.

Ned darted forward to grab hold of a rope flapping inches above Alec's head. Where was young Bob? He was meant to take charge of the water barrel for the flood effect. "I got no time to talk now," Ned said. "You'd best get going. The doors are set to open in ten minutes." Alec worked out front, taking tickets and helping keep the peace when the pit goers got overexcited.

"Oy, I know me job and all," Alec said. "You might think yer the king of shit back here, but I don't take no orders from you."

Ned grinned as Alec pushed past him, eyes squinting into the darkness but his lips twitching. Alec never had much patience for anger.

୫୦ଔ

On his way out of the theater at the end of the evening, Ned stepped in to see Mrs. Beecham. She laughed at him when he told her his quest, particularly when he blushed to recall Grace's figure. Eventually, she gave over teasing him and piled a gown and light wool spencer into his arms.

"Don't tell Mr. Kemble," she said. "I trust you to get them back to me in decent shape. Tell your mystery girl to keep them clean and to take care not to tear the muslin. Does she require a bonnet?"

Ned nodded. "And if you've also got a shawl, I'd be obliged."

"I'm not a mantua maker." She gathered up a sturdy woolen shawl—a plaid pattern Ned recognized from a recent production of *Macbeth*. "Go on with you, quick now, before anyone sees you in here with me."

"Ah, Mrs. B., it's not as if I don't talk with you plenty of an evening." Ned grinned down at her. Although a few years past thirty, Mrs. Beecham was still a fine-looking woman. Her husband had been in the navy and gotten himself killed at the Battle of Trafalgar back in '05, leaving Mrs. Beecham to shift for herself. Fortunately, she was more than up for the challenge. Ned turned quickly. It wouldn't do to let Mrs. Beecham see him blush. She'd likely get the wrong idea.

Grace was asleep by the time he got home, so he undressed in the dark and laid her new clothes at the foot of her bed. Alec had grudgingly gone to spend another night with Daisy at Mrs. Gellie's. Ned knew the arrangement couldn't last much longer. Alec's pay didn't extend to many more full nights with a whore.

℠∓

Grace saw the clothes as soon as she woke up the next morning. Ned lay on Alec's bed, his back to her, the blanket not quite high enough to hide his bare shoulders. A thin cord rested at the base of his neck, almost covered by tufts of blond hair. She slid out of bed. The night before, she'd peeled off her filthy dress and worn only a chemise and her sleeveless petticoat. She'd removed her stays, their absence making her feel virtually naked as she pulled the gown Ned brought over her head. With her ribs so sore, she'd need to keep the stays off a while longer. God only knew how she'd get the gown fastened up the back, but at least it felt much cleaner than her own, even if the fabric was coarser.

If—no—*when* she finally returned to her father's house, she'd slip in when he was out and bundle the soiled dress into a closet before Betsy saw it.

"Do you need help with the back?"

She jumped at the sound of his voice and then chided herself. If he'd wanted to harm her, he'd already had plenty of opportunity. "Yes, please," she said. "Not too tight, if you don't mind. My ribs . . ."

"'Course. I know what it's like havin' bruised ribs."

She kept her gaze on the blank wall in front of her. "You do?"

"Sure. You don't get to my age livin' round Covent Garden and not be in your share of fights." She felt a slight tug as his fingers took hold of the laces. Breath warmed the bare skin of her neck. She'd never had a man stand so close before, and she felt suddenly nervous. As soon as Grace felt him tie the laces at the base of her neck, she stepped forward and picked up the bonnet. She put it on and expertly tied the blue satin ribbon in a bow before turning to face him.

"I am obliged to you, Ned."

"I reckon you're used to having a maid take care of your things." He was buttoning his own shirt. Grace saw a flash of silver at his chest. A medal or coin of some sort appeared to be threaded through the cord she'd seen earlier. Probably it was some kind of token from the theater.

"I do. And I won't pretend to not miss warm water and a clean chemise." She laughed at the look on his face. "Truly, Ned, you are a man of many surprises. You bring me a gown and a bonnet and then blush when I mention a chemise."

"I brung a shawl too. Mrs. Beecham, our costume lady, loaned everything to me. She'll want them back, but no hurry."

Grace untied the bonnet and threw it onto Alec's bed. "I won't be staying much longer."

Ned didn't say anything, because they both knew she was not wrong. Whatever world she came from, she had no business sleeping in a rough room in a Covent Garden lodging house.

"Before you go, you got to let me keep my promise," Ned said.

"What promise?"

"To take you to the theater. Tomorrow they're putting on *Othello* and then a cracker of a melo-drame. You got to see it! I'll find a place for you to watch, out of the way of the machinery. Thank goodness we got no live animals on tomorrow." Ned rolled his eyes and plugged his nose. "They're the worst. Mr. Kemble favors having them, but some of the other managers don't, so it's only every so often we get them in. 'Course, we just about always got dogs."

Grace laughed. "I was hoping for camels and horses."

"Don't you worry. We have them more often than I'd like. You don't want to know about the mess."

"I can imagine." She settled herself on the bed and smoothed the skirt of her new gown. For the first time since coming to London, she felt like she had something to look forward to.

ᔥᲗᲒ

Ned was not a man to renege on a promise, but as he got closer to the stage door, holding Grace's arm so she didn't slip in the mud, he had his doubts. At any given time, before and during a performance, a good fifty people milled around the cavernous backstage spaces crammed full of scenery and props and dressing rooms and all the complicated machinery used to create the spectacles—the thunder drum and the rain box, the wooden waves on long sticks of doweling, the windlass for the enormous curtain.

"Mind your step," he said. Her arm pressed lightly against him. For a woman almost as tall as he was, she felt delicate—like one of the weeping willows in the park, with arms like long fronds, swaying and supple. But like a willow, she seemed to possess a core of strength that Ned suspected could not be easily snapped.

"I don't wish you to get into trouble on my account," she said.

A clutch of actresses flitted past on their way into the stage entrance, chattering and laughing like they always did—a flock of pigeons with the odd dove. Olympia flashed a smile at Ned as she passed, and he swallowed convulsively. Grace's eyes as she watched the girls go into the theater shone with anticipation in the late-afternoon sun.

What kind of a man would he be to deny her pleasure?

"Don't worry about me, Grace. Just keep close to me when we go in. I'll make the introductions to old Mr. Harrison, who takes charge of the stage door. He don't act no more, but Kemble won't let him go. He's like that, is Mr. Kemble. Loyal." Ned fervently hoped that Kemble's loyalty would extend to him should he get wind of Grace's presence. London was full of men who would be glad to take his job. And why not? He had it good—warm and dry inside, with all the pomp and excitement of the theater swirling about.

He pushed open the door. "Come on then. Move smart. I got a mountain of things to do before the plays go up."

৪০৫৪

Grace stepped into paradise at precisely 4:50 in the afternoon. All those days when her father was away from home and she'd sat with her mother and recited scenes from Shakespeare had not prepared her for the reality of the theater. Her first impression was of a bustling kind of chaos, like a busy London street but enclosed and pulsing with an energy she'd never experienced before. Boys and men scurried past her, carrying props and ropes, shouting, jostling, laughing. A woman dressed in a gown thick with rich embroidery, panniers wide in the style of the last century, turned sideways to pass them. Brightly rouged cheeks startled Grace. Paint was for fallen women, and yet as she walked deeper into the theater, every woman — and a fair number of the men — wore thick makeup — eyes brightened with azure and jade and gold, lips like open wounds.

"Keep close to me," Ned whispered behind her. "No one will notice you."

He hustled her along the dark corridor. A door to their right opened, and out spilled a young woman. She didn't move so much as dance in place, her small feet just visible under her skirt. She rushed up to Ned.

"Ned! I'm at my wit's end. Mrs. Beecham was to have my costume ready for tonight, but it's nowhere to be found, and she's gone off home with a headache."

"I didn't know you were on tonight."

"I'm taking the part of Elvina in the melo-drame. Mr. Kemble's put me in, although he knows I prefer comedy."

"You'll be splendid."

Grace looked sharply at Ned, saw his blush even in the dim light. So that was how it was. She was glad to see it. Ned deserved a bit of love in his life.

"Grace, this here is Olympia. She's one of the actresses."

"I surmised as much." Grace smiled and held out her hand. "Very pleased to meet you, Olympia."

"Olympia's a cracker with the comic roles," Ned said. "'Specially the breeches parts."

"Dear me, Ned, you'll have this lady thinking all sorts of dark thoughts about me."

"I can't imagine anything more wonderful!" Grace exclaimed.

Olympia smiled and glanced up at Ned. "I didn't know Mr. Kemble was taking on a new actress so late in the season."

"Oh no!" Grace said before Ned had a chance to answer. "I'm not an actress. I'm, ah, staying with . . ." She stopped, confused. "I mean to say that . . ."

"Grace is stopping with a cousin of mine," Ned said. "I've brought her backstage to see the plays. Don't tell Mr. Kemble."

"Good heavens! I'm hardly likely to do *that*." Olympia nodded at Grace, apparently taking at face value Ned's ridiculous story about a cousin. She must have noticed that Grace was genteel by her speech, even if the clothes supplied by Mrs. Beecham were plain. "I'm pleased to meet you," she said.

Ned took Grace's arm and angled her away from
Olympia. "I'll see to your costume as soon as I get Grace
settled," he said over his shoulder. "You needn't worry."

"I never worry when you're in charge, Ned!" Olympia
called down the corridor with a laugh.

Grace sensed Ned smiling as he led her down the
corridor, and felt a longing she'd never felt before. The easy
way in which these people talked to each other, laughed,
and made promises tugged at her heart, making the pain of
having to leave this new world all the sharper.

"Oy, Ned!" One of the callboys ran up, his face ashen.
"We got a problem with the waves—the second set's
sticking."

"I'm on it!"

"Waves?"

"Painted ones on rollers. They're a bugger to work with.
Beggin' pardon, Grace."

"You don't need to beg *my* pardon, Ned, not when you're
being so kind as to bring me backstage."

"Aye, well. Ain't no trouble. The rollers, see, they stick if
one of the boys forgets to oil 'em." He grabbed the arm of a
passing callboy. "You! Go get the oil can from the paint
room. Yes, now!" He turned back to Grace and walked with
her a few more yards to a dark space in the wings from
which she could see the smooth boards of the stage,
gleaming in brilliant candlelight. "Sorry, but I've got to
leave you."

"I'm perfectly fine, Ned. Please, don't worry about me."

"Make sure you stay put here, to the side, like. Don't get
in the way of the actors and actresses as they come through
to the stage. Mr. Kemble always comes in on the other side,

so you'll be safe enough. It's a good thing Mrs. Beecham loaned you a dark dress."

"Are you sure, Ned?"

"Just stay quiet and out of sight. I'll be back later to check on you."

ﻼﻼﻼ

Ned joined her for a few minutes during the second of the evening's two performances. *Othello* had already been performed, and now was the afterpiece—a musical melodrama called *The Blind Boy*. The look on Grace's face as she watched the actors, and especially as she listened to the music, made any risk Ned ran of bringing an outsider into the theater worth it. And truly, what harm was there in giving her a bit of fun?

"What's happening?" Grace whispered.

"That's Oberto—he's a peasant. He's raised a blind baby who was left in his care."

"Someone left a baby?"

"Common enough even now," Ned said. Grace was surprised by the bitterness in his voice. He put his hand on her arm. "Listen to this bit. It's one of my favorites."

A messenger strode onstage and handed a letter to Oberto, who was being performed with great pathos by one of the older actors. The violins shivered out a stream of notes meant to indicate Oberto's agitation.

"*Edmond, the son of Stanislaus, Heir to the Throne of Samartia . . .*"

"Here comes the important part," Ned said. He stayed by Grace's side to watch. The music turned softly lyrical, and the actor wiped tears from his eyes. "*My Edmond! My dear boy, my Prince?*"

"He's just found out that the blind boy he's raised is a prince," whispered Ned. "I still get choked up, even if it's make-believe and all."

Oberto strode around the stage, his arms slicing the air with great vigor as the music swelled. The orchestra wove in and out of the action with strings quaking and woodwinds trilling.

"He looks upset."

"How'd you like to find out yer livin' with royalty?" asked Ned.

"I shouldn't think there is much chance of *that*."

Grace heard him chuckle as he moved off to attend to a scene change. She continued watching the action unfold onstage, her heart banging with delicious pain against her bruised ribs. How did these people do this night after night? The women especially! Grace had never before thought of a future beyond her father's house and perhaps a dutiful marriage.

And now this.

ଚଉଗ୍ଷ

For the first time in many months, Ned sensed a touch of warmth in the night air, a promise of spring. He drew Grace's arm through his as they walked along Bow Street, quiet now an hour after the theater closed. Olympia had been so grateful when he'd found her costume. She'd thanked him with a peck on his cheek. Hours later, the memory of her lips on his skin still made him blush.

"Did you enjoy yourself?" he asked Grace.

"I never thought I'd see such things!" she exclaimed "That Mr. Pope in *Othello*? He was marvelous."

"It's Shakespeare and all, ain't it? Folks in the theater are always banging on about Shakespeare like he was some sort of god. Give me a lively melo-drame any day. I like the music."

"Yes, but the play! It was . . ." Grace sighed. "I've read it but never seen it performed. I don't know the best word to describe it."

"Long?"

"No! It was wonderful. And poor Desdemona! She died so beautifully. Who was the actress?"

"That would be Louisa. She's settin' herself up to be the next Mrs. Siddons, but if you ask me, she ain't got what it takes."

"Why?"

"Can't say exactly. I don't spend a lot of time worrying about what most of the actors and actresses do once they get onstage. I'm more worried about helpin' the prompter get them on and off at the right time and makin' sure the scenery don't fall on them."

"Olympia was delightful in the melo-drame."

"You'll get no argument from me about Olympia." Ned wanted to say more, maybe even tell Grace what he felt, but what purpose would that serve?

"Does Mrs. Siddons act often?" Grace asked.

"Oh, aye. There ain't no one like Mrs. Siddons for making people believe in what she's acting."

"What about Mr. Kemble? Why did he not take the part of Othello?"

"Don't know, but Mr. Kemble always takes Iago."

"I can see why he is so admired. He made my skin crawl."

"He's a wonder, and that's for certain. You should see him when he plays Macbeth."

Ned resolved to find another opportunity to take her backstage. The season would be over in a few weeks, but as soon as the plays started up again in September, he'd find a way.

And then he remembered that Grace would be gone from his life long before he had a chance to take her anywhere. The realization left him feeling hollow and vaguely uneasy. He didn't like the idea of Grace going away with no one to look out for her.

Chapter Four

Why yet I live to say "This thing's to do,"
Sith I have cause, and will, and strength, and
means,
To do't.

Hamlet (4.4.44–46)

*F*or the first time since her mother's death a year earlier, Grace slipped into a dream that she did not want to end. The light and color and noise of the stage embraced her. Even in sleep, the sharp tickle of sawdust in her nose mingled with the miasma of drying paint and strong perfumes and overheated bodies. She was alive to the promise of happiness to come, just like she used to be when she stood upon the cliffs at Clevedon and imagined a world beyond the sea.

The last moments before waking from her dream exploded with the sounds of metal scraping across rock and a horse's anguished neighing. Blood flowed across a leather seat and dripped onto sodden grass.

"Oh!" She sat up so quickly that the blanket fell away from her bare arms and shoulders. Ned was already up and dressed. He had his back to her as he knelt in front of the fireplace and poked the coals into flame.

She pulled the blanket around her before he turned. "I'm sorry," she said. "Did I startle you?"

"Don't worry about me, but you look as if you've had a proper nightmare. You was moaning something fierce before you woke up. I figured I'd get a fire started and go out for pies."

"You are very kind, Ned."

"Ah, well, so you keep saying."

"I cannot stay."

Ned scrambled to his feet and sat heavily on Alec's bed. "Have you got a place to go?" He stared down at his hands. Not for the first time, Grace was surprised at their fineness—long fingered with narrow nails and strong, slim wrists. "You'll be safe?"

"I hope so."

He clenched his hands into fists. "Hoping ain't what I want to hear."

"It's the best I can do, Ned. You know it's not right for me to stay."

"No, I suppose not, but give me a few more days. I'll ask one of the girls at the theater to find you a place to stay. They's mostly good girls, respectable enough, all things considered, 'specially Olympia."

"You've been very good to me, Ned, but I can't stay here or with Olympia, or anyone."

"It ain't no trouble." He ducked his head, blond hair still tangled with sleep. "Will you at least stay until later today? I got to get to the theater early, but I can be back midafternoon and go with you to wherever you're going, make sure you don't get lost. London's awful big."

"I'm quite capable of making my own way, Ned. My father's house is not far." She clapped her hand over her mouth, eyes wide.

"Your father? You ain't tellin' me that *he* was the one what hurt you?"

Grace shook her head, but she could tell that Ned did not believe her. "It was just the one time, and I'm sure he doesn't remember anything. My father has had difficulties . . ."

"Ain't no excuse. No man hits a woman."

"Yes, well, Ned, you know that isn't true."

"I suppose not, but it still ain't right." Ned stood up and went to the door. "It's not my business to stop you, but are you sure you won't let me ask Olympia about you bunkin' in with her? She lives with her mother and is respectable enough, although there's some talk about a general who pays the bills." Ned shrugged. "Ain't none of my business."

"I can't, Ned. I must return to my father's house." Grace sat back against the bedstead.

He stayed a moment longer, looking down at her. She had a sudden urge to gather him in her arms, to soothe the hurt from his face like he was a child. She straightened her spine and regarded him evenly, drawing a veil around her heart and pinning it tight.

"I will be perfectly fine, Ned," she said.

"You're sure 'bout that?"

"I am, Ned. Please don't worry about me."

The look on his face as he turned toward the door tore at her heart. She'd had so little time to get to know him, but

41

she'd begun to suspect that Ned lived with a hurt so deep that he didn't know what to do with it.

"Don't be a stranger," he mumbled, then opened the door to the landing and started down the stairs. Moments later, the front door opened and then slammed shut, the sound of footsteps quickly swallowed by the clatter and clash of the London street.

Grace threw off the blanket and planted her feet on the rough floorboards. If only for her mother's sake, she had to give her father another chance.

৪৩૩

"There you are! I was all set to send out the constables." Mr. Harrison was out of his chair and leaning against his cane. "We've got a problem!"

"What's happened?" Ned asked wearily. With the certainty that Grace was about to leave him, he felt flat, as if he no longer mattered in the world. "Mr. Kemble hasn't gone and gotten camels again, has he?"

"No, no, nothing like that." Mr. Harrison's knees cracked like gunshot as he lowered himself back into his chair. "We're short a girl for tonight's performance."

"Who's out?"

"Agnes."

"Again?"

"She said she was feeling poorly when she left last night, and this morning she sent a note. I don't want to be the one to tell Mr. Kemble."

"What about a replacement?"

"Do you know anyone?"

Ned shook his head and then stopped. Well, why not? There wasn't any law against asking. "As a matter of fact, I do!" He pulled open the door. "Don't say a word to Mr. Kemble. I've got someone who'll fit in just fine in the chorus. Agnes don't have no speaking parts tonight, does she?"

"Not so far as I know," Mr. Harrison said. "She's scheduled for the procession in the afterpiece, so you just need someone who can sing. Failing that, she can mouth the words so long as she's got the looks. Mr. Kemble don't like seeing ugly faces in the chorus."

But Ned wasn't listening. He was already out on to Bow Street and sprinting in the direction of Hart Street. When he got to his lodgings, he wrenched open the front door and took the stairs to his room two at a time.

ಬಂದ

Olympia's costume shimmered and shifted as she moved — and in the short time Grace had known her, she seemed always to be moving. "Stay close to me and copy my actions," she whispered.

Grace thought Olympia was very much like a seabird — compact, graceful, poised to take off when the wind was right. "Shall I sing?" she asked.

"If you wish. Do you?"

"Sometimes." In Clevedon, Grace had been the center of her mother's small social circle of respectable families — her singing a welcome addition to evening parties so long as her father was away. And she often sang on her solitary walks. With the wind as accompaniment, Grace would stand alone on the cliffs overlooking the Bristol Channel and let her voice soar, relishing the tang of freezing air in her lungs and accepting with a curtsy the caws of the seagulls for applause. Her mother had often told her that she had a beautiful voice, sometimes smiling wistfully and joking that she was as good as any professional.

Grace smiled down at Olympia. With hair neatly coiled around a headdress of white feathers, her head barely came to Grace's shoulder.

"I am a trifle nervous," Grace said.

"I'd be surprised if you were not."

Grace smoothed one hand over the fabric of her own costume—it was rough with tiny glass beads that she guessed would catch and fling the light thrown from the candles. A crescendo rose from the orchestra.

"Here we go!" whispered Olympia.

With eight other young women, Grace and Olympia marched with slow solemnity from the stifling dark wings into an inferno. The stage blazed with light and heat. Grace squinted and stumbled but was saved from falling by Olympia's hand on her arm. The music was so loud that Grace was sure her ears would burst, and at the same time, the sound made her feel like she'd been picked up and taken on a golden chariot to a glorious new heaven.

The other girls started to sing. Much to her surprise, Grace recognized the song. Her mother had taught it to her years earlier. She said she'd learned it when she was at school in Bath.

Grace opened her mouth and let the notes spill out, blending at first with the voices of the other girls and then soaring high above theirs with perfect tone and clarity. Dimly, she was aware of Olympia pulling her hand. Mr. Kemble, black eyes snapping, posed downstage, resplendent in a jewel-encrusted gown.

The song ended, and the girls circled the stage in front of Mr. Kemble. A huge yellow star rose above them, and the wind machine cranked up and blew their skirts so they billowed out like silver-tipped clouds. Grace followed Olympia's lead and held out her arms and twirled. A procession of actors carrying spears, faces thick with blue makeup, gathered upstage on various levels, some peeking out from behind cutout slabs of wood painted to resemble large boulders. The orchestra reached a shattering climax with Mr. Kemble standing center stage and the entire company singing the final chorus. A shower of sparks burst upward, and the thunder box rumbled. Gears under the stage ground and rattled, and seconds later Mr. Kemble was borne aloft on a square of stage pushed up from below. When he was five feet above the stage, the curtain fell in a swish of red velvet.

Grace joined hands with Olympia and another girl and stepped forward. When the curtain rose, the massed company took their bows and then stood with their arms raised while Mr. Kemble was lowered back to the stage. He stood unsmiling and in profile to accept the cheering and stomping of the crowd.

"What do you think?" Olympia shouted in Grace's ear. She had no need to speak lower with the noise rolling and cresting from every corner of the auditorium.

Grace did not reply. She could not.

ଈଔ

"I'll be a while yet," Ned said. "Do you mind waiting? Mr. H. will keep you well entertained. He acted with Garrick back in the seventies."

Grace had never before felt so full—brimming over like a river in flood. A thousand smooth pebbles clacked and clattered around her skull, bouncing off bone, smacking into each other. How did the other actors and actresses go about the business of winding down after performances— scraping off makeup, pulling gowns and tunics from sweat-damp bodies, taking a quick drink to soothe nerves sharpened to steel by the applause?

"I'll be fine, Ned," she said. "Take your time. I'm too excited for bed anyway."

"The stage can do that to people, especially when they're new." He smiled. "I won't be more than an hour. Promise you'll wait?"

Grace remembered her own headlong flight through the streets before collapsing on Bow Street. "I'll stay with Mr. Harrison," she promised. She walked along the dark corridor to the small room adjacent to the stage door, reaching it at the same time as several actresses, many of whom she recognized from the procession.

"Grace! There you are!" Olympia bustled forward. "You're a sly one. What a voice!" She gazed around at the other girls. "Did you hear her?"

"We weren't likely to miss her." The girl who spoke was close to Grace in age and decades beyond her in experience. Grace recognized her as the actress who had played Desdemona the night before. She had a brazen kind of beauty—all apple cheeks and staring eyes that regarded Grace with all the warmth of a desert-dwelling lizard.

"Don't pay any attention to Louisa. She sings like a frog."

Grace burst out laughing and had the satisfaction of seeing Louisa recoil and turn away in a huff.

"I'm obliged to you," Grace whispered to Olympia. "For helping me."

"I didn't need to do much," Olympia said cheerfully. "Far as I can see, you belong on the stage."

"Thank you."

"Olympia!" called one of the other girls—a bouncy, smiling one, who Grace thought might be called Caroline. "We best get going. I'm that parched."

Olympia took Grace's arm and pulled her toward the door. "Come with us. We go to a tavern across the Piazza. Mr. H. here will tell Ned where you are."

"A tavern? Oh no! I couldn't."

"Too much the lady, are you?" asked Louisa. She swept past them to the door. "She's got no business being here, and I'll wager Mr. Kemble won't be happy with what she done." Louisa hooked arms with Caroline and another girl and slammed open the door, leaving Mr. Harrison to half rise with arthritic protest. Grace hurried to catch the swinging door and then pulled it in against the damp spring night.

"Those girls could learn more ladylike behavior," he grumbled. "Are you two going out? I don't fancy spending half the night sitting in a draft."

"You have your hands full tending to us, Mr. Harrison," said Olympia. "I'm sorry for Louisa's rudeness. She's just angry because Grace here put us to shame with her singing tonight."

Mr. Harrison sank gratefully into his chair. "Is that so? Grace, is it? You're new, aren't you?"

"Yes, sir."

"And what is your genius?"

"Sir?"

47

"He means what do you do onstage, your passion, what delights you," Olympia said.

"I can't say." The brimful feeling was back. Grace wanted to laugh out loud with the novelty of her new situation. Fancy being asked what delighted her! She'd never really felt passionate about anything, unless it was wanting to disappear from Clevedon during her parents' long silences. "I think," she began and then stopped and looked at Olympia, who was smiling encouragement. "I am very new, but perhaps, if I was given the chance, I'd like to excel at tragedy. Like Louisa as Desdemona."

"Tragedy, is it?" Mr. Harrison's gaze was frank and assessing. Grace wondered if she ought to feel affronted, but sensed that he was regarding her only with curiosity. Ned had told her that Mr. Harrison was a formidable tragedian in his day. Would he see something of the same potential in her?

"Yes," he said finally. "You have the height, and your features appear capable of expressing strong emotion. You are not a beauty, and for tragedy that will serve you well."

"How so?" Grace had no illusions about her own beauty, but she'd never thought to hear its lack described as an asset.

"Pretty girls like little Olympia here are made for comedy. But when it comes to tragedy, audiences want to see the face of suffering."

"Dear me, Mr. Harrison, you'll scare Grace away from the stage just when we've found her." Olympia grasped Grace's arm. "Come out with us." She encircled Grace's waist and turned her toward the door. Grace gasped at the pressure against her ribs.

Olympia drew back. "Are you injured?"

"Please, don't trouble yourself. I just need a moment."

While Olympia watched with concern, Grace leaned one hand against the wall, then wrapped her other arm across her chest and breathed shallowly.

"Grace?"

"I am perfectly well." She stepped forward and took Olympia's hand, let her lead her toward the door, the sensation of willingly giving up control unfamiliar and welcome. She had so long been used to ceding control of her life to the will of her father. How intoxicating to choose to give herself over to lovely Olympia.

Olympia steered them toward the Piazza, still bustling with carriages and ablaze with light from the torches carried by boys running in front. Dogs barked and horses stamped. Grace had never seen London like this—another world from the cloistered life at her father's shabby townhouse in Russell Square. And as for comparing the scene before her to sleepy little Clevedon, the two locations may as well be on different planets.

"It's so noisy," she said.

"You've never been in the Piazza at night?"

Grace shook her head. "Ned brought me to the theater from Hart Street."

"It is a bit overwhelming, I suppose."

"I've lately come from a house overlooking the sea. The nights were exceedingly dark."

Olympia did not ask for details, which Grace was glad about. This dream could not last—she had to drink it to the dregs.

A man stepped in front of them.

"Excuse me, sir," said Olympia. "We are respectable women. You will allow us to pass." She drew Grace closer.

"Come, Grace. This gentleman does not mean any harm. He is merely mistaken."

Grace did not move. A wide-brimmed brown hat too provincial for London perched atop greasy gray curls. Her father held his ground like an aging elm in a windstorm.

She was at least relieved to see that he was sober.

Chapter Five

The smallest worm will turn, being trodden on.

Henry VI, Part 3 (2.2.17)

*M*r. Tobias Johnson paced back and forth in front of the fire, as usual built too high for the size of the room. Grace thought she might faint from the heat.

"You have made a fool out of yourself and of me."

"No one at the theater knew me."

"And how long did you expect to keep up the charade?"

When Grace didn't have an answer, her father shook his head. "As I suspected! You paid no thought for any consequences. I'd not have believed a daughter of mine capable of such behavior."

Still Grace remained silent. She could not let him rattle her. Not this time, not now that she'd glimpsed another life.

"You cannot be so cavalier of your mother's memory."

Grace clasped her hands in her lap, felt bone grind on bone. Her ribs still ached from his blows. "My mother did not expect her husband to lay hands upon her daughter."

"What the devil are you talking about? I've never laid hands on you in my life—not that you don't deserve it. If you were a child, I'd have every justification for laying you across my knees and teaching you your duty."

Grace jumped up. She was taller than her father by several inches, and half his width. "You don't remember what you did the night I ran away?"

"I did nothing. You cannot begin to comprehend my shock when I realized you were gone—and concern I might add, although I see now that it was sorely misplaced. You were hardly worried about *my* feelings when you exposed yourself onstage—little better than a harlot. At least I have Providence to thank that I was in the audience and was able to find you after."

"Why *were* you there, Father?" Grace asked, distracted for a moment. "You despise the theater."

To Grace's surprise, her father's cheeks flushed. He turned toward the mantel and absently stroked a figurine of a shepherdess that had once belonged to Grace's mother. "Not that it is any business of yours," he said to the wall, "but an acquaintance of mine procured a ticket for me. I deemed it polite to accept."

"I was not aware that you knew anyone in London."

"You are misinformed." He turned back to her, his expression again angry. "I can at least thank God you were well disguised in that absurd costume."

Grace walked closer to her father and with one hand held back the hair she'd arranged to cover her forehead. "*This* is what you did to me, Father—*and* you shoved me so hard my ribs are bruised."

"Ridiculous! I have no time for such nonsense." He pushed past her without even glancing at her forehead. "You are deluded."

⟡

Mr. Kemble still wore the costume of an oriental potentate. The turban, crouched like a plump peacock on top of his head, added another foot to the man's already-considerable height. Black soot outlined his eyes, and a robe shot with gold swept to his knees. A jeweled belt cinched his waist.

"Who was she?" he demanded.

Ned gripped his hands behind his back and took a deep breath.

"Ned?"

"Her name's Grace, sir. She was, ah, stopping with me for a few days. Agnes was out sick, sir, and Grace being willing and all and the right size for Agnes's costume, well, she stepped up, like."

"And you did not see fit to inform me? I am still manager of this establishment, am I not?"

"Yes, sir, sorry, sir. There weren't time. And no one heard, sir. Did they? The orchestra was loud, and she was at the back."

"*I* heard."

"Sir." Ned knew better than to give more excuses — Mr. Kemble loathed excuses — so he stared at the floor, feeling like he was six years old and being scolded by Mrs. King at the Foundling Hospital. What had he been thinking putting the only good job he'd ever had at risk? He'd end up back on the streets, lucky to get taken on to push a dust cart, ringing a large bell and calling *Dust O!*

Mr. Kemble paced the length of the room. A rack of costumes lined an entire wall, and a jumble of hats, gloves, and belts covered a small table. He stopped abruptly and turned on Ned. "Did I not warn you, Ned, the last time you let Renfrew go onstage when he was drunk? I have a mind to dismiss you now and be done with it."

Ned stayed silent. He hadn't prayed since he was a lad and couldn't find the words, so he just waited. His fate was in Mr. Kemble's hands, anyway. Praying couldn't do any good.

Mr. Kemble stopped pacing and slid into the chair in front of a burnished mirror. For several minutes, Ned waited and watched, the only sound the clinking of pots full of chalk and pigment powders that Kemble's hand brushed past in his efforts to clean the heavy stage makeup from his face.

"Are you familiar with the story of Miss Peg Woffington?" he asked without looking at Ned. Leaning close to the mirror, he wiped a scrap of linen across the smudges of black cork above his eyes.

"What? No, sir." At least Mr. Kemble was still talking. That was something. Maybe he'd steer clear of the dust cart after all.

"I don't suppose you could have. She died back in the sixties." He put down the linen and turned to face Ned. "Miss Woffington was an Irish actress of some renown. She also lived quite openly with David Garrick, among many others, but *that* scandal is not relevant to our purpose. The point is that she was discovered singing on the street in her native Dublin and rose to become one of England's finest actresses."

"Yes, sir."

"You don't get my drift?"

"Ah, no, sir. Sorry, sir." Ned hoped Mr. Kemble would get on with it. If he wasn't going to get the sack, then he had a thousand things to do to put the theater to bed for the night. "This girl who sang, she's got the potential to be another Peg Woffington. Do you understand?"

"Not really, sir."

Mr. Kemble sighed loudly, his dark brows furred into one thick line above piercing black eyes famous for making the ladies in the boxes swoon. "Bring her to me, Ned. I may have a position for her next season."

"Sir?"

"You heard me. I can forgive you for bringing her into the theater without my consent, although I ask that you never do such a thing again. But I cannot be angry about her voice. Have her come see me tomorrow afternoon." He nodded toward the door. "Now get back to your duties, man. I'd like the theater closed up before dawn."

Ned bolted from the room.

৪০৫ঙ

Ned went first to Mr. Harrison's room to look for Grace. He was surprised to find Olympia, her eyes red from crying. He rushed forward and grabbed her arm. "What's wrong? Are you hurt? Why are you crying?" For a moment, he forgot all about Mr. Kemble and the pressing need to bring Grace to the great man or risk losing his job.

Olympia looked down at his hand on her arm and then back up at him. "Grace is gone, Ned."

He dropped his hand and stood back. "What do you mean *gone?*"

"We was walking out into the Piazza, and this man came to stand in front of us—like a brick wall, he was. He wouldn't step aside when I asked him to. At first, I thought he'd taken us for Cyprians, but then Grace didn't move when I tried pulling her away. She looked at him like . . ." Olympia shuddered. "I don't know what, but her face got deathly pale, and I was afraid she'd swoon."

"Did he lay hands on her?" Ned had not expected the anger that flushed through him like a cold rain in November. It was not as if he had improper feelings for Grace. If anything, he felt a kind of warm regard that had nothing to do with desire. But he did know that he'd cheerfully disable any man who tried to harm her.

"No, not like that. He just held out his hand palm down like you would to a child. And she took it." Olympia's lips quivered, and it was all Ned could do not to wrap her in an embrace. Instead, he waited patiently, arms at his sides.

"Did she say anything?"

"She told me not to worry, that she was in no danger. And then before I could think what to do, she was walking away with him to a carriage."

"Did you see a crest? Footmen?"

"No, it was a hackney coach." Olympia sank to the only other chair in Mr. Harrison's room and gratefully accepted the cup of hot tea he'd made the moment she'd slammed open the stage door. "I should have stopped her."

"Sounds as if she went freely," Ned said. "You said this man didn't force her?"

"No, but oh, Ned, her face! I've never seen anyone look like that before—so resigned—as if she knew there was no escape."

Ned rested one hand on Olympia's warm shoulder and was gratified when she didn't pull away. Olympia was the only one of the young actresses who treated Ned like he was more than a big lad to be flirted with.

"We didn't have much hope of keeping her," he said. Now that he knew Olympia was safe, all he could think about was what on earth he'd tell Mr. Kemble.

ᏵᏆᏅ

Alec slapped Ned on the back as they walked into the Piazza. "What's wrong with you? She's just another dolly, and there's no shortage of them around here. And if you're not wanting to avail yourself of the local talent, then come with me to Miz Gellie's. Daisy's got some fine-looking friends."

A man held out a basket brimming with flat cakes of hot, spiced gingerbread. Alec threw him a halfpenny and took up the cake in both grubby hands.

"I'm not looking for a whore," Ned said. "And it ain't like that with Grace."

"You just keep telling yerself that." Alec transferred his cake to one hand and dodged out of the way of Ned's fist. "So she's gone off, and you got no idea where? Is that about the size of it?"

"Pretty much. I got to find her, Alec. Mr. Kemble heard her sing last night, and now he wants to meet her. He thinks she might be a great talent. I can't tell him that I don't know where she is. Hell, I don't even know her surname."

"She's ladylike, right?"

"That's how she talks."

"That's a start. Did she mention any family? Friends?"

"Just her father, and she didn't want me to know that he was the one what beat her up. She did say once that she's not been in London long. Came up from some place in the West Country."

"You remember where?"

"Naw — Cleve something. Does it matter?"

"It could." Alec hopped back and forth on small feet, bits of gingerbread spraying the cobblestones like dried currants. A plump rat slipped between Alec's legs and swiped tiny claws at the crumbs.

"If you've got an idea how to find her, then tell me. I got until this afternoon."

"Did you check our room?"

"What? Why? She wouldn't leave nothin' there."

"Yer sure 'bout that?"

Ned stared at Alec and then smiled. "No, I ain't. Come on then. Let's go take a look-see."

∞⊂⊗

"I've made up my mind," Tobias Johnson said the next morning at breakfast, which he took with Grace — an unusual occurrence. "We leave in a week. I trust you will be ready."

"Leave?" Grace asked. "Where are we going?"

"Home."

"To Clevedon?" Grace stared at her father, her heart racing. "You said we needed to start again, that London was where you could find your way after Mama . . ." Her voice trailed off. She could not return to Clevedon, to a life of solitude with no mother to lighten the days, not after what she'd seen at the theater.

"I was wrong," her father said. "I miss the sea. This house does not suit me." He rose from the table and stood aside, waiting for Grace to precede him into the sitting room. No candles had been lit to soften the shadows cast in the half light of a spring morning on a cloudy day.

"I can't go with you," Grace said.

"And how do you propose to stay in London? Have you a husband waiting in the wings? I won't give you money, and there's nothing you can do to earn your keep." Grace sat in a hard chair while Tobias settled himself in a stuffed chair next to the fireplace. He stretched out legs grown too stout for his tight breeches. Two unshined brass-buckled shoes gleamed dully. Grace was glad her mother could not see how her death had reduced the man she'd called her husband for over twenty years.

"That's not true," she said.

"I suppose you think you'll get an engagement with that theater."

"Mama used to say that my voice was as good as any professional's."

"Your doting mother's opinion is irrelevant to this discussion." Tobias crossed thick arms across a sunken chest. "She knew nothing about the theater."

"I want to try." Grace rose from her chair and stepped toward her father. "Will you at least allow me to do that?"

"Make a fool of yourself?" He shook his head. "No."

"I could ask my aunt if I may stay with her. I won't need much money to live."

"Augusta?" To Grace's surprise, her father's scowl deepened. She knew he'd never had anything good to say about his wife's sister, but there was something menacing in his expression that she'd never seen before.

"She wrote to me," Grace said.

"What's this?" He gripped the arms of the chair with his hands and started to rise. "Show me."

Grace stepped back. "I, ah, I no longer have the letter."

Tobias settled back into his seat. "Whatever it says, you can depend upon it that Augusta is no friend of yours. And even if she were, I'm not giving you money to live in London. No, Grace, you will return with me to Clevedon, and that's an end of it. I do not wish to live alone, and your place is with me."

"I said that I cannot go with you, Father."

For a man well into his fifties and not in robust health, Tobias Johnson moved much faster than Grace thought possible. He shot to his feet and gripped her wrist. She tried to step back, but he held on, his fingers tightening.

"I am not afraid of you." She kept her voice steady, trusting that he was too distracted by his own anger to notice her flushed cheeks or hear the pounding of her heart. She breathed shallowly, her ribs still sore. Surely he'd not dare hit her again, not after he'd sworn that he'd not struck her the first time. Grace kept her eyes on his, noting with some satisfaction that even when standing, he had to crane his head back to meet her gaze.

"No?" He drew back one hand and slapped her hard across the side of the head.

The room exploded. Grace fell back against the side of the fireplace. He lunged forward to grab hold of her again. She flung her arm up and swept from the mantel to the hearth the figurine of a shepherdess swathed in a white toga and cradling a lamb.

Tobias teetered back on his heels and fell back into his chair, his reddened palm outstretched as if to catch the figurine before it hit the hearth tiles. But he was too late. Brightly painted shards scattered and bounced. He let out a low moan. "That was your mother's favorite! She brought it with her when we married."

Grace staggered to her feet and clutched the mantel with both hands. Only the head of the shepherdess—her red smile painted and pert—remained intact. She remembered her mother stroking the length of the figurine from tight curls to sandaled feet with one finger, her face clouded with memories she never shared with Grace.

Tobias nudged the head with one scuffed toe. "She said it was one of a pair but that she'd lost the other one."

Her father man slumped into the chair next to the fire, his eyes closing, blue-veined hands splayed across his knees. The burning of her cheek was nothing to the shame that twisted her heart. Her father blamed her for the death of her mother, and nothing she could say or do could change that—or bring her mother back.

"You know it was an accident," she said. "The mare bolted. I did everything I could to control her."

"Yes, yes." He nodded toward the sputtering fire. "Call Betsy to clean up the mess and tell her to build up the fire. It's getting cold in here."

"I miss her too," she said.

"Get out," he said. "You've done more than enough damage."

"Father . . ."

"Go."

She stood a moment longer and then turned and left the room.

ಬಂಗ

Alec brandished a letter. "I told you we'd find something."

"What?" Ned asked.

"It must have slipped under the bed." Alec gave the letter to Ned. "Go on and read it. You know I ain't able to."

Ned took the single sheet of paper and held it to the light of the candle. The writing was all loops and flourishes—a lady's hand.

"What's in it?"

"Give me a minute."

"Read it aloud. It's bound to tell you somethin' about where she's gone."

Ned felt somehow dirty reading Grace's private letter, but there was nothing for it. He had to find her or risk losing his position at the theater.

"All right." He cleared his throat and began to read—slowly and with plenty of pauses to decipher the words. At the theater, he mostly read printed playbills and prompt books annotated with Mr. Kemble's spiky handwriting.

"*My dear Grace. I trust this finds you well. I have heard from mutual acquaintances that you have arrived in London. To my dismay, I was obliged to employ subterfuge . . .*"

Ned looked up. "What the hell kind of word is that?"

"Don't ask me." Alec nodded at the letter. "Go on."

Ned sighed and began reading again.

" *. . . to employ subterfuge*—whatever that word means— *to discover your address since your esteemed father did not see fit to supply it. I am at least glad that you are finally in the city. My sister always wanted to live in London, but your father never saw* *fit to indulge her and now it is too late. I hope you will find the time to visit me in Grosvenor Square. Mr. Knowlton has left me a house tolerably fitted up although nothing like I was accustomed to in Jamaica. Percival asked after you recently and will be happy to see you. I myself am well enough, all things considered. My sister's death affected me most cruelly. She and I were such friends in our youth, and I mourn our . . ."*

Ned stopped again.

"What?"

"Hold on a mo." He mouthed the syllables and then cleared his throat and continued.

". . . estrangement these past several years, although the cause of it is unjustified. But we must put such things behind us. I await your reply."

"Blimey," Alec exclaimed. "I ain't understood one word in ten. What's she on about?"

"She sounds like a right old bat."

"Who do you think she is?"

"It's signed Augusta Knowlton. I'm guessing she's Grace's aunt."

"Is there an address?"

"Naw. The envelope's gone. But leastways we got something. An Augusta Knowlton in Grosvenor Square. Let's go see what we can find."

"I ain't going," Alec said. "Far as I can see, this Grace girl is just going to get you into trouble. If you want my advice, tell old Kemble that she's gone and then forget about her. He might rage a bit, but he won't let you go. You've made yourself too useful backstage. Besides, Mr. K. knows as well as any of us that London's full of stage-struck girls. And plenty of them can sing."

Ned folded the letter and tucked it into the waistband of his trousers, then led the way out of the room. "We best get back to the theater. We got *Hamlet* tonight, and I need to make sure the props are in place. Last time we lost the skull."

"You're not going to go lookin' for this Knowlton woman?"

"I didn't say that."

Chapter Six

*If this were play'd upon a stage now, I could
condemn it as an
improbable fiction.*

Twelfth Night (3.4.116–17)

*G*race left the house in Russell Square the next day while her father was still sleeping off his brandy from the night before. He'd gone out shortly after breakfast and returned in the small hours of the morning, his thumping and blustering waking her. She'd huddled under the bedclothes, eyes wide in the darkness, and counted the minutes until morning.

The day was fine, and Grace walked rapidly in the direction of Covent Garden. To her relief, no one paid her any attention. London was too full of people for anyone to care about a young woman alone. She reached the theater and lingered under the portico enclosed with Doric columns that fronted the principal public entrance on Bow Street. The bells at Saint Paul's tolled twelve times. She tried the door, knowing it had to be locked at this time of day, and was surprised when it opened easily. She slipped inside. The filtered light from high windows revealed a large and spacious saloon. Small stoves used to keep the space warm in the winter months lined the outer wall. A double staircase led to the upper circles. A door in front of her was open, revealing a shadowed view of seats in the lower circle just beyond. At night, hundreds of people—up to three thousand if one of the principals like Mrs. Siddons or Mr. Kemble was performing—crowded through the Bow Street and other entrances and with fans fluttering, milled around this saloon, mounted this staircase, and made their way to seats in the circles and benches in the pit. Grace sank onto one of the padded benches in the saloon, unsure now what she should do. The theater during the day felt somehow ominous—cold and uncaring in its emptiness. A coil of fear erupted at the base of her stomach.

A career in the theater? For her? Her mother would be horrified. Charlotte Johnson had never talked about any other future for Grace beyond making a good marriage that would take her away from her father's house.

Grace left the saloon and returned to Bow Street. She walked quickly toward the stage door. She'd just poke her head in and say goodbye to Mr. Harrison, maybe ask to see Ned one last time.

"Grace!"

Grace turned to see Olympia running toward her. As soon as she reached her, she threw her arms around Grace. "You've come back! Ned's been in a right state since Mr. Kemble told him to find you."

"Mr. Kemble wants to see me?"

"Mr. Kemble's always on the lookout for a new star, and maybe you're the one. A voice like yours is no common thing." Olympia linked her arm through Grace's. "I'm so glad you're back."

"But . . ."

"What's wrong? You're that pale. Come on inside. I can brew us a cup of Mr. Harrison's tea. The man lives on tea, when he's not living on gin." Olympia giggled.

"I don't know, Olympia. My father . . ."

"That man in the Piazza."

"Yes, but how did you know?"

"He was far too old to be your husband, and he appeared too respectable for a cock-bawd."

Grace stopped walking so suddenly that Olympia was pulled backward.

"Did you really think I was . . . ?" Grace could not even say the word.

Olympia laughed at the horrified expression on Grace's face. "Don't look so affronted, Grace. The theater can be a rough place, and I didn't believe Ned's story about you being his cousin for a second. I heard him talkin' with Alec about finding you in the streets. But you won't find people here care much about where you come from, so long as you get your lines right. You've got to be tough if you want to join us."

"Join you?"

"It's why you came back, isn't it? To join the company? And you should, if Mr. Kemble will have you. And from what Ned's said, he's already well disposed. The season's ending in a few weeks, but maybe you could join our summer troupe and then come back with us for the fall season. What with Agnes out sick and not likely to return, we *need* you to join us. Well, almost all of us, and you've got to learn not to mind Louisa."

"What are you talking about, Olympia? What is a summer troupe?" Grace wanted to press her hands down on Olympia's narrow shoulders to keep her still. A new future that she hardly dared to imagine glimmered just out of reach. She wasn't sure if she was terrified or hopeful.

"What it sounds like. We're actors and actresses who go around the country in the summer. The provincial theaters are pleased to have us. You could do a song or two to start, and then, as you got your confidence up, try your hand at acting a few scenes. We don't generally put on full plays in the summer. People enjoy a bit of variety—some singing, a bit of dancing if the stage is fit—and it isn't always—and a few of the famous soliloquies and the best bits from the plays that everyone knows." Olympia took Grace's hand. "Let's go in and talk with Mr. Renfrew. He's been put in charge of us what with Mr. Kemble and his sister going off to Ireland for the summer."

"What? No, Olympia! I can't go with you." Grace dug her heels in and pulled back, but Olympia just tugged harder.

"We're a jolly lot, and what's to stop you?"

"Well, ah, my father . . ."

"Excuse me, Grace, but he does not own you."

"Olympia!"

"Well, it's true. Mr. Renfrew should be in the script room. There's no harm in asking and no guarantee he'll say yes, anyway." Olympia opened the stage door and stood aside to let Grace pass, then let the door bang shut behind her. Grace blinked in the dim light. The room was empty but still smelled of old man and burning coals.

"Where is Mr. Harrison?"

"Sleeping it off somewhere, I should imagine. He never comes in before four. Now, take off your bonnet so that Mr. Renfrew can see your face, and stand up straight. Your height's an advantage in this business. Don't look as if you'll get the vapors at the sight of your own shadow."

Grace removed her bonnet and laid it on Mr. Harrison's chair. The notion that she could join the company was absurd at best—and dangerous at worst. But she could not turn away. What harm would it do to see this Mr. Renfrew and find out if he'd even consider her? There was no use tying herself in knots before she knew the score. That's what Mrs. Gale used to say—their housekeeper back in Clevedon. Her practical good sense and sympathy had often saved Grace when one of her mother's frequent bouts of melancholy put her beyond Grace's reach.

Grace followed Olympia down a long corridor to a small room carved like an afterthought into a corner behind the stage. Shelves overflowed with stacks of tattered scripts, most with the pages scrawled upon and dog-eared. She smelled musty costumes and stale perfume and gin.

"This is Mr. Renfrew," Olympia said, gesturing to a stocky young man who was reading a script. He glanced up and inclined his head in Grace's direction.

"Good afternoon."

"You remember Miss . . ." Olympia stopped and turned to Grace. "Dear me, I just realized that I never learned your surname."

"Ah, Green. My surname is Green."

Grace Green? She sounded like the gardener's wife. Even if Mr. Renfrew believed her, Olympia had to realize that she was lying. But to Grace's relief, neither of them even blinked.

"Charmed, Miss Green," said Mr. Renfrew. "I am delighted to see you back with us. Mr. Kemble was very taken with your voice and quite put out when you disappeared."

"Miss Green wants to join us this summer," Olympia said. "With Agnes poorly, we'll have need of her."

"Perhaps." Mr. Renfrew looked Grace up and down like she was livestock at a county fair. "We know already that you can sing, but have you any acting experience, Miss Green?"

"No, sir, but in addition to encouraging me to sing, my mother often had me recite scenes from the great plays."

"Do you have any notion of the hardships of a summer spent traveling from town to town? Miss Adams has likely not told you about the inferior accommodations, the drafty playhouses, some no better than barns leaking in the rain, and the often-impertinent audiences. You don't appear to me as if you could last a week."

Mr. Renfrew reminded Grace of a work-hardened sheepdog—the small, short-haired kind with a pointed nose and darting eyes. But instead of the usual black-and-white coloring of a sheepdog, he had bushy red hair and pink skin like a fresh-washed piglet.

He was not a handsome man, but he had a self-assured air about him that set him apart from the few young men of Grace's acquaintance.

"I am not accustomed to luxuries," she said stiffly.

"And you'll find none on a summer tour. You are sure you have the stomach for it? You're not going to squeal at the first sight of a rat in your lodgings?"

"I was brought up in the country and am familiar with the creatures. While I would not relish seeing them in the place where I sleep, I may be counted upon to take a broom to one without fainting." She refused to let this sheepdog man get the better of her.

"You are set on joining us?"

"Yes, sir." She kept her chin up and her eyes fixed on Mr. Renfrew. If she was to be an actress, she had better learn how to manage her emotions.

"The pay is dependent on the size of the audiences."

"Pay?"

"You don't think we do this purely out of our love for the drama, do you, Miss Green? We are working players, and the stage is our livelihood. We are not a haven for misplaced ladies and gentlemen." He started to turn away.

"No! Forgive me, sir. I did not mean to sound naive. I accept whatever terms are offered."

He turned back, red whiskers quivering, eyes narrowed. Grace half expected him to run around her and Olympia to herd them into a corner. "Good. We leave for Margate in two weeks and will be gone until the middle of August. Can you be ready?"

"Yes, sir." Excitement battled jolts of panic. What was she thinking? Her father would never allow her to travel around the country with a troupe of actors.

He'd sooner see her dead.

෨෬

"Ned!" Thomas Renfrew emerged from the men's dressing room and caught Ned by the arm. The last performance of the season had ended ten minutes earlier, and the theater still buzzed with the chattering of the company backstage

71

and the muted rumble of the audience moving out of the theater into the night.

"Sir?" Ned tried to keep the impatience out of his voice. His dislike for Mr. Renfrew increased daily. The actor's drinking before performances either made him belligerent or sick—and neither option made Ned's job any easier. Even worse was how he prowled around Olympia, who, to Ned's dismay, had so far done nothing to discourage him. He didn't think Olympia had succumbed to Renfrew's dubious charms, but she did not appear immune to them.

"What are your plans for the summer season?" Mr. Renfrew asked.

"I'll stay here as always. There's plenty to do organizing props and scenery backstage to get ready for the fall."

"You know that Mr. Kemble has put me in charge of the summer troupe."

"I heard as much."

"Yes, well, I don't believe his trust will be misplaced." Renfrew cocked his head to one side and smirked. "Mr. Kemble agrees that you will be better employed coming with us."

"I don't understand, sir."

"On tour, man. We need you to help backstage and to be a strong man when necessary. You're a fine, tall fellow capable of keeping unruly audiences in line. What say you?"

"I ain't never been out of London, sir. And if it's all the same to you, I'd just as soon not go. As I said, I got plenty to keep me busy here."

"That's as may be, but Mr. Kemble has given his blessing. You must come."

"I ain't got a choice in the matter?"

"I didn't say that, now did I? But I thought that you'd be wanting to come, seein' as that new girl — Grace Green? She's coming too."

"Grace? She's come back?" Ned couldn't hide a broad smile. It was a good job that he hadn't gotten himself into trouble going to see that aunt of hers.

"You and Miss Green — there is, I trust, nothing untoward going on?"

"What? Oh, no. 'Course not, Mr. Renfrew. Miss Green's a friend."

"Good. Keep it that way."

"Sir?"

"I would not wish to get in your way, although I confess it unlikely Miss Green would be attached to a man such as yourself." Mr. Renfrew smiled. "No offense intended." He pursed fleshy lips. "Miss Green intrigues me."

Ned swallowed the desire to smash his fist into Mr. Renfrew's smirking red face. "Miss Green is not your common sort." ·

"Which is why she intrigues me. I'm bored with our current crop of girls. Little Olympia has a bit more to recommend her than the others, but even she pales next to Miss Green. There's a quality about her that I'd like to investigate further, if you get my drift. I've already cleared her engagement with Mr. Kemble. He's charged me with watching her progress over the summer and letting him know if he should consider her for the fall season. Mr. Kemble trusts my judgment. Well, I'm sorry you don't wish to join us this summer. I'll ask Alec. He's good with his fists, and I don't know if we'd be better off with him. Good day to you, Ned."

"I'll go with you," Ned said quickly.

"Excellent. I shall tell Mr. Kemble."

Ned watched Mr. Renfrew scurry off, as much like a red-furred rat as any man had a right to be. Although relieved to hear Renfrew's waning interest in Olympia, the image of him sniffing around Grace almost propelled him to the pot he'd put in the wings to catch Mr. Renfrew's vomit.

ঙ০৫৪

"Go if you must. I'll not stop you." Tobias wrapped stubby fingers around a large glass of wine. Drops splattered the already-dirty tablecloth and speckled his cravat like bloody pinpricks.

"Thank you, Father." Grace stayed out of arm's reach and kept her voice cool — water to his fire. She would not show her surprise at his sudden change of heart. She'd accept it and worry later about what she'd do come fall when the company returned to London. Maybe by then she'd have made herself so indispensable that Mr. Kemble would take her on, and she could be free of her father forever. The prospect was bewitching.

"I'll not be thanked. Go and make a fool of yourself. I suppose I can't lock you in your room." He held the wine up, examined it in the candlelight like it was a fine claret and then spoke to it rather than look at her. "You should get married. That's what your mother wanted."

"And whom do you suggest I marry, Father?"

He set down the glass and scowled at her. "I'm sure there are plenty of men foolish enough to take you on. You're no beauty — not like your mother was — but your figure does well enough, and you're easy to do with when you don't get ridiculous notions into your head. Find someone rich."

"Some of the actresses receive considerable compensation. I do not need to be married."

"And you think *you'll* be one of them? You're an even bigger fool than I thought." Moodily, he swirled the wine in his glass and then took a long swig. He set the glass down but did not take his eyes off it.

"The theater has become a respectable place for women." Grace realized she still longed for her father's approval, never mind his forgiveness. She had not stopped being the child who years ago discovered that she mattered much less to him than did her mother.

"The theater will *never* be respectable."

"I will make sure I'm not exposed to censure."

"See as you're not. I don't want my name sullied."

"My stage name is Green."

Tobias squinted up at her. He was not wearing his wig. Unwashed strands of hair splayed across his skull— bleached out kelp on damp sand. For just a moment, his eyes flashed an agony so acute that Grace stepped back. And then it was gone, replaced by a sneer as he raised his glass in a mock toast. "How thoughtful of you. Miss Grace Green? Ridiculous. Now leave me. I have an engagement this evening."

"I will write, Father, if you wish."

"Do not trouble yourself."

Chapter Seven

To business that we love we rise betime,
And go to't with delight.

Antony and Cleopatra (4.4.20–21)

Ned hadn't expected to get much enjoyment out of touring the country with the company — and he was proven right. Carriages bumping across rough roads from one drafty inn to the next and provincial theaters in varying states of decrepitude made him long for the bustling Piazza and the solidly built Theatre Royal. To add to Ned's troubles, Mr. Renfrew was a poor manager, who picked favorites and paid little attention to anyone else's comfort but his own. Ned spent more time soothing the ravaged feelings of various members of the company than he did keeping track of props and costumes and sets.

The one bright spot in an otherwise grueling summer was seeing the growing friendship between Grace and Olympia. The two girls shared a room at the inns and went off to explore the towns when they had free time away from rehearsals and performances. He liked watching them laugh and chatter—one tall and gliding when she wasn't bumping into things, the other a blur of energy.

"Ned! Where's my dagger? I left it here on the props table, and now it's gone."

Ned kept his sigh to himself. Louisa Warren bustled into the tiny room that he'd commandeered at the theater in York to keep the props organized. He held out the wooden dagger.

"I took it to touch up the gold paint on the hilt," he said. "You'll not be needing it for another hour yet."

Louisa Warren snatched the dagger from Ned. Most of the time, he steered clear of her. If she wasn't fussing about a prop, she was demanding to know her cue or sidling up to him and asking him to tie a loose ribbon on her costume or pick off imaginary threads. He couldn't deny that Louisa was a fine-looking girl for those who liked the loud sort— all blooming cheeks and big teeth and masses of piled-up hair that from the back made her look like she was wearing lumps of coal on her head.

"How do you like my gown, Ned?" Louisa twirled around to show off the red velvet gown she wore to play the balcony scene from *Romeo and Juliet*.

"It looks well enough."

"Oh, Ned! You have no idea how to talk to a girl."

He didn't bother replying in the hope that she'd leave him in peace to get ready for the start of the evening performance.

"What a fuss last night with that fly," Louisa said, her coal head nodding, teeth bared in a smile.

"It worked out fine in the end."

"Yes, but such a crash! I thought the whole theater was caving in on top of us—scared me out of me wits."

"You were far enough downstage. The fly didn't get nowhere near you."

Ned didn't want to let on how mortified he'd been when a large fly painted with a castle scene crashed forward onto the stage. He prided himself on running a tight ship backstage, no matter how grim the theater. A few times that summer, they'd performed outdoors, and Ned had been obliged to use all his wits to figure out how to prop up the scenery. The night before, one of the lads charged with moving the fly had tripped, and the whole bleedin' thing had crashed to the boards.

"I heard you come onstage, although I didn't dare look around," Louisa said.

"I didn't have much choice, did I? I grabbed the end of the blasted thing and hoisted it up. The lad what tripped got back far enough to steady it, and then we wrestled it to where it was supposed to go."

Louisa laid a hand on his arm and widened her smile. Her breasts spilled over the top of the low-cut gown like freshly laundered pillows just begging for a man to lay his head on. "You saved the day."

Ned swallowed hard. "Aye, well, I didn't much like being out onstage. Don't know how you lot stand it. Bright as midday and hot as a bleedin' inferno with all them candles."

"I can't speak for everyone else, but I relish the heat."

"I'll stick to backstage. I got to get going now. Curtain's up in ten minutes."

"I can wait for you," Louisa said. She fluttered her lashes. He tried to take a step back, but she reached out and twined her fingers through his, lifting his hand with tantalizing slowness to her lips. "Later? I got a room to meself tonight."

"No. I don't think . . . I mean to say, I got work to do."

"You have to sleep somewhere, Ned." Louisa guided his hand to her chest, splayed his fingers across the creamy skin. "You don't need to be alone *all* the time."

"Oh!"

Ned stepped back so quickly that Louisa lost her balance and fell into his arms. Instinctively, he wrapped his arms around her to break her fall. Over her shoulder, he saw Olympia staring. For a few seconds, she held his gaze and then shrugged and turned away.

Ned tried to follow, but Louisa was like a dead weight in his arms. When finally he untangled his arms from hers, little Tommy—son of one of the older actresses—popped out of the wings and ran toward them.

"Ned, sir? Me mam needs you to come right away. The candle what she's supposed to carry in the sleepwalking scene's burned down so's it won't light, and she don't know what to do."

"I'm on it, Tom. Go tell your mam I'll be there in a shake."

Ned escaped with profound gratitude into the darkness of the wings.

ℰ൦ℭ

Grace quickly adapted to the life of a traveling player. She cheerfully endured bumping along the rough roads in drafty coaches to arrive at a new town every few days. To be sure, some theaters were close to falling apart, and she didn't much fancy the nights they performed in barns, but a fair number of the theaters were solid, well-built affairs that reproduced in miniature Covent Garden's massive

Theatre Royal, and she never once saw a rat. Her contribution to each night's performance was confined to singing two songs immediately following the interval.

She learned how to wrap her whole self around the nerves that soared and dived like gulls fighting over scraps on the beach. In the minutes before she walked onstage, she'd be convinced that her legs would give way under her, but then she'd feel Ned's hand on the small of her back, gently urging her forward, and her courage would return. Audiences loved her—stamping and whistling their approval. Grace felt as if she was finally stepping into the enchanted life she'd only dared visit in the fantasies of a lonely child.

One morning in Gloucester, Grace opened the newspaper and smoothed her hand across the page. She had become accustomed to seeing her name in print, but not yet hardened to the thrill of reading praise of her performance.

"Careful, Grace," said Olympia. "You'll get ink smudges all over you." Grace turned her hand palm upward. "Ah, well, too late. Read what they wrote about you this time."

"Miss Grace Green is a Talent to be reckoned with," Grace read. She looked up at Olympia. "Oh dear! I hope that's good."

"'Course it is. Go on."

"Madame Catalani had best watch her Back when she returns to the London Stage. Miss Green is poised to step into her Italian shoes and show that a British Voice does not need to play second fiddle to any Foreigner." Grace put down the paper. "Who is Madame Catalani?"

"Just the most famous singer in the world," Olympia said, clapping her hands with delight. "Oh, Grace! It's a great honor to be compared to her. You must let Mr. Kemble know when we get back to London."

"I suppose you think you're better than the rest of us." Louisa snatched the newspaper out of Grace's hands and threw it in the fire. "That so-called critic's a fool. I've seen Madame Catalani perform, and she is magnificent."

"Grace should be very proud of what she's accomplished since coming on the tour," Olympia said. "You're just upset because he wasn't so complimentary about your Juliet."

"I never take any notice of critics. They're a vile lot."

"Then why should you care what they say about Grace?" Olympia laughed. "Come now, Louisa. We don't want to be quarreling among ourselves. We've got enough to cope with tonight what with the barn of a theater we're supposed to perform in. I don't know how Mr. Renfrew thinks it's fit for anything but livestock."

"Is it so very bad?" Grace asked.

"Bad enough. Ned's spent the afternoon sanding down the worst of the splinters on the stage and finding rugs to put over the holes. We'll need to be careful where we step."

"Grace doesn't need to worry," Louisa said. "All she's got to do is stand at center stage and sing. The rest of us need to move around. Ned said that the platform rigged up for the balcony scene ain't fit to climb. I'll be risking my neck."

"Why don't you complain to Mr. Renfrew?" Olympia asked.

"And give him an excuse to replace me? Not on your life."

"There's no one to replace you, Louisa. You know that. What with Caroline gone off home to her mother and Grace with no experience with acting — and you know I never touch tragedy if I can help it—your position's safe enough. And if you're that worried about the balcony holding you, go tell Ned. You seem to be getting more than your fair share of his attention."

Grace was surprised to hear sunny-natured Olympia sound so cross. She'd long suspected Ned's feelings for Olympia but had not realized that Olympia might return them.

"I don't need *you* to tell me what to do," Louisa said. She stalked out of the room, and moments later they heard her calling for Ned.

"Ned's always so eager to help," Olympia said.

"Do you care for him?" Grace asked.

"Me? 'Course not. And as for Louisa, I wouldn't worry about anything she has to say. She's jealous."

"Why?"

"You're such an innocent! She's worried you'll take her parts, don't you see?"

"But I've never acted before."

"Yes, but you want to."

"I shouldn't think of it."

"I don't see why not. You got as much right as anyone to try."

Grace blushed and rubbed at the ink on her hand.

୫୦୧ଓ

Ned spent the afternoon working on the structure that held up the balcony platform. He had no confidence that the mechanism used to slide the platform out from the wings with Louisa perched on top would work. At least solving the problem of how to keep Louisa from falling headlong to the stage kept his mind busy and away from Olympia.

Three hours later, he couldn't help sucking in his breath when Louisa stepped out onto the platform to deliver her first line.

"O Romeo, Romeo! Wherefore art thou Romeo?"

The platform creaked, and Ned heard an ominous splinter. It would be a miracle if Louisa made it to the end of the scene without tumbling six feet to the stage. But to Ned's relief, the platform held, even when Mr. Renfrew scaled a rickety ladder and leaned his full weight against the balustrade. Ned had warned him not to, but Mr. Renfrew was never one to be told what he didn't want to hear.

As soon as Louisa and Renfrew made it through the scene, Ned signaled a boy to lower the curtain. He wiped the sweat from his forehead while the crowd roared their approval. The balcony scene was always a crowd-pleaser, although Ned couldn't see much in it.

Louisa clambered down from the platform and came to stand next to him, her chest heaving from the exertion. "Have you got the dagger?"

"Here." He handed her the wooden dagger. "Mr. Renfrew's changed the order of the program. Grace is to sing next, and then you'll do the death scene."

"What? He didn't tell me that."

"Mr. Renfrew does what he likes. Stand aside, if you don't mind." He looked around her into blackness. He didn't dare have candles lit; the old building was as dry as kindling. "Grace? Are you there? Two minutes."

"She's likely off preening. Fancy anyone comparing her to Madame Catalani. It's indecent, if you ask me."

Ned wanted to say that he had no intention of asking her, but he kept his mouth shut and kept peering into the darkness. Where was Grace? If he didn't get the curtain up soon, Mr. Renfrew would have his head. He'd exited to the other side of the stage after the balcony scene, but it wouldn't take him long to make his way around the back to find and yell at Ned.

Ned sensed movement just ahead of him. "Grace?"

"I'm sorry, Ned! I didn't know I'd been moved up." Her elbow caught him in the ribs as she teetered forward in the dark, and then, before he could grab hold of her, she slammed her full weight into Louisa.

Louisa crumpled to the floor, her scream and the crack of a bone muffled by Grace's body collapsing on top of her.

ༀൠ

"The physician has set her arm, but it's a bad business. She'll not perform for many weeks, perhaps months," said Mr. Renfrew. "Dry your tears, Miss Green. No one blames you."

Grace nodded and sniffed. She felt like a fool. Mr. Renfrew was being kind, but surely he couldn't keep her on after this. It wasn't the first time her clumsiness had gotten her into trouble. One night a few weeks back, she'd tripped over a loose floorboard onstage and got so close to the candles that she almost set her gown on fire.

"When we get to Bath in two days, you will go on as Juliet. Can you be ready?"

"You want *me* to take Louisa's place?"

"You're all that's left."

"But I have not yet acted," Grace said, her heart banging. She loved singing, loved it when people in the audience went quiet to listen to her, loved especially the way singing let her forget the life she'd left behind. But acting? That was something different altogether.

"Yes, but I believe you wish to act," said Mr. Renfrew.

"How do you know?"

"Miss Green, Grace, it is my business to know what my actresses are thinking and feeling." He reached for her hand. "You need not worry. I will be your Romeo."

"I know the part," she said.

"I expect you do. What young hopeful does not know Juliet?" He smiled. "I suggest we start this afternoon. Ned has commandeered a room behind the stables that we may use to rehearse in. You can be ready?"

"Yes." His palm felt like damp wool left to steam by the fire. She tried to extricate her hand, but he held on, not quite crushing her fingers.

"See as you are."

Just when she thought she'd gotten her nerves under control, a surge of panic threatened her breakfast.

ഇറയ

Several hours later, coached by Olympia and feeling marginally surer of herself, Grace arrived in the stables to meet with Mr. Renfrew. She knew her lines in the three scenes she was to play—the ballroom scene where Romeo and Juliet meet, the balcony scene, and finally the death scene. How many times had her mother sat on the sofa, clapping her hands in delight, as Grace declaimed Juliet's lines? Sometimes, her mother had even made suggestions about how to move and which words to emphasize. Grace was often surprised at the intensity with which her mother supplied direction, and wondered how she knew so much. Only once she asked her mother if she'd ever acted onstage. Her mother's snapped denial was enough to make Grace never ask again.

Mr. Renfrew took her hands between his and held them with the same damp grip, just tightly enough that she could not easily get free. "We will start with the balcony scene, my dear," he said. "Will that suit?"

"Yes, of course," Grace stammered. "You will need to guide me."

"I intend to." He caught and held her gaze. She'd never had a man look at her like that and she wasn't sure how it made her feel. Bathed in the afternoon light slanting through the window, Mr. Renfrew's face did not appear quite so plain. He had an open countenance and had already shown himself to be passionate in his opinions, even if she didn't always agree with them.

The words in her script danced and blurred. She took a deep breath.

"O Romeo, Romeo! Wherefore art thou Romeo?"

She broke off, laughing. "Oh dear! That sounds terribly wooden."

"It sounds perfect," Mr. Renfrew said gallantly. "But you could linger a trifle longer on the second Romeo, as if you're trying out the name on your tongue and deciding if it suits you."

"I'm already supposed to be in love with you." For the first time, Grace noticed that his eyes were a very deep brown—soft and admiring.

"That is true. Even so, a slight questioning might not come amiss. But of course, you must be the final judge of how you are feeling."

"I'm not sure what I am feeling." The words were out before Grace could draw them back.

"You are declaring your love for Romeo to yourself."

"Yes, of course." The pages of the script fluttered in her hands. She threw the thin volume on a table and turned away from him. "I'll try again."

"Romeo, Romeo! Wherefore art thou Romeo?"

She paused. "Better?"

"Perfect the first time, sublime the second."

Feeling more confident, she spoke the next few lines into the room, away from his gaze.

"And for that name which is no part of thee, take all myself!"

She turned to face him as he delivered his next line at full volume the way he'd do when calling from the stage to the balcony.

"I take thee at thy word.
Call me but love, and I'll be new baptized.
Henceforth I never will be Romeo."

He stepped forward and tried to take her hands, but she kept them firmly clasped behind her and raised her voice for the next line.

"What man art thou that thus bescreened in night,
So stumblest on my counsel?"

"I believe you'd sound more frightened," Mr. Renfrew said. "You're a young, inexperienced girl who is startled by a strange man in the middle of the night. Wouldn't you be terrified?"

"I'm not sure about that. Juliet is not an ordinary girl."

"Perhaps not, but I still maintain that she would be alarmed by a man's voice. Juliet is little more than a girl." He smiled and quoted, *"She hath not seen the change of fourteen years."*

"We're getting rather too carried away looking for hidden meanings," Grace said. "Let us continue." She felt she must keep her dignity, ignore the knocking of her heart, the warmth flushing her cheeks.

"As you wish."

Grace and Mr. Renfrew continued to trade lines, inching ever closer to the declarations of love that would seal the fates of their doomed characters.

"My bounty is as boundless as the sea," she said. This time when he reached for her hand, Grace let him take it. He drew her hand to his chest and held her palm flat over his heart. The fine cotton of his shirt was cool to the touch, but she sensed his heart beating under her fingers.

Before she could get out her next line, he pulled her close, bent back his head to gaze up at her, his lips inches from her lips. "You do not need to be afraid of me," he murmured.

His breath smelled faintly of last night's wine. Although shorter than she, he was broader, making her feel small and suddenly unsure of herself. A strange fluttering gripped deep in her belly — more pleasure than pain.

"My bounty is as boundless as the sea," she said again, stronger this time.

Would he kiss her? Did she want him to? She had so little experience of men. In Clevedon before her mother's death, the local curate had taken a liking to her. He sat near her at dinner parties, applauded when she sang, and did everything he could with limited personal charms to make himself agreeable. Grace had not paid the curate any serious attention, which was just as well. After the death of her mother, the curate no longer wanted anything to do with her.

She tried to step away, but Mr. Renfrew tightened his hold on her.

"I don't think . . ." she began.

The large wooden outside door creaked open, and Grace heard footsteps. Mr. Renfrew released his grip, and she stepped back, her face crimson. Ned strode into the barn. He did not glance at her, but she sensed his disapproval in the grim set of his jaw.

"Beggin' pardon, sir, Mr. Renfrew, but I got a matter to discuss with you 'bout the ticket arrangements for tonight."

"What is it, man? Can't you see I'm in the middle of rehearsal?"

"Aye, I can see well enough. The box office keeper says we can't charge more than what's normal for the performance tonight."

"We are from the Theatre Royal at Covent Garden," Mr. Renfrew said loftily. "We can charge what we wish."

"Will you come talk with the man?"

"Tell him I'll be there directly." He turned his back on Ned and spoke softly to Grace. "I am sorry, my dear. It appears that our rehearsal must be cut short. Do you feel confident?"

"Yes, thank you, Mr. Renfrew." She barely recognized her own voice.

Renfrew placed the palm of his hand against her cheek. One finger stroked downward toward her top lip. "I can help you if you let me."

Grace glanced back at Ned, who stood in the middle of the room, his arms crossed, blond brows furrowed. He would not look at her. Mr. Renfrew's meaning was clear even to her, but surely a liaison with him was impossible, unthinkable. Grace shook her head and stepped back. "Thank you, Mr. Renfrew. I believe I will manage."

When he brushed past her to follow Ned, she saw squinting eyes and lips pressed together, his irritation plain. Grace wondered if she would come to regret turning him down.

Chapter Eight

I have no other, but a woman's reason
I think him so because I think him so.

The Two Gentlemen of Verona (1.2.23-24)

A few yards from the open door of the makeshift dressing room Grace shared with the other actresses, the entire company pounded through the ballroom scene, the whirl of color and noise a prelude to her entrance as Juliet.

Ned appeared at the door. "Five minutes!"

She couldn't move. Singing was one thing, but this . . . acting? Saying lines and pretending to fall in love with Mr. Renfrew? She should never have come away with the company.

"Grace?"

"I can't, Ned. I . . ."

He held out his hand, palm upward, long fingers steady. "You can, Grace. I got faith in you."

The memory — never far from her mind — of rocks grinding against the wheels of the new gig — a light, two-wheeled affair — threatened her confidence.

The gig was more suited to smooth roads than the rough track that skirted the cliff edge at Clevedon. A stone wall curved with the track just ahead — too close. Grace pulled on the reins, but she could not stop the poor mare.

No! Grace rose to her feet. She could not let what happened to her mother hold her back.

"I am Juliet Capulet. I am Juliet Capulet," she said to herself as she followed Ned along the short corridor to the wings. Light blazed from the candles floating in oil baths placed in front of pieces of polished metal ringing the stage perimeter. Grace closed her eyes and breathed deeply into her belly to confront the fear that rose and swirled like sea foam.

"Go!" Ned's voice was hot in her ear.

She opened her eyes and walked slowly down the slight incline. The heavy train of her gown tugged at her shoulders, tipping her backward so she was in danger of losing her balance. She stiffened her spine and took small, shuffling steps. As the dancers swirled around her, Grace glanced up. Beyond the candles, Bath's New Theatre Royal heaved with people. Fashionable dandies preened themselves in the front rows of the pit. On benches behind them lounged tradesmen and clerks, with a sprinkling of gentlemen and the occasional rouge-cheeked whore. From the three tiers of boxes, elegant arms waved fans to paramours across the narrow expanse of the auditorium. The theater was as brightly lit as the stage.

The music faded, and a hush fell over the audience. Grace lowered her eyes and stopped a few feet from the front of the stage to wait for Mr. Renfrew. She held her hands in front of her stomach to keep them from shaking.

Mr. Renfrew stepped forward and grabbed Grace's elbow.

"If I profane with my unworthiest hand . . ."

He half turned to the audience, his features arranged in a sentimental leer. Instead of looking at her as he'd done in rehearsal, he declaimed his lines into the auditorium. He had not forgiven her.

"This holy shrine, the gentle sin is this;
My lips, two blushing pilgrims, ready stand . . ."

In Renfrew's case, the blushing pilgrims owed a great deal to a pot of red paint. Grace cocked her head to one side to indicate her struggle between doubt and curiosity. She would not let him get the better of her. Mr. Renfrew brushed the top of her hand as lightly as possible so as not to smudge the paint.

"To smooth that rough touch with a tender kiss."

When Mr. Renfrew drew back, Grace held her arm out, her fingers just grazing his chest. She delivered her first line.

"Good pilgrim, you do wrong your hand too much . . ."

Mr. Renfrew sighed with such vigor that her next line stopped at the first few rows of the pit.

"Which mannerly devotion shows in this . . ."

A few titters rose from the pit. She shouted her next two lines.

"For saints have hands that pilgrims' hands do touch,
And palm to palm is holy palmers' kiss."

She placed her two palms together as if in prayer. Out of the corner of her eye, she saw a pair of young men stroll across the empty space between the first row of the pit and the orchestra. One cuffed the other's shoulder and tossed him a small purse. When they reached the end of the stage, they turned to walk back. Mr. Renfrew nodded at the men, who both hallooed greetings. She'd seen Mr. Renfrew greet acquaintances from the stage before, sometimes in the middle of his most tragic soliloquies, but this was *her* debut. Grace drew herself up to emphasize the height difference and heard a few chuckles. Mr. Renfrew looked up at her with surprise, but at least he looked at her.

They played the rest of the scene like two pugilists circling each other in a ring of blood-steeped sand.

Mr. Renfrew lunged at her for his final kiss just as Olympia, dressed outlandishly as the Nurse, swept across the stage.

"Madam, your mother craves a word with you."

Olympia's shameless mugging soon had the crowd roaring their appreciation, all the pretended tenderness of Grace's scene with Mr. Renfrew forgotten. At least three times, Olympia's antics drew so much laughter that Grace's lines were lost. She had to look ridiculous mouthing words no one could hear. Grace forgot about feeling anything other than rage as she shouted her newfound love for Romeo.

"My only love sprung from my only hate!"

A man in the front row let out a loud guffaw that set off several of the other men. Her face flamed the color of her dress. When Mr. Renfrew stepped forward to speak with the Nurse, Grace fled from the stage.

ಔಂಗ

The next morning Ned rose early with the intention of finding and destroying any of the newspapers that might be delivered to the inn. He was too late. Renfrew was already up and fuming. He threw a copy of the paper down on the table, splattering grease from a plate of half-finished eggs. Ned was at least grateful that none of the girls had come down to breakfast yet.

"Stupid girl. I thought better of her."

"She did all right, sir," Ned said loyally. "She just needs some time to get used to acting."

"I don't have time. We have two weeks left on the tour, and I can't risk putting her onstage again. That business in the death scene! People were laughing."

"That weren't Grace's fault, sir."

"She dropped the dagger, for God's sake! What kind of an actress drops the dagger in the death scene? No wonder people laughed. It was a good job I was already dead, or my lines would have been lost. As it was, I wanted to sink through the floor. I should never have put her on."

"Grace will work hard to get better. You can't just dismiss her."

"I most assuredly can, and I believe I will." Mr. Renfrew squeezed his nostrils together as if he'd just scented a particularly plump fox. "Don't look at me like that. I'll send her off with her pay. She mentioned that she grew up in Clevedon, which isn't too far from here. She can get a coach from Bristol tomorrow."

Ned felt as if he'd been punched in the gut. Mr. Renfrew believing he could have his way with Grace was bad enough, but this anger toward her was worse. Much worse. It was all on account of that damn critic.

Wooden and unlifelike . . .

A Shadow of a Girl without a Hope of exciting Passion in herself, let alone her Romeo (played masterfully by the incomparable Thomas Renfrew), and most certainly not her Audience . . .

Miss Green is best advised to attend to her Needlework. Acting is not for her.

"When will you tell her?" Ned asked.

"I see no profit in wasting time." Mr. Renfrew mounted the stairs leading to the rooms, and moments later Ned heard him banging on the door to the room shared by Grace and Olympia.

The seagulls were making almost as much racket as Mr. Renfrew when Ned emerged from the inn and inhaled a noxious mix of sulfur from the baths and fresh horse droppings. He'd rarely felt so helpless. Anger at Renfrew was mixed with worry about what would become of Grace when she left the theater.

He wished the tour was over and he was back in London where he knew the lay of the land. Bath unnerved him—too much cream-colored stone with every house looking just like the one next to it. And the theater was far too small. He missed prowling the dark corridors backstage at Covent Garden and the convenience of a well-stocked prop room.

"Excuse me, but do you work at the theater?"

A man as tall as Ned stepped forward. He was dressed with the casual elegance of a gentleman—snowy cravat elaborately pleated, black coat of fine wool, boots shined.

Ned touched his hand to his forehead. "Sir."

"I am looking for one of the actresses—a Miss Johnson? I was told the Covent Garden company was staying at this establishment."

"We don't got no Miss Johnson in the company, sir," Ned said. He couldn't say why, but something about the gentleman put him off. He reminded Ned of one of those big cats that he'd seen at the menagerie — sleek and well fed, sleeping most of the time, but deadly when it got its claws out.

"That is not true," the man said. "I saw her perform last night."

"I ain't lying, sir," Ned said. "You must have mistook her for someone else."

"I assure you that I have not."

"Percy?"

Ned turned to see Grace standing in the doorway to the inn. Tears streaked her face.

"Do you know this gentleman?"

"Hello, Grace," the man said and bowed.

ஐ

Grace grimly appreciated the irony that the last time she'd encountered her cousin Percival Knowlton was during her first and only visit at the age of twelve to the very same theater that had witnessed her disgrace the night before. Grace's father had been away on one of his crusades to the shipyards of Liverpool. If he'd been home, Mrs. Johnson would never have dared take Grace with her to stay with her sister Augusta in Bath. And she certainly would not have taken Grace to see *Hamlet* at the old Theatre Royal. Grace remembered seeing the actor who played the doomed Dane standing alone at the front of the stage, one hand raised to the candles flickering in the massive chandelier, the other at his hip. He was very handsome — tall and commanding, his broad forehead shining in the candlelight.

"To be or not to be, that is the question."

Grace's mother leaned forward, her elbows resting on the edge of the box, her fan drooping from her wrist. In profile, her mother appeared almost young again, the lines of disappointment smoothed out, her lips mouthing Hamlet's well-loved speeches. Aunt Augusta sat on the other side of Grace. Directly behind her lounged Percival, a lanky youth of fifteen.

"Pretty poor specimen if you ask me," he hissed in Grace's ear. "Mama's right to despise him."

Grace ignored him.

"Whether 'tis nobler in the mind
To suffer the slings and arrows of outrageous fortune . . ."

She knew the speech, having practiced it many times with her mother. Sometimes Grace overheard her parents arguing about her.

"She's never to set foot in a theater, Charlotte. I forbid it."

"I see no harm in teaching her to speak well."

"There is a very great difference, my dear, between speaking well and acting. We must not raise another actress."

"He's an ass," whispered Percival. Grace resisted the urge to swing around and smack him across the face with her fan. She closed her eyes to hear the actor, without the distraction of the people seated in the boxes across from them — so close that Grace could see jewels glinting at the throats and wrists of the ladies.

The actor finished his soliloquy and accepted the enthusiastic applause with a graceful bow. Aunt Augusta rose to her feet and shook out her fan. Grace glimpsed a painted scene of ocean waves and palm trees.

"Come, Percival. We will not stay."

Charlotte Johnson twisted around to look up at her sister. "You can't mean to leave now, Augusta."

"I cannot bear another moment. His acting has become insufferable. Are you coming?"

"No. We will find our own way home. It is not far."

"Suit yourself." With more noise than she needed to make, Augusta scraped her chair out of the way and swept from the box. Percival pinched Grace's arm between two hard fingers and then laughed when she gasped and turned red.

In the ten years since Grace had seen Percival Knowlton, he'd grown very tall and some would say exceedingly good-looking. His smug self-assurance had definitely increased. She allowed him to take her arm and walk with her along the street to a tearoom.

"Dear Cousin, I am impossibly chagrined!" Percival said as soon as they were seated. "Your charming mother! My most beloved aunt! I was otherwise engaged when she was laid to her rest, and was not able to come."

"My mother has been dead for close to a year."

"I can only plead the demands of business and society." He sighed theatrically and placed one long-fingered hand against his chest.

"My aunt is in good health?"

"Ah, dearest Mama manages as well as can be expected. The news of her poor sister's death distressed her terribly."

"Aunt Augusta and my mother were hardly the best of friends."

"My dear Cousin, you are too harsh. My mother *doted* on her sister. When the news came of your mother's untimely passing, dear Mama took to her bed for *days*. I feared for her health." Percival closed his eyes as if to hide the excess of emotion brought on by worry for Augusta Knowlton.

"My aunt appears to have recovered, Cousin. The writing in the note she sent to me when I was in London showed no signs of feebleness."

"Well, yes," Percival opened his eyes. "I am glad to report that my mother appeared remarkably robust when I saw her last."

"And that was?"

"About a fortnight ago. She so looks forward to my visits."

"She is a lucky woman."

"Quite."

For a few seconds, they sat in silence, pleasantries exhausted. Grace knew she had to speak first or risk surrendering the upper hand. She suspected that Percival would be only too happy to seize it.

"I—"

"You—"

The words clashed in midair. Percival held up one hand and rotated his wrist with conscious delicacy. Grace caught a whiff of expensive soap.

"What do you want, Percival?" she asked.

"Even as a child, you were always charmingly direct," he said, sitting back and crossing one leg over the other. Every inch of Percival screamed privilege. *His* mother had married a man of rank and wealth. "Do you remember the time you threw a soup spoon at me when you were six?"

"It is one of my most cherished memories." Grace met his gaze squarely. "You have sought me out for a reason, Percival, and I'm quite sure that it has nothing to do with extending condolences for my mother's death or reminiscing about a childhood we never shared."

"I have always admired you."

"I doubt that." She wanted to be gone from the noisy tearoom full of gossiping women and ancient men waiting to dip their gouty legs in the baths.

"A month ago, your father came to me."

Grace's attention snapped back to Percival. "What are you talking about? My father has never had anything to do with my mother's family."

"People change, Grace." Percival smirked. "I anticipate that the news I must impart will be unwelcome, and I regret it, but there is no remedy for it."

"Please, Percival, get to the point. I have a great many things to do today."

"You are performing again tonight?"

"Just tell me," she said wearily.

Percival took a sip of tea and then carefully set his cup onto a saucer painted with a pink butterfly fluttering above a cluster of small purple flowers. An elegant, two-tiered cake plate rested on the table between them. The sight of the tiny cakes and sandwiches turned Grace's stomach. She'd told Percival that she was not hungry, but he'd ignored her and ordered the food anyway.

"As I said, your father and I met. He wished to consult with me about the disposal of his estate."

"Why you?"

"Because, dear Grace, he has decided to make me his sole heir."

Grace sprang to her feet, knocking the small table and toppling the overloaded cake plate. Crustless sandwiches, iced cakes, and other delicacies tumbled to the black-and-white-tiled floor. Several scones rolled as far as the elegantly slippered feet of two ladies seated nearby.

Chapter Nine

What's gone and what's past help
Should be past grief.

The Winter's Tale (3.3.219-220)

Grace hated the pity on her friend's face. It pushed and prodded at her heart like a hot knife through butter.

"That's so unfair! Why would your father be so cruel?" Olympia took Grace's hand and led her to a bench placed alongside the Gravel Walk leading away from the Royal Crescent. Grace had never been to this part of Bath with its uniform houses sweeping in elegant arcs and circles. She'd run headlong into Olympia after leaving the tearoom. They'd walked quickly up the hill from the Theatre Royal, Grace not knowing or caring where they went, trusting Olympia to keep her close.

"My father was very angry at me for joining the company," Grace said as they sat on the bench. "He doesn't want me in the theater."

"But to cut you out of his will!"

Grace despised people who felt sorry for themselves, but at this moment, she could not help the desolation that filled her heart in the wake of Percival's announcement. He had been surprisingly compassionate of her feelings, but that did not take away from the precariousness of her position. She took a deep breath and pushed back tears. She must *not* give in. "I agree it is a harsh thing for my father to have done, but he is right about me not belonging in the theater." She inhaled another ragged breath and caught a whiff of orange-scented cologne from a pair of passing dandies. She wondered if they were the same men who had waved at Mr. Renfrew during her performance as Juliet the night before. Unlikely. In Bath, every other young gentleman squeezed his legs into leather breeches and wore a blue coat with brass buttons. Most of them also wore white cravats so stiff and high that they could not look down to see their boot tops. Remembering the dandies brought Percival to mind. His dress had not been quite as extravagant as the two young men walking past, but he would not be out of place in any collection of fashionable men.

"For goodness' sake! It was just the one performance. You'll improve. The first time I got onstage with a speaking part, I forgot half my lines."

"Mr. Renfrew thinks I am not suited to the theater. Tomorrow, when the company goes on to London, I will return to my father's house in Clevedon."

"You can't give up so easily! And what about me? I will miss you! And Ned too. You can't go!"

"I'm sorry, Olympia, but it's impossible for me to stay." Grace smiled sadly. She'd never had a friend like Olympia—so loyal and funny, so full of warmth and kindness. In fact, she'd never had an intimate friend of any kind. The young ladies in her neighborhood in Clevedon had envied Grace's singing voice but had no use for her company. She was too tall and too serious, and most of all, she was the daughter of Tobias Johnson, who everyone knew had radical opinions about everything from impressment to the slave trade. And after the accident that took her mother's life, no one wanted anything more to do with the family.

"You must at least stay to watch Mrs. Siddons tonight," Olympia said, taking Grace's hand. "I'll never forgive myself if you go away without seeing her."

"She's performing?"

"Yes! You've been so preoccupied that you must have forgotten. She's stopping in Bath on her way back to London from Ireland. Her brother has gone ahead, but Mrs. Siddons spent a great deal of time here when she was younger and has decided to favor the Bath Theatre Royal with her presence. Oh, Grace! Tonight, she's playing Lady Macbeth. You can't miss the sleepwalking scene. Stay and watch with me backstage. I'm on just the once as the servant girl."

"What about Mr. Renfrew?" Grace knew she was foolish to even consider staying. Why torment herself? She resolved to return to her father's house without delay and confront him about the will. He could not be allowed to leave her penniless. But Mrs. Siddons! Grace might never get another chance to see the great actress perform. Although past fifty and almost at the end of her career, "The Siddons," as she was known, was larger than life—the epitome of the sublime, celebrated throughout Britain as *The Tragic Muse*. Some said that Mrs. Sarah Siddons was the finest actress of this age or any age.

"Mr. Renfrew can go hang," Olympia said. "He can hardly throw you out into the streets. He'd have to get Ned to do it, and you know he wouldn't."

"I will miss Ned. It's thanks to him that I got onstage in the first place."

"Yes, we all depend upon Ned." Olympia jumped up and seized Grace's hand. "Come on. We have time to get back to the inn and pack your trunk and then have a bite of supper before the performance."

Olympia's cheerful humor—even if a trifle forced—encircled Grace like a gust of sparkling air bringing with it abandoned hopes. She let her friend pull her along the pathway that led into Back Lane and then made a sharp right onto Barton Street and the way back down the hill to the theater. There would be plenty of time for misery and recriminations in the days ahead. If she did not see Mrs. Siddons now, she might never get another chance.

⁗⁖

A plump, middle-aged woman with a striking profile bustled along the corridor leading from the outside door to the dressing room allocated for her use. Grace's first impression was that Mrs. Siddons appeared to be a respectable lady who wouldn't be out of place presiding over a whist table. She reminded Grace of her own mother—taller than average and with the same strong features Grace saw in her own mirror every morning.

"Should I introduce myself?" Grace whispered.

Olympia shook her head. "I wouldn't risk it until after the performance. Mrs. Siddons may appear affable, but I've heard that she's very reserved and particularly objects to anyone distracting her from her preparations."

Grace followed Olympia to a vantage point backstage from where they commanded an excellent view of the stage. A buzz of voices filled the pit; the theater would soon be full. No one wanted to miss Mrs. Siddons's performance as Lady Macbeth. Mr. Renfrew paced nearby. He was to play Macbeth—a role he'd performed many times but never opposite such a formidable partner. His ashen face and jerky movements betrayed his nervousness. Grace was not above feeling some satisfaction.

Even from Grace's position offstage, the heat from the candles penetrated her bones. The mingled smells of smoke and face powder, sawdust, and excited bodies mocked a future stinking of salt air and damp earth.

"Look!" Olympia clutched Grace's arm. "She's making her entrance."

Mr. Renfrew was no match for the commanding presence of Mrs. Siddons as she swept onstage for their first scene together. Mrs. Siddons delivered her lines with a riveting force that silenced the packed theater. Grace moved away from Olympia and wrapped her arms around herself. Perhaps by holding fast to her own body, her feet would stay on the ground. When Mrs. Siddons turned her head toward Mr. Renfrew, the burning of her eyes pierced Grace's soul.

"Screw your courage to the sticking place and we'll not fail."

An hour later in the sleepwalking scene, those eyes glowered with such unseeing ferocity that Grace needed to lean against Olympia for support.

"Here's the smell of the blood still.
All the perfumes of Arabia will not sweeten this little hand."

Grace bit her tongue to prevent herself from crying out when Mrs. Siddons stopped rubbing her hands and faced the audience.

"*O, O, O!*"

The wail filled every corner of the auditorium, caught hold of every heart, the awed silence so profound that Grace was sure she heard the squawking of gulls cresting the winds high above the theater.

"Well?" Olympia asked when the play was over and Mrs. Siddons had retired, flushed and triumphant, to her dressing room. "Was she not wonderful?"

"Wonderful does not even begin to describe her! Thank you for making me stay."

"You're sure we can't find a way for *you* to stay?"

"A miracle?"

Olympia laughed and patted Grace's arm. "At least you still have your sense of humor. I refuse to believe that you'll bury yourself forever in that Clevedon place." She rose on her tiptoes and kissed Grace's cheek. "Depend upon it, Grace. You will be performing again within the year."

Grace did not reply. She could not.

8003

Ned watched Olympia and Grace standing in the wings during the sleepwalking scene. Grace was leaning against Olympia for support. For just about all the years he'd been a man, Ned had more or less sworn off women. The risk of doing to one of them what had been done to his own mother was too great.

So how had his life become so complicated? He almost longed for the days before he'd come to the theater, when he'd kept himself to himself, only occasionally following Alec to the brothel for a random push. Ever since Olympia—and now Grace—had come into his life, Ned barely knew up from down.

Ned wished he could grab Renfrew by the scruff of his scrawny neck and shake him like the dog he resembled. Where did he get off dismissing Grace like she was little better than a housemaid? Ned decided to speak with Mr. Kemble when the company returned to London. The chances of Kemble listening to him were remote—after all, Ned was just the backstage man, while Mr. Renfrew was a real actor—but he had to try.

The two girls turned away from the stage and joined him in the wings. Out front, the audience exploded with applause as wild and unfettered as a fusillade of bullets raking distant battlefields.

"Ned!" Grace exclaimed. "I've seen her at last."

"Aye, she's a wonder and that's for sure." He smiled down at Grace. "Can I do anything for you? Help you with your trunk and all?"

"Thank you, no, Ned. Olympia's already found a boy at the inn to take the trunk to the coach yard. I leave early in the morning."

Ned stood awkwardly in front of the two girls. Olympia was holding tightly to Grace's hand. "I'd best get her back to the inn," she said.

"Yes, 'course." Ned stood aside to let them pass.

Grace stopped in front of him. "You've been so terribly kind to me, Ned. I won't forget you."

"Weren't nothing, Grace. You take care of yourself now."

"I will try." Impulsively, she kissed him on the cheek and then turned and hurried with Olympia down the dark corridor toward the stage door.

"Ned! The rain effect's buggered. We need you to come."

Sighing, Ned followed Tommy around the back of the stage to tend to the box full of pebbles that, when shaken, was meant to imitate the sound of rain on a roof. A jagged cut in the box had emptied out the pebbles. Ned ordered Tommy to look for them while he figured out a way to repair the hole.

Maybe it was just as well that Grace was leaving before Renfrew got the better of her. She was too innocent for her own good. And as for Olympia, Ned resolved to stay away. It did no one any good to complicate life.

⁖⁗

Dressed in black with her pale hair hidden by a wide-brimmed bonnet, Grace attracted no attention when she stepped down from the coach in Bristol at noon the next day. The yard teemed with activity and noise. Compared to refined Bath with its uniformly constructed modern houses, Bristol was a much rougher town—its docks and harbor crammed with ships. Most of them sailed into port packed with sugar from the West Indies and then journeyed south to Africa with holds overflowing with bolts of cloth and other manufactured goods to trade for slaves bound for the islands of the Caribbean. Grace's father had often railed against the enormous profits reaped by those responsible for keeping the ships plying the Atlantic triangle afloat with human misery.

One of the few times Grace remembered seeing her father smile with satisfaction was a year earlier—just a month before her mother's death—when an Act of Parliament ended the trade of souls for sugar, but not the practice of slavery itself. Her father had been tireless in his efforts on behalf of the abolitionists—writing pamphlets and encouraging anyone who would listen to abstain from using sugar in order to protest slavery on the Caribbean plantations. Grace had grown up torn between resenting her father's frequent absences and being happy to share the solitude with her mother.

Rather than stay in the noisy yard to wait two hours for the coach back to her father's house in Clevedon, Grace walked toward the docks to watch the bustle of boats and men. When she was a child, her father had spent a great deal of time in Bristol, talking with sea captains and sailors. He'd once staggered home with blood caked to his face and his right arm dislocated after being beaten for distributing his pamphlets critical of the slave trade.

A block from the coach yard, a young woman ran into the street, her hair unpinned and cascading in tangled ropes down her back. The woman gaped at Grace, her eyes wide.

"Gone!" she shrieked. "My Robert!" The woman gripped Grace's arm, drew her close. "Do you hear? He's gone."

"I'm sorry!" Grace stammered. "What's happened? Is Robert your child?"

"My husband. They've taken him." The woman lurched away from Grace and stumbled a few steps down the street before turning back. "The sailors. They're getting that bold. Mostly they take men from the tavern for their filthy navy, but my Robert was no tavern goer. They came into our house before dawn. Our house, ma'am! I screamed and tried to stop them, but they threw me to the floor so's I hit my head." Tears splashed down the woman's cheeks. "Poor Robert! What am I to do?"

"I'm sorry." Grace's heart bled for the woman—the despair in her eyes a reproach.

"It ain't your fault, ma'am," she said. "It's this damn war. Beggin' your pardon, but the King's Navy got no right takin' respectable men."

Run-down houses lined both sides of the street. Grace suspected that the woman, and her children, if she had any, would be confined to the workhouse long before her husband returned home—if he returned. Grace had read about the naval battles in the Atlantic campaign. The Royal Navy had been victorious in restricting the movement of French ships between the West Indies and France, but at the cost of how many lives? Suddenly, Grace felt ashamed. *She* had a warm house to return to, and, however grudgingly, her father would not let her starve, at least so long as he remained alive. *She* did not need to fear press-gangs or cannon fire or workhouses or the degradations of poverty. Grace reached into her small purse and pulled out a handful of coins.

"Please," she said as she pressed the money into the woman's hand. "It's not much, but it might help, and maybe your husband will escape."

"He'll not escape, ma'am. No one does." Hard living and deprivation had etched gray lines into a face that must once have smiled with love for a man likely chained in the reeking hold of a ship at anchor in the harbor. "But I thank ye for your kindness." A child cried and she turned away, her shoulders slumped with the weight of an unknown future.

Grace wanted to follow her, but knew she had no more help to give. Her father had often railed against the cruel work of the press-gangs.

"They kidnap Englishmen!"

"Does that mean they should not be taken?" Grace asked. *She was ten years old and had already noticed that her father's blustering softened when she asked questions. He might not have been a fond father, but he rarely neglected an opportunity to instruct her.*

"Indeed, it does, my dear. An Englishman has rights. He is not a slave."

Grace walked on to the coach yard. She remembered her mother telling her that Mrs. Siddons had incited the ire even of her admirers when she revealed that she watched people in despair so she could mimic their misery when she was onstage. Grace thought of the poor woman in the street. She had never seen such anguish. Could it ever be right to counterfeit it? And would she ever again get the chance? Grace answered her own question with the expected no. Her future stretched before her with numbing predictability—empty days and lonely nights with only her memories for comfort.

Just as Grace reached the coach yard, a fresh gust of wind roared in from the Bristol Channel, making the horses stamp nervously. An old man—the spitting image of Mr. Harrison—clutched at his soiled wig. Grace stopped walking so suddenly that her heels sank into a steaming pile of manure. She jumped back and steadied herself against a post.

"Careful there, miss," called the man. "Ye've got to watch your step in here."

"Yes, thank you," she called back. The answer to her troubles, the chance she needed, was within her grasp. Why had she not seen it earlier? Well, no matter. She saw it now. All she had to do was reach out and take it, grasp hold with both hands, and shake it into submission. *She* would not be like the poor young wife bewailing the loss of her Robert, powerless to change her fate.

Grace would not face defeat without a fight.

Chapter Ten

Get thee a good husband,
and use him as he uses thee.

All's Well That Ends Well (1.1.200–01)

*M*r. Kemble walked with Ned through the dark wings to the stage at the Theatre Royal, Covent Garden. All around them, men and boys hammered and sawed, getting the flies and props and machinery ready for the new season.

"He dismissed her?"

"Yes, sir. I tried to tell him not to. Grace, Miss Green? She weren't that bad."

"Quite right. Renfrew had no business telling her to go. I don't care how poorly she performed. I am not in the habit of turning my actresses out to the street. Can you get her back, Ned?"

"I can try, sir. Olympia's her friend. She'll have an address."

"Good. When I said I thought the girl had potential, I meant it. Mr. Renfrew should learn not to cross me."

Ned couldn't help feeling gratified and hoped a time would come when Mr. Kemble found a reason to dismiss Renfrew. The man was nothing but trouble.

"I hear poor Louisa is still laid up," Mr. Kemble said. "I gather she'll not be ready for the start of the season?"

"No, sir. She's gone back to her mother's house in Kent."

"We're still short an actress and only a fortnight left to find one."

"Yes, sir."

"Miss Green deserves another chance. See to it that she's brought back. I'll deal with Renfrew. He needs to remember that he is in *my* theater on *my* sufferance."

"Sir!"

ᘒᘓ

Grace was surprised that her aunt's house in London was not as grand as she expected. A door scarred with peeling paint rose from a dusty stoop. Most of the other houses in the square were well maintained, which made her aunt's house look even shabbier. Grace checked the number again, and then took a deep breath and started up the stairs. Exhausted after the long journey up from Bristol, she caught her foot on the top stair. The door opened while she was still gripping the bannister with both hands to regain her balance.

"Yes?" The young woman regarded Grace with curious insolence. "You want to see the mistress?"

Grace nodded. "Tell her that her niece is here."

"She's in the front room. You can go in yourself. The footman's off today, so ain't no one to announce folk."

Grace followed the girl into a damp hallway.

"She's in there. Go on."

The cramped parlor smelled hot and stale with an underlying sweetness—lavender, Grace thought. Her aunt was sitting on an upholstered chair facing the fireplace.

"Aunt Augusta?"

The woman swiveled her head to peer up at Grace. An involuntary spasm of grief shook Grace as she regarded features so closely resembling the face she'd last seen lying lifeless on a bed in Clevedon. With a composure worthy of Mrs. Siddons, Augusta replaced a flicker of alarm with a slight curl of her upper lip. "I lost hope of ever seeing *you* again."

Grace sat uninvited in the chair opposite her aunt and removed her gloves and bonnet. "You are well?"

"I am alive. What do you want?"

"I need to come live with you, Aunt, here—in London."

"You don't waste time, do you?"

"No."

"Your father's house in Clevedon isn't good enough for you? Hardly surprising. My sister loathed it there."

"She was not always unhappy, Aunt."

Augusta stared at Grace, her eyes red-veined bulges in a face that had once been beautiful. The ends of the pink ribbons dangling from her lace-trimmed cap had faded to the color of thin gruel. "Are you going to tell me why I should take you in?"

"For my mother's sake." Grace sat up straighter, determined not to let her aunt see that her words were capable of hurting her.

"Your mother would not have done the same for my Percival."

"You don't know that."

"Yes, I do."

Grace bit back a sigh. "I know that you and my mother were not friends, Aunt, but she is at peace now, and I cannot go back to my father's house."

"Percival has told me all about it. You are disinherited, and now you expect me to take you in. You presume a great deal."

"It will be a temporary arrangement."

"Until when?"

"Until I find another position at the theater."

Augusta threw back her head and laughed so hard that her cap slipped over one eye, giving her a rakish look. She pushed it back into place. "You are still set on the theater? You know it is not respectable."

"The status of an actress is much improved, and I'm sure you agree I must do something to earn my keep."

"You could get married or, failing that, go to work as a governess. At least then you'd have some chance of falling into good society. It is not unknown for a governess to snag herself a respectable husband. Some members of the clergy are not fastidious, and there are always second sons."

"I have no training or inclination to be a governess."

"You don't know what you are wishing for, Grace," Augusta said, sitting forward, her usual smirk replaced with an expression almost like concern. "An actor's life is one of great anxiety. One moment he—or she—is idolized and fawned over, showered with enough flattery to turn any head. But when the charm of novelty wears off, the actor sinks into cold and silent neglect."

"I don't believe that," Grace said. "Look at Mrs. Siddons. She is loved everywhere she goes."

"Sarah is an exception, I will grant you."

"Sarah? Do you know Mrs. Siddons?"

Augusta snapped open her fan and rang the bell to summon the maid. "I do not wish to talk further on the subject. You may stay with me until you find an alternative. Now, where is your trunk?"

౸ඏ

"You're off to do Mr. Kemble's bidding again, are ye?" Alec sat on his bed in the same clothes he'd worn the night before—and countless more nights before that.

"It's me job, Alec. Besides, I'm that pleased that he wants Grace back." Ned pulled on his boots. "You got in late."

"Stop changin' the subject. You're right stuck on her, ain't you? I've said before that she'll cause you grief."

"And I've said before that it ain't like that with Grace. She's just a friend, like."

"Since when are women friends?" Alec grinned. "You'll get yourself in trouble one of these days being so friendly and all."

Ned gazed around the cheerless room and sighed. He was glad to be back in London after slogging around the country, feeling at times more like a pack mule than a stage manager, but sometimes he wished he had more to look forward to after work than bunking in with Alec.

"So what *is* it like? You know she'll not have someone like you."

"I'm just fond of her, is all." He wasn't about to tell Alec how he felt about Olympia. He'd never let him hear the end of it. "Anyways, Grace didn't deserve Renfrew letting her go. He's a proper arse, that one."

"How will you find out where she's gone? You were that lucky she came back last time, but who's to say it will happen again?"

"I know," Ned said glumly. "She's gone off to the West Country to stay with her father. He's a right bastard."

"You can't be interferin', Ned. Remember your place and all."

"Ain't much chance of me forgettin' that."

"Mr. Kemble can't hardly expect you to go fetch Grace from so far away. Haven't you been saying that you're done with travelin'?"

Ned sat down heavily on the bed. "I reckon."

"What are you going to do?"

"Ask Olympia to write to her, I guess. If anyone can get Grace back, it's Olympia."

"Mr. Kemble won't like it if you come up empty-handed."

"I thought you didn't want me to find her."

Alec shrugged his skinny shoulders. "I don't, but I also don't want you in hot water with Mr. K. You've done well for yourself at the theater, and I ain't one to like seeing you lose your place."

"You're gettin' proper soft, Alec," Ned said, grinning.

"Shut yer mouth." Alec climbed out of bed and pulled on his boots. "I got me a spot of work over at the market today. Don't pay much, not as much as takin' tickets at the theater, but it's somethin'. Damn good thing the theater's starting up soon. I'm getting skint and all."

"We're opening in two weeks. I'm as eager as you to get back at it. Mr. Kemble is too, so far as I can tell. I don't think Ireland was to his liking."

ဆဝသ

The sharp tang of shriveling leaves freshened the late-August air in Hyde Park. Grace had not expected to enjoy a walk through the shady paths with Percival. His appearance at her aunt's house a few hours earlier had been a surprise, but not an unwelcome one. After a week of sitting through excruciatingly dull evening parties with her aunt, Grace longed for diversion. Percival wasn't quite what she had in mind, but a walk in the park with him was preferable to another afternoon watching her aunt doze in her chair by the fire, rousing only occasionally to find fault with the room temperature, the tea, Grace's hair, the slovenliness of her maid—anything and everything.

Grace had been dismayed to find Olympia more difficult to contact than she had anticipated. The letters she'd sent to Olympia in care of the theater had not been answered, and she didn't dare approach Mr. Kemble directly—not after Mr. Renfrew had so summarily dismissed her. And as for Ned, Grace didn't think it right to involve him. She didn't want to get him into trouble with Mr. Renfrew.

"You are staying in town?" Grace asked. They had so far kept the conversation light, avoiding any mention of Grace's father and his estate, or the theater.

"I keep a house in Bedford Square," he said. "You must visit."

"That would hardly be proper, Percy," Grace said.

He stiffened. "Could you not use that odious diminutive?"

"Percy? It's a perfectly suitable nickname."

"I loathe it."

"Then you have my apologies. I will try to remember to call you Percival." He really was a prig, she thought, stealing a look at his finely chiseled profile. His top hat almost brushed the low-hanging foliage shading the path. She amused herself by imagining his hat speared on the tip of a particularly aggressive branch.

"Yes, thank you," he said. "I did not mean to offend."

"You did not." They lapsed back into silence. Grace decided to enjoy the outing with or without amiable conversation from Percival. To be outdoors in nature was soothing to nerves rubbed raw by the noises of the city. A pair of fine horses carrying elegantly attired ladies, hat plumes swaying, trotted past on a nearby bridle path.

"Do you miss riding?" Percival asked when the horses had passed.

When she did not reply, he stopped walking so suddenly that Grace almost lost her balance. "Forgive me! I had forgotten." His blue eyes clouded with concern. "What must you think of me?"

"I think very little of you, Percy, ah, Percival," she said, her voice strangled by the sudden, sharp memory of a horse's anguished squeals. "Perhaps we should turn for home. I am fatigued."

"Yes." They walked on in silence, her hand still wrapped around his arm. Another pair of horses trotted past. The clinking of harnesses and the crunch of hooves on gravel filled her senses, gave her time to think. Percival could not be blamed for the past. There was so much he didn't know.

"I do not hold you responsible for my father's decision," she said after a long pause.

"I'm relieved to hear it. I did try very hard to dissuade him."

"You did?"

"Yes, but to little purpose. He was determined to have the will changed, and no argument that I put forward had any effect on him. He is unjust to you, Grace."

"He believes he has reason."

"The theater?"

"That—and other reasons." Why had she said that? He'd want to know what she meant.

"Do you wish to tell me?"

"No."

They walked on, their feet rustling through the dry leaves pockmarking the gravel. They were almost to the edge of the park when Percival stopped again and this time drew her around to face him. He was handsome, there was no doubt about that—half a head taller than she was, with a broad forehead and elegant manners. He would make a dashing figure onstage—more like stately Mr. Kemble than conceited little Mr. Renfrew.

"If we were to marry, you would not lose the benefit of your father's estate. After your father's death, we can live at Clevedon for part of the year, or sell it. I am willing to go along with whatever you decide on that score."

"Are you proposing to me?" The surprise in Grace's voice caught him off guard.

He blushed. "I, ah, yes." His haughty mask slipped, and Grace glimpsed another man—a man who kept himself well hidden from the world. She thought she might be able to like that man.

She disengaged her arm from his and stepped backward. "Why?"

"I wish to make amends for your father's actions," he said, quickly recovering his dignity. "And I feel that we may get along well. I must marry, and I have always thought you would be a suitable choice."

"You have rarely seen me since I was twelve years old."

"It is a fair offer," he said. "And considering the circumstances, you may not expect a better."

Grace set off down the path, too agitated to reply. She had not gone more than a few yards before she tripped over a stone. Percival came up behind her and caught her before she lost her balance and tumbled into the dead leaves.

"You do have a propensity for clumsiness, my dear," he said.

"I am not your dear." Grace turned away from him. "I am going back to my aunt's, and I'll thank you not to follow me."

"I will see you home."

She had no choice but to let him accompany her, although she walked several paces ahead, so that by the time they reached Grosvenor Square, she was out of breath and longing for the quiet of her room where she could cry in peace.

My bounty is as boundless as the sea.

The line from *Romeo and Juliet* looped through her head. He'd not mentioned love or even regard. And as for her own feelings—she did not exactly dislike Percival—but marriage?

She'd go to work as a governess in some dismal northern estate before she'd consent to become Mrs. Percival Knowlton.

ࠐ࠙ࠑ

"Ned!"

He was standing in front of her aunt's place, cloth cap in hand. Grace ran toward him. "How did you find me? Oh, Ned! I'm so glad to see you!" She wanted to throw her arms around him—big, solid Ned, who had taken care of her when there was no one else. Kind Ned, who asked for nothing from her. She stopped a few feet from him and acknowledged his awkward head bob with a curtsy. Percival came up behind her, panting slightly.

"Is this the fellow from the theater with whom I spoke in Bath?"

"Yes, Percival," she said without turning around. "This is Mr.—what *is* your surname, Ned? I don't believe I ever heard anyone use it."

"Plantagenet," Ned said.

"How very royal," Percival said with a sneer.

"I ain't got nothing to do with it. They gave it me at the Foundling Hospital." Ned thrust his chin out. He was as tall as Percival, but with broader shoulders and the air of a man able and willing to fight. Grace doubted that Percival had ever done more than engage in a bit of light fencing when he was at school.

"Ah." Percival turned to Grace. "I suggest we go in, my dear. My mother will be waiting on us."

"Tell my aunt I will be in shortly," Grace said. "I wish to talk with Ned."

"I should like to announce the good news to Mama without delay."

"I have not given you an answer."

"No, but I believe you will. Do not be long." He touched the brim of his top hat to Ned and then mounted the steps to his mother's front door.

"What good news?" Ned asked as soon as the door closed behind Percival.

Grace shook her head. "It's nothing. My cousin has made a mistake. So why are you here? Did the theater not forward my letters to Olympia? Please tell me something hasn't happened to her. How is everyone in the company? I miss them all so much!"

"I don't know about any letters. Mr. Brandon—he's the box office keeper? He's out this week, so happen he didn't get them to send on. Or could be Mr. Renfrew kept hold of 'em. He was workin' in the office this week."

"Mr. Renfrew is not my friend," Grace said ruefully.

"Maybe not, but he don't make the decisions. And Olympia's fine. She told me that she can't wait to see you."

"How did you know to come here?"

"I didn't really, not the exact house and all, but remember when you stayed with me?"

"I'm not likely to forget."

"You left a letter there. From your aunt. I figured you might have come here, and if you hadn't, I'd ask around a bit, find out where she lived."

"You were willing to take all that trouble to find me? Why? I'm sure you're not here just to tell me that Olympia misses me."

"With any luck, she'll be seeing lots more of you soon."

"How?"

"I come direct from Mr. Kemble, Grace. He wants you in the company."

Grace stared at Ned and then started to laugh.

Chapter Eleven

Double, double, toil and trouble;
Fire burn, and caldron bubble.

Macbeth (4.1.10–11)

*T*he company warmly welcomed Grace back. Little
Tommy presented her with a posy he'd bought in the
market, and Mr. Harrison kissed her cheek. Any doubts she
had about turning down Percival were quickly dispelled.
How could she even consider any other future? Her aunt
had threatened to throw her out on the street, but Percival,
surprisingly, had taken Grace's part with his mother and
did not appear to despise her for refusing him. She felt a
tiny nugget of disappointment. She had been used to
thinking of Percival as a haughty, proud man with no claim
on her affections. She hadn't expected to like him.

But all that was past now! She was back at the theater,
and although still living with her aunt, Grace was confident
that within a year or two she'd rise through the ranks and
begin making enough money to afford a tolerable
independence. Perhaps she and Olympia could find

lodgings together. Grace knew Olympia hated living with her mother and the general.

Mr. Renfrew made his displeasure at her return known to Grace and by extension Olympia, but he had the sense to keep his opinion from Mr. Kemble. *He* welcomed Grace with his usual stiff formality and assigned her to the chorus for the opening night performance of *Pizarro*. She made no objection. She'd keep her head down and her ears open, and spend every morning learning the parts that she'd one day play onstage.

Olympia had told her once that Mrs. Siddons was renowned for how carefully she studied the texts to prepare for her performances. Well, Grace would work just as hard. The future was paved with opportunities. Maybe London really would be the place for dreams.

☋☋

Ned knew he should be tending to the thousand and one backstage details that cropped up during every performance, but several nights after the start of the fall season, he couldn't resist stopping in the wings to watch Olympia onstage in a breeches role. She was playing Rosalind in *As You Like It* and looked enchanting. She wore a pair of red breeches, wide at the hips and ending at garters just below the knees, her ankles shapely in soft leather boots. A wide lace collar framed her face above a tightly fitted gold jacket.

The audience—disappointed that the role was not being taken as it usually was by Mrs. Dora Jordan—hissed and booed during Olympia's first scene. Any actress who took a role associated with the most famous principals ran the risk of inciting the ire of the crowd. Fortunately, after a few minutes' uproar—mostly from the young men in the pit—the crowd quieted and allowed Olympia to charm them.

In Ned's opinion, Olympia at the age of twenty-four made a much more convincing Rosalind than Mrs. Jordan, a mother of ten children with the Duke of Clarence. In her day, she had been the toast of London, but at close to fifty, Ned thought she was getting a bit too old to be squeezing herself into breeches.

Ned stood aside to let Olympia pass as she skipped offstage, smiling broadly, the applause still ringing in her ears.

"Oh, Ned!" she exclaimed. "I can't believe it!"

"You've won them over, to be sure." Ned only just stopped himself from wrapping his arms around her and lifting her off her feet, then carrying her to the paint room where they could . . . He blushed and turned away. Who did he think he was? After this night's performance, Olympia Adams could well be on her way to becoming one of the principals herself—a star to be fawned over and celebrated. She'd then be even less likely to consort with a lowly orphan from the Foundling Hospital. She deserved the best, did Olympia.

And the best wasn't Ned Plantagenet.

ఴుౖౘ

Ten days after opening night, Grace waited in the wings to go on with the chorus at the end of yet another production of *Pizarro*. Since starting at the theater, she'd several times sung her heart out in the chorus and had the satisfaction of hearing Mr. Kemble tell her she was coming along well. She hadn't had the nerve to ask him when he'd offer her an acting part, but she knew it was only a matter of time. Mrs. Siddons, wonderful as she was, could not take on *all* the tragic roles. To be sure, the company included a handful of younger actresses all vying for parts, but Grace was not worried. Her voice was by far the strongest, and she'd been working diligently on her acting. Almost every day, she practiced with Olympia, who had no taste for tragedy herself but knew how to project her voice and wring emotions out of the text.

Mr. Renfrew barreled offstage and handed Grace the still-smoking prop gun that he'd used to shoot Rolla, played with incomparable zeal by Mr. Kemble. Grace was too surprised to do what she should have done, which was throw the gun right back at him. Mr. Renfrew had barely spoken to her since her return to the theater. He had not forgiven her for Bath and, worse, for coming back to the theater at Mr. Kemble's invitation. Grace had already resolved to keep well out of his way, although when Mr. Kemble finally got around to giving her real acting roles, she'd inevitably be acting opposite Mr. Renfrew.

The prop gun was heavy and still hot.

"Come on, Grace!" Olympia ran up and grabbed Grace's hand just as a flourish of trumpets signaled the start of the funeral procession that ended the play about the conquest of Peru by the Spanish conquistador Francisco Pizarro.

Grace dropped the gun onto a table piled with scripts. Ned would see to it later. With Olympia, she joined several young women dressed as Incan priestesses to walk alongside six male utilities dressed in pagan priest costumes and carrying Rolla, the doomed Incan commander, on his funeral bier. Grace and the other girls chanted a dirge while the actor and actress playing Alonzo and Cora knelt on either side of the bier and kissed Rolla's hands, their expressions somber with the misery of loss.

The pathetic scene ended finally with the slow descent of the curtain. The cheers and calls of the audience shook the stage. Grace squeezed Olympia's hand.

"Aren't you glad you refused your cousin?" Olympia asked as the curtain rose again.

Grace stepped forward with the other actresses and swept into a curtsy. Nothing could stop her now—not her father nor her aunt nor even the memory of the accident that had claimed her mother's life. She would learn to replace the past with this glittering present and an even more enchanting future.

€C&#x08;

The mildness of the September night suited Ned's good mood as he walked the short distance from the stage door on Bow Street to Hart Street and home. The theater had been open for less than two weeks, and so far no crises had marred any of the performances. Grace was settling in nicely, Olympia was still basking in her triumphal turn as Rosalind, and Mr. Renfrew was keeping out of Ned's way. And as for Mr. Kemble, he reigned with his usual stern benevolence over them all.

That evening, both the play and the afterpiece had gone off well. All the actors and actresses attended to their cues, and Mr. Kemble himself took the trouble to commend Ned for making sure the prop gun fired as planned in the climax of *Pizarro*. Ned had spent a fair bit of time fussing over the gun used to shoot Rolla. The wadding needed to be dry and the small explosion neither too loud nor too soft.

He remembered seeing Mr. Renfrew, who had fired the gun, hand it to Grace, who was standing in the wings waiting to go on for the finale. He'd not had a chance to ask Grace where she'd put the gun, but surely she'd know enough to place it on one of the property tables. He should have checked before leaving for the night, but the truth was that he was done in. Every production of *Pizarro* was a nightmare for the backstage crew — the spectacular sets, large cast, and multiple effects required split-second timing. The production even included a collapsing bridge. Ned promised himself to go to the theater early the next day and have a good look around to make sure everything was neat and tidy for the evening performances.

Four hours after he fell exhausted onto his bed, Ned woke up so suddenly that he wasn't even sure he'd slept. He sat up and peered into the darkness, his head still stuffed with sleep. In the distance, the church bells struck five, and then into the silence following the last peel burst the one word capable of striking the most fear into the hearts of all city dwellers.

"Fire!"

Ned bounded out of bed and dashed to the window. A pillar of flame shot into the night sky. He called out for Alec and then saw that his bed was empty. Ned pulled on a shirt and his boots and clattered down the stairs to Hart Street and raced toward the Piazza. He'd gone only a few yards when he crashed into a dark form running around the corner from Russell Street.

"Oy!"

"Alec!" Ned recognized his friend only by his voice. He looked like a stick of charcoal set against the flames licking the black sky ahead of them. "What's bloody 'appened? I woke up real sudden and saw the fire from our window."

"We ain't had no warning—no smoke, nothing!" Alec cried. "I was comin' out of Miz Gellie's place—having my time with Daisy. There was this awful noise and then so many flames. I swear I could see to read if I was able. Come on! We'll go round to the Bow Street entrance."

Ned ran with Alec toward the theater. Watchmen swinging rattles joined them, the crackling din competing with the roar of the fire. People—most still in nightclothes—emerged from houses on both sides of the street. Shrieks of terror brought the dead night to life.

The Piazza Coffee House burst into flames along with three tall houses on the other side of Hart Street. Ned and Alec rounded the corner into the Piazza just as several water engines drawn by neighing, stamping horses pulled up in front of the theater. A half dozen firemen surged through the front entrance. Across the Piazza, Covent Garden market disgorged hundreds of people. At this time of the morning, the market was packed with farmers and merchants bringing their goods in from the countryside.

"We should go into the theater!" Ned cried. "Get out what we can."

"No!" Alec grabbed Ned's arm and pulled him away. "We'd best find water." Bright embers glowed in Alec's shock of black hair. Ned lunged forward and swatted at his friend's head.

"Never mind that. We got to help."

Ned followed Alec to the market where they plunged into a melee of screaming people. Alec found a bucket and filled it with water from a rain barrel. He passed it to Ned, who yelled for others to help. The bucket bobbed from hand to hand, finally splashing into the flames to produce a fizzle of smoke. Ned broke from the line and ran toward the theater. He had to get close enough to salvage what the firemen brought out.

A blazing piece of debris fell at his feet. He recognized one of the wooden stage swords, its gold-painted hilt charred black. All around him bits of stage life fluttered to the ground from a scarlet sky. Ned kicked at scraps of costume, fragments of scenery, props, scripts with edges curled and singed. The air was alive with burning splinters tossed by an east wind. He bumped into Mr. Brandon, the box office keeper.

"Mr. Brandon! Are you hurt?"

"What? No. I escaped in time." He clutched a pile of books and papers. "I got out some of the accounts, but not all. Mr. Kemble will be angry."

"Mr. Kemble!" Ned looked past Mr. Brandon to where the great man himself stood before the front door of the theater. "No! You must not!" He rushed forward and grabbed his arm. "It's too dangerous!"

"My theater! I must save it!"

"No, sir. Please, step back. The heat's too much. You'll be burned alive."

Mr. Kemble, his hair wild with sparks, looked like a pagan god. "Stand aside, man," he said with quiet authority. "You'll not keep me from it."

Ned let go of Mr. Kemble's arm and watched as he strode toward the burning building. Firemen swarmed around the engines, pumping water in streams too weak to quench the flames. For over an hour, Ned scurried back and forth across the Piazza, helping to carry buckets of water, encouraging anyone not able to help to seek safety. To his disgust, the area soon teemed with pickpockets taking advantage of the distracted crowds. Ned caught hold of a lad no older than eight and yanked him off a large man so engrossed in watching the fire that he failed to notice the dirty fingers clutching at his watch. Ned stopped carrying buckets and applied his fists to the pickpockets until, just before sunrise, a troop of Horse Guards clopped into the Piazza and restored order.

As Ned returned to helping fight the fire, he wondered how it could have started. He was always so careful. One of his jobs was to pile blankets soaked with water on either side of the stage before every performance. Their purpose was to smother the first hint of a spark. Once ignited, the heavy curtains and wooden scenery, the densely packed costumes and piles of books and scripts, would provide enough fuel for a fire to feast upon until everything was reduced to ash. The theater had been empty, except for Mr. Brandon, since midnight. Ned was one of the last people to leave, bidding Mr. Brandon goodnight and locking the stage door behind him.

That damn pistol! Ned should have tracked it down and made sure the wadding was fully extinguished.

Was the fire his fault?

Several firemen emerged coughing from the front door of the theater. A few carried props and other objects, but most were empty-handed. Their sweat-striped faces and grim expressions proved the hopelessness of the fight. Ned ran toward them. One of the firemen staggered into him, his eyes streaming. "We can't stay inside any longer. Get back!"

With a crash loud enough to rouse everyone within a mile of Covent Garden, the roof of the theater caved in.

"Is anyone hurt?" Ned asked the fireman, who just shook his head and with several of his companions lumbered toward the portico to the left of the entranceway to join at least half a dozen firemen operating a water engine under the stone canopy.

Mr. Kemble was talking intently to a fireman. Ned ran to his side. "What can I do, sir?"

"Ah, Ned. They've stationed one of their largest engines under the vaulted passage. Help me convince the firemen to move it back. The passage roof is not stable."

"Don't you worry, sir," said the fireman, his teeth flashing in his soot-streaked face. "We've got it sorted. The big engine's got more water than the others. We'll save what we can of your property."

"We should go back into the Piazza, sir," Ned said. "The firemen know what they're about."

"Pray God that is true," Mr. Kemble said, turning away. Despite the cacophony of bells and screams and clashing pistons from the water engines, his voice was as measured as if he were giving orders to the scene changers. "I will be ruined, Ned."

Ned kept his hand on Mr. Kemble's shoulder as he took one step backward and then another, raising his other arm to shield his face from the scorching heat. The theater was a smoking, empty cavern abandoned by most of the firemen, who were now under the stone-vaulted portico, helping to operate the water engine.

Ned and Mr. Kemble had walked only a few yards into the Piazza when the paving stones under their feet shuddered and bucked. A shower of sparks shot skyward and then slowly, with almost balletic grace, began to fall—a parody of the fireworks that in summer burst across the sky above the Vauxhall Pleasure Gardens. When they were boys, Ned and Alec often snuck out of the Foundling Hospital and ran across the bridge to hide in the bushes and marvel at the spectacle put on for the toffs.

"Run!"

Ned would never forget—no, not until his dying day—the sickening crash of stone striking stone. A blast of heat roared toward him. He sprinted into the open Piazza. His back was being roasted over blazing coals. Later, he'd discover that much of his shirt had been burned away. He swung around to see how he could help others to safety. Mr. Kemble's long legs had taken him well out of danger, so Ned searched for Alec's black head. The bells tolled seven. The fire had been raging for over two hours with little progress made to contain it. In the east, a thin strip of light ushered in the morning. Where was Alec? He must have outrun the flames. Alec was a survivor.

Bodies littered the ground, some screaming, others staring with eyes like pinpricks set in bloodshot whites. A few people rushed to help them. Ned ran toward the smoldering portico, sure that at any moment Alec would grab hold of him and laugh at how close they'd come to death. They'd been through plenty of scrapes together. This was just one more.

A wild-haired figure rushed from a side street toward Ned. He recognized Daisy. She was dressed only in her shift, her stays flapping. Daisy stopped and dropped to her knees in front of a body.

Her wail tore open the dawn.

Chapter Twelve

Things without remedy
Should be without regard: what's done is done.

Macbeth (3.2.11–12)

The place was reduced to ash in just three hours," said Mr. Madison, a wide man with a cherry-cheeked face, who presided over his company with all the complacency of an emir.

Grace was seated to Mr. Madison's right, across the table from her aunt and several places above Percival. She had spent the day in a restless agony of uncertainty — the stink of smoke a pall over the city. She would have rushed to the theater to see the damage for herself but was forestalled by the arrival of Percival. Her aunt had insisted that Grace accompany them to dine with the Madisons, and Grace had no choice but to comply.

"I heard that a poor girl who made her bed under the portico was roused by the smell of smoke and knocked up the box office keeper," said one of the women at the table, her eyes shining.

"Scandalous the way these vagrants sleep wherever they please. London's not fit for respectable people," Mr. Madison said.

The rest of the company nodded and murmured.

"Quite."

"Terrible business."

"Something should be done."

"Does anyone know how the fire started?" asked Mrs. Madison, a tiny woman with a large mouth, who rarely took her eyes off Percival.

"Oh, dear me, yes," said Mr. Madison.

"Well?"

"The fire chief believes that the wadding in a pistol that was used in the play caught fire."

"What play?"

"*Pizarro*. By that ubiquitous Sheridan fellow."

Grace ground her hands into her lap. A pistol? Impossible. Ned would have seen it on the script table and stored it away safely.

"Ah!" Several of the ladies and gentlemen nodded.

An eager woman to Percival's right leaned forward and assured everyone that the play was first rate. "I saw it at Drury Lane two years ago in '06. Charming performance by Mrs. Siddons. Her Elvira was so *pathetic*. I got chills watching her."

"She never disappoints," said a gentleman seated across from her. "I saw her last week in *Macbeth*." He raised his eyes to the elaborately decorated ceiling. "A triumph, particularly considering her age."

"Dear me, quite so. She must be well past fifty, and yet she still has such a *powerful* presence," said Mrs. Madison. "I dare say this fire will not sit well with her. She's firmly entrenched in her brother's company. I've heard that she's gone completely away from Drury Lane, a circumstance which I'm sure must not suit Mr. Sheridan."

Laughter and nods of agreement rippled around the table. Grace wanted to scream. How could they be so easily distracted? So unmoved? The fire had just wiped out everything she cared about. She took advantage of a brief pause.

"Does anyone know if people were hurt in the fire?" she asked.

"You haven't heard? Almost two dozen souls perished!" Mr. Madison delivered the news with what seemed to Grace unnecessary relish.

"Most of the dead were firemen," said Mrs. Madison. The three white feathers on her cap quivered like a panicked goose. "Shocking business! A dozen or so of the poor wretches were operating a water engine under the stone portico and were crushed when the roof fell in on them."

Several ladies sat forward, their cheeks flushed and lips parted in contemplation of such dreadfulness. Few things were more fascinating than a tragedy that did not affect them.

"This may perhaps change your answer, my dear." Percival's voice, so close to her ear, startled her. She hadn't noticed that the young man placed to her right had left the table and that Percival had slipped into his empty seat.

"There is still the Theatre Royal at Drury Lane."

"Yes, but you have no connections at Drury Lane. They already have several excellent singers in their employ, and you can't expect to be taken on ahead of the more seasoned actresses who will now be looking for work." Percival moved even closer. "Perhaps it is a sign."

"What do you mean?" she asked through clenched teeth. The hostess gave the signal for the ladies to retire. People rose from their seats, the men bowing, the ladies gathering fans and proceeding through double doors into the drawing room.

"You should accept my offer, Grace," he said, his smile close lipped and confident.

"Why now?"

"You cannot stay with my mother forever."

"I can make my own way."

"Not easily." Percival reached for her hand. "What could you do? A governess? I think not. Such a life would not suit *you*. I suggest you reconsider. I was sincere when I told you that I wish to make amends for your father."

"Ladies? Shall we retire?" Mrs. Madison bustled over.

Grace pulled her hand away and followed the chattering flock of overdressed women into the drawing room.

৪০০৪

The smoke still rising from the theater's charred remains mingled with Grace's tears. A few beggar children, their skins gray with ash and squalor, picked through the rubble, squealing with excitement when they found something worth selling—the tassel from a costume, a half-melted candleholder, a slab of metal. Everything disappeared into bags slung over thin shoulders. Grace let herself get distracted by their antics rather than dwell on what the devastation of the theater meant for her. Pulling her cloak around her to ward off the damp, she kept her gaze fixed on the children. They laughed and hallooed as they combed through the debris. Such easy pickings were rare in their miserable lives.

"Grace?"

Ned plodded toward her, his face fixed in a scowl, his eyes red rimmed. "What do you make of this?"

"Oh, Ned! How can we bear it?"

He shrugged. "We don't got much choice."

"Did you help fight the fire?"

"I did." He continued staring straight ahead. His defeated look was almost worse than the destroyed theater.

"I read in the *Chronicle* that a subscription is being solicited for people from the theater who have been put out of work by the fire," she said. "I hope that's true."

"A subscription, is it? That'll be the day when the quality give money to support actors and actresses, never mind the rest of us backstage."

"Do you think people are so uncaring?"

"I've not often seen different, Grace," he said, his gaze moving to the children picking through the ruins. "Have you?"

"We can't let this disaster turn us into cynics, Ned."

"I can't say as I know what that is, Grace, but if you mean people that's only out for themselves, then I hope I ain't one of them." He nodded at the children. "If everyone's a cynic, what chance have they got?"

Grace put her hand on his arm and felt even through her glove the soot sliding across his wool jacket. He appeared ready to collapse.

"I got to ask you something," he said after a long pause. "Do you remember the pistol you took off Renfrew?"

"I do." Grace turned and stared at Ned, her eyes wide with horror. "You don't think . . .?"

"Dunno, but I've heard talk."

"I should have taken the pistol right to you."

"Don't get yourself worked up about it," Ned said. "They can't prove nothin', and besides, it's Renfrew's fault if it's anyone's. Mr. Kemble hasn't said one thing or t'other about it. So long as he gets the insurance, he ain't bothered."

"I won't say anything, Ned."

"Thanks."

"What will happen now?"

"I wish I knew. I guess I'll try for work at one of the other theaters, or get somethin' in the market. Maybe Mr. Kemble and the other managers will decide to rebuild the theater."

"I've already heard talk of it."

"Mr. Kemble ain't a man to let grass grow under his feet."

"I hope you're right."

Ned grinned, dull gray teeth almost white against his blackened face. "I learned early on that you can't change what you can't change."

"Wise words."

"Them's words I can't quarrel with, and maybe it's better than being a cynic." He leaned forward as if to embrace her and then appeared to think better of it. "I'd best get going, Grace," he said, touching two fingers to his forehead.

"Goodbye, Ned." She stood very still and watched him tramp back to the steaming pile of rubble, scattering the children with a shout. They squealed and pretended to run, but Grace noticed that none of them ran far. She suspected that Ned was well known as someone who showed them kindness when most others in their lives kicked them to the gutter.

A gust of wind swirled the ashes around her feet, the soft sound a counterpoint to her desolation. Ned had been the first person since her mother died who had been truly good to her, who did not blame her.

છ৩৫

Ned watched Grace walk back into the Piazza. She'd been crying when she stood before the smoking ruins. His heart turned over for her. She might have a more comfortable home to go back to, but her future was probably even more uncertain than his.

Alec hopped across a blackened beam to come and stand next to Ned. The top of his head grazed Ned's shoulder. Apart from the filthy sling supporting a broken arm and the blood-streaked bandage circling his head, Alec was as ready as ever to take on the world and win. When Daisy had found him sprawled unconscious in the Piazza, she'd assumed the worst. It had fallen on Ned to carry Alec back to Mrs. Gellie's establishment and hold him down while the surgeon set his arm.

Ned gestured to the children creeping back into the debris. "I've told 'em three times to leave off their scrambling."

"Yer too soft on them," Alec said. "They know you're all bark and no bite."

"And you'd do better?"

"'Course." To prove his point, Alec picked up a charred piece of wood with his good hand and rushed forward. He bared his teeth and roared a string of expletives. One of the boys squealed in terror and backed up to his mates, urging them to run. Within seconds, the ruins were deserted.

"They'll stay away at least for today," Alec said, dropping the wood. A whoosh of ash rose and subsided.

"What's going to happen to us?" Ned asked.

Alec kicked at the ashes. "You want to be the one to ask him? He's over there talking to the newspaperman." Several yards away, Mr. Kemble stood with hands clasped behind his back, his distinctive hooked nose wrinkled against the reek of charred wood. In a world that had very little use for him, Ned had seen his share of men bowed with despair and anger, but never any with such a look in their eyes — the eyes of a man who had climbed to the top of the world before plummeting to its depths. Perhaps it was harder to accept defeat when you'd spent most of your life at the top.

The newspaperman backed away, and Mr. Kemble swiveled his gaze to Ned and Alec.

"Why are you not working?" he barked. "I don't pay you to stand around."

Ned stepped forward, emboldened by Mr. Kemble's mention of payment. Maybe he'd keep them on — to do what, Ned couldn't imagine. But if there was any chance . . .

"Please, Mr. Kemble, sir."

"Yes? What is it?" His penetrating eyes bored into Ned.

"What's to become of us, sir?"

"Become of *you*? I am ruined! How can I know what will become of you?"

"I heard there was a subscription, for the workers, like."

"Some such nonsense is in the papers, but I wouldn't go putting much stock in it." Mr. Kemble glanced down at Alec. "You were hurt?"

"Yes, sir, but I'll be right as rain in no time. I can do whatever needs doing. Me and Ned both."

"We will rebuild."

"Sir?"

"My theater. I will rebuild it." He waved one arm toward the ruins. "I'll build the most magnificent new theater in London."

"How, sir?" Ned asked.

"Let me make something clear to both of you," Mr. Kemble said. "The question is not *how*. The question is *why*."

Alec laughed nervously, but Ned hushed him with a flick of his wrist. He met Mr. Kemble's gaze. "You mean why build a new theater, sir?"

"Exactly. And what do you say to the question?"

"That you must rebuild, sir, because London cannot do without you." A flash of resentment burned across his mind. Mr. Kemble would always have a place to live and clothes on his back. Both he and Mrs. Siddons were to go over to the King's Theatre the following week. *They'd* not suffer from the destruction of the theater—not like Ned and Alec would.

"You're a good lad, Ned," Mr. Kemble said. "I'll see to it that you don't lack for work." He nodded at Alec, who was grinning like an idiot. "You too, Alec. Now, get back to cleaning up this unholy mess. We've got a great deal of work ahead of us."

He stalked off, his feet plowing trails through ashes that noiselessly collapsed in on themselves.

Chapter Thirteen

. . . for the very substance of the ambitious is
merely the shadow of a dream.

Hamlet (2.2.157–58)

*T*wo weeks after Covent Garden's Theatre Royal burned to the ground, Percival pulled a chair out for Grace at the small table set for three at his mother's house. Grace was in no mood for his gallantry. She had been all set to spend a quiet evening alone in her room when Percival had arrived and announced he would dine with Grace and his mother.

"I have procured tickets for the theater tomorrow evening," he said as he took his own seat.

"What theater?" Grace asked indifferently. Why should she care how Percival spent his leisure hours? The life she wanted for herself was as good as over.

"The King's Theatre at the Haymarket. I wish you to accompany me."

"I hardly think that would be proper."

"Dear me, Grace, you are a fine one to talk about what is proper."

"That is unkind," Grace said.

Augusta dismissed the footmen who had seated her, and once again took command of the conversation. "I heard you mention the Haymarket, Percival. Surely you are not intending to go to the performance tomorrow?"

"Indeed, I am, and I am hoping that my fair cousin will come with me."

"I have no wish to go, Aunt."

"I'm surprised to hear that," Percival said. "I thought you were a great admirer of Mrs. Siddons, although I suppose you have seen her several times by now."

"What are you talking about?"

"Mrs. Siddons and Mr. Kemble are performing. Did you not read that the principals have moved to the King's Theatre?"

"You should not even suggest it," Augusta said. "Grace's career on the stage has thankfully been cut short. What is the point of upsetting her?"

"The King's Theatre only puts on operas," Grace said.

"As a rule, yes, but these are extraordinary circumstances."

"Are they acting *Macbeth*?"

"Regrettably, no. I believe the play is *Douglas* with Mrs. Siddons as Lady Randolph, but I have heard the term *transcendent excellence* used to describe how she handles the role. Ridiculous overstatement, of course, but that is the theater for you."

Grace glanced over at her aunt, who was scowling her disapproval. Her heart leaped with excitement at the prospect of again seeing Mrs. Siddons, even if now Grace was in the audience and not backstage. With an effort, she kept her voice cool. "Thank you, Percival. I will accompany you."

"Capital! Mr. Kemble is to give an address before the play goes up."

୫୦ଔଓ

Ned headed for Piccadilly, where he knew Olympia lived with her mother, the mistress of a retired general and a former actress herself. With the theater in ashes and the company out of work, he knew his chances of getting close to Olympia were even less now than they'd been, but he had to at least make sure she was well. The three-story building had quite recently been converted into sets—apartments that were home to many of London's dandies and a fair number of retired military men.

There was a time, when he was younger and job prospects were dim, that Ned thought about signing himself up for the army. He fancied carrying a gun and wearing a red coat. But after he got his first position at the theater as a scene changer, he realized he had it good compared to the poor buggers limping back to England with legs and arms shot off by Boney's cannons.

He entered the building. His inquiry about the whereabouts of a Miss Olympia Adams brought a disapproving look from the sour-faced footman and a grudging direction to a set of rooms on the second floor. Ned mounted the stairs with growing trepidation. Would Olympia thank him for coming? The building was very grand—nothing like the mean lodging house he shared with Alec. With each step up the marble staircase, Ned grew more uncertain. Olympia was used to living like this? His pay would never extend to such a place, especially now when he had no pay.

He reached the door to the general's rooms and stopped, thinking he should write a note instead. But that was the coward's way out, and besides, he had no paper, and his penmanship was worse than bad. At the Foundling Hospital, training in basic reading and some number work was deemed sufficient for children with dismal prospects.

The door opened before Ned got up the nerve to knock.

Framed in the doorway was the reddest-faced man Ned had ever seen. He wore a tight jacket and shiny black boots pulled to his knees. Pale breeches puffed out over ample hips, and his stomach expanded under a grubby white waistcoat. A hint of grease slicked his chin.

"Yes? Who the devil are you? Tradesmen go around the back. Didn't they tell you?" The general was a good foot shorter than Ned, but he had an air of command that made Ned step back. He could well imagine this barrel-shaped little man standing atop a hill, surveying his troops from a safe distance—barking orders and sending men to their deaths before tea.

Ned drew himself up. "I'm come to inquire after Miss Adams," he said as clearly as he could, acutely conscious of his rough accent.

"What's someone like you got to do with Olympia?"

"I'm from the theater."

"Ah, yes. The blasted theater. Damn good thing it's been burned down, if you ask me. It's high time Olympia got herself married."

"Sir?"

"Not that it's any business of yours, man. What do you want with her? Brung her wages, have you?" He chuckled. "Old Kemble's in a helluva bind now, ain't he? Serves him right — preening around that theater of his like he owned the place."

"I believe Mr. Kemble *is* one of the owners," Ned said stiffly. How did Olympia live with such a man?

"He's just an actor when all's said and done," the general said. "Olympia's not here right now. If you got something to give her, I'll take it." He held out one pudgy hand. The baby finger was missing. Ned wondered if it was ripped off by a stray musket ball, and was sorry the ball hadn't been better aimed.

"Just tell her that Ned came to say hello," he said, ignoring the general's outstretched hand. "She'll know who I am."

The general stepped back into the vestibule of his rooms and slammed the door in Ned's face.

৪০৪৪

Grace clung to Percival's arm as he shouldered his way through the crowd into the lower lobby of the King's Theatre in the Haymarket.

"We appear to have come too late," Grace said. She tightened her grip on his arm. "I did not expect such crowds."

"You underestimate my concern for your well-being, my dear. This morning, I sent a message to Mr. Madison, asking him to save us seats in his box."

"The Madisons are here?"

"You'll be obliged to put up with their society again, although I trust you'll find the sacrifice worthwhile." Percival steered Grace up a flight to stairs to the second level, where the quality of the people filling the lobby was several cuts above those on the ground level. Percival swept open a curtain and stood aside to let her pass into a box. "After you, my dear."

"Please don't call me that," Grace whispered as she passed in front of him. "We are not engaged."

"Not yet."

She ignored him and nodded to Mr. Madison, who struggled to his feet and held out his hand to guide her to a seat at the front. "Miss Johnson," he said. "A pleasure." Next to him, his wife looked past Grace to Percival. She fluttered her eyelashes and her fan in equal measure. Grace expected Percival to take the hint, but to her surprise, he settled into the chair next to hers.

"Since this is your first visit to this theater, Grace, you will not be aware of the alterations made this past week."

"Oh?"

"The inside of this theater is usually resplendent with crimson curtains, but as you can see, they have all been removed." Percival gestured to the party of people seated in the adjacent box. "The partitions between boxes have also been taken out, which I must say is an improvement. We are now able to more easily see the stage."

"Is this theater always so crowded?" Grace asked.

"Not quite. This is a special night." He waved to acknowledge the arrival of a fashionably dressed couple. Grace recognized them as Mr. and Mrs. Lawrence Jackson. The wife was yet another one of Percival's admirers. Grace acknowledged them with a nod and a quick flick of her fan as Percival rose from his seat and bowed. When he resumed his seat, he turned away from Grace to speak with Mr. Jackson.

Grace leaned forward to more clearly see the stage. At that moment, backstage would be bustling—actresses smoothing skirts, tucking lace into bodices, powdering faces one last time in front of stained mirrors; actors rubbing rouge into their cheeks; the prompter climbing into his box and spreading out his script; callboys prowling the wings, checking the scenery, making sure props were in place. Every actor and actress waiting to step onto the stage would be starting to breathe a little bit deeper. No matter how many times they performed, the tingle and flap of nerves were never completely stilled. Grace imagined that even Mr. Kemble himself was tamping down the excitement that was always part of life in the theater. It was that excitement—and the fear never far removed from it—that attracted people to seek a life on the stage. Its sudden lack in her life was an iron ball lodged in the pit of Grace's stomach.

Chandeliers bristling with candles were suspended above the pit. With the performance about to begin, the benches were packed with people, the noise of their talking and laughing amplified in the small space. The band struck up "God Save the King," and the audience rose. Grace joined in the wild clapping as, moments after they were again seated, Mr. John Philip Kemble strode onto the stage. Gravely, he acknowledged the applause, which built and crested until it seemed to Grace as if the entire theater would be rocked off its foundations. Goodwill flowed from the crowd to land at Mr. Kemble's feet. After many minutes, he ended the applause with a modest dip of his head and then fixed his famous eyes on the farthest boxes.

"Ladies and Gentlemen."

Skirts rustled and fans clicked as, all around Grace, people leaned forward to listen.

"The power of utterance is almost taken from me by the very great kindness of your reception on my reappearance before you. Be assured that, however words may fail me, I can never be wanting in the gratitude which is due for your patronage on many former occasions and still more particularly for your favor on the occurrence of that calamitous event which is the cause of our opening the King's Theatre this evening."

Next to her, Percival murmured, "Nicely said, man." He nodded toward the stage. "I wouldn't be surprised if he announces his intention to build a new theater at Covent Garden."

Perhaps Ned had been right. In a flash, Grace's imagination soared to a future where she was taken on at the newly rebuilt theater. But it would take years for Mr. Kemble and his partners to raise enough money. By the time the new theater was ready, Grace would be too old to act her favorite roles.

Mr. Kemble continued. "Proprietors are already occupied in preparations for constructing a theater that they trust will, by next September, be worthy of your attendance and patronage, and build the appropriate ornament of a British metropolis."

"There you go, Grace," said Percival, leaning so close that his lips almost touched her bare neck. "You need only wait another year."

"I thought you didn't approve of the theater."

"I may reconsider if . . ."

Grace knew what he meant. Other actresses continued careers after they were married—many even had children. Mrs. Siddons had produced six children; and Mrs. Jordan, ten.

Grace settled in to watch the performance, but her mind was elsewhere. A decision needed to be made, but, like Hamlet, she preferred to put it off to another day.

ഇറെ

Two weeks later, with fall already snapping at the air, Mr. Kemble gestured for Ned to stand to the side of the small group of men grouped around the table in a room above a Piazza coffeehouse. Ned's rough working clothes set him apart from the other men who wore black coats and pressed trousers. A thin beam of sunlight fell across a table that was spread with a large drawing that showed the outlines of a stage and pit and boxes.

"It will be the largest theater in London, Mr. Kemble!" exclaimed an older man with ink-stained fingers and a sloppily tied cravat. His name was Mr. Bowles, and he worked for Mr. Robert Smirke, the architect commissioned to build the New Theatre. The great man himself was absent. He would not begin work until the managers amassed sufficient funds.

"Have you had word from the insurers?" asked Mr. Brandon. The fire had deprived the theater's box office keeper of both his position and his home, forcing him to take up residence with his spinster sister. He was almost as eager as Mr. Kemble to see the theater rebuilt.

"We will get the full fifty thousand pounds," Mr. Kemble said gravely.

"That is not even half of what's needed!" exclaimed Mr. Brandon. "We cannot start rebuilding on so little."

"I am well aware of our situation, Mr. Brandon," said Mr. Kemble. "So much of what was lost—Handel's organ, the costumes, even the wines we stored for the Beefsteak Club—was not insured. My poor sister even lost several yards of lace that once belonged to Marie Antoinette. She is inconsolable." He placed both hands flat on the table, either side of a drawing depicting an elegant facade of columns.

Ned wondered why Mr. Kemble didn't build something smaller with the insurance money, but he knew better than to ask. He was still getting over his shock that Mr. Kemble had made him his assistant, worthy of staying in the room with Mr. Brandon and Mr. Bowles. He'd wanted to run straight to Olympia to tell her and then remembered the general and thought better of it. Alec hadn't been too happy about Ned getting so high and mighty, what with working directly with Mr. Kemble, but there wasn't much Ned could do about that.

"We will set up a subscription," Mr. Kemble said. "The people of London will support us."

"To the tune of fifty thousand pounds?" asked Mr. Brandon. He smoothed his hand across a waistcoat darkened with spots of wine. "It will take years."

"It will not!" Mr. Kemble snapped. "We must start building by Christmas."

"But, sir, that is less than two months hence," said Mr. Bowles. "It's impossible."

"I promised the people that a new theater will rise upon the ashes of the old within a year of its destruction, and I will not be made to take back my words."

Mr. Bowles regarded the toes of his shined boots; Mr. Brandon picked fluff from his sleeve.

"Ned!" Mr. Kemble strode toward the door. "We have work to do. I need you to deliver some messages for me."

"Yes, sir." Ned followed Mr. Kemble down the stairs to the street. He didn't know or care what his new duties would be. So long as he was of use to Mr. Kemble, he had a job and could be on the lookout for work that Alec could do. Ned wasn't bothered about Alec living off his shilling for a time. When they were boys, they'd had a pact—whoever got work helped the other. No exceptions.

ಞಲ

On a dreary afternoon in the middle of October, a handful of weeks after the fire, Grace sipped a tepid cup of tea in her aunt's stuffy parlor. Hannah, her aunt's maid, seemed incapable of delivering a hot one, and Grace had given up asking. She'd awakened that morning from a dream in which she'd stepped onto the London stage. Young men in the pit cheered and stamped, and the boxes spilled over with the cream of London society all clapping for her. Throughout a tediously wet day that kept her indoors, Grace tried erasing the images from her mind. Why upset herself? She knew what she had to do, and the sooner she got the opportunity, the better.

But her resolve weakened. When she set aside a worn copy of *Othello* to take tea, she relaxed back against the sofa cushions and imagined herself bowing with imperious charm in front of an audience, her expression both grave and humble. Her hand shook as she brought the thin china cup to her lips.

"A visitor, miss." Hannah stood at the door.

"Who is it? I'm not expecting anyone."

"It's Mr. Knowlton, miss," Hannah said. She jumped forward to catch Grace's cup before it hit the floor. "Steady on. The mistress will have me head if any of the china's broke."

Grace rose from the sofa, and *Othello* slipped to the carpet. Now that Percival was here, she was no longer so sure of her decision. It wasn't too late to change her mind. She could take the position as a governess that her aunt had told her about. Within weeks, she could be ensconced in a Hampshire country house where she'd be well treated, have useful employment, and be able to pass her love of Shakespeare on to the two young girls in her charge.

And she'd give up forever any chance of returning to the stage.

Screw your courage to the sticking place.

Percival sailed into the room, cleaving apart the stale air with all the aplomb of a decked-out navy frigate.

"Hello, Percival."

He peeled off his gloves. Grace gestured to a chair while she settled herself on the sofa. He ignored the chair and lowered his legs sheathed in impeccably cut trousers next to her.

She took a deep breath. The arm of the sofa dug into her back, preventing her from moving when he leaned toward her. Any woman would be glad to have him. He was charming, clever, and rich enough to keep a house in town. *And* he was respectable, considering his father's connections to trade. It wouldn't do to have him too high up in society, not if she intended to continue her career on the stage.

"I have decided to accept your proposal of marriage," she said before he could say anything.

Percival shifted back but kept one hand resting along the top of the sofa, inches from her shoulder. "As always, your directness is charming."

"So you've said. Does your offer still stand?" She'd chosen this route; she'd stay the course. "Yes or no."

Before she could stop him, he reached for her hand, swiveled to the side, and dropped to one knee. He arranged his face into an expression of romantic devotion. "My offer still stands, dearest."

Grace wasn't sure if the heaviness gripping her chest was relief or dread. "You can dispense with the *dearest*," she said as she tried to extricate her hand.

"If we are to be married, you must allow me to treat you as a wife." He tightened his hold. She jerked her hand free and jumped up, cheeks flaming, fingers tingling. Percival lost his balance and teetered on one knee, then clawed himself forward. First one elbow and then the other found purchase on the overstuffed sofa. With a grunt, he leveraged himself onto it. Grace was glad of the opportunity to calm her own breathing and take a chair opposite him. He smoothed his open palm across his hair and regarded her with narrowed eyes.

"Forgive me."

"No need." Grace straightened her spine and met his gaze, fiercely ignoring the sick thudding of her heart. "I have one condition."

"Yes?"

"When the opportunity arises, I wish to continue my career on the stage."

"Ah." Percival sat back against the sofa and recrossed his legs. "The fire has not dampened your ardor? You must see that good society prohibits your continuing."

"I do not care for good society, Percival."

"No, but I do. My father's history in trade is such that I cannot afford to court additional stains."

"You'd consider me a stain?"

"Always so charming," he murmured. "You are well aware what I mean."

"My condition still stands, Percival. I want to act, and when the theater is rebuilt, I need to be free to return."

"If they will have you."

She inclined her head. "Of course."

"You are certain this is what you want? You will not lack for money."

"If it weren't for the fire, I'd still be at the theater. It's *all* I want."

"Then why do you wish to marry me?"

"My aunt has made it very clear that she wishes me gone. Two days ago, one of her acquaintances asked me to consider a position in her home as a governess. If I do not marry you, I will have no choice but to accept it."

"That is the only reason? If we're to be married, do you think perhaps you should have some regard for me? I assure you I will have no difficulty returning it." His frankly appraising gaze was as disconcerting as his touch. "I would not be ashamed to have you as my wife."

"I prefer to consider our marriage as a business arrangement. I get the security of a steady income while I pursue a career on the stage."

"And I get you? I see." He let his words hang in the air, the silence lengthening as he continued to stare at her.

"Percy?"

"Please, my dear, call me Percival or, in company, Mr. Knowlton."

"Fine. Percival. Do you agree to my terms?"

"Yes. I will marry you and not stand in your way should you decide to return to the stage."

"Thank you." She wasn't absolutely comfortable that his promise was sufficient security, but she was out of options.

"We have said what needs to be said for now," Percival said. "I confess myself relieved."

"When shall we marry?"

"You are in a rush?"

"If it were done when 'tis done, then 'twere well it were done quickly."

"I do hope you'll not make a habit of trotting out Shakespeare every time you wish to make a point."

"I'll endeavor to restrain myself."

He smiled thinly. "Sarcasm does not become you, my dear. I suggest we marry in mid-November."

"That will be fine. We should keep the news from your mother until we are married. She won't approve."

"I have no objection. Do you wish to order wedding clothes? You'll find me a generous husband, so far as I am able."

"I assure you that wedding clothes are the furthest thing from my mind."

"All to the good."

"Good afternoon, Percy." She paused. "Percival."

He stood and bowed. "I shall wait upon you again tomorrow." He turned on one heel and left the room. A moment later, Hannah's drawling voice rose and fell with the shutting of the front door.

A swift inhale expanded into Grace's head and prodded at her eyes and lips. She wished she had lines to say, because she had no words equal to the task of expressing what she felt.

Her mother had married for love and lived to be miserable with the man she chose. Grace was determined not to make the same mistake.

ⅎ∓

On Grace's wedding day, the clouds leaked rain like a gently squeezed sponge. Only the union of Romeo and Juliet officiated by Friar Lawrence had included fewer people than attended the union of Percival and Grace. A distracted clergyman and two witnesses — neither known to Grace — were all the law required to make her into Mrs. Percival Knowlton. Olympia sent her regrets without explanation, and Percival did not invite his mother. There was no wedding breakfast and no lace on Grace's gown.

"You could at least *pretend* to be cheerful," Percival said when they arrived at his house in Bedford Square after the ceremony.

Grace seated herself by the window and gazed out at the passing carriages. The gold band on her finger felt like it weighed ten pounds. She covered her left hand with her right and did not turn around when Percival came to stand behind her. Her reflection in the window showed huge eyes and a mouth set in a firm line. Juliet had loved her Romeo so much that she'd chosen death rather than life without him. Grace smelled starched linen and another, deeper smell that made her belly lurch with that strange sharpness that was more pleasure than pain. This feeling could not be love—not the pure, sacrificial love of Juliet for her Romeo. Grace shifted her position slightly, enough to squelch the sharpness and leave behind a quiet ache. Real life was nothing like the stage.

"Grace."

She didn't move, but neither did she resist when Percival stepped in front of her and leaned back against the window seat, blocking out her reflection. He reached for her hands. "You don't need to fear me."

She wanted to pull away but realized that she must not. He was her husband now, her Romeo.

My bounty is as boundless as the sea.

My love as deep . . .

Slowly, with a deliberation that deepened the strange sensation in the pit of her stomach, Percival leaned forward and for the first time pressed his lips against hers. For a second, just a second, she let herself soften into his kiss, let herself feel something. And then sense prevailed. She tightened her lips and opened her eyes.

Chapter Fourteen

But shall I live in hope?

Richard III (1.2.199)

*L*etter for you, sir," Ned said as he walked into Mr. Kemble's office above one of the coffeehouses overlooking the Piazza at Covent Garden. As usual, Mr. Kemble was working at a table placed under the window, a wool scarf wrapped around his neck to ward off the freezing air. A few hours earlier, Ned had cracked ice to get water for his tea.

Mr. Kemble rubbed his hands together to warm them. "Leave it on the table, Ned. I'll see to it later."

"You'll want to be opening this one right away, sir," Ned said. He held it up to show Kemble the coat of arms pressed into the seal. "It looks important."

"Really, Ned, I believe I may be trusted to decide which letters are important and which are not." Mr. Kemble wrote for a few moments more before laying down his pen and holding out his hand. "Very well. I can see that you're fit to burst. What's so special about this letter?"

"It was hand delivered, sir. The footman what brought it was very grand."

Mr. Kemble glanced at the seal. "I say, Ned, you're right. It's from the Duke of Northumberland."

"Sir?"

Mr. Kemble waved him to silence. Ned watched anxiously as Mr. Kemble broke the seal and scanned the contents, his expression grave as always. The only time Ned had ever seen Mr. Kemble's face betray emotion was when he projected to the highest galleries.

One dark eyebrow rose. "I say."

Ned leaned forward. "What is it, sir? Do you need me to deliver a return message?"

Mr. Kemble's mouth curved into a rare smile. What news could the letter possibly contain to rouse him from his customary gravity? Mr. Kemble spent every waking minute soliciting funds for the New Theatre. Subscriptions were coming in, but Ned had overheard Mr. Brandon say that they were still many tens of thousands of pounds short. November had already clamped gloomy skies over London, and plans were underway to start construction of the New Theatre at the end of December.

"Well, Ned, you were right to press me. This letter does indeed contain good news. Very good news indeed." Mr. Kemble laid the letter flat on the table and smoothed it with one hand. "Do you wish to know what His Grace says?"

"Sir! Yes. That's kind of you, sir." Fancy him being privy to a letter from a duke! Alec would get a laugh out of that.

"Yes, well, I confess myself inclined to share the news, and since there's no one else here, you'll have to do." He smiled again to take any offense from his words, although

Ned hadn't taken any. "As I said, the letter is from the Duke of Northumberland. You will have heard of him?"

"Yes, sir, I mean, well, not exactly, sir."

"It's no matter. The duke will be sorry to hear that his fame does not extend to the lower orders, but we'll not be the ones to tell him, eh?" Mr. Kemble laughed. "Several years ago, I had the great good fortune to tutor the duke's son in the art of elocution."

Ned had no idea what Mr. K. was talking about, but there was nothing new in that. He waited and listened, a polite look on his face. Mr. Kemble rarely passed up the opportunity to show off his superior knowledge.

"*Speaking*, Ned. The duke wanted his son, who was ten years old at the time, to learn how to speak well in company. Owing to my modest success as an actor —"

"Sir!"

"You are right. False modesty is most unbecoming in a man such as myself. The duke had seen me perform many times and considered me a fit teacher for his son. I was happy to oblige. I gave the young man lessons for a few months at most. He was a likely lad and learned quickly. Well, let's to it. Here's what the duke says." He picked up the letter and began to read:

"*My dear Mr. Kemble, I have been looking these past ten years for a way to repay you for your kindness in teaching my son how to speak well. You will be happy to know that he is now at Oxford and by all accounts doing well. The loan of ten thousand pounds I sent some months ago for the rebuilding of the theatre is forgiven. I do not require a penny to be repaid, nor do I wish to collect any interest. Your services to me and to the nation deserve nothing less.*"

"He's *giving* you ten thousand pounds?" Ned asked. How rich must the duke be to part with so much?

"It appears so." Mr. Kemble put down the letter. "There is a lesson in this, Ned. Our actions, no matter how insignificant we consider them, can have undreamed of repercussions."

Ned nodded gravely. "Of course, sir." He sometimes wondered if Mr. Kemble ate dictionaries for breakfast.

"I never thought that my helping the duke's son could result in such an act of generosity."

Ned brightened. "The duke must be a very great man."

"That he is, Ned. Give me a minute to write my reply, and then you can take it to him. We'll not trust the post with such a message, eh?"

Mr. Kemble chuckled to himself as he dipped his pen in the inkwell.

ം‍ങ്ങ

Olympia stood in the middle of the gravel path bordering the Serpentine in Hyde Park, her small figure shaking with anger.

"You *married* him? Grace, how could you?"

Sun played across the lake, but the mid-December air was icy, making Grace glad of the new woolen cloak Percival had insisted on having made for her. "You must understand my situation, Olympia. I cannot stay in my aunt's house forever, and with the theater gone—"

"London is full of theaters."

"Yes, but only two are licensed to perform serious drama, and I have no connections at Drury Lane."

"Times are changing in London, Grace. The newer theaters are finding ways to get around the old patent-theater system. Some are even putting on Shakespeare plays—or at least excerpts. And maybe you could get taken on as a singer."

"I must be practical."

"And so you decided to marry a man you do not love."

"I am fond of him," Grace said.

"Really? You don't act like you are."

"He is not a bad man, Olympia, and he's very handsome, which you'd know if you'd have come to our wedding."

"I was otherwise engaged," Olympia said. She gazed out at the lake for several moments and then sighed—her breath a white cloud in the glittering air. "I may as well tell you."

"Tell me what?"

"I've found work over at Astley's."

"The circus?"

"I stand in the ring and clap my hands while the acrobats do their contortions. It is not satisfying work."

"Well, at least you still have your sense of humor."

"My mother wants me to find someone with money to marry, but I have refused. She doesn't approve of Astley's, but for now I have prevailed. At least the pay is good."

"Percival has promised that when the Theatre Royal is rebuilt, he will allow me to contact Mr. Kemble."

"How very generous of him."

Grace fixed her gaze on the frost speckling the grass bordering the path. Olympia's attitude surprised and dismayed her. Gone was the easiness of the summer when she and Olympia had spent hours together—laughing, practicing lines, suffering with great good humor the hardships of constant travel.

The fire had changed everything.

After several more minutes of walking along the frozen path, boots crunching, Olympia took Grace's arm. "Forgive me. I am giving in to bitterness, and I should not. You must know that being married is no guarantee of anything. Mrs. Siddons's late husband squandered a shocking amount of her money on poor investments, and look at Mrs. Jordan! Her position is precarious at best."

"Fortunately, Percival is not a duke, and I have no plans to have ten children," Grace said drily.

"Poor Mrs. Jordan will be thrown off soon enough, and then where will she be, with all those children to care for?"

"Perhaps if she had married, she'd not be in danger of suffering such a fate."

"The Duke of Clarence can hardly marry an actress. No, he'll have to give her up soon and marry someone royal. I've heard that he and Mrs. Jordan were very happy for decades, but that will not save her."

"Then I suppose I'm lucky to have Percival. You won't believe how many hearts I've broken by accepting him. Half the young ladies in London had their eye on him."

"I suppose if you are to be married, you may as well marry someone worth looking at."

"What about you, Olympia?" Grace asked. "You must know that Ned thinks the world of you."

"My mother wants me to marry well, although she is hardly a model for matrimonial bliss. I am better off staying in the theater—the circus now—and having some measure of independence."

"You care for Ned. I know you do."

"Since when does caring for someone make any difference to anything?"

Grace could not dispute it.

ဆၢ

"By God, Ned, we're on our way! Have you had a message yet from His Highness?" Mr. Kemble stopped pacing to face Ned as he entered the shabby room above the coffeehouse. In the dismal light of a rain-drenched day a week after Christmas, Mr. Kemble practically crackled with nervous energy.

"No, sir, not yet, but he said he's coming, right? He's not the kind of gentleman to disappoint, is he?"

Mr. Kemble frowned. "If I did not consider you incapable of irony, Ned, I would accuse you of disloyalty to our prince."

"Sir?"

"Never mind." Mr. Kemble struck a pose, one hand on his hip, the other raised to the low rafters. "How do I look?" In honor of the occasion, Mr. Kemble wore knee breeches, white stockings, and shiny black shoes with silver buckles.

"Very fine, sir, although you might want to take an umbrella. It's awful wet out today."

"Good heavens, no! I'll not stand before His Highness holding an umbrella. The rain will stop soon."

Ned held out Mr. Kemble's cloak. "Shall we go, sir? Your sister is coming?"

"Dear Mrs. Siddons wouldn't miss it for the world. She's as fond of royalty as any woman in the kingdom." Mr. Kemble barked out a laugh. "I doubt even she can count how many times she's played a queen."

"People say, sir, that you and your sister be the king and queen of the London stage."

"Nonsense! You should never believe everything you hear in this town." Mr. Kemble pretended to scowl, but his lips twitched into a smile. "We don't want to keep the people waiting. We'll join the procession when it reaches Bow Street."

The laying of the first stone of the grand New Theatre Royal at Covent Garden on December 31, 1808, began with a procession from Freemasons' Hall in Great Queen Street. Ned had never seen anything so splendid. The masters, along with the tylers, deacons, and other officers from the individual lodges, carried their insignia with measured solemnity along Bow Street. Their destination was a gallery covered with green cloth that led to an elegant marquee at the northeast corner of the building site.

His Royal Highness, the Prince of Wales, arrived at the marquee at the same time as the procession. A royal salute of cannon boomed out to welcome the prince, and then six bands struck up "God Save the King."

Ned shivered in the snow-streaked rain that pooled at the base of his neck and seeped under his collar to his skin. He stood a few feet away from Mr. Kemble, who had stationed himself as close as possible to the prince—who was also the grand master—and the deputy grand master. Mud spattered Mr. Kemble's stockings, and droplets of water trickled across his brow and glistened in his soaked side-whiskers. But the rain had no power to dampen the spirits of the hundreds of people gathered for the ceremony, most singing lustily.

After the anthem, Mr. Robert Smirke, the esteemed architect, stepped forward and presented to the prince a rolled-up plan of the building. His Royal Highness then deposited a brass box into a cavity hollowed out of the foundation stone. Ned learned later that the box was filled with medals and coins of the realm. He and Alec had a good laugh over the folly of burying perfectly good money. The deputy grand master presented a silver gilt trowel to the prince, who stepped in front of the foundation stone suspended above a prepared bed of cement. He bent at the waist and smoothed the cement and then nodded for the stone to be lowered.

After fussing with various tools presented by other important people, the prince took up a mallet and knocked in the stone with three sharp strokes. Ned craned his neck around Mr. Kemble's shoulder. Next to him stood Mrs. Siddons, the black ostrich feathers in her hat drooping in the rain. She also had scorned an umbrella.

With a sweeping gesture worthy of an actor in the throes of a tragic soliloquy, the prince poured over the stone an offering of corn, wine, and oil from three different silver vases. Finally, Mr. Smirke stepped forward and, after waiting patiently through several fine speeches and returning numerous bows, received back the plan of the New Theatre.

A burst of cannon fire made Mrs. Siddons jump, her ostrich feathers quivering like startled cat tails. Moments later, His Royal Highness swept off with all the other dignitaries, including Mr. Kemble and his sister.

Ned joined in the cheering. Throngs of spectators gathered within the bounds of the new building; hundreds more hung out of windows, many waving flags. A band of Highland bagpipes squealed.

As soon as the procession moved away, dozens of small bodies swarmed over the stone to scoop up the scattered corn. Ned recognized a few of the boys as the pickpockets and scavengers who prowled the Piazza. He made no move to stop them. It seemed only fair they got something out of a building they'd never enter.

"Quite the to-do, ain't it?"

Ned grinned as he turned to greet Alec. Not long after Ned had gone to work for Mr. Kemble, Alec had landed his own job. Most nights Alec got home after Ned was asleep and was still snoring when he got up. "I didn't expect to you to be here. They keepin' you busy over at Drury Lane?"

"I got no complaints."

"Ain't that a new jacket?"

Alec held up one arm to show how the raindrops beaded on the thick black wool. "Drury Lane's paying me better than old Mr. K. ever did."

"Just to stand at the door and let people in and out?"

"Yeah, well, that's just part of me job," Alec said. "I get to crack a few heads now and then when lads in the pit get rowdy."

"I'm glad for you," Ned said. "Let's go get ourselves a drink to celebrate the new year. Mr. Kemble don't need me until Monday."

Alec laughed and slapped Ned on the back. "Me and you done good for ourselves, all things considerin'."

"Who'd have thought it when we was growing up at the hospital?"

"Not old Mrs. King, to be sure," Alec said. "She'd be twirling in her grave if she knew Alec and Ned got anywhere other than gaol or transported." The matron at the Foundling Hospital had particularly loathed Alec and Ned because she had never been able to control them.

"You ever wonder about your mother, you know, the one what left you off?" Ned asked.

"Naw. Why bother? You've seen yourself how desperate girls can get when they got babies they can't take care of."

"Do you blame her?" Ned asked.

"No." Alec opened the tavern door. A stream of light and noise spilled into the darkening afternoon. Before going inside, he turned to Ned. "Let the past lie where it fell, Ned. Maybe one day you'll have your own babe to care for. Pray you won't need to give it up like we was."

Ned pushed past his friend into the welcome heat, his jaw set.

ॐ

Grace sat alone by the fire in yet another drawing room, enduring yet another evening of empty conversation. Like most of the ladies around her, she pretended interest in the polite chatter while at the same time keeping an eye on the double doors leading to the dining room. Finally, cigar smoke and laughter ushered in the men.

Three of them bowed to Grace and took chairs close by to continue their conversation about the laying of the foundation stone for the New Theatre Royal at Covent Garden.

"The rain was abysmal, but I'm not sorry I went. Plenty of pomp and fine speeches." The youngest of the three men wore a blinding white cravat that buttressed a pink chin.

"Mr. Kemble and his partners are going to be stretched to the limit to recoup expenses," said the second man.

The third man cut in. "If you ask me, the whole enterprise is absurd. Admission prices are bound to rise."

"Yes, but you must agree that would be a good thing."

"How so?"

"Higher prices will keep out undesirables."

"True," the second man said. He had large teeth and blotchy cheeks. "They never should have pushed the start time for performances to past six o'clock."

"Now every Tom, Dick, and Harry thinks they've a right to come in."

"Drawn to the dreadful melo-drames and spectacles, more's the pity." The older man shook his head. "I've heard that the New Theatre is going to be enormous — bigger even than the last one. The words of our great poets are lost in such cavernous spaces."

"There is nothing to be gained watching an actor's lips move when we cannot hear the words," said the pink-chinned man.

"Can't be helped," said the dark-haired man. "Old Kemble will reap his profits even if it's at the expense of art."

"Shall we join a table?"

"Quite."

Grace sat very still. Brandy-fueled voices doubled the sound level in the room, and the candles seemed to burn hotter. She imagined herself on the stage of the New Theatre. She'd heard that it was designed to seat more than three thousand spectators. What would it be like to speak lines into such a space?

"Grace?"

She looked up, startled. "Mr. Renfrew?"

"At your service."

"What are you doing here? Are you a friend of our hostess?" Surprise robbed her of manners.

"*Friend* is perhaps too strong a word. I am the younger brother of Mrs. Partridge, our host's wife." Mr. Renfrew gestured to the free chair next to Grace. "May I?"

"Please." She could hardly refuse him and make a scene in the drawing room.

"I trust you are well, Miss Green," he said. Away from the theater, his bluster was somewhat diminished, replaced by a kind of awkward attempt at urbanity that did not suit him. He'd even grown a pencil-thin mustache that sat above his upper lip with all the elegance of a severed mouse tail.

"I am Mrs. Knowlton now."

"Ah, you have married since we last met?" Like twigs against a sunset sky, strands of thinning hair covered a ruddy-skinned skull.

"Obviously." Grace nodded toward Percival, who was deep in conversation with an elderly matron across the room. "My husband is Percival Knowlton. Have you met?"

"No, although I believe my sister is acquainted with his mother. Now that you are married, you perhaps do not wish to be reminded of the past." He bared his teeth in a smile. "We did not part as friends."

"That is true, Mr. Renfrew, but since we now find ourselves in the same room, we can, I'm sure, be civil. Did you attend the laying-of-the-stone ceremony yesterday?"

"It was a damp affair, but we are all happy to see the New Theatre on its way."

"I wish Mr. Kemble well with it."

"You will return in the fall?"

"I do not know. My husband . . ." Grace glanced over at Percival. He had promised to help her, but as the months wore on, she could not help worrying. Five nights out of seven he arranged for them to go out to dinners, dances, whist parties — the extent of his acquaintance in London was alarmingly large. Every day, the likelihood that he'd allow her to return to the stage grew dimmer.

A group of musicians at the other end of the room struck up a jig. Ladies rose with alacrity; the younger men moved among them in search of the fairest hands. The melee of pairing up soon resolved into ten couples forming along the length of the room. The successful women flushed with anticipation; the rejected ones settled, with bruised hopes, into chairs lining the dancing area.

Percival strolled over.

"This is Mr. Renfrew, Percival," she said. "From the theater."

"Good evening to you, sir." Percival scarcely moved the air with his bow before leaning down to speak with Grace. "You do not care to dance, my dear?"

"No, thank you. I am no dancer."

With a brusque nod, Percival moved off as Mr. Renfrew rose to his feet. "I am pleased to have met with you again, Grace, Mrs. Knowlton," he said. "My sister is waving for me to join a whist table. Good evening."

"Good evening, Mr. Renfrew." She inclined her head in response to his bow and then snapped open her fan. Red poppies flashed in the candlelight. She stood and walked to the edge of the dance floor. Couples whirled and laughed.

"Will you dance?"

The youngest of the men who had spoken earlier about the New Theatre bowed and offered his hand.

Grace caught Percival's surprised look across the room. She turned to the gentleman and smiled.

"With pleasure, sir."

Chapter Fifteen

I have no spur
To prick the sides of my intent, but only
Vaulting ambition, which o'erleaps itself,
And falls on th' other . . .

Macbeth (1.7.24–28)

The last time Grace had seen her father's house high on a cliff above Clevedon, she was still in mourning for her mother. She'd certainly never expected to enter the musty sitting room on Percival's arm. Her father rose as they entered. He swayed slightly, one hand wrapped around a full glass of wine.

"You must think yourself very clever, marrying your cousin so you can keep your hold on my property," he said by way of greeting.

"No, Father, I do not think that."

Tobias turned to Percival. "You played a pretty trick on me, sir."

"It was no trick, sir. I love Grace."

Grace glanced at her husband in surprise. Love? What was this? He'd never said, and surely it was impossible in the face of her indifference. She took her seat and said nothing. The sitting room at the house near Clevedon that Grace had lived in for most of her life was as small and dark as ever. Her father walked over to the window. Against the white glare of the late-January day, he turned into a black wraith with no distinguishing features. Beyond the window stretched an unkempt expanse of brown grass—a view as confining as the dankest prison. The sea in all its shimmering glory was not visible—a defect in the placement of the house that had always depressed the spirits of Grace's mother. She often complained that the house should be moved a few hundred feet closer to the cliff edge. No matter how many times Grace's father explained that, first, the house could not be moved and, second, the current aspect protected them from the ferocious winter winds, Charlotte refused to relent. She professed herself exempt from tedious logic. In rare moments of connection, Grace traded resigned looks with her father behind her mother's back.

She did not dare look at Percival, although she sensed him looking at her.

"I suppose you plan on staying with me," Tobias said.

"We wrote to you, Father, and you replied with an invitation."

"Did I? More the fool I. Can't imagine what I was thinking. But I can't turn you out, considering Percival's claim on the place."

"You are very gracious, Father," Grace said. The smell of wine encasing her father like a thick London fog made him impervious to sarcasm. Percival, however, was not. She heard him stifle a laugh.

"I was on my way out," Tobias said. "Business in the town."

"Percival and I will take a walk along the cliffs until your return."

"We are grateful, sir, for your hospitality."

"Tell her to show you the place."

"Sir?"

"Good afternoon, Father. We shall see you at dinner." Grace seized Percival's arm and steered him out of the sitting room into the narrow, dark hallway. "This way," she said grimly. "The path to the cliffs starts behind the house." She should never have agreed to come to Clevedon. But Percival had been so insistent. He believed that reconciliation with her father was not only desirable but possible.

He had no idea.

"Slow down, Grace. Your father will be out for some time. We have no need to rush."

She didn't reply as she passed through the kitchen to the back door. As soon as she was outside, she let go of Percival's arm and ran ahead along the path bounded by a high hedge that led through the garden to a gate. Without stopping to wait for Percival, she flung open the gate and emerged onto the path that led to the cliff edge. Spreading her arms wide, she embraced the wind like an old friend — her only friend. Grace had always loved the sea, loved the wind whipping off cream-topped waves, loved the fresh edges and clean smells. So often growing up she had escaped to the cliffs to avoid her father's rages and her mother's silences.

"I say!" Percival said when he came to stand next to her. "This is a fine view. I so rarely get to see the ocean."

"It's the Bristol Channel, Percival."

"You have missed your calling, Grace."

"How so?"

"If you'd been a man, you would have made a fine lawyer. Fancy quibbling at my calling this stretch of water an ocean! I see waves and water and wind. What more do I need?" He offered her his arm. "Shall we walk?" Below the cliff swirled gray water bubbling with foam. Seabirds dipped and soared through a brittle blue sky. A freezing wind reddened their cheeks.

"I'm sorry, Grace," Percival said, breaking the silence after several minutes. "I did not realize."

"Surely my father's changing his will must have been a clue as to his state of mind concerning me."

"I see that now, but at the time, I was thinking only about the increase to my fortune. Can you forgive me?"

"My agreeing to marry you is forgiveness enough."

"You are coldhearted, Grace."

"I have learned to be rational. As you well know, marrying you was my only option in the circumstances."

Percival said nothing. As they walked on in silence, Grace was surprised to find herself wishing that she *could* think more fondly of Percival. She wondered if his reasons for marrying her were more to his credit than she wanted to admit.

"Your father . . . ," Percival began and then stopped.

"Please, go on."

"Your father's actions are not those of an honorable man," he said quickly. "Forgive me."

"You don't need to spare *my* feelings, Percival. My father has rarely been amiable." She took a deep breath. Perhaps now was the time to finally tell Percival the truth. Up ahead, the path narrowed, bounded on one side by a stone wall and on the other by a sheer drop to the shingled beach below. This was the place. She broke away from Percival and rested gloved hands against the wall. The wind had been sharp that day as well, but not so frosty. It had been April — a bright and breezy day in April.

"My father blames me for my mother's death," she said quickly before she could change her mind. A line from *Richard III* came to her. *An honest tale speeds best being plainly told.* Yes, the tale she had to tell was honest. Painfully honest.

"You told me it was an accident."

Grace shook her head. "My father does not believe it. He tells me that I am at fault." She paused, the hurt not lessened by time. "He said it was my clumsiness that crashed the gig — that if it hadn't been for my poor driving, we'd never have overturned."

Percival came to stand next to her, but he did not touch her. His presence reassured her, emboldened her. She'd never spoken of the accident to anyone except her father.

"My mother often suffered from bouts of melancholy, Percival. She responded sometimes to fresh air, so that morning I decided to take her out. She was particularly low. Most of the time, when my father was home, they maintained a civil silence, but the night before, they had quarreled — violently. I heard him shouting, but I could not make out the words. The next morning my mother would not rise from the sofa. I begged her to let me take her out for a drive to restore her spirits. She did not want to go." Grace gulped a ragged breath that tasted of the sea. "I persisted."

"And your father? Why did he not try to stop you if he was worried about your driving?"

"That was the strange thing. He did not. In fact, he told old Patrick, our groom, to harness the horse to the new gig that he'd bought just the week before and to lead it out to the pathway along the cliff top. I had not yet driven the gig, and for my first time, I'd have preferred to drive farther inland where the track was smoother and easier for the horse. But my father—I remember him saying that sea air was what my mother needed."

"And so you took her out and . . . ?"

"The track was rocky, just as I expected. I still can't say what happened. I was driving carefully along the cliff edge, and my mother had roused herself enough to speak to me." Grace paused, remembering the words that were to be her mother's last. She shook her head and continued. "One minute my mother was talking, and then the next minute the horse bolted. I don't know why. It was a calm day with little wind."

"Had an animal run across the path?"

"I'm sure I would have seen it, and an animal would not have startled the mare. She was a placid horse."

"What happened next?"

"The horse reared up, and I lost control of her. She crashed her shoulder into the wall . . . this wall. The gig overturned, and I was thrown clear. But my mother . . ."

"Do not distress yourself, my dear. I understand."

Before Grace could object, he gathered her in his arms, held her close, her cheek softening against the fine wool of his jacket. For a few blessed moments, she let herself feel safe.

And then she pulled away and started back in the direction of her father's house, not turning to see if he followed.

൪൚

Grace and Percival stayed three days in Clevedon—three days of dreary dinners and dark looks and the anguish of being reminded of her mother at every turn. Percival thankfully did not ask again about the accident that had taken Charlotte Johnson's life. He engaged Tobias in conversation about politics and accompanied Grace on silent walks along the cliff top. In the long evenings, he did not object when she retired early.

On her last afternoon in Clevedon, when Percival and her father had gone into the town, Grace finally entered her mother's room. She sat on the bed and let herself remember.

In death, her mother's radiant face was a soft mask, the eye sockets sunken, the cheeks flaccid. A layer of blankets hid most of her broken body. Grace gently placed her mother's hand over her mother's heart. The flesh felt solid, like one of Mrs. Gale's overstuffed sausages. Grace wanted to be weeping. Why was her heart not breaking? It beat its regular rhythm in her chest—the pulse of life forever denied her mother.

Charlotte Johnson looked smaller in death, as if she'd already started shrinking back into her bones. Grace wanted to reach up and catch her mother's soul before it ascended to heaven.

"Mercutio's soul is but a little way above our heads."

Yes, that was exactly right. Shakespeare always got it right. Her mother's soul was but a little way above Grace's head. Was it too far to grasp back? Just two nights earlier, Grace's father had been away from home, leaving Grace and her mother free to indulge their favorite pastime. They'd read Othello that night, but many other times, they'd sighed over Romeo and Juliet.

Grace lifted her eyes to the ceiling. A brown water stain bloomed across the plaster. When her father was at home, he never concerned himself with house maintenance. He was gone again from the house, but this time it was to make arrangements for her mother's burial.

The emptiness vanished in a sudden, sharp pain — like a squall battering the cliffs below the house. Grace's heart fractured in two. She let one long, low sob escape and then breathed it back. She saw her father's face dark with fury. He'd stood above her like an avenging angel, his fists clenched, iron-colored curls wild in the wind.

"Murderer."

Grace smoothed a wisp of blonde hair off her mother's cold forehead and bent to kiss her cheek.

The door latch turned, and Mrs. Gale lumbered into the room. "Ma'am? I'm sorry to disturb you, but I thought as you'd want to see this."

Grace glanced up from the empty bed. Mrs. Gale had been a part of her life for as long as she could remember. Charlotte had often said that she could never do without Mrs. Gale. "Yes?"

"This here, it belonged to your mother, ma'am," said Mrs. Gale. She filled the small room like rising dough. "The master don't know about it, but I be thinking as you should have it. She'd have liked that."

Grace took the small wooden box from Mrs. Gale and opened it. She gasped. The box overflowed with glittering pieces of jewelry—rubies, emeralds, sapphires, pearls, all set into sparkling tiaras and golden bracelets and necklaces thick as ropes.

"What's this?" Her mother had never worn any jewelry except a plain amber cross. Grace picked up a string of pearls that were each the size of her thumbnail.

"They's glass and paste, of course," Mrs. Gale said, "but your ma thought the world of them."

"Why have I never seen them before?"

"Don't know, ma'am. Your ma, she had things from her past that she didn't want anyone to know about."

"What things?" Grace wanted to shake the housekeeper. "What are you talking about?"

"Beggin' pardon, ma'am, I've said more than I should. I just thought you'd be wanting the box and all, seeing as you be married now. The master never comes into your mother's room, but I keep it dusted and swept in memory of her. I'm not sure your father ever knew about the box. Your ma was very particular to keep it well hid. She had a special place for it at the back of the closet. No one else but me knew about it." Mrs. Gale's broad face quivered. "You'll not be telling the master, would you?"

"Of course not, Mrs. Gale. And thank you."

"I'm glad you come, ma'am. The master, he's not well. I wanted to write to tell you, but I didn't have your address, and I didn't dare ask him. He's not been right since your ma died, but then I guess you know that."

"He is still grieving, Mrs. Gale."

"Aye, that I know. It's why he drinks so much."

Grace picked a tarnished round disk out of the jewelry box and held it to the light. With her fingernail, she scratched the surface. The gleam of silver shone through.

"What's this?"

"It be a button, ma'am. You see the two holes in the middle. Your ma told me it come from the costume she wore

185

to play Juliet. She told me it was one of a pair specially made. Unique, like."

"My mother played Juliet?"

"Yes, ma'am. She told me it be her favorite role. When she was first married and you were just a babe, she'd tell me about the roles she'd played—and who with." Mrs. Gale's plain face puckered into a smile. "She missed the stage, but the master, your father, he don't like to hear nothing about it. Whenever he was around, your ma never said where she come from, and then when you got older, she made me swear not to ever say. But, ma'am, you be grown now, and it's time you knew. You got her voice. I don't forget hearin' you sing when your mother was alive. Gave me goose bumps."

"My mother sang?" Her mother had always encouraged Grace to develop her singing voice, but never had she joined in.

"Dear me, yes. She had a beautiful voice, but your father never wanted to hear her—or you for that matter, but you knows that."

"My mother told me it was because the noise gave him a headache."

"Your singing weren't never noise, ma'am." Mrs. Gale bobbed a curtsy. "I'd best get supper ready. The master don't like it being late."

"Yes, thank you, Mrs. Gale."

Grace rubbed the button between her fingers. Her mother had played Juliet? On impulse, she picked up the box and dumped the contents onto the bed. The heat and clamor and wonder of the stage flashed before Grace's eyes. She plunged her hand into the mound of jewelry, let the ropes of heavy gems wind around her fingers, brushed her fingers across smooth stones and rough edges. Now that she held the jewelry, she could see the pieces were not real. The paint was scratched and peeling, the weight too light. She picked up and gripped the button from her mother's Juliet costume in her palm. How could she not have known? She saw again her mother's face when she watched the actor perform *Hamlet* at Bath's Theatre Royal all those years ago. She had been transformed — another woman entirely whom Grace had not recognized.

The future spread before Grace, rich and obvious.

"Grace?" the door opened, and Percival walked in. He'd been very kind to her the past three days while they stayed with her father. "There is an hour of daylight left. Shall we take a walk? The rain has stopped." He came farther into the room. "What's this?"

"My mother's jewels."

"Good lord! It looks like Aladdin's cave. Surely they are not real." He picked up a tiara studded with egg-size rubies and sapphires.

"Of course not, Percival. Don't look so avaricious."

"Why would your mother have such a gaudy collection? She could never wear them in good society."

"I think, Percival, that we must pay a long overdue visit to your mother when we return to London."

Chapter Sixteen

Reputation is an idle and most false imposition;
Oft got without merit, and lost without deserving.

Othello (2.3.259–60)

Ned had never in his life crossed the river to Lambeth to find the big tent in which Mr. Astley produced his circus. He thought he was well versed in theatrical effects and splendid productions, but Astley's Amphitheatre was a whole other world. He had never seen anything like it— the noise and the color and the heat made the Theatre Royal, with its measured speeches and rich costumes, look almost staid by comparison. At Astley's, everything seemed to be moving at once. Acrobats slipped up and down ropes and stood on horses galloping at speed around a sawdust-covered ring; a curtain at one end of the ring opened to reveal sumptuous pantomimes and even staged battles; troops of performing dogs barked and twirled. The vast amphitheater was almost brand-new—built just a few years earlier in 1804 after its predecessor was also destroyed by fire. That morning, Alec had told Ned that he was crazy to go over the river looking for a girl. There were plenty of them at Covent Garden. What did he need a special one for?

It was thanks to Louisa that Ned learned where Olympia had gone after the fire. Louisa had come by the building site a few weeks' earlier, looking for Mr. Kemble to take her back once the theater was built. Her arm had healed, and her brashness and bosoms loomed as big as ever. She'd sidled up to Ned and pecked him on the cheek, right in front of the lads on the building site. They'd had a good laugh at his expense.

Louisa told Ned that Olympia was gone over the river to Astley's Amphitheatre. She didn't say how she knew, and Ned didn't ask. He thanked her and moved off, hoping she wouldn't follow, but she pursued him right to Mr. Kemble's office and wouldn't leave until he went upstairs and asked Mr. Kemble to see her. Thankfully, he refused, and Louisa flounced off.

Olympia was standing in the middle of the ring, dressed in a top hat striped red and blue and wearing a skirt that fell just above her knees. The costume she wore for the breeches roles revealed far less of her than this costume, and Ned blushed to see her. She skipped around the ring, clapping, bowing, gesturing expansively with both arms at the performers as they tumbled and twirled and twisted. Her wide smile looked false to Ned.

After the performance, he waited outside the small tent where he'd seen the performers go to shed their sweat-soaked costumes. Absently, he pulled out the silver button he wore on a cord around his neck and rubbed his fingers over it, loving as always the feel of its serrated edge. Ned too had rough edges — too rough for someone like Olympia, he knew, but still he had to see her.

When she emerged, makeup gone and dressed again in a sober brown gown that blended with the beaten earth, Ned barely recognized her.

"Olympia!"

She turned at her name and stared blankly at Ned, her face lined with exhaustion. Then, recognition dawned, and she turned quickly away. Ned's heart sank. She took several steps and then paused, her narrow shoulders slumping as she turned back.

"Hello, Ned," she said quietly. "I didn't expect to see you here. How did you find me?"

"Louisa."

"She came a few weeks ago. I asked her to promise not to tell anyone from the old days, but I should have known not to trust her."

"I'm glad she told me, Olympia. I've been that worried about you."

"Why, Ned?"

The question took him by surprise. Didn't she know why? How could she not know? He stepped closer to her and tried to take her hand, but she kept both hands behind her back.

"Are you happy here?" he asked.

"I don't mind it."

"Kemble's got the theater well underway. Will you come back?"

"I don't know."

"I can see to it, Olympia."

"Mr. Kemble's taken to consulting with *you* about who he hires, has he?"

"No, but . . ." Ned didn't know what to say.

Olympia shook her head ruefully. "Don't mind me, Ned. I'm that weary."

"The theater's comin' along faster than anyone thought possible," he said in an attempt to get her to smile, to see again the Olympia he remembered. "We've just started, but Mr. Kemble thinks we'll be ready to open in the fall."

"And Mr. Kemble is always right."

"We have to hope he is this time."

Olympia's eyes widened as she looked past Ned. He turned to see the general shoving his way through the crowd. A woman, the spitting image of Olympia in twenty years and as many pounds, followed along behind. They both stopped next to Olympia.

"Ready?" the woman asked.

Olympia rose on her tiptoes, her breath warm against Ned's neck. He leaned into her. "I'm to be married," she whispered in his ear, and then, without meeting his eye, ran off to meet her mother.

The general hung back. "Stay away from her," he growled.

Ned only just managed to keep his hands at his sides. Smashing a fist into the general's nose, squashing it even more, would be the most satisfying thing he could think of doing at that moment. The general waited, almost as if he was hoping Ned would react so he could have him clapped in irons—maybe pressed into the navy. That would serve him right for setting his sights on Olympia.

An elephant—laden with an elaborately tasseled saddle and led by a man dressed in a flowing robe—lumbered toward them. The gray wrinkled skin hung slackly from the beast, and streaks of blood dripped down its flanks from under the saddle. Massive, trunk like legs ending in rounded feet lifted up and set down, each time shaking the ground under Ned.

By the time the beast had passed, the general was gone, and Ned faced the same solitary future he always had. But now, the shell he'd built around his heart to protect it was shattered.

ৡড়ঃ

Augusta Knowlton acknowledged Grace's curtsy with a complacent nod. "At least no one can say that we are not a well-formed family," she said. "You, of course, don't have your mother's beauty, but you have her figure and her coloring, and when neatly dressed, you do very well. Unquestionably, your mother was never loath to flaunt her good looks." Augusta patted the seat next to her on the sofa in her cramped sitting room. "Sit here next to me and we shall have a chat before dinner is served. Percival will continue to stare out the window with his back to us. Beastly manners."

Grace perched at the opposite end of the sofa from her aunt. "You are well?"

"Middling. At my age, robust health is too much to expect. Percival tells me that you plan to stay in London permanently. You are pleased with this arrangement?"

"Yes."

"I hope you realize how hurt I was that you did not invite me to your wedding." Eyes sharp as flint shards made Grace think of Lady Macbeth reading the letter from her husband, announcing his untimely elevation to Thane of Cawdor.

"It was a very small affair."

"That is obviously *not* the point. I should have been invited. I never expected my only son to go behind my back. The first I heard of your marriage was the note you left me on your wedding day. Abominable behavior. And then you go off to that dreadful Clevedon place to see your father. A lesser person would be offended."

"It was you, Aunt, who told me I should be married." Out of the corner of her eye, Grace saw Percival's shoulders tense and then shake ever so slightly.

"That is as may be. However, I do not believe I am being unreasonable to expect Percival to consult with me about his choice of bride, particularly in light of our connection."

"He was, perhaps, carried away with passion."

For the briefest of moments, a glimmer of humor lit Augusta's eyes and then, finding unfamiliar territory, disappeared. "You have your mother's odd wit." Augusta's toad-green turban trembled.

"You approve the match?"

"No. I'd have stopped it if given the opportunity."

"Then I suppose I must be grateful that the opportunity did not arise."

"Impertinent. Just like your mother. The truth is that I have no control over whom Percival chooses to marry. He is of age." She pursed her lips. "Your note inviting yourself to dinner implied that you have something that you wish to consult with me about."

Grace could not fault her aunt for beating about the bush. She closed her fingers around the handle of her fan. "I need to ask you what my mother did before she married my father."

"Did? Whatever can you mean?" Augusta snapped open her own fan and sliced at the stifling air. A faint blush crept up her neck and spread across her cheeks. Grace waited, the silence stretching for several more seconds, during which time Augusta looked anywhere but at Grace. Finally, she threw down her fan. "We shall go in to dinner now."

As if on cue, Percival sidestepped several chairs and small tables to take his mother's arm and help her to her feet. Grace saw no need for such attention. Augusta was about as helpless as a jackal. Percival went forward with his mother into the dining room, and Grace had no choice but to follow. Whatever her aunt knew, she did not appear inclined to share it, which only deepened the mystery of her mother's past.

As a footman in faded livery seated her at the small Pembroke table in Augusta's dining room, Grace kept her gaze fixed on a pair of heavy candlesticks.

"You are comfortable, Mama?" Percival asked after helping her into her seat.

Augusta smiled tightly. "Pour me a glass of wine."

"You have not answered my question, Aunt," Grace said.

Percival glanced over at her, his eyebrows raised. He didn't need to say anything. In the carriage coming over, Grace had established with Percival that she would broach the subject of her mother's background.

Percival poured wine into the three glasses, then took a sip and smiled at his mother. "Excellent vintage, Mama. I'm glad you still have some of Father's stock of French wine left. Shocking that we cannot get more these days, although I suppose it is unpatriotic to say so."

Aunt Augusta motioned for the footmen to bring forward the first course—a smooth white soup. "This is not an appropriate topic of conversation for the dining table."

"I have a right to know what my mother did before she married," Grace said.

Aunt Augusta's spoon clattered into her bowl, sending a splash of soup across the tablecloth. "A right? If that's how you feel, then I suggest you ask your father."

"You know that he and I are no longer on good terms."

"Hardly my concern."

Grace caught Percival's eye. He shrugged. She clutched her own spoon, her knuckles white. For the rest of the meal, she ate to suppress her physical hunger while her whole being ached to know more.

Chapter Seventeen

When sorrows come, they come not single spies,
but in battalions.

Hamlet (4.5.75–76)

Ned's days started at dawn and rarely ended until well into the evening. He delivered messages to and from gentlemen eager to contribute to an edifice being talked about as the greatest theater that London had ever seen, and acted as Mr. Kemble's eyes and ears at the building site — cajoling foremen, keeping an eye on the workers, making sure building materials didn't go missing at the end of the day. The harder he worked, the more chance he had of forgetting about Olympia. Every night, he fell exhausted onto his narrow bed, not even rousing when Alec came reeling in, stinking of gin and whores.

"Yer working too hard, Ned," Alec said one afternoon when he convinced Ned to knock off early and meet him at the tavern for a mug of ale. "Miz Gellie's got some new girls in — real lookers, a few of them. Daisy's gone off sudden, like — don't know where — but there's plenty more to take her place. How about you come with me tonight? I ain't got to be over at Drury Lane until tomorrow."

"I'm fine here," Ned said, raising his mug. "I'll take another and then be on my way home to my bed."

"You're not a monk, man! What's wrong with you? Yer not still pining after Olympia?"

"I just don't want to throw my money away at Mrs. Gellie's."

"What else you got to spend it on?" Alec grinned. "I seen plenty of gentlemen at her place. Her girls are good enough for them. Why not you?"

"I told you, Alec, I ain't interested." Ned took a long swig of ale. He wouldn't admit it to Alec, but he sometimes wished he *could* feel like going to Mrs. Gellie's.

"Ah, well, more's the loser you. I'll be off now." Alec drained his mug and slammed it down on the scarred table. "Here's to that theater of yours gettin' built. I'm content enough over at Drury Lane."

"Mr. Kemble says we'll be ready to open in September."

"I wouldn't bet money on that."

Outside in the street, a woman screamed. The two men jumped up and rushed to the door. A cloud of acrid smoke blotted out the sky. Dread clawed at Ned's heart as he followed Alec into the street, suddenly full of people running toward them, some yelling 'Fire!'

"Move it, man!" Alec yelled. "The smoke's comin' from Drury Lane."

"Can't be," Ned said. "Not again." He and Alec dodged the people coming toward them and dashed along the narrow street toward the fire.

∞∞

"Well, my dear, it appears that God has a sense of humor."

"What are you talking about, Percival? And stop pacing around the room. You're making me dizzy."

Percival leaned against the mantel of the front parlor. "The fire needs stoking, my dear. Shall I call Betsy? It is cold in here, and we can't have you risking your health."

"My health is perfectly fine, and I prefer a cooler room. Are you going to tell me your news, or will I be reduced to guessing? If so, I'd just as soon not do so. I was pleasantly occupied with my reading before you burst in." Grace held up a slim volume.

"*Hamlet* is it? I take it that you are still hoping to play Ophelia. It would be something to see you throw yourself around the stage with your hair unpinned."

"You'll have to wait awhile longer before you see that," Grace said. "You've told me often enough that you have no connections at Drury Lane, and Mr. Kemble's theater is a long way from being finished. But I gather you did not come barging in here to talk about Ophelia."

"My dear Grace, I never barge."

"Well?"

"Quite. I am gratified to learn that you hold no aspirations for Drury Lane. If you had, then my news would be doubly painful."

"Please get to the point, Percy."

"The Theatre Royal at Drury Lane has just burned to the ground."

"What?" She dropped her book. It landed face down and open on the carpet.

"London has now lost both of its patent theaters. I'm afraid there will be precious little Shakespeare for the next many months." He stroked the starched folds of his cravat. "I'm sorry if the news distresses you."

"It is beyond belief!"

"If only that were so, but these oversized theaters are dreadful firetraps. If it's any consolation, a few days ago, I was introduced to Mr. Sheridan, the manager at Drury Lane, to name one of his many accomplishments. He'd heard of you through his connection with Mr. Harrison, who I believe was once quite the tragedian. Mr. Sheridan said he'd be delighted to meet with you."

Grace stared at him.

"Shame it won't come to anything now. You do rather have bad luck when it comes to theater managers. Well, enjoy the remainder of your afternoon, my dear, and remember that we are to dine tonight at the Jacksons'. My mother will be there. I'll have the carriage sent around at five and would appreciate your being in the vestibule." He stooped to pick up her book and handed it to her without closing it.

As the door clicked shut behind him, Grace glanced down at the open page.

When sorrows come, they come not single spies, but in battalions.

The line, spoken by treacherous King Claudius after Ophelia goes mad, wove like counterpoint through the tuneless melody her life had become.

ജ)03

The London drawing room of Mr. Lawrence Jackson, one of Percival's richest acquaintances, buzzed with clinking teacups and murmuring females. Grace had hoped to avoid conversing with Percival's mother while waiting in the drawing room for the men, but Augusta had taken Grace's arm as soon as they exited the dining room and steered her to seats by the fire.

"I trust your health is improved," Augusta said.

"Aunt?"

"Percival informed me at dinner that you've been unwell." Aunt Augusta's mouth stretched to a thin smile. "You are not . . . ?"

"No!" Grace exclaimed a little too loudly.

Several heads turned. Augusta frowned at the two ladies sitting nearby who were pretending not to eavesdrop. She snapped open her fan to shield her words. "Really, my dear, you do not need to raise your voice."

"Forgive me, Aunt." Grace accepted a cup of tea from a footman, conscious of the eyes still turned on her.

"Why, pray, would such a happy event be so abhorrent? Percival must produce a legitimate heir, and I wish for grandchildren."

"I am sorry we've not yet obliged you," Grace said.

"I trust you will not keep me waiting much longer." Aunt Augusta leaned close. Lavender-scented powder clogged the fine web of wrinkles just starting to take up residence on her face. Grace took some small satisfaction knowing that her aunt must loathe above all things the fading of her beauty.

"I assume you have given up all pretensions to the theater," Augusta said.

"Who told you that?"

A flicker of amusement crossed her aunt's face. "No one, my dear. I am merely trusting to your good sense."

"You've never yet satisfied my curiosity about my mother. Was she an actress?"

"You could say that."

Grace waited.

"I suppose the answer is yes. Your mother did go onstage for a time."

"She was successful?"

"Middling," Augusta said. "You would do well to put aside foolish notions about the stage. It is a dreadful place for a woman."

"I intend to return when the New Theatre opens."

"I am aware that you do not believe me, my dear, but I have your best interests at heart. The stage cannot make you happy."

"Pardon me?"

"Your mother stayed too long and paid a high price for her stubbornness."

"What do you mean?"

Augusta rose from the table and signaled for the footman. "Enough questions. Go home with your husband and forget about the stage."

༄༅

The New Theatre Royal rose with white-columned splendor at the edge of the Piazza. All of London praised Mr. Kemble and the other managers for making good on their promise to rebuild the theater in less than a year.

It was two weeks before the theater was set to open, and Ned was having a mug of ale in a nearby tavern. A weedy young man with a face that looked like it never turned to the sun started talking loudly about the theater.

"Will you look here?" he said, holding up a piece of paper announcing the opening of the New Theatre. Ned was glad to see the notice being read — he'd gotten Alec the job delivering a sheaf of them around the Covent Garden coffeehouses and taverns.

"We ought to get tickets," said his companion. "I hear the New Theatre's very grand."

"That's what it says in the newspapers, but see the notice here? The prices have changed."

"What? Let me read that!"

Ned was gratified by how avidly the two men studied the notice announcing the opening. The evening would begin at six with a speech by Mr. Kemble followed by a full production of *Macbeth* with Mr. Kemble in the title role and his sister, Mrs. Siddons, as Lady Macbeth. Ned was confident that everyone who came would not fail to be astonished. The New Theatre Royal was the largest and grandest in all of London, maybe even the world. Ned couldn't attest to such a lofty claim, but he could not imagine any other people on earth capable of building such an edifice in so short a time.

"It ain't right," said one of the young men. He slammed his mug down so hard that ale slopped over the paper.

"What's he playing at?" The other man snatched up the notice and shook off brown drops. "Here, listen to this." He put on a posh voice and began to read.

"The proprietors, having completed the New Theatre within the time originally promised, beg leave respectfully to state to the public the absolute necessity that compels them to make the following advance on the prices of admission."

"Necessity, is it? What do they mean by advance?"

"Boxes are now seven shillings and the pit's four shillings. They've kept the lower and upper galleries at the old prices, which I guess is some comfort."

"That ain't no comfort at all. One of the carpenters told me that the top gallery is so high up that anyone in it will be lucky to see the actors' feet, never mind anything else."

"Sounds to me like the management wants to keep the likes of us out of their precious New Theatre."

"You mean Mr. Kemble's theater. He's running the show, and if you ask me, he's forgotten what he owes John Bull."

Ned drained his glass and stood up. He was tempted to say something to the men. As soon as they saw the magnificent interior of the New Theatre, they'd stop resenting the few pennies' increase in the ticket prices. Did they think the money to pay for the theater came from thin air? Ned had learned a great deal in the year since the old theater burned down. He often heard Mr. Kemble complain about the knife edge he and his partners existed on to keep the New Theatre from crumbling under debt as crushing as the ashes that buried the old theater. John Bull indeed! The ridiculous nickname for the common man was trotted out every time someone didn't agree with something done by the quality. Well, Ned wasn't quality, but he didn't see how anyone could object to what Mr. Kemble built for the people of London. John Bull and his ilk should be grateful.

Chapter Eighteen

True hope is swift, and flies with swallow's wings.

Richard III (5.2.23)

*M*r. Kemble favored Grace with a distracted bow. With just ten days before the theater opened, he had the air of a man with no time to spare. "So you have returned, Miss Green."

"I have married, sir. My name is Knowlton."

"I wish you joy."

"And may I also offer my congratulations on the New Theatre? It's being spoken of as the toast of London. No one expected it to be rebuilt so soon after the fire."

"People have made a habit of underestimating me," said Mr. Kemble. He frowned. "To their detriment. What do you wish to see me about?" He gestured to the piles of papers on the desk tucked in the corner of a large dressing room. Shelves were half-built, and no costumes yet hung from the large wooden rack extending across one wall. "I am exceedingly busy." He peered at her in the light thrown by the weak-flamed lamp on his desk. "And how did you get in? I left strict instructions with Mr. Harrison to keep the doors closed to actors."

"Mr. Harrison was not at the door when I arrived, sir. I should have waited, but I am wishing most fervently to speak with you." She took a few rapid, shallow breaths. Nerves fluttered and gnawed—as acute as any she'd felt before a performance. Mr. Kemble's expression as he regarded her was far from friendly.

"I suppose you wish to return to the company."

She nodded.

"Your eagerness is understandable. Who would not want to be a part of this grand enterprise?" Mr. Kemble flung one arm vaguely in the direction of the stage. "However, I regret that I cannot offer you a place."

"Why?" she blurted.

"I did have hopes for you, Miss Green, ah, Mrs. Knowlton, but you have heard, no doubt, about the expenses incurred to build my new theater?"

"Yes, of course."

"Sacrifices must be made, madam. I've engaged the incomparable Madame Catalani, who, as I'm sure you know, is one of the finest singers in all of Europe. In the interests of economy, I am obliged to reduce the number of players I take on this season. You understand, of course."

"I am happy to sing in the chorus, sir." Grace straightened her shoulders, conscious of the way in which the maroon cloth of her new gown molded to her figure. She'd come to the theater without telling Percival. As the summer wore on, he'd become increasingly resistant every time she'd mentioned returning to the stage. "I can also act, sir. Tragedy is my delight."

"Your delight, is it?" The celebrated dark eyes appraised Grace. "My dear sister takes most of the tragic roles, and you lack sufficient experience. I am sorry, Mrs. Knowlton, but I have no place for you. Perhaps try again after Christmas. Many things can happen over the course of a season, and I may again have need of you."

Grace did not move, even when Mr. Kemble picked up his pen, signaling with a curt nod that the interview was over. She could not let him dismiss her with such careless disregard. Ned told her how Mr. Kemble had compared her to the famous Peg Woffington, who had risen to stardom from very humble beginnings in Dublin.

"That will be all, madam. Please be careful on your way out. The theater is not yet complete. Loose boards and the detritus of construction are making the corridors hazardous."

"Mr. Kemble, sir?" The door opened and Ned strode in.

"Ned!" Grace almost ran into his arms, restraining herself just in time, but she could not mask her smile.

"You've come back!" Ned grinned, his pleasure at seeing her so genuine that she felt like weeping.

Ned winked at her and then placed a stack of letters in front of Mr. Kemble. "These come for you, sir. Looks like more donations."

"Thank you, Ned."

"Will Miss Green be joining us for the season?"

"No. Please escort her from the theater."

"Sir?" Ned stood like an oak tree in the middle of the room, his hands on his hips, blue eyes steady.

"You heard me. I have no place for her."

"I'm content to be of service wherever I am needed," Grace said. Ned's presence fueled her courage. If it hadn't been for him, she would never have even entered the theater, much less got onstage.

Instead of replying, Mr. Kemble picked up one of the letters Ned had brought, scanned the contents, put it to one side, and then picked up another. He read it quickly and then to Grace's surprise looked up. "Your husband is Mr. Percival Knowlton?"

"Yes, sir." Surely Percy would not have stooped so low as to try influencing Mr. Kemble against her.

"How very curious. Your husband has just donated a generous sum to our building fund." Mr. Kemble smiled. "A *very* generous sum. You should have told me."

"I knew nothing about it, sir." Grace did not dare look at Ned, but she could feel his eyes on her—sensed that his hopefulness matched her own.

"Your husband is not a stupid man, Mrs. Knowlton. He recognizes a good investment when he sees one."

"I am glad, sir."

"If you were not aware of your husband's donation, then you are also not aware that it comes with a condition."

Grace shook her head. That Percival was in a position to donate money to the theater was surprise enough, but a condition?

"Your husband wishes me to engage you for the season, and I confess that the generosity of his donation is such that I must reconsider my earlier refusal. I cannot promise you speaking parts, but I can assign you as understudy for my sister. Can you be ready should something happen to her? We open in ten days with *Macbeth*. I presume you are familiar with the part of Lady Macbeth?"

"Yes, of course, oh yes, Mr. Kemble. I'd be delighted." Grace clamped her mouth shut and did not dare look at

Ned. Kemble's cheek twitched—disdain or amusement? Impossible to know. Lady Macbeth! Her despair evaporated like snow on the flanks of a galloping horse.

"You are not likely to be needed," Mr. Kemble said. "My sister's health has improved considerably over the summer. She is as eager as the rest of the company to get back onstage after such a long time away."

"Yes, sir, thank you. And may I ask one thing?"

Mr. Kemble sighed audibly. "Yes?"

"May I continue to be known as Miss Green?"

To her surprise, Mr. Kemble laughed. "You would not be the first actor to adopt an alias for the stage, my dear. I will grant your request. Miss Grace Green it is."

Grace curtsied. "Thank you, Mr. Kemble. I am obliged to you."

"Good day to you. Please tell your husband that I appreciate his assistance with the New Theatre." Mr. Kemble dismissed her with a nod. "Ned! Show Miss Green to the stage door and then go ask Mrs. Beecham when I'm needed for a fitting of my new kilt."

ᔥᔥ

Grace almost collided with Mr. Harrison on her way out of the theater.

"Miss Green! This is a welcome surprise! But you appear agitated. May I be of assistance?"

Grace smiled as the old gentleman managed an arthritic bow. He'd been kind to her in the few weeks she'd been with the company—and now she'd be seeing him almost every night. Grace was already determined that her position as understudy to Mrs. Siddons must soon expand to other roles.

"Thank you, no. I'm sorry if I startled you. I have just come from meeting with Mr. Kemble, and it appears that I am again to join the company."

"Wonderful news, my dear. You will be a charming addition." Mr. Harrison leaned over his cane, his legs splayed and trembling. Grace leaned forward to take his arm. He tried to wave her away, but when she would not let go, he gave in and gripped her elbow, lips tightening over clenched teeth. Wincing with sympathy at the sight of feet twisted and swollen with gout, Grace helped him shuffle to his chair.

"Ah, that is better. I am glad to have you back, Miss Green."

"Thank you." Grace was about to turn away, anxious to get back to Percival and ask him about his donation to the theater, when an object on a shelf above Mr. Harrison's small coal brazier caught her eye. She picked it up and turned it over, her hands shaking.

"Mr. Harrison?" Her voice sounded strangled.

"Yes, my dear?"

"This figurine? Is it yours?"

"Ah, yes. I received it many, many years ago. By great good luck, I did not have it here when the old theater burned down. I brought it only today from my lodgings. I am a foolish man, and he reminds me of better times."

Grace carefully set down the china figurine of a shepherd holding a lamb—the twin, she was sure, to the smashed shepherdess that had belonged to her mother. "It is very beautiful."

"Indeed." He peered up at her, his face shadowed. "You have a quality about you, my dear." He seemed about to say more and then shook his head and pointed at a footstool just out of his reach. Grace pushed it toward him.

"Thank you. The fire destroyed my old chair, you know, but this new one is doing very well, although I miss running my hands over the shiny bits on the arms." He smiled up at her. "The brocade had rubbed off over the years, you see, rough edges smoothed as it were, rather like me in my old age. Well, mind how you go. I believe the streets are wet."

Grace chose to walk home rather than ask Mr. Harrison to find her a hackney coach. He must have known her mother, which of course made sense if her mother had been an actress. Their paths could have crossed. She shook her head. What did it matter now? More important was to make sure she did not give Percival any reason to change his mind. She arrived home, breathless and windblown, to find him in the sitting room, standing next to the mantel, one hand wrapped around a glass of wine.

"Why?"

"Charming and direct as always," Percival said. "You have come from the theater, I gather."

"Answer my question."

"Really, my dear. You are hardly in a position to bark orders."

Grace waited.

"You can be most exasperating." He took a careful sip of his wine. Beautifully dressed as always, every inch of Percival screamed indolence and ease. He rested one elbow on the mantel, exposing a waistcoat brightly embroidered in the latest fashion. "If you must know, my mother came to me several days ago and told me to do everything in my power to keep you from the stage."

"I don't understand." Aunt Augusta was the last person Grace expected to thank for Percival's change of heart.

"It is not obvious?" He took another sip, his lips full and red.

"Not to me."

He nodded toward the sofa. "Will you at least sit so that we may converse in a civilized manner?"

She sank onto the sofa while Percival returned his attention to the wine. He held the glass up just as a beam of early-evening sunlight pierced the rain clouds, flooding the room. For several moments, he turned the glass, as if absorbed with the play of light and liquid. Finally, he drained the wine, then walked over to a side table and filled his glass to the brim from a decanter before taking a seat opposite her. "It is of no importance. You've got what you wanted, and I trust it will make you happy." For a second, she saw a flash of hurt in his eyes, hastily mastered.

"Thank you, Percival."

"Just do me the honor of not making a fool of yourself, or of me."

"At the theater, I will be known as Miss Green," she said. "No one will connect us."

"That is thoughtful of you."

"The New Theatre is very grand," she said. "You can be proud of your contribution. Apparently, the admission prices are to be raised, even for the pit."

"And a good thing too. Mr. Kemble and his partners must recover their investment. The higher prices will dissuade the more unsavory elements from attending. The theater's no place for shop assistants and tradesmen."

"Who is it for then?" Grace was surprised to find that she was enjoying talking with Percival. They so rarely spent time together.

"Gentlemen and ladies, my dear, gentlemen and ladies. Mr. Kemble knows what he's about by putting up the prices. The clientele can only improve, which is good news for you. A more cultured audience will be a more attentive one. Mind you, in my opinion, Mrs. Siddons is getting too on in years to play Lady Macbeth. I've been watching her since I was a lad, and she was past forty then."

"Mrs. Siddons is a legend!" Grace sat forward. "She is so tall and stately! And her eyes! Mr. Kemble has made me her understudy, but I am determined to get my own roles. It is only a matter of time, and I am still young."

Percival chuckled. "It is gratifying to see you so passionate, my dear. I have not often the pleasure of it." His eyebrows rose as he stroked his cheek with one finger. "Perhaps tonight, we could retire early."

Grace flushed but was prevented from replying by the appearance of Betsy, who placed a bowl of ripe peaches on a side table. "Please, ma'am. These be fresh."

"Peaches? A fine treat! Tell Mrs. Granger well done, Betsy." Percival patted his flat stomach.

"Please excuse me." Grace rose from the sofa. "I must review lines."

"What for? Mrs. Siddons may be getting old, but her stamina is as legendary as her acting. She's birthed, what, six children and outlived at least three of them?"

"I believe it is seven children, and she has outlived four. Good evening, Percival."

Grace escaped to her dressing room. Keeping her voice low, she recited her lines and practiced gestures. She would not wish ill upon so great a lady as Mrs. Siddons, but if something should happen to her—nothing terrible of course, a slight cold would be enough—then Grace would be ready to step in and show Mr. Kemble that he was wise to take her back into the company. Percival was right. Mrs. Siddons was no longer young and rumored to be considering retirement. She'd certainly earned it. Most of the other actresses at the theater would be vying for the chance to replace Mrs. Siddons, but Grace was convinced she had as much chance as any to be chosen.

The successor to Mrs. Siddons! If only her mother were alive to watch Grace make her debut on the London stage—finally stepping into the life she was born for!

Two floors below her window, the door to the street opened and then closed. Percival had not let her down—that was something. She should make more of an effort to speak civilly with him. She could not love him—not as a wife should—but she did not hate him. A hairline crack splintered through one of the protective layers she'd hardened around her heart against him.

Still, by the time Percival returned from his club, Grace would make sure she was long asleep, with the door to her bedchamber firmly shut.

৪৩

"We should tell him, Alec. He's got a right to know something's up." Ned cocked his head at the group of men gathered around the table next to them in the crowded tavern. "This lot looks like they mean business."

"It's all just talk, Ned. They wouldn't dare."

"Maybe not, but there's been plenty of talk these past weeks."

A young man slapped the table with the flat of his hand. "Damn me, we'll teach him a lesson!"

Ned raised his eyebrows at Alec. "You might get the chance to crack a few heads after all these months away from the theater."

Alec scowled. "We'd be a lot better off if your precious managers hadn't raised the prices. There's going to be trouble."

"They ain't *my* precious managers. Besides, I only work for Mr. Kemble."

A watchman's rattle cracked. A young man held it aloft by its smooth wooden handle and cranked. The business end—a wooden rectangle about eight inches long and three inches high—rotated around the handle like a spindle. The grinding, grating sound set Ned's teeth on edge. Several young men guffawed at the din and banged their fists upon the table. Heads turned, and more young men came over to investigate.

"Old prices!"

A chorus of jeers and cheers drowned out the rattle.

"You sure they mean no harm?" Alec shouted over the noise. "If I was you, I'd go straight to Mr. K."

More men brandished rattles as the tavern erupted with cries of "Old prices!" Ned set down his mug and stood up. "All right, Alec. I'll go see him. But I still think nothing will come of it. It's just high spirits."

Alec followed him out of the tavern into the Piazza. "I hope you're right."

"'Course I'm right. Everyone in London wants to get inside the theater. No one will dare make a ruckus. I'd stake me job on it."

Chapter Nineteen

His rash fierce blaze of riot cannot last,
For violent fires soon burn out themselves . . .

Richard II (2.1.33–34)

*O*n the afternoon of September 18, 1809, Grace arrived at the theater several hours before the doors would open at 5:30 p.m. She walked onto the empty stage in front of the crimson curtain and gazed out over the immense auditorium. Five tiers rose into the gloom—three tiers of boxes and two more above that to accommodate the upper galleries, with the top one crammed with seats so close to the ceiling that patrons would be obliged to peer straight down at the stage. All the walls and box fronts were painted a light shade of pink embossed with Greek designs intended to echo the neoclassical style of the theater's exterior.

The stage was the largest Grace had ever seen. Two yellow pillars held up the proscenium and supported a wide arch that spanned the width of the stage. Grace stepped to the very edge of the stage above the orchestra and turned to peer up at the carved entablature—a broad horizontal frieze emblazoned with the royal coat of arms just visible in the light thrown from sconces set into the walls.

She knew, because Ned had told her, that ten feet below the stage was a second stage where the machinery used to work the traps and the wings was placed. Below this stage was a cellar deep enough to accommodate the massive flies that were sunk down through slats in the floor.

Grace stretched out her arms and turned slowly on one foot. She wanted to laugh out loud. If only her father could see her. He'd be apoplectic with rage—and powerless to stop her.

"It's not yet three, sir, and there's thousands of people out there!"

Mr. Kemble, dressed in his Macbeth costume, entered the stage from the back, trailed by Ned. Before they could see her, Grace darted into the wings and waited in the darkness to watch and listen.

"There's too many to take in," Ned said. "What should we do?"

Mr. Kemble whirled around. He was as tall as Ned but with the commanding presence of a man accustomed to taking charge. "What's the problem?"

"They's pushed so hard against the gate at the Bow Street entrance that the chain's broke, sir."

"Is the crowd contained? We still have at least two hours before we open the doors."

"Yes, sir. Most of them are milling around in front of the theater now, crowding the doors. But there's too many, sir."

"So you've said."

"What do we do?"

"Do? We do nothing. If my theater has attracted such a mighty crowd on opening night, then the only thing we can *do* is be grateful. Those who can't get in will return tomorrow." Mr. Kemble clamped one large hand on Ned's shoulder. "Tell the lads to be at the doors when they open and to keep the crowd orderly. They'll be no trouble."

"Yes, sir."

Grace heard the dismay in Ned's voice even if it seemed Mr. Kemble did not. The night before, Percival had mentioned some nonsense about people being upset by the new admission prices, but surely that would not account for such a large crowd. Mr. Kemble had to be right. Everyone was eager to get inside the New Theatre. And who could blame them? In just a few hours, the boxes and pit would spill over with patrons ready to be enchanted by the great Mrs. Siddons—and Mr. Kemble too. Everyone proclaimed his Macbeth was a marvel.

On her way back to the dressing area, Grace passed Mrs. Siddons's private room. The door was slightly ajar.

"To alter favor ever is to fear:
Leave all the rest to me."

The line was from Lady Macbeth's first scene with Macbeth when she plots with him to kill King Duncan. Even in practice, the full, rich tones of Mrs. Siddons's voice thrilled Grace. She'd watch and learn from the great actress so that one day she too could earn the adoration of thousands. Grace hugged herself, smiling into the gloom.

ဨႺဗ

A few hours later, Grace stationed herself in the wings so she had a good view of Mr. Kemble striding onstage. The theater was full to overflowing. She'd heard Ned say that the box office had turned away several hundred people — mostly young men who wanted to gain admission into the pit. Just yards from where Grace stood, over three thousand people shuffled feet and adjusted fans. The New Theatre Royal at Covent Garden was the largest theater ever built in London, which meant, so far as Grace knew, that it must be the largest theater in the world.

Mr. Kemble stopped at center stage and stood bare legged in his new Macbeth kilt, his fists resting on either side of his hips. The orchestra struck up "God Save the King," and the theater exploded with lusty singing. Grace felt as if her own heart would burst with pride as she joined in. She grinned at the three actresses dressed as the witches ready to go onstage as soon as Mr. Kemble finished his welcome speech. Under their hideous makeup, they also flushed with pride, their voices clear and sweet. Grace had never experienced the tug of patriotism with such fervor. The smell of fresh paint and the twitch of newly hung curtains were a reminder that she stood at the precipice of a new life.

As soon as the anthem ended, Mr. Kemble stretched out his right arm. "We feel, with glory, all to Britain due," he declaimed. He then paused and lifted his other arm, symbolically embracing every man and woman in the audience. "And British artists raised this pile for you!"

A mighty roar, a volley of boos and hisses and jeers, rose and crested through the vast theater. Grace clapped her hands over her ears. Onstage, Mr. Kemble did not flinch. He continued speaking, although not one word was audible except perhaps to Mr. Kemble himself. The witches crowded in front of Grace, their olive-tinged faces aghast.

The crowd came together in a crescendo of booing—the sound long and sustained like foghorns on the river. Seconds later, whistles took up a counterpoint of malice, weaving in and out of the rumble of stamping feet and rough shouts—seabirds in a storm. Ned came up behind her.

"They'll calm down soon enough," he said.

Mr. Kemble finished his speech and stood tall and haughty for another minute. The noise swirled around him—chaos bumping against rigid defiance. Finally, with a sniff of his famous hooked nose, he strode offstage.

"Go on, girls!" Ned said. "They've got no quarrel with you."

The witches edged onto the stage to be greeted with a renewed bout of jeers and heckles. Like frightened puppets, they lurched through the scene, their jerky movements so clumsy that one of them kicked over the cauldron. A cascade of dirty sand skittered across the stage. Raucous laughter destroyed any chance the witches had of setting a fearsome tone for the play. Grace remembered her own disastrous debut as Juliet and shuddered with sympathy.

"We're in for a long night," Ned said.

"They can't keep it up," Grace whispered, although she needn't have bothered keeping her voice low.

Howls of protest greeted the reappearance of Mr. Kemble at the other side of the stage. Oblivious to the noise, he strode in front of the witches and waited with his chin held high to be hailed Thane of Cawdor. For all the crowd knew, he was being hailed Thane of Cheapside. The theater erupted with more yells and catcalls. The terrified witches struggled to shout lines that no one—not even Mr.

Kemble—had any hope of hearing. Grace would not have believed it possible for an audience to keep up such a racket.

Kemble's bare knees under his kilt glinted like swollen white fists in the light thrown from the candles. For a few seconds, the noise lessened and his words boomed out.

"Stars, hide your fires;
Let not light see my black and deep desires . . ."

The hoots and catcalls and hollers started again, even louder than before. Mr. Kemble mouthed a few more lines and then stamped off the stage, his face purple with rage.

"Intolerable boors!" he hissed. "They can't keep it up."

But for the next two hours, they did keep it up from scene to scene and act to act—sometimes swelling in volume, occasionally receding so the odd, disembodied word hung in the air only to be smothered by an even greater uproar. The rumbling of the crowd bubbled through the theater like carriages over cobblestones. The loudest yells were reserved for Mr. Kemble. Each time he stepped onstage, the noise in the theater trebled. When Mrs. Siddons as Lady Macbeth joined him, the line that always sent shivers down Grace's spine was swallowed in a thunderous cry.

"Screw your courage to the sticking place and we'll not fail."

"It's a bleedin' disgrace." Ned came to stand next to Grace. "Mr. Kemble's told me to call in the magistrates. As soon as the play's done, they'll read the Riot Act."

"What do they want?" Grace asked.

"They want the prices put down."

"Will Mr. Kemble oblige them?"

"Mr. Kemble don't bow to no man, and especially not to a crowd like this. It's bad enough they're yelling at him, but Mr. K. won't want them doing the same to his sister."

Mrs. Siddons reeled off the stage after her final scene—the famous sleepwalking scene when she rubs unseen blood from her hands and stares with mad, dead eyes at the horrors of her past.

"Insufferable!" she exclaimed. "Where is my brother?" Mrs. Siddons turned on Grace. "You! Take my place. I will not set foot on the stage again until this outrage is ended."

ᘒᘗ

Two magistrates arrived to read the Riot Act at 11:00 p.m. Mr. Kemble, still in his Macbeth kilt, stood next to them and scowled out at the crowd that had not yet dispersed after the end of the final act of the afterpiece—a farce called *The Quaker*. Although the shouting and hallooing did not stop, the mood was more festive than vicious. Even if the magistrates' threats had been audible, no one in the seething crowd seemed remotely inclined to heed them.

At Mr. Kemble's command, Ned was stationed below and to the right of the stage where he could see out over the pit. The musicians had packed up their instruments and left the theater for the comfort and relative quiet of a nearby tavern. Ned wished he could join them, but there was no chance of that for many hours yet. He'd ushered the actors and actresses out through the stage door and did his best to calm Mr. Harrison. The poor old man railed about the riot caused decades earlier when he'd taken Mr. Garrick's place as Hamlet. But loud as the crowds had been then, they'd never kept up the disturbance for the entire evening. This new breed of theatergoers was insufferable! The lot of them should be banned.

"They'll not be budging," said Alec, who came to stand shoulder to shoulder with Ned.

"They can't stay here all night," Ned said. He grinned at Alec. He was glad that he'd been able to convince Mr. Brandon to take Alec back on as ticket taker out front. It felt good to be working with his old friend again.

"What a fine mess! I never expected them to keep it up so long."

A young man jeered at Ned. "Whatcher smilin' at? Ain't nothing to smile about." The man raised his fist and bellowed, "Old prices!"

Others near him took up the cry with renewed energy. Onstage, one of the magistrates gestured and shouted, his face plum purple. The other held him by the arm and appeared to be telling him to give it up as a lost cause. Mr. Kemble continued to scowl at the crowd. Ned wondered if Mr. K. would have more success with the crowd if he listened to their complaints. After all, the prices *had* risen. Maybe people had a right to be angry.

"The magistrates have given up," Alec said, jerking his head toward the stage. "Does that mean we can go home now?"

"I wish, but so long as there's patrons in the theater, we got to stay. Let's hope they get tired soon."

The young man staggered toward them, his arms and legs moving independently, reminding Ned of an ineptly handled marionette. The lad landed at Ned's feet and smiled up at him with gin-fueled confidence. "Old prices, mate! Whatcher mean just standin' there not making a noise with the rest of us?"

Ned seized the lad's arm above the elbow. "We work for Mr. Kemble," he said. "And the performance is over." He gave the lad a none-too-gentle shove toward the side door. "Theater's closed."

To Ned's relief, the lad executed a mock salute and then lurched out the door. Ned turned his attention back to the seething pit and sighed with dismay. Several men hopped up on the benches. They stomped their feet and bellowed at the now-empty stage, and then laughed uproariously.

"You'd better resign yourself, mate," said Alec. "We ain't going nowheres for a long time yet."

Alec was right. By the time he and Ned staggered out of the theater, the September sky was starting to lighten, and the bells of nearby Saint Paul's tolled five times.

ଧୠ

"Intolerable!" Mr. Kemble exclaimed. "Ned, listen to this!" He spread open the *Times* and began to read, his deep voice booming off the walls of his dressing room.

"It was a noble sight to see so much just indignation in the public mind; and we could not help thinking, as Mr. Kemble and Mrs. Siddons stood on the stage, carrying each of them five hundred pounds upon their backs in clothes, that it was to feed their vanity and to pay an Italian singer, that the public was screwed."

Mr. Kemble flung down the paper. "Screwed, are they? Preposterous. The public wants fine acting and the best singing. How the devil am I to finance it without assistance? The rise in prices is trifling! They should be grateful!"

Ned picked up the newspaper and folded it over the offending article that described in painstaking detail the proceedings of the previous night.

"It's bound to blow over soon, sir."

"We'll not give in, I can guarantee you that. Is everyone ready for tonight?"

"Yes, sir."

"Damn good thing we scheduled *The Beggar's Opera*. I've said before that whenever there's any danger of a riot, always set an opera."

"Why, sir?"

"The music will drown out the troublemakers. I'll go myself to tell the conductor to play as loudly as possible. That will show them."

For the first half of the evening, Ned and the performers were relieved by the relative quiet of the audience. A handful of people waved banners, and in the pit several men stood with their hats on and their backs to the stage, but for the most part, the performance continued without interruption. The theater was not full, particularly the pit, but a respectable smattering of people in the boxes and galleries was enough to encourage the company.

Everything changed after the third act—the traditional half-price-admission time when patrons paid half the full rate to enter the theater. Within minutes of opening the pit to the half timers, mysterious bulges under black coats transformed into rattles and horns and dustbin lids. Men brandished placards emblazoned with the new letters of the protest—OP.

Old Prices.

From the pit, rioters hoisted dozens of signs scrawled with a litany of grievances. A popular theme was the patriotic objection to employing Madame Catalani. Although admired for her florid singing style, many people objected to her exorbitant salary of seventy-five pounds for every performance, and also that she was a foreigner—an

Italian! Ned had listened to the grand woman in rehearsal and thought her wonderful, but when Catalani appeared for her first turn onstage, the rioters drowned out her aria with screams of *Cat* and *Nasty Pussy*.

Ned rushed around backstage, overseeing the entrances and exits. Anxious faces greeted him at every turn. None of the actors wanted to go onstage, particularly the principals who sang song after song with only their memories of the music to accompany them. The orchestra played valiantly, but despite Mr. Kemble's orders to play *fortissimo*, the musicians might as well have put dampers on their instruments. Ned wondered why Mr. Kemble did not go onstage himself and call a halt to the evening. But while the actors sang and acted in dumb show, Mr. Kemble paced the corridors and wings, hands behind his back, his brow furrowed.

The actors responded to the tumult by rushing through their parts so briskly that the second piece—a farce called *Is He a Prince?* that entertained no one—ended at ten o'clock, a full hour earlier than normal. Ned was glad of the early stop. Now perhaps the pit would clear, and everyone could gather at the taverns to enjoy their tankards.

A cry went up from the pit. "Get on the stage!"

The stamping of feet and roar of male voices reached backstage to where Ned stood in the wings. Mr. Kemble grabbed his elbow. "Alert the constables!"

Ned ran back along the corridor on the side of the building that housed the dressing rooms for the actresses. The actors were accommodated on the other side. The women, most half-dressed, their makeup dripping from tired faces, crowded into the corridor. Grace put her hand on Ned's arm as he passed. She had not performed that evening but had stayed to help soothe the nerves of some of the older actresses upset by the riots.

"What's happening?" she asked.

"They're storming the stage!" He opened his arms to shepherd the women back into the dressing room. "Ladies! Get behind locked doors. The constables will be here soon."

The Bow Street police station was just steps away. Ned dashed into the street and almost collided with a posse of constables.

"We've heard," a constable said grimly. "Stand aside."

Ned followed them back into the theater and out onto the stage.

"Open the traps!" Mr. Kemble's voice cut like a scimitar across the tumult. Ned veered into the wings where he met Alec leading a group of backstage boys into battle. A crowd of rioters climbed from the pit to the stage and rushed toward them. Alec banged open one of the trap doors and then stood back, his arms crossed, laughing, as a man pitched head first into the abyss. He'd land on a mattress on the second stage ten feet below and have the wind knocked out of him. Ned hoped he got good and terrified on the way down.

The other boys opened the rest of the trap doors. For the next several minutes, unmanly shrieks drowned out the yells of *OP*. A young lad—he couldn't have been more than nine years old—landed in the thick of the struggling men. Ned rushed forward to whisk the lad away from the stomping feet, but two rioters caught the boy and hoisted him to their shoulders. Ned glimpsed a white face and wide eyes before the boy rode to safety, with memories that he'd dine out on for decades.

The Bow Street constables flowed from the stage into the pit. Slowly, methodically, they rounded up a dozen or so young men. The sight of men being led away eventually calmed the ones who remained. Within another half hour, the crowd dispersed, leaving Ned and Alec and the other backstage lads to clean up the mess. Someone had kicked a stage door off its hinges, and in the pit, rioters had upended benches and littered the floor with ribbons, OP badges, and torn placards. But for all the mayhem, the damage was surprisingly light. Ned didn't think the young men meant any real harm. They had grievances that Mr. Kemble refused to hear. No wonder they were frustrated. The next night had to be calmer.

Chapter Twenty

Chewing the food of great and bitter fancy.

As You Like It (4.3.100)

"Ready?" Ned came up behind Grace, his lips close to her ear.

"I hope so," she said.

"Keep yer wits about you," Ned said, moving to stand in front of her so she could see the concern on his face. "You're a brave girl to be doing this."

Grace managed a small smile. "Each of us is brave in our own way, Ned." Of all the parts available to her in the repertoire, the role of the doomed Lady Anne in *Richard III* was one of the most difficult to play convincingly. In one short scene, Lady Anne went from cursing Richard, the murderer of both her husband and her father-in-law, to accepting Richard's offer of marriage. The role of Lady Anne belonged to Miss Norton, but she had pleaded a violent cold. From being the understudy to Mrs. Siddons, Grace had been quickly promoted to general understudy. That afternoon, Mr. Kemble had dispatched Ned to Grace's home with the message that she was to come early to the theater to prepare for Lady Anne. Fortunately, Percival had been out; otherwise, Grace was sure he'd have tried to stop her. The subject of the riots—and Percival's worries for her safety—had formed the chief of their conversation at breakfast.

Ned returned her smile. "I suppose you're right, Grace, but that don't make you any less brave yourself." He nodded toward the auditorium. "It's quiet for now. After two nights, them that's makin' the noise have likely had enough. I'm guessing we'll have an easy time of it tonight."

"Thank you, Ned." She took a deep breath and walked to where she could see a portion of the auditorium. It was alarmingly empty. A cannonball shot through the pit might damage the wainscoting but not necessarily hit a human being. "Where is everyone?" she whispered.

"It's just the pit's that's empty. The boxes are full." Ned grinned. "As usual."

Grace had heard that Covent Garden's whores—popularly called Cyprians—often used the private boxes to service their well-heeled clients. One of the grievances of the so-called OPs was that two tiers of expensive private boxes had replaced two tiers of regular gallery seating. People objected to the boxes being used for more than just watching the plays.

She watched Mr. Cooke as the evil Duke of Gloucester, later crowned Richard III after he'd killed everyone in his way, exit to the other side of the stage. Two of the utilities—the dozen odd players who performed the walk-on roles—pushed forward the casket containing the corpse of King Henry VI, the murdered father of Lady Anne's murdered husband.

This was her time. Grace took a deep breath. The polished stage boards glowed with the light thrown by over three hundred oil lamps trained upon the stage and scenery.

"Go now," Ned said. "There's a girl." He gave her the slightest of pushes to propel her forward. She took three steps downstage and then knelt and laid her hand upon the casket. The few people sitting in the pit rustled and talked, but no one made any commotion. She launched into her long, lamenting soliloquy, her gaze fixed on the coffin. Halfway through, she glanced out at the pit to see a few young men sauntering to a bench in the front row. As soon as they got there, they clapped tall beaver hats on their heads and turned their backs to the stage. The insult sent a surge of power through her. She spoke louder and added more pronounced gestures. When she finished her speech, the utilities returned to take up the coffin, only to be stopped by Mr. Cooke limping toward them, his shoulder overpadded and his neck bent to one side in imitation of a hunchback. Ned had warned Grace that Mr. Cooke had already drunk several cups of wine. When he croaked out his line, the fumes knocked Grace back a foot.

"Stay, you that bear the corse, and set it down."

Mr. Cooke swayed and regained his balance, his eyes widening as he squinted past the two men lifting the coffin, obviously only just realizing that Grace had replaced Miss Norton.

Grace delivered her line in a strong, clear voice:
"And what black magician conjures up this fiend,
To stop devoted charitable deeds?"

Mr. Cooke ordered the utilities from the stage and then, with an unctuous smile, focused bleary-eyed attention on Grace. For the next several minutes, they played the scene—

her shrill protests inexorably wilting in the face of his flattery. Out of the corner of her eye, Grace saw one of the young men standing with his back to the stage turn around. His companions admonished him, but he shushed them with a gesture before taking off his hat and sitting.

She aimed her lines like darts to wipe the smug look off Mr. Cooke's face. He advanced, she countered, finally throwing up her hands and saying her line with careful, deliberate emphasis on each word, drawing out the last word with vicious pleasure.

"And thou unfit for any place but hell."

Mr. Cooke stepped so close to Grace that she saw wine-laced spittle drying at the corners of his mouth. She tried to step back, but he took hold of her arm.

"Yes, one place else, if you will hear me name it."

Even drunk, Mr. Cooke made a good Richard—smooth, dark, evil. Grace pulled back and spat her line.

"Some dungeon."

Mr. Cooke's lips curled into a leer.

"Your bed-chamber."

Grace threw him off and strode downstage. Mr. Cooke followed her, beginning his assault with lines calculated to appeal to Lady Anne's vanity.

"Your beauty was the cause of that effect;
Your beauty, which did haunt me in my sleep,
To understand the death of all the world,
So I might live one hour in your sweet bosom."

Back and forth the dialogue went, with Mr. Cooke throwing out line after line about his desire for her. Grace continued to resist Mr. Cooke until he brandished a dagger and urged her to stab him. They had not had time to rehearse the scene, so Grace acted on instinct. She turned away from him, one hand shielding her face—an exaggerated move that she hoped Mr. Kemble would approve.

The curtain dividing a box on the second tier from the private corridor behind flew outward, and several young wags emerged. They yelled *Old prices* at the men in the pit, who pulled out large wooden rattles and swung them with noisy enthusiasm. The young man who had turned to watch Grace stomped and hurrahed.

Her next line—*I will not be thy executioner*—fell at her feet.

Mr. Cooke cast away the dagger and launched himself at her. "Let's get it over with, girl," he muttered as he dropped to one knee. He shoved the heavy stage ring onto her finger, almost bending it backward in his haste, and then yelled a few more lines. Grace wasn't positive they were the right ones. Mr. Cooke glared at the audience and then limped to the side of the stage and leaned against the column holding up the proscenium.

As Grace turned to exit, she glanced up at the box on the first tier closest to the stage. Percival was leaning forward, his forearms resting on the railing. She was so startled that she walked right into Mr. Renfrew, who was waiting in the wings to go onstage as Lord Hastings after Richard finished his soliloquy.

"I say!" For a second, his sturdy arms tightened around her. She smelled greasepaint and hair powder. He let her go, and she reeled back, tripping over the hem of her gown.

"Mr. Renfrew!"

Ned came up behind Grace. "Your cue, sir."

"Thank you." Before he went onstage, Mr. Renfrew leaned toward Grace and whispered, "You make a most compelling Lady Anne, Grace. Perhaps I misjudged your potential last summer."

She stayed to watch the next scene. Mr. Renfrew lacked the imposing presence of Mr. Kemble, or even Mr. Cooke when he was sober, but the earnestness of his expression as he delivered his lines was not without merit. She turned away from the stage and hurried back to her dressing room. Although more confusing than pleasing, Mr. Renfrew's praise of her performance was not altogether unwelcome.

In Act 3 of the play, she returned to the wings to see Mr. Renfrew's Lord Hastings meet his death. A pair of utilities dragged off his body—splayed loose limbed and convincing. When Mr. Renfrew saw her standing in the wings, he jumped up and bowed.

"That's me done," he said cheerfully. He jerked his head toward the constant assault of whistles, horns, rattles, and boos coming from the audience. "Poor Mr. Cooke hasn't got a chance tonight. How are you holding up?"

"Well enough."

"We hadn't reckoned on them protesting for three nights."

"Do you think they'll settle soon?"

"It's impossible for them to continue on much longer." He smiled at her, his teeth gleaming in the dim light.

"Your cue, Grace," said Ned coming up behind her.

She walked into a wall of noise. It engulfed her like a fire-heated blanket on a summer night. She spoke her lines into air that felt solid. With every ounce of her strength she amplified her gestures to compensate for the impossibility of making her voice heard.

The pit was a sea of placards; the boxes, festooned with crudely lettered banners.

OLD PRICES FOREVER!
NO PRIVATE BOXES!
NO CATALANI!

When she finished her speech and returned to the wings, Mr. Renfrew was still there. He clapped his hands. "Well done," he said.

Grace bobbed a quick curtsy. "Thank you, Mr. Renfrew. That is kind of you to say."

"It's not kindness to say the truth." His smile dimmed the clamor beyond the stage. In the eight months since she'd last seen him, his looks had improved. He had gained a few pounds, which softened the foxlike sharpness of his features, and he had shaved off his mouse tail moustache and trimmed his whiskers so he no longer resembled a sheepdog.

She could not admire him, but now that she was back with the company, it was wiser to have him as an ally than as an enemy.

ȘOCȘ

That night after the performance, Percival railed for a short time about the insolence of the mob and then rang for soup and made Grace drink a glass of wine and water that he mixed himself—something he had never before done for her.

"Can I bear it?"

"You are not obliged to, my dear. I'd not be unhappy to see you leave. The disturbances are shocking. During the last act of the play, some miscreant let fly a pigeon from the upper gallery."

"People object to the design of the top gallery," Grace said wearily. "It's said to be no better than a row of pigeon holes." She took a sip of the wine and let the warmth soothe away her exhaustion. She felt as confused as the poor bird that had flapped from the gallery to the stage and back, circling round and round the ceiling while people below shouted and pointed. Mr. Cooke had been in the middle of his famous speech during the final battle of the play.

A horse, a horse, my kingdom for a horse.

He may as well have been bellowing for a pair of earmuffs.

"Mr. Kemble made a good case for the price increase when he came on after the farce," said Percival.

"Oh? I didn't hear him."

"Few did." Percival smiled. "He told the crowd that the prices had not increased for over a hundred years and that, consequently, the profits were negligible. Of course, they didn't believe him."

"They will soon, I'm sure." Grace drained her glass.

"Who was the fellow who played Hastings?" Percival asked. "He looked familiar."

"He's the brother of Mrs. Partridge, who I believe is also acquainted with your mother. We met Mr. Renfrew in early January."

"I spoke with him briefly. Tiresome fellow."

"That's unkind, Percival!"

"You take an interest in him?"

"I know him from the summer tour last year."

"I want you to leave the company, Grace. Mr. Kemble cannot expect you to act under these circumstances, and I cannot have you risking your health."

"No, Percival. I have no such plans."

She had to stay the course. Rising quickly, she hurried to the door, hiding her red cheeks from Percival.

She must screw her courage to the sticking place.

She must not fail.

৪০তেও

"See here, Ned," Mr. Kemble said, rattling his copy of the *Examiner*. "The management is accused of exhibiting, and I quote, the 'merest feelings of tradesmen.' What do you suppose they mean by that?"

"I think, sir, that people don't understand how much the theater costs to run." Ned sorted and folded the London newspapers that lay open and scattered across the table. Each one contained an account of what was now being referred to as the Old Price Riots at the New Theatre Royal, Covent Garden.

"What? They expect us to operate on air?" Mr. Kemble tossed the paper at Ned. "Insufferable!"

"If you could explain to people . . ."

"Explain? I tried that, and they refused to listen." Mr. Kemble bounded to his feet and began pacing around his combination dressing room and office. The rack lining one wall was now crammed with costumes while the new set of shelves held hats, gloves, and shoes. "Don't people realize that it's no longer profitable to cater only to the tastes of the gentry? We built a theater large enough to accommodate over three thousand spectators. It's a glorious accomplishment." Mr. Kemble stopped pacing and glared at Ned. "Why can't they understand that?"

"Forgive me for saying so, sir, but I'm not sure they're going to stop."

"They must stop—and soon." Mr. Kemble sat at his desk and picked up a pen. "I'll appeal to their sense of fair play," he said. "They are Englishmen, after all." He wrote rapidly for several minutes and then thrust the paper at Ned. "This will calm them. Take it to the printer and tell him to add it to the playbill for tonight."

"Yes, sir." Ned took the paper and left the building to run across Bow Street to the print shop. The sour-faced printer scowled at the new paragraph.

"He thinks this will help?"

"Just get it set and printed," Ned said. "Mr. Kemble knows what he's doing."

"Lots of people don't agree."

"Make that sentence bigger than the others." Ned pointed to words that Mr. Kemble had underlined.

"I can read directions same as you. Mr. Kemble's added a note for large type." The printer shook his head.

TEN YEARS HAVE NOT BEEN SIX PERCENT.

"He means the theater's not making enough profit," Ned explained.

"Profits? What's he on about? I read that he pays himself and his sister a bleedin' fortune. Maybe he should look in his own backyard if he wants profits—not gouge the pockets of respectable men."

"I ain't in the mood to argue with you." Ned turned to the open door.

"That's on account of me being right about your Mr. Kemble," the man called after him. "People have christened him King John, and they don't mean it as a compliment."

Ned didn't bother to reply. He sat on a bench outside the shop and lifted his face to the warm September sun. The truth was that he couldn't care less about defending Mr.

Kemble and his damn theater. For three nights in a row, he'd seen the morning sky lighten. When the printer came out with the sheaf of notices, Ned was snoring gently, his long arms and legs soft in sleep.

"Oy!"

Ned's head jerked back, and he banged his elbow hard against the bench. He squinted up at the printer.

"Good luck with these." The printer thrust the notices into Ned's hands. "You got your work cut out for you with old Kemble."

Ned stood up, towering over the printer, who was a short man with one arm noticeably more muscled than the other from working the presses.

"Send the bill to the theater," Ned muttered, taking the notices and blinking the sleep from his eyes. He felt as if he'd been thrown under a speeding coach and left for dead face down in the mud.

The disturbances couldn't possibly go on for another night.

Chapter Twenty-One

Wilt thou, after the expense
of so much money, be now a gainer? Good body, I
thank thee. Let them say 'tis grossly done; so it be
fairly done, no matter.

The Merry Wives of Windsor (2.2.126–29)

Mr. Kemble was wrong. His notice only served to inflame the rioters until finally he was forced to do what Ned dreaded.

"Mr. K.'s closing up shop, is he?" Alec leaned against one of the four thick columns that held up the portico in front of the Bow Street entrance, his arms crossed as usual over his chest.

Ned peeled off one of the new notices that he'd carried from the printer and held it up to show Alec. The largest word set in thick black letters was CLOSED. "That's what it says here."

Alec waved away the notice. "I overheard Kemble talkin'. What's it mean?"

"It means that Mr. K. is giving in. I got to say that I didn't expect him to cave so quickly. The notice says that a committee of swells is goin' to get together to examine the accounts."

"Yeah? They'd be better off examining their heads," Alec said. "It's a right fix they've got themselves into."

"Let's just hope Mr. K. and the other managers can sort things out so we can get back to work."

"What if the committee says the new prices are justified, like?"

"Then we just got to hope the mob takes their word for it and stops their bellyachin'."

"You don't think they got a point? The rioters, I mean?"

"Nah, and neither should you. Remember, we work for the theater." Ned grinned. "At least they got rid of Madame Catalani."

"Poor old Nasty Pussy," Alec said, laughing. "I gotta say I'm glad to hear it. We don't need to be payin' no Eye-talian to squawk like an old crow."

"I can't say I minded her singin', but I agree she had to go. Lots of people want the second tier of private boxes ripped out as well, but that ain't going to happen overnight. People got to be reasonable. Mind you, I'm not objectin' to a few days off."

"You coming for a drink? You can paste up some of them notices on the way."

"Mr. Kemble might need me to run more errands."

"You're his boy and all now, ain't ye?"

"Until he no longer needs me, yes." Ned held out half the notices. "Go and put these up, will you?"

Ned entered the theater and headed for the property room, passing the women's dressing rooms on his way. The door to the main room shared by the young actresses was closed, but he could hear the girls chattering and laughing. He missed hearing Olympia's voice. Ned had heard nothing about her since the day he'd left her at Astley's. If she was married, she'd not seen fit to inform any of her friends at the theater. And if she was married, it wasn't right for him to keep thinking about her so much.

ಬಂಛ

"Where did you get it?" Grace picked up the thin pamphlet with the tips of two fingers as if any more contact would taint her by association.

"They're being sold all over." Mr. Renfrew leaned against a table in the company rehearsal room where Grace had gone to practice lines. She had a small part to play in the afterpiece — another farce. It was Monday, September 25, and the riots had raged for one week.

Grace read the title printed in large letters on the front piece of the pamphlet: BROAD HINTS AT RETIREMENT. AN ODE TO A TRAGEDY KING. PRICE ONE SHILLING. She glanced up. "They get money for this?"

"People are angry, Miss Green. We are at their mercy."

"These riots must end soon."

"We are all on edge."

"I don't understand why people can't see for themselves that the New Theatre cost a fortune to build and run. The price increase is minor."

"Many people do not agree." He nodded at the pamphlet. "Will you read it?"

Grace opened the pamphlet and scanned the first page. The so-called ode was fashioned in mock heroic style complete with rhymes.

"Dost thou not hear the Critics scoff?
That damning cry of Off! Off! Off!
Canst thou plead ignorance to sounds
With which the theatre rebounds?"

"That's the most dreadful rhyme," Grace said.

"It gets worse." Mr. Renfrew grinned and motioned with one hand for her to continue. Grace noticed lean fingers and hastily turned her attention back to the pamphlet.

"Go, take the hint, and take thy flight,
And with thy Witches fly by night
Go, go, John Kemble, quickly go,
While the stormy winds do blow."

She stopped again. "Oh, honestly, they're even quoting Shakespeare? This is ridiculous."

"You must admit it's rather amusing." Mr. Renfrew smiled. "We must side with Mr. Kemble, but I can't help being diverted."

Grace threw down the pamphlet. "How can you say that? You know how it feels to act in front of such a load of ruffians."

"Most of them are clerks and tradesmen. Some are gentlemen. They're not criminals to want the ticket prices lowered."

"You take their side?"

"I see no sides, Miss Green. Kemble's made a mistake, and he needs to fix it or risk losing the theater."

"There's no danger of *that*. People will get tired of these silly protests, and everything will go back to normal."

"Tell that to Mr. Kemble. He's closed the theater tonight."

"What are you talking about? I'm to perform in the afterpiece."

"Not anymore. I'm afraid you've come to the theater today for nothing. On my way here, I ran into Ned coming from the printer. He was carrying a sheaf of notices announcing that the theater will be closed until a committee of gentlemen completes an investigation of the books and accounts. That's good news, I'd say."

"How can this be good news?"

"It shows that Mr. Kemble is prepared to have the accounts examined. People deserve an explanation. Once they have it, they'll settle down."

"Why didn't you tell me this when you first came in?"

"And miss the opportunity to have you read to me?" Mr. Renfrew smiled and reached for her hand. "I think not."

ഇൻറെ

The financial report on the New Theatre appeared in the *Times* nine days later on October 3, the day before the theater was to reopen with another performance of *The Beggar's Opera*.

"They're spending thirty-one thousand pounds just for salaries? No wonder people are angry." Alec lounged against the wall alongside his bed as Ned read out loud from the newspaper.

"That's what it says here." Ned held the paper out.

"Just read it to me."

"The sum includes everyone, even us. See here, it says *'Salaries, including Band, Painters, Supernumeraries,*

Carpenters, and all other Servants throughout the Theatre.'
We're the Servants."

"Mrs. Beecham told me that the big stars like Mrs.
Siddons make fifty guineas for every performance. No one's
that good."

"I guess they think Mrs. Siddons is. And what are you
doing talkin' with Mrs. Beecham? We've been closed all
week."

"Never mind. Keep reading."

Ned scanned the remaining list of expenses. "It says here
that it costs almost fifty-seven thousand pounds a year to
run the theater. Even in a good year, the box office don't
take in more than sixty thousand pounds."

"You're making my head ache with all them numbers."

"Mr. K. says the riots will stop when people read that he
was right to put up the prices," Ned said.

Alec chuckled. "Old Kemble ain't got a clue what people
want."

"And you do?"

"You're like a bantam cock, standing there defending the
honor of Mr. Kemble. He can look after himself."

"He pays our wages."

"But that don't give him the right to treat us like dirt.
None of us got paid this past week."

"We got to get back to normal, Alec. It's awful the way
people carry on. It ain't right."

"If you ask me, it ain't right to charge an arm and a leg
to watch a bunch of fancy people prancing around a stage
as if they owned it."

"If that's what you think, why stay at the theater?"

"I got a right to complain, same as anyone," Alec said. "You think the sun shines out of Kemble's backside, and I don't. It's as simple as that."

"Yer callin' me a flunky?"

"If the shoes fits." Alec bounced off his bed. "I'm gone to Mrs. G.'s. When you see sense, you can come join me."

As soon as he left the room, Ned balled up the paper and threw it at the door. Damn Alec.

&OCR

The large crowd filling the pit and boxes included a great many young men wearing OP badges and OP hats. From the wings, Ned watched Mr. Kemble brandish a page detailing the accounts and profits of the New Theatre.

"Will they be satisfied?" asked Grace, who came to stand next to him. Although Ned hoped for an end to the riots, he'd hate to see Grace demoted back to Mrs. Siddons's understudy when the great actress returned. Grace had not succumbed to the melancholy that infected most of the rest of the company.

"I hope so. Listen. He's explaining the position of the managers."

Mr. Kemble launched into his defense of the new prices. "The independent auditors have proven us right!" he shouted and then swept his arm across the wide expanse of the theater. "The expenses associated with building the New Theatre have made the increase in prices essential. As people of London, you must understand our obligations to pay for this magnificent new building."

The theater erupted. From the pockets of hundreds of coats emerged rattles, whistles, dustman's bells, postboy horns, trombones, and dozens of other noisemakers. Angry voices rose to the ceiling, heels pounded, the din so loud the floor creaked. A thousand hands waved a sea of placards, proof that the mob had decided Mr. Kemble's fate long before he opened his mouth.

SUPPORT KING GEORGE, RESIST KING KEMBLE!

NO PRIVATE BOXES FOR INTRIGUING!

PRIVATE BOXES FOR YOUNG CATS AND OLD FOXES!

OLD KEMBLE BEGINS TO TREMBLE!

Ned couldn't help smiling at the last one, although he hastily suppressed it when Mr. Kemble stormed offstage. He touched Ned's shoulder, told Grace she'd go on the next night, and stalked off to his office.

Ned sprang into action. He signaled the scene changers to lower the flies for the first scene and dispatched a callboy to tell the conductor to cue the orchestra. Ned then ran to the dressing rooms and shouted a two-minute warning to the actors. Most of them looked more resigned than frightened—better another night playing to chaos than going through another week without pay.

Chapter Twenty-Two

The pale-faced moon looks bloody on the earth
And lean-look'd prophets whisper fearful change . . .

Richard II (2.4.10–11)

Dressed as the ghost of the doomed Lady Anne, Grace waited patiently onstage for her turn to speak. Next to her stood Mr. Renfrew playing the ghost of Lord Hastings, and on either side of them ranged the ghosts of Richard's other victims. Downstage lay Mr. Cooke as Richard III. He mimed a fretful sleep as one by one the ghosts stood forward to curse him on the night before his final battle.

Like a poorly harmonized overture, the constant clattering and rumbling in the audience intertwined with the words spoken by the actors. Grace watched the two youngest actors who played the princes murdered in the Tower of London speak their lines and then exit from the stage, her cue to step forward. She glided downstage to stand over the sleeping Richard and delivered her lines with as much intensity as she could muster, sweeping her arms wide and then clutching them before her breast.

"Richard, thy wife, that wretched Anne thy wife,
That never slept a quiet hour with thee,
Now fills thy sleep with perturbations.
To-morrow in the battle think on me . . ."

For the last line, she raised one arm, holding her hand palm down above Richard's head so that she appeared to be giving a benediction and not a curse.

"And fall thy edgeless sword: despair, and die!"

This was the second time that Grace had played Lady Anne. She should have felt more comfortable in the part, but she felt only relief to have it done with when she exited the stage and waited in the wings to watch Mr. Cooke rise from his sleep and plod through the rest of the scene. From her vantage point offstage, she could also see a portion of the pit. A young man wearing a large hat emblazoned with the letters *OP* clambered onto a bench. Three men joined him, and then all four took up heavy staves and turned their backs to the stage. A roar from the audience was their signal to begin.

Mr. Cooke flinched and kept acting.

The men raised their staves at least two feet off the bench and crashed them to the floor with a hollow boom. Although Grace could see only their backs, she noticed the stiff way in which they held themselves, as if they were a quartet of ceremonial guards.

"What are they doing?" she asked Mr. Renfrew, who had also lingered to watch the final scenes of the play. She didn't bother to lower her voice.

"It's the OP dance," Mr. Renfrew said. "I've heard they practice it in the taverns and then come here to cause their mischief."

"Do you still agree with their grievances?" Grace asked.

"I can understand them."

"Yes, but must they keep up such a racket? We may as well not act, for all the good it does anyone."

"Old Kemble will not bend."

"Miss Green? Mr. Renfrew? A word."

Grace whirled around to see Mr. Kemble standing directly behind her, frowning.

༄ ༅

Several hours after the end of the performances on October 9 of *Richard III* and an afterpiece called *Raising the Wind* that should have been called *Riling the Crowd*, Mr. Kemble walked out onto the empty stage and called for Ned to gather the lads who worked as ticket takers and dealt with troublemakers.

"You've got to admire his nerve," Alec whispered when he joined Ned on a bench in the pit.

"I've gathered you here for two reasons," Mr. Kemble said. He spoke as if he were delivering one of Hamlet's soliloquies rather than addressing a handful of men seated a few yards in front of him.

"He ain't backing down, that's for sure," Alec said.

"Shut it!" Ned whispered. "You know he won't tolerate talking." He'd not forgiven Alec for calling him a flunky, but that didn't mean he wanted to see his friend get in trouble. Alec exhaled a curse. Ned ignored him and fixed his attention on Mr. Kemble, who paced back and forth across the stage, his voice rising as he warmed to his subject.

"First, I commend you for your efforts in keeping control of these so-called rioters. You've comported yourself with restraint and dignity, and I want to assure you that your efforts have not gone unnoticed."

"Get on with it, man," Alec said under his breath. He flexed stubby fingers, flecks of dried blood still clinging to his knuckles. The night before, Ned had watched Alec use his fists to control a young rioter with more drink in him than sense who'd tried climbing past the spikes installed in front of the stage to keep back the rioters.

"That said," Mr. Kemble continued, "I have decided that you require assistance."

"What's this? We ain't in need of no assistance," Alec muttered.

"I've hired professional pugilists whom I have charged with controlling the crowd, particularly those ruffians making a commotion in the pit. I ask that you accord them every courtesy. You will continue to station yourselves at the entrances, where it is to be hoped you can waylay some of the more boisterous sorts."

"What's that he's saying?" Alec asked. "He talks like a bleedin' book."

"What do you expect? He's an actor."

"Oy!" Alec's voice cut across Mr. Kemble's.

"Alec!"

"Sir!" he called again.

Mr. Kemble stopped talking and glared down at him. "What is it, man?"

"Yer not serious 'bout bringing in boxers, are you, sir?"

"Very serious. You must know by now that I am not in the habit of saying what I do not mean."

Ned pulled at Alec's arm and tried with his bulkier body to step in front of his friend until he had the sense to keep his mouth shut. Alec didn't know that Kemble had a formidable temper.

"It's a mistake, sir!"

Ned dropped his hand from Alec's arm.

"If that is how you feel, then you are not obliged to stay in the employ of this theater. You are dismissed." Mr. Kemble scowled at the other lads. "Does anyone else think it's a mistake for the management to defend our property?"

Ned knew he should step forward and defend Alec. How often had the two of them gotten into scrapes in the old days? They'd always stuck together, always taken the blame for each other's misdeeds. But Ned had never told Alec what Mrs. King at the Foundling Hospital had said to him one time after he and Alec were caught and punished for stealing apples from Covent Garden market.

Mrs. King called him into the dank room she used as an office. Ned expected more scolding – Mrs. King was a great one for scolding. What he got was maybe worse, maybe better.

"You're not like Alec," she said.

"Alec's me mate." What was she on about? He'd known Alec since they were both four years old and brought back to the Foundling Hospital from the country, where they'd been sent as babies. Ned had few memories of the woman who had cared for him beyond the smell of sheep and smoke and the feel of the husband's broad hand slapping his backside.

"I want to tell you something that I hope you'll take to heart," said Mrs. King.

Ned glowered at the floor.

"Now that you're ten, you'll soon be leaving us."

"I know." Not for the world would he let old Mrs. King see the terror that haunted his nights when he imagined the world outside the hospital. He'd be apprenticed to do some kind of job, but he

didn't know what. At least he was already too tall for the chimneys.

"You're kind, Ned," Mrs. King said.

He looked up. She'd always been such a grand, forbidding presence in his short life — to be avoided and reviled. Now he saw a woman creeping toward old age, her hair dry and gray, her cheeks pocked like thin porridge.

"Looks like I'm gone," Alec said as soon as Kemble strode off the stage. "And a good thing too. I don't fancy playin' second fiddle to a load of boxers."

"You shouldn't have talked to him so disrespectful, like."

"I ain't any man's lickspittle, even your precious Mr. Kemble."

"What yer goin' to do now?"

The habitual black-toothed grin that Alec wore to defend himself against the world folded into thin lips. "What do you care?"

Before Ned could say anything more, Alec pushed his way through the crowd of lads, all muttering about Mr. Kemble's harshness and, it had to be said, Alec's stupidity. Moments later, one of the side doors leading from the pit to the street slammed shut.

If Ned was really as kind as old Mrs. King thought, he'd follow Alec and talk sense to him. But Ned stayed put. Alec had made his own damn bed, and he could lie in it and starve, so far as Ned was concerned.

Ned also couldn't spare another minute for anger on Mr. Kemble's behalf. The evening performance would go up in two hours, and he still had a thousand things to do. He made his way backstage and down a corridor to Mr. Harrison's room next to the stage door. They were short two girls for the chorus that evening — both gone after declaring they'd rather sell hot pies in the market than go onstage to be hissed at. He hoped Mr. Harrison would know where to find some replacements.

Ned was almost to Mr. Harrison's room when he heard a voice he'd heard lately only in dreams. He paused at the doorway. She was bending toward Mr. Harrison, smiling, shaking his hand. She'd grown thinner over the summer. When she turned to see him watching her, he saw sallow cheeks.

"Hello, Ned."

He bobbed his head. "Miss Adams."

Her eyes widened slightly at the formal greeting, and he fancied that she looked a little bit hurt, which was at least some compensation for the months he'd spent trying to forget her.

"Olympia here's come back to us," Mr. Harrison said cheerfully. "And not a moment too soon after we lost them two from the chorus."

"These riots are shocking," Olympia said sympathetically, "but surely they can't last much longer. There have been riots before."

"Aye," Mr. Harrison said, "but never so bad as this. I remember, oh, early seventies it must have been, when people made a right fuss because Mr. Garrick didn't appear in *Hamlet* when the playbill said he would. People booed and carried on something fierce." Mr. Harrison grimaced. "I should know. I was the poor sod who played Hamlet in his place."

Olympia laughed and patted his arm. "I am glad to be back," she said. "Your new room is much more spacious than the one in the old theater, and I see you've gotten yourself a new chair."

"More's the pity. There's a shocking draft, and as for my chair . . ." He sighed loudly. "Well, my dear, you'd best go with Ned here to get yourself sorted out for tonight. Ned? You're standing there like a great pillock. What's wrong with you? Olympia here's come back."

"I can see," Ned said stiffly. She hadn't said anything when he called her Miss Adams, and so far as he could tell, she wasn't wearing a ring. He knew he didn't have any right to hope, but being human and all, he couldn't help himself.

☙ଓ

Grace arrived home early from the theater, still flushed with confusion and some delight after her hurried conversation backstage with Mr. Renfrew. He'd not said anything improper, but the expression in his eyes when he looked at her had made her feel somehow different, admired. Did he care for her? She didn't have a word for how she felt about him. She only knew that she no longer wished to avoid his company.

Grace refused Betsy's offer of charred toast and took only tea in the sitting room, in front of the fireplace brimming with ashes in an unswept grate. She noticed that Betsy's hair was trailing from her cap and her apron was askew. Grace really needed to have a word with Mrs. Granger, the housekeeper.

She opened her script of *Romeo and Juliet*, but after a few minutes, with the light from the single candle flickering across her exhaustion, she pulled her shawl tight around her shoulders and let her head loll back against the sofa. Yes, Mr. Renfrew cared for her. Every time Grace was waiting to go onstage, he came up to her and whispered encouragement and was in the wings again when she came off, smiling at her, complimenting her. She had never wanted a man to care for her. And yet . . .

She closed her eyes and relaxed into the blessed silence, letting her mind drift back to the stage. She imagined an audience that watched her with breathless fascination, taking in with willing ears and open hearts every word she spoke. Even the rioters were quiet for once, charmed by her skill and beauty. Everywhere was warmth—the lamps, the faces rapt with wonder, Mr. Kemble smiling his approval. Grace owned her place on the stage and no one could take it from her. She smiled and curtsied, accepting the applause with eyes downcast and cheeks flushed.

An arm encircled her waist, and strong fingers pressed the bare flesh of her wrist. She moaned and softened into the touch.

"My dear!"

Percival's voice dashed against her pleasure like sharpened nails. She sat up and brushed his hand away. The script slithered to the carpet where it fell open.

"Are you unwell?"

The concern in his voice disconcerted her. "I must have fallen asleep."

"Obviously." The usual drawl was back. "But really, my dear, it is hardly the thing. You have a perfectly good bed upstairs."

"I did not intend to fall asleep," Grace said with as much dignity as she could muster. "This evening—"

"Was trying. Yes, I know."

"You came again to the theater?"

"Yes." He moved closer and placed his open palm against her cheek. "You were even lovelier this time. I believe you are improving. Those ruffians in the audience could not have seen a better Lady Anne." He'd never used such a gentle tone with her. "You are fatigued."

She rose swiftly to her feet. "I am perfectly well, Percival. We are learning to ignore the commotion in the pit."

"The fighting is getting out of hand. I cannot have it, Grace."

Rather than reply, she bent to pick up her script.

"Another role?"

"Juliet."

"Ah, well that must please you. But you can't want to play her under these circumstances. If the rabble is not content *now*, what more can Mr. Kemble do?"

"Perhaps Mr. Kemble will give in and lower the prices."

"Unlikely. He believes such a course would ruin him, and I'm inclined to agree."

"I have no wish to discuss it, Percival," Grace said. "I'm sorry if I startled you." She turned to the door.

"Grace."

She whirled around. With no fire lit, the room was chilly, and yet an unwanted heat settled over her shoulders. Before she could stop him, he reached for her, enfolded her in his arms, pressed her cheek against his shoulder. His lips grazed the top of her head. "I am sorry, Grace. Truly, I am. But you cannot continue."

"You said I could." Her voice was muffled by his jacket.

"That was before these ridiculous disturbances. I can't have it, Grace. You must see that."

For a few moments, Grace let herself find safety in his embrace.

My bounty is as boundless as the sea. My love as deep.

"I can't stop," she said, pulling back from him.

He dropped his arms from her shoulders and strode around her to the door. With a click of his heels and a bow, his face averted from hers, he held the door open for her. "Good evening, my dear. I trust you can find your own way to your room."

She passed out the door into the vestibule and then stopped at the bottom of the staircase. The clock struck one. Rain spattered against the glass panes of the front door. Percival fastened his cloak and picked up an umbrella.

"You are not going to bed?" she asked.

"No."

It would be the work of a moment, the flick of a shoulder, a flash of her eyes. He was her husband. She did not move to climb the stairs, almost wishing he'd reach for her again. One word would be enough to stop him.

He opened the door and stepped into the darkness.

She mounted the stairs alone.

ಶಲ

The presence of professional boxers in the pit enraged the OPs so much that fights broke out every night the theater was open. Gone was the spirit of fun that had infused the actions of even the loudest rioters. Now, young men faced off with deadly earnest against the infamous pugilists, Dutch Sam and Dan Mendoza, along with a gang of their boxing cronies. Bloody noses and cracked skulls turned the pit into a battleground.

"What do you think about these boxers, Ned?" Grace asked one evening as she waited to go onstage. Dressed as a servant girl, she was good-naturedly replacing one of the female utilities in a small role that required little acting skill beyond standing in the right place at the right time.

"Don't let Mr. Kemble know, but I think it's daft havin' them in the theater. The magistrates have gone and put up signs announcing that anyone caught rioting will be prosecuted, but that ain't right neither. I don't like what the rioters are doin', but they ain't criminals."

"Why did Mr. Kemble hire the boxers?"

Ned shrugged. "I guess he thinks they'll control the crowds better than our own lads can."

"It's not working."

"True enough." He peered past her to the stage. "Your cue's coming up."

He handed her the tray she was to carry, and then glanced out at the pit seething, as usual, with angry men. A short man with a black-toothed grin was standing on one of the benches and brandishing a trumpet. In response to yells of encouragement, the man blew a cacophony of off-key notes.

Ned lunged forward. In another step, he'd be on the stage.

"Ned! Where are you going?"

With a sigh of frustration, Ned stepped back into the shelter of the wings.

"You almost walked onstage!"

"I forgot meself. Please don't mention it to Mr. Kemble." Damn Alec. What was he playing at, raising a ruckus in the pit along with the other troublemakers?

"Of course not."

Onstage, Mr. Cooke raised his arm to call for the maid, Grace's signal to enter. As the riots continued to rage, the actors had developed their own set of visual cues to compensate for the noise.

"Off you go, Grace."

"Thank you, Ned." She flashed him a smile before hastening onstage.

Ned watched Grace go with mixed feelings. Her growing partiality for Mr. Renfrew worried him. Had she forgotten Renfrew's treatment of her the year before? He peered out at the pit again. Alec had got hold of a rattle now and was cranking it round and round over his head. What a fool! He'd get himself arrested or beaten up by one of the hired bruisers.

Ned was finally able to leave the theater half an hour after the end of the afterpiece. The crowd had dispersed more swiftly than usual, thanks in large part to the efforts of Mr. Kemble's pugilists. At least they were good for something.

Ned said goodnight to old Mr. Harrison, who was nodding off in his chair, and left the theater by the Bow Street entrance. He got as far as the corner of Hart Street before walking straight into the middle of an ambush.

Chapter Twenty-Three

Cowards die many times before their deaths;
The valiant never taste of death but once.

Julius Caesar (2.2.32–33)

*L*ook there! He works for Mr. Kemble."

Ned swung around and narrowly dodged a fist aimed at his head. Instinct took over. With all his strength, he drove his elbow into his attacker's stomach.

"Oy!" Another man leapt onto Ned's back and clutched at his neck. Ned spun around and kicked. The man dropped into the mud, arms flailing.

"Get off home with you!" Ned yelled. "The theater's closed."

The man on the ground struggled to his feet while a third man plowed one fist and then the other into Ned's ribs. A white-hot rage catapulted Ned into a fourth man, who raised both elbows, catching Ned square on the jaw so he doubled over, his cheek grazing his knees. A heavy boot lashed out at his ankles. Just in time, Ned sidestepped it and then pivoted, landing a solid punch into a soft stomach.

Another fist caught him in the eye, which immediately started to close. But he didn't need to see to fight. The men were coming at him on all sides—punching, kicking, cursing. Ned flailed his arms like the vanes of a windmill, catching one man and then another and flinging them down.

"Leave him, lads! He ain't one of the fighters."

Ned recognized Alec's voice, dimly aware of his friend dancing on the periphery of the fight and trying to pull off one of the attackers. Ned started to turn his head to tell Alec not to try helping him. He'd only get himself hurt. Another fist smashed into his cheek.

"He works for Kemble, don't he?" yelled the man who hit Ned. "I seen him come out the stage door."

"I said leave him!" Alec shouted.

Faces blurred and shifted—angry faces, leering faces. With a roar, Ned reared up and swung his fist. He connected with flesh, heard a cry and a curse. He had them now. From his good eye, Ned glimpsed an arm coming at him. He drove both fists into the face above the arm, bellowing his rage.

"Ned!"

Ned dropped his guard and whirled around to see Olympia running toward one of the men, her small fists flailing. As he lunged toward her, hands snatched at his waist from behind. He threw back his head and banged into a skull with a solid, satisfying thunk.

One man was down now, rolling in the mud, groaning. Olympia was still beating on a second man, and Alec was grabbing at a third, yelling something Ned couldn't hear. The face of the biggest man, the only one Ned hadn't gotten the better of, loomed in front of him, snarling through cracked teeth.

Moments later, Ned's forehead exploded.

ଛୠ୕ଔ

The cut on Ned's forehead streamed blood. He heaved himself to his feet and staggered back to the theater, his face striped red so he looked like Banquo's ghost. Alec had run off with the attackers rather than stay to help. His friend's betrayal hurt Ned almost more than his cut forehead. The stage door opened just as he got there and he collapsed into Grace's arms.

"Dear God! Ned!" Grace's knees almost buckled under Ned's weight. Olympia rushed up behind him and took hold of an arm.

"Quick! We need to get him to Mrs. Beecham," Olympia said. "She'll know what to do."

Between them, Grace and Olympia hobbled with Ned down the corridor to the costume room. Mrs. Beecham was coming out the door, the candles in her room already extinguished. She stood aside to let the women and Ned through and then found and lit a fresh candle.

"What happened? So much blood!" She didn't wait for Ned to speak. "Sit."

She flew into action, a dervish on a mission as she gathered up a bundle of cotton and then barked out orders to Grace and Olympia to find water and another candle. Ned couldn't deny that his head ached, but he suspected the cut looked much worse than it was. Watching three women run around on his behalf was a new experience for him. He couldn't help feeling just a little bit glad that his injury was capable of inspiring such alarm, particularly in Olympia. She'd tried to help him. That had to mean something.

Mrs. Beecham plunked the basin on the table and set to work tearing the cotton into thin strips.

"It's not too bad," he said, putting on a brave face. He was very aware of Grace and Olympia standing nearby. They were clasping hands and watching Mrs. Beecham soak the cloth in water and dab at his forehead. He would *not* wince, not with Olympia looking so concerned. Why had she come back?

"You hush," Mrs. Beecham said. "I'll be the judge of what's bad. What happened? Did you see who did this?"

Both women shook their heads. Ned opened his mouth to explain and then closed it with a snap when Mrs. Beecham applied more pressure to the cloth with one hand while she glanced around the room. "My sewing things. Where did I put them?"

"Sewing things?" Ned asked. He saw Olympia go pale.

"Don't be a baby," said Mrs. Beecham. "The cut's deep. I'll need to sew it."

"You can't sew skin!"

"Of course I can." Mrs. Beecham turned to Olympia. "Come over here and hold the cloth with a firm hand. You'll need to put some muscle into it to stop the bleeding."

"But—" Ned protested.

Olympia's hands were very soft—much softer than Mrs. Beecham's. She stood close to Ned, her arms shaking with the strain of holding the cloth steady over his wound. Ned relaxed a little bit. He knew for sure now that she didn't wear a wedding ring. Mrs. Beecham came back into his line of sight. She was holding something up in one hand, something that glinted in the candlelight.

"No!"

"Don't worry. I've done this before."

"You have?"

"Hush! Olympia, you hold his hand, and, Grace, you stand behind him and press his shoulders down. I can't have him moving while I work."

"I ain't going to move. Ai-yee!" The needle was a hot poker slicing through his flesh. He gripped the sides of the chair with both hands; sweat popped out all over his body. The urge to pull away was overwhelming, but even if he'd wanted to, he'd be hard pressed to break free of all three women at once. Mrs. Beecham sewed with slow, deliberate care. He counted the stitches. One, two . . . The pain was appalling. He had to cry out. He saw tears glistening in Olympia's eyes. Three, four . . . Mrs. Beecham was insane to put him through this. He'd never heard of anyone sewing flesh. Five . . . He couldn't endure another second.

"There. That should do it. You'll look a right mess tomorrow, like you've been in the wars."

Mrs. Beecham bound strips of cotton around his forehead and then removed the blood-filled basin to another table. "You'd best sleep here tonight."

"In the theater?"

"Why not? Go into Mrs. Siddons's room. It's not like she's using it, and she has a sofa. I'll get cleaned up here, and the girls can get on home. You're not going to die, leastways not tonight."

"There was four of them, maybe more."

Mrs. Beecham laughed and even Grace smiled, but Olympia still held his hand. She squeezed it before letting it go.

"This is all because of Mr. Kemble and those pugilists he's hired," Olympia said. "The OPs are madder than ever."

"I don't suppose we can blame them." Ned wished she'd take his hand again. The stitches felt like red-hot screws digging into his flesh.

"I can blame the ruffians who attacked you." Olympia smoothed the hair from his forehead.

"One of the prats swung his rattle at me."

Olympia helped him to his feet and then went to stand next to Grace. "You must take it easy tomorrow, Ned." she said. "I'm sure Mr. Kemble will understand."

"Fat chance of that."

He gave the women a clumsy salute, then felt his way down the dark corridor to the room allocated to Mrs. Siddons. No other actress had dared take it over since she left. When she'd get back to the theater and onstage again was anyone's guess.

The riots had now raged for twenty-two nights since the New Theatre opened on September 18. The longer the riots dragged on, the more entrenched became Mr. Kemble. He was oblivious to the numerous cartoons depicting him in all manner of undignified ways, the insulting placards, the constant calls for his removal from the theater.

Ned settled himself on the sofa and crossed his arms over his chest like a dead person. Olympia was back, and Alec was running with the OPs.

Why had the world suddenly turned upside down?

Chapter Twenty-Four

The jaws of darkness do devour it up:
So quick bright things come to confusion.

A Midsummer Night's Dream (1.1.148–49)

*D*ear Grace, you can't be serious." Olympia pulled Grace aside in the crowded dressing room. "You told me you hated him."

"That was last season." Grace smiled at the look on Olympia's face. "You have missed a great deal. But please don't worry about me. I have no intention of letting anything happen."

"You don't know what Mr. Renfrew's like."

"What do you mean?"

"Never mind. You're such an innocent, Grace."

"I am a married woman."

"Yes, and that state never gave any woman sense." Olympia turned around for Grace to unlace her costume.

"I promise to stay away from Mr. Renfrew. Will that satisfy you?"

Olympia twisted her head around. "I don't trust him."

"No, but I presume you trust me." Grace leaned forward to plant a kiss on her friend's cheek. "Let's not quarrel. I have enough to worry about with Percival. The last thing I need is a lover."

"Grace!"

"Dear me, Olympia. Look who's shocked now!" Grace would have liked to say more about Percival—how he often stayed out long past the time she returned home from the theater and then avoided her at breakfast, and how if he chose, he could forbid her from ever setting foot in the theater again. Not for the first time, she wished she could have pursued her career on the stage without tying herself to a husband.

"Will you come with us tonight to the tavern?" Olympia asked.

"I can't. Percival will know if I come home late. I'm glad you're back, Olympia. Are you ever going to tell me what happened?"

Olympia shook her head. "Please don't ask me. Just know that I'm here to stay this time."

"You are living still with your mother and the general?"

"With my mother, yes."

Grace wanted to know more, but Olympia pushed past her to join a group of actresses leaving the theater.

⊱⊰

"But he can't do that!" Grace wanted to stamp her foot like a child.

"As actor-manager, Mr. Kemble has complete dominion over us all."

"You are not happy with the decision. You cannot be."

Mr. Renfrew did not immediately reply. They were strolling through the Piazza on a drab afternoon in late October, the sky swollen with clouds of unshed rain. Grace took his arm as she stepped over a rivulet of filthy water running across the pavement. If they were seen walking out together, tongues would wag, but Grace no longer cared. All around them swarmed the street life of the great metropolis—beggars and whores and pickpockets vying for the notice of neatly dressed merchants and black-frocked clerks and gentlemen wearing tall beaver hats and gloves of fine leather. With Mr. Renfrew—Thomas—so close that his arm pressed against hers, Grace felt protected. The noise and clatter gave her energy where they had once tired her. Strange and wonderful sensations filled her waking hours with anticipation and her nights with a new kind of dream in which her husband played no part.

"I confess that I am put out." Mr. Renfrew steered them around a cart rumbling toward the market. "It would have been my first turn as Romeo on the London stage."

"And mine as Juliet."

"But *you* will still perform. You should be pleased."

"It won't be the same without you."

"And I am sorry for it," he said quietly. He stopped walking and turned to look into her eyes. He was just a little shorter than she was, but he filled the space in front of her with a comforting solidity that anchored her, made her feel like she could do anything. How had she ever thought him plain? When he smiled, as he was doing now, his soft lips parted, and his eyes—a very deep brown—regarded her with a pleasing earnestness so different from the piercing blue of Percival's gaze.

"Miss Green."

"Grace," she said.

He shook his head. "No, I must not be so bold. I would not expose you to scandal. Your husband . . ." He started walking again, guiding her with light pressure across the Piazza.

Her heart, so long closed, was a rose on the point of blooming, petals unfurling to the sun—insistent, unstoppable. She wanted him to touch her skin, to hold her against his chest and make her feel like she mattered. But she was not free, and no amount of hoping could change that.

"What do you think about Mr. Charles Kemble?" she asked to turn the subject.

"He is Mr. Kemble's brother."

"Yes, but can he act?"

"Well enough. He will make a creditable Romeo. Mr. Kemble is not wrong to exchange me for him. Mr. Charles Kemble won't embarrass you."

They reached the Strand, beyond which a maze of small, stinking lanes led to the river. A steady stream of carriages rumbled up and down the busy thoroughfare. Mr. Renfrew spotted a rare gap and pulled Grace across and into one of the lanes. The overhanging houses almost obliterated the sky.

"Grace," he whispered. He held her chin with his gloved hand.

She knew she should pull away. Love was for doomed ingenues on the stage, not for wives. But one kiss . . . What was the harm? No one would find out if she gave in—if just this once she let herself be Juliet. A fine, misty rain leaked through the narrow gap between the buildings. If she lifted her face, she'd feel it wet her cheeks while his lips closed over hers. One kiss. What harm in one kiss?

"Blast!"

Mr. Renfrew broke away from her so abruptly that Grace staggered back against the blackened bricks of the building running alongside the lane. She saw a blur of movement next to Mr. Renfrew that sharpened into the figure of a young boy shouting in triumph and holding aloft a gold watch.

"Mr. Renfrew! Thomas!"

But he was not listening. He set off after the boy, who darted down the lane and around a corner. Grace heard a cry and a scuffle, and then, minutes later, Mr. Renfrew climbed back up the lane, his face a mask of fury.

"Damn the little rascal!" He clenched his fists. "He slipped out of my grasp."

"He's only a child and likely starving!" Grace exclaimed. The violence of his anger shocked her.

"He's little better than vermin!" Seeming to recollect himself, he bowed absently. "Forgive my language, madam."

"Please, walk me back to the theater, Mr. Renfrew. I am not scheduled to perform this evening, and my husband expects me home." Her heart, so recently opened, snapped shut.

With a scowl, he held out his arm.

She took it, and they walked in silence for most of the way back across the Piazza to the theater. He made one half-hearted attempt to engage her in conversation, but she suspected his mind was more on his stolen watch than on her comfort.

They arrived at the theater to find Ned standing in the open stage door. He still looked a mess after his ordeal four nights earlier—one of his eyes was swollen closed, and his forehead was a mass of crisscrossed lines.

"There you are, Grace!" he said. "I've been looking all over. Mrs. Beecham is in a state. Turns out the gown you're to wear for the death scene's been torn. You'd best come right away."

Grace followed Ned into the theater without a backward glance at Mr. Renfrew.

৪০৫৪

On the last day of October, Ned stood at the Bow Street entrance to usher out the constables and their charges. At half time that evening, dozens of London's young wags had crowded into the theater, sometimes to cheer on the rioters with their placards and badges, at other times to pick fights with the "New Price" supporters that Mr. Kemble paid to attend performances. Ten arrests were made—a larger number than usual, mostly laborers, clerks, and tradesmen, with one or two gentlemen.

"Alec?"

A constable held Alec by the elbow. His stained waistcoat was missing a few buttons, and one sleeve of his jacket was torn. Alec twisted around. "Tell 'em, Ned. I ain't done nothin' wrong."

Ned hesitated. Alec's eyes bored into his. Gone was the cheeky grin at a world that had never wanted him. Hollow cheeks streaked with dirt hinted at a hard few weeks after his dismissal from the theater. Alec hadn't been back to the lodgings he shared with Ned and had left no word about his whereabouts. Ned was still too angry with Alec for not helping him after the attack to investigate. But then he remembered Mrs. King's words.

"I know this man," Ned said. "He worked for Mr. Kemble."

"Don't matter to me," said the constable. "He was seen throwing punches at a gentleman in the pit and hallooing at the stage."

"He and dozens of others, Constable. And I'm sure he's very sorry." Ned glared at Alec, who had the sense to hang his head.

"Sorry, Constable," he mumbled. "I ain't never meant no harm."

Reluctantly, the constable let go of Alec, who stumbled over to Ned, his head still down, although Ned knew the grin was creeping back.

"I'll make sure he stays out of trouble," Ned said. "There's plenty more need arresting. Mr. Kemble will appreciate you clearing the theater."

"It would be a damn sight easier to clear the theater if it weren't for them pugilists that Kemble's hired. They cause more trouble than they're worth." The constable hefted his truncheon and headed toward the auditorium where he'd find enough heads to bang together to keep him busy for at least another hour.

"Told you so," said Alec.

"Shut up," Ned hissed. He pushed Alec back along a narrow corridor to a dark area backstage. "What on God's earth are you playing at? Why did you leave me?"

"Honest, Ned. I chased after the fellow and got the rattle off him and then gave him a good swipe of me own. But when I went back to help you up, you'd gone." He peered up at Ned's forehead. "He got you good, I see."

"No thanks to you."

"I tried to get 'em off you." He grinned. "Leastways, it looks like your girl's back. That ought to make you happy."

"She ain't my girl." Ned grabbed Alec's arm. "You shouldn't even be in the theater. Mr. K. let you go."

"I got a right to come into the pit, same as anyone. I paid me way."

"What if you'd gotten arrested?"

"That weren't goin' to happen. I'd have given that constable the slip long before he got me to the station. Besides, I ain't in the wrong here. Kemble's the villain for raisin' the prices."

"Come off it. Since when do you care 'bout theater prices? You've never been in an audience in your life."

"Don't mean I haven't wanted to." Alec pulled himself to his full height, still a foot shorter than Ned. "Can I go now, or are you wantin' to keep me here another hour to lecture me?" Alec spat on the floor. "Yer as bad as old Mrs. King."

"Get on with you then." Ned crashed his shoulder into the wall as he turned, sending a shuddering pain through his arm. "I got work to do." He stomped down the corridor to the wings where a couple of scene changers were shunting the flies along narrow tracks set into the floor at the back of the stage.

Fuck Alec.

⁎⁎

Grace lay on her funeral bier, her eyes tightly shut. She breathed shallowly to prevent anyone seeing her chest rise and fall. It was November 9—almost two full months since the theater opened. After a few blessedly quiet nights, the mob had returned with a vengeance. The solitude of her closed eyes amplified the cacophony of whistles, bells, shouts, and thumps.

Old prices!
No private boxes!
No pigeon holes!
No Kemble!

Grace imagined herself floating high above a battlefield, untouched by the fray. If only Mr. Renfrew stood over her and not Mr. Charles Kemble. The lace from Kemble's sleeve brushed across her nose, tickling it so she needed every ounce of willpower to hold in a sneeze. Mr. Renfrew would never be so clumsy.

While she waited for Charles Kemble to take the poison and die, she wondered if she'd been too hasty in condemning Mr. Renfrew. He'd been understandably upset at having his watch stolen. People said things in anger; even the best of men swore on occasion. Just look at her father.

The chants rose and fell, the voices sometimes in unison, more often not. In a few moments, Mr. Charles Kemble would kiss her and utter his last line—*Thus with a kiss I die.* He'd then collapse artfully against her bier. His kiss was her signal to wait a few beats and then wake up. In the interests of economy, Mr. John Kemble had cut out the scene with the Friar that bridged the death of Romeo with the death of Juliet.

Charles Kemble's lips grazed her cheek. She wrinkled her nose against the stench of stale wine, trusting that his body shielded her face from the audience. The bier shuddered as he slumped against it. She counted to three and opened her eyes.

A mighty roar shook the theater to its rafters.

"Dead! Dead! Kemble is dead!"

Grace shut her eyes and increased the count to ten, twenty, thirty. The ugliness of the crowd paralyzed her. After over two months of almost nightly riots, the counterfeit death of a Kemble—any Kemble—was inflaming the audience to fever pitch.

Charles banged his fist discreetly against the bier. Grace felt as if a lead weight was pressing against her, grinding her into the unpadded slab of wood painted to imitate marble. Through half-closed eyes, she peered up at the ceiling above the stage—a mass of ropes and pulleys that supported the grand spectacles. The New Theatre really was huge. From the galleries, Grace would look like a child in her flowing yellow gown. Her facial expressions as she played out the last minutes of an ill-fated life were invisible to three-quarters of the audience. She might as well be acting to a flock of high-flying birds. A crushing sadness overwhelmed her—for Juliet, for the theater, for Mr. Renfrew, and especially for herself. Tears burned and fell. What did it matter if no one saw them or cared if they did?

With one swift movement, she sat up, gazed around with mock surprise, and then down at Charles's dead body splayed across the floor. As she'd rehearsed, she flung her arms wide and howled—the sound lost to everyone but herself. She leaned down, plucked the wooden dagger from Charles's belt, and held it high above her head. She'd not drop it this time.

The noise stopped as if smothered by a giant hand. Thousands of eyes watched Grace, the horns and whistles and rattles still. What was her line? She knew it like she knew how to breathe. But she held the line in, held the dagger steady so it pointed directly at her satin bodice. Her loosely dressed fair hair cascaded over her back in waves that blended with the satin so that from a distance her entire figure appeared dipped in sunshine. She exhaled shallowly into the hush. The gold paint on the dagger glinted in the candlelight as she raised it higher into the air. Finally, she threw her line out across the wide auditorium.

"*Oh, happy dagger! This is thy sheath; there rust, and let me die!*"

With all her strength, she plunged the dagger toward her heart, veering at the last moment to hide the point under her arm. A long, low moan started from her belly and grew to fill the theater. She swung around to face the audience—a blur of faces and black hats, of hands holding aloft noisemakers and rattles for once silent. She let her body go limp and slumped with slow elegance onto the bier. Just as her head touched the painted pillow, she let her right arm drop as if relieved of every muscle and bone. Her motionless fingers grazed the top of Kemble's head. She let out one long, last sigh, closed her eyes, and waited.

For several more seconds, silence pulsed into the ears of every man and woman in the theater. She began to count. *One, two, three . . .*

At eight seconds, the theater erupted. After weeks of boos and hisses and rattles, the noise that spread to every corner of the massive theater was the one most welcome to any actor.

Applause.

The ovation lasted for only a few minutes before the yells and jeers resumed, but in those few minutes, Grace's spirits soared. Finally, she was free to be who she wanted to be. Nothing else mattered—not Percival, nor Mr. Renfrew, nor even the memory of her mother's body crushed into the cliff-top mud. She was Juliet, and the crowd loved her.

"Wonderful performance!" Mr. Renfrew met her in the corridor outside the women's dressing room at the end of the evening and walked with her to the stage door. "Magnificent." He leaned closer and whispered. "Forgive me?"

"You were provoked."

"That was no excuse to distress you. I would not have you angry with me." Mr. Renfrew's eyes were still outlined in black from his turn on the stage in the afterpiece—a musical farce called *The Poor Soldier*.

"I am not angry."

He moved closer. "Then perhaps we may go walking again one day?"

The stage door opened to let out several actors on their way to the tavern. Bits of debris swirled in—ticket stubs and crumpled playbills and cigar butts. Grace wrapped her cloak more firmly around herself.

"Grace!"

"Damn the fellow!" Mr. Renfrew said under his breath. Ned crowded into the small room. His collar was unbuttoned and his neck cloth untied, the wound on his forehead glowing pink with new skin. He sagged with exhaustion. The flash of silver at his throat, which Grace had first seen that morning in Ned's room, again caught her eye.

"If you please, Miss Green, Mr. Kemble's asked me to see you home."

"That is not necessary, Ned. My husband always sends a carriage to fetch me."

"Carriages can't get through." Ned was panting slightly. The thin cord circling his neck was threaded through a round disk—the flash of silver. She smiled to herself, remembering how she'd spent three nights sleeping in a bed not three feet from Ned. Except for the one time she saw his naked back, Ned had always been fully dressed in front of her, shirt buttoned and brown neck cloth wrapped neatly around his throat.

"The streets ain't safe. A crowd's planning to head toward Mr. Kemble's house in Bloomsbury."

"What for?"

"To cause more mischief. Two nights ago, over a hundred of them marched to his house and threw mud, coins, even rubbish. They broke windows and terrified poor Mrs. Kemble half to death."

"I can see Miss Green home," Mr. Renfrew said. "She will be safe with me."

"No, sir. Mr. Kemble's asked me. Thank you, sir." Ned took Grace's arm, blocking Mr. Renfrew with his broad back. "Please, Grace, we got to get going."

Grace glanced back at Mr. Renfrew and shrugged as she let Ned take her arm. To insist on having Mr. Renfrew see her home would not be wise. She turned to say goodbye to him, but he was already stalking back along the corridor, the red cloak of his soldier's costume flapping when he rounded the corner to the men's dressing room.

"It's uglier than usual tonight," Ned said as he led Grace out to the street. Several groups of young men pelted past them, laughing and shouting. Ned steered her around a pile of horse droppings. "Mind the dirt."

"Mr. Kemble must regret hiring the strong arms," Grace said. "Have they finally been sent off?"

Ned flashed a grin. "Long since, Grace, although Mr. K.'s not one to admit he was wrong to have hired them in the first place."

"I think we already knew that." They shared a laugh and then settled into a comfortable silence, their footsteps muffled by the filth of the street. They walked the length of Bow Street and then turned into Long Acre on their way to Bedford Square.

"That object you wear around your neck," Grace said, "It looks like silver."

"Ain't nothing special. Just a bauble." His large hand closed around the disk as he pulled it from his shirt. The silver flared in the light of a torch fixed to a passing coach.

Grace stopped walking and reached up to gently pry the disk from his fingers. She rubbed the serrated edge, felt the two small holes. It couldn't be. And yet she felt certain the button was the mate to the one in her mother's old jewelry box.

Chapter Twenty-Five

'Tis dangerous when the baser nature comes
Between the pass and fell incensed points
Of mighty opposites.

Hamlet (5.2.60–62)

*O*lympia sparkled as Constance in the farce *Animal Magnetism* by the indomitable Elizabeth Inchbald. Ned noticed a sharp drop in the noise level from the rioters every time Olympia Adams stepped onstage—and who could blame them? She played her part with such spirit. Her small, neat body appeared to float above the polished boards. He had no illusions about his chances with Olympia. She might not have gotten married, like she said she was going to, but that didn't mean she'd look twice at him. He wasn't a toff—not the kind of man she deserved.

It was Saturday night—the busiest night of the week for the rioters. The pit and boxes overflowed with noisy young men, many jingling pockets full of the new medals struck in honor of the riots. The chiseled shape of a head meant to represent Kemble appeared on one side of the medal, with the letters *OP* on the other. Above the head were etched the words OH MY HEAD AITCHES. Ned couldn't believe the lengths the rioters were going to make their point. Someone had paid good money to have the medal struck and copies made—a criminal waste in Ned's opinion.

Grace came to stand next to him in the wings. She'd finished her turn in the chorus of the comic opera *Love in a Village*, which opened the evening.

"She's wonderful," Grace said, nodding toward the stage where Olympia was delivering her lines.

"Aye, that she is."

"You know that she's left the general's house? I hear she's trying to support her mother on what she makes at the theater."

"I'm glad to hear it. He's a right old bugger." He grinned. "Beggin' your pardon and all, Grace."

Grace laughed. "I'm not so innocent anymore," she said. "That button—the one you wear around your neck? How did you come by it?"

"Why do you want to know?" Ned turned from watching Olympia and motioned for Grace to follow him away from the stage.

"I have the same kind of button. It belonged to my mother."

He fished the button out of his shirt and held it in his palm. The memory of how he got it was never far from his mind, although it wouldn't ever do to tell Grace. Or anyone. "I don't think it can be, Grace."

"May I borrow it? Just for a few days?"

"Why?" He couldn't imagine what harm it would do, but the request was strange, even coming from Grace.

"I want to see if it's the same as my mother's."

"Your mother? What do you mean?" Surely Grace didn't think . . .

"I, well." Grace blushed.

"Take it if you like, Grace," he said, pulling the cord over his head and thrusting the button at her before he could change his mind. "But it won't make no difference."

He remembered a night many years before—hot and sticky it had been, not like the November chill that honed the air outside the theater tonight. He'd left his bed to wander the halls of the Foundling Hospital, drawn by the sound of a woman's cries in the darkness. He smelled the blood before he saw it—a black pool that coated the scrubbed floor like liquid coal.

The woman left a few days later, but the child—a girl so small that six-year-old Ned could have cupped her in his hands—only lived long enough to be christened.

"I got to get on, Grace," Ned said. "The scene's about to change."

He escaped back into the wings in time to see Olympia skip off the stage, her cheeks flushed.

ဆဩ

Grace wasn't sure if she was relieved or dismayed to find Percival waiting in the vestibule for her when she arrived home. He was still wearing his cloak.

"I did not hear a carriage," he said.

"The carriages could not get through the crowds. Ned walked me home again."

"Good of him. Is he still out there? I'll give him a shilling."

"No, Percival. He'd be insulted." Ned's silver button felt as heavy as a piece of lead shot in her hand. She should wait for the morning to talk to Percival, but that would be the coward's way out.

If it were done when 'tis done, then 'twere well it were done quickly.

"Would you come into the sitting room with me, Percival? I have something I wish to tell you."

"Of course, my dear." He helped her out of her cloak, then paused a moment to hold her shoulders. His warm breath on her neck was soothing. She bit back a sigh and broke away from him, just glimpsing a flicker of hurt on his face as he took a lit candle from its wall holder. A blast of damp air swirled around her legs. She and Percival so rarely used the sitting room now that she spent six evenings out of seven at the theater.

"I can wake Betsy to see to the fire if you're cold."

"Thank you, Percival, but it's not necessary to disturb her. I am quite warm." Grace sat on the edge of the sofa, her back ramrod straight to stave off shivering from the cold — and nerves. Perhaps she shouldn't tell him. Percival would hardly rejoice at even the possibility he may be related to someone of Ned's class.

Percival used the candle to light several more around the room and then lowered himself into a hard chair opposite her. Black leather shoes gleamed in the soft light. He crossed one leg over the other and then clasped both hands to the side of one knee where the white stocking met the cuff of his silk breeches.

"What is so pressing that you must keep us from our beds?" he asked.

Grace held out the button still threaded on a cord burnished black with dirt.

"This button belongs to Ned," she began. And then, with halting words and many pauses, she described her suspicion. When she finished, Percival sat in silence for several minutes, his expression impassive as he stared at the fire. She knew that what she'd told him was shocking, unbelievable perhaps. But she needed him to want the truth as much as she did.

"So you are telling me that, because of a button, you think this Ned fellow is your *brother*?" Percival made the word sound obscene.

"Half brother. And I said I wasn't sure."

"We must talk to my mother."

"Your mother?"

He sighed with exaggerated patience. "Your own mother is dead, and Ned can't be expected to know about his origins. Your assertion that a silver button leads to a relationship with your mother and by extension *you* is no more than surmise." He held up his hand to forestall Grace. "Hear me out, my dear. I understand that you are feeling somewhat emotional at this suspicion about Ned's parentage, but believe me when I assure you that it cannot be true."

"I don't know why you think that. I was never told about my mother's life before she married my father. You remember how surprised I was to find her stage jewelry. If she was indeed an actress, then she may well have gotten herself in trouble."

"Are you suggesting that because your poor mother was once associated with the theater that she had loose morals?"

"No, Percival. But I am not so innocent that I don't know what can happen to a young woman who strays."

"Your father would not have married her if she'd borne an illegitimate child." Percival sat back, his expression smug.

"My father likely knew nothing about it." Grace stopped as she remembered her father's voice raised in anger the night before her mother's death. Was *that* the reason—so many years later? "I brought my mother's jewelry box with me to London. It contains a button that is identical to the one Ned wears around his neck. Mrs. Gale told me it was one of a pair that came from my mother's Juliet costume and that my mother had always prized its uniqueness."

"Coincidence."

"Normally I would agree with you, Percival, but please hear me out as to why I believe the two buttons are related." Grace took a deep breath. "A few weeks ago, Ned and I got to talking backstage while I waited for my cue. He told me that he'd been born at the Foundling Hospital. I know that the wretched mothers who gave their babies away after giving birth at the hospital often affixed a token of some sort to their child's blanket—brooches, thimbles, charms, that sort of thing. The button must be the token that Ned's mother—my mother—left for him."

"How can you know this?"

"One of the actresses at the theater told me about the tokens."

"Thereby proving my point about the moral quality of the people you work with."

"Let us not quarrel. We have an agreement."

Percival rose to his feet and nodded down at Grace. "I will inform my mother that we wish to speak with her. If your mother bore a child, my mother must have known about it. Ned is likely hoping that fabricating a connection with you will help him get on in the world. He is sadly mistaken."

"Ned is a good man, Percival. I doubt he has any idea of the connection. How could he?"

"Alleged connection, my dear. His kind's always looking to take advantage of their betters. We must sort this out as soon as possible. I presume next Sunday will be convenient?"

"Yes, of course."

He stood and indicated the door. "Goodnight, my dear." He extinguished the candles and stood aside to let her pass. She did not look at him as together they mounted the stairs to their separate beds.

ଚ୍ଚOଔ

Augusta received Percival's description of Ned with perfect composure, the slight sneer on her lips barely fading, even when she regarded the two identical buttons he set before her.

"How fascinating." She kept her eyes on Grace, ignoring Percival. "You believe this Ned fellow is your mother's bastard son?"

Grace flinched. "The evidence is compelling."

"You call this evidence?"

"The buttons are identical. Mrs. Gale—my mother's housekeeper—said the button came from Mama's Juliet costume."

"*Her* costume?"

The malice in Augusta's voice surprised Grace. Why should her aunt care what roles her mother had played? "Mrs. Gale told me that Juliet was my mother's favorite role. And I know about the tokens left by mothers for their babies at the Foundling Hospital. This button could have been left by my mother."

"Your mother never acted Juliet."

Percival was on his feet, pacing around the small sitting room that faced the unkempt back garden at his mother's London house. "What are you talking about, Mother? I saw the stage jewels that Aunt Charlotte left behind. She could not have come by them if she had not been an actress."

"I never said that Charlotte was not an actress, only that she never played Juliet." Augusta had regained her composure and spoke with perfect calm, as if commenting on the weather and not the genesis of a good man's life.

Grace stared at her aunt. Why would she be so hostile about her mother's roles? Augusta had to be hiding something. Grace longed to take hold of the faded ribbons hanging from her aunt's lace cap and pull them—make her tell everything she knew about her sister. Nothing was right about any of this. She remembered hearing her father tell her mother that *we must not raise another actress*. Another? Her father must have known about Charlotte's background, and yet he'd married her anyway.

Had her father seen her mother act and been enchanted? Grace could hardly imagine her stern, black-browed father enchanted about anything. And yet for all his sour moods, Grace knew with complete certainty that even if he was indifferent to his daughter, her father had loved her mother.

"Please tell us what you know, Aunt."

Augusta gazed down at her clasped hands as if hoping to find the answer there. Finally, she let out an irritated sigh. "I can see that you will not be satisfied with anything but the truth."

"If you know something about Ned, then you must tell us, Mother. Grace has no wish to be related to such a man."

"That is unkind, Percival! I've said no such thing."

"Enough." Augusta's voice still commanded attention. She glared at Percival until he stopped pacing and seated himself next to the window. "Thank you. Grace, the button that your mother kept all these years did indeed come from Juliet's costume, but it was *my* costume, not hers."

"*You* were an actress?"

"Yes, Percival, to my shame, I was."

"Why did you never tell me?"

"It was not necessary that you should know. My father managed a small company of traveling players. He took my sister and me all over the country, even to Ireland one dreadful summer. Both of us were onstage almost before we could walk. When I was sixteen and Charlotte eighteen, we were taken on at the Theatre Royal in Bath. Those were difficult years, Percival, that I wish to forget. Your father saved me."

Grace glanced over at Percival, who was looking like he'd been run over by a speeding carriage.

"This is all very distressing to have to talk about so many years later," Augusta continued, apparently not noticing the effect of her words on Percival. "Particularly so with your mother in her grave, Grace. The truth was that my sister cut the button off my costume after I left the theater to marry Mr. Knowlton. She was always jealous of my greater success on the stage. You are mistaken about your mother's connection to Ned, although correct in assuming a connection between the two buttons." She held up her hand. "I shall explain. The theater has not always been a respectable place for young women. Some would say it still is not." She glanced up at Percival. "Which reminds me, Percival. You must put a stop to Grace's continued involvement. It is unwise, particularly in light of the current disturbances. The theater is not respectable for a decent married woman. I do not approve."

"Please do not change the subject, Mama. You were speaking of Ned."

"We had in our company a young woman who, by her actions, put the reputations of all of us at risk."

"She had a child," Grace said.

"Yes. And as you correctly surmised, Grace, this young woman—I forget her name—took one of the buttons from my costume. She must have pinned it to her baby's blanket at the Foundling Hospital. Heartbreaking story, but not an unusual one. Mind you, I am distressed to learn that this Ned fellow had gotten hold of the button. I was under the impression that the governors of the hospital kept these tokens and the identities of the mothers a secret."

"Do you know if the woman is still alive?" Grace asked.

"Of course not!" Augusta snapped. "When I left the theater to marry Percival's father, I never had anything more to do with the stage. I am not like your mother, Grace. *She* regretted leaving. *I* did not. Now, I trust this explanation will relieve you of your anxieties. You are not related to Ned, and that is an end to it. The woman who bore him was an inferior actress and jealous of your mother and of me." Augusta spoke with such calm assurance that Grace felt chilled to the bone. Nothing about the young woman's pathetic fate appeared to distress her aunt in the slightest.

"I'll have a word with Mr. Kemble," said Percival. "Get him to dismiss Ned."

"No!" Grace exclaimed. "Ned has done nothing wrong."

"Leave the young man where he is. I'm sure he meant no harm."

"If you wish, Mama. Well, Grace, there's an end to it."

"Quite right." Augusta picked up the bell to ring for tea. "We will not speak of it again." The expression on her face was perfectly serene, but Grace noticed that the hand holding the bell shook just enough to keep the bell tinkling for several seconds after she stopped ringing it.

Chapter Twenty-Six

. . . we know what we are, but know not what we may be.

Hamlet (4.5.41)

*N*ed!"

The sound of Mr. Kemble's voice snapped Ned to attention. He followed Mr. Kemble to his office and waited at the door while Mr. Kemble shuffled papers on his desk, his movements almost agitated.

"May I help, sir?" Ned asked.

"You heard about Brandon?"

"Yes, sir. He's that upset about it."

"Brandon has nothing to be ashamed of. It's that blasted Clifford fellow who should be ashamed of himself—bringing trumped-up charges of false arrest against my box office keeper. Mr. Brandon should be commended for his actions, not made to answer to charges like a common criminal. By arresting Clifford, he was protecting the theater—*my* theater. Henry Clifford is a radical. People should be grateful that our box office keeper turned him over to the magistrates."

"I believe, sir, that some people think of Mr. Clifford as the leader of the OPs."

"Don't say that loathsome abbreviation in my hearing! But yes, you are right. It's no doubt because of the mob's support that Mr. Henry Clifford, damn him, was released from custody so quickly. The magistrates haven't the courage of their convictions."

"Yes, sir." Ned wished Mr. Kemble would hurry up and tell him why he was summoned. He needed to get backstage and make sure that Mr. Renfrew was ready for his entrance. That afternoon, he'd seen the actor enter his dressing room carrying a full bottle of rum.

"And now Clifford's saying that Brandon laid hands on him unlawfully. Unlawful, is it? Clifford was causing a disturbance, and Brandon handled it." Mr. Kemble picked up a newspaper, read it quickly, and then threw it back onto his desk. "God save me from these newspaper men. Now they are accusing *me* of being un-English. I, who have done so much for Britain! Listen to this fellow. He thinks I should suppress the very *idea* of private boxes, never mind the boxes themselves. And do you know why?"

Ned shook his head.

"Because they are foreign! Can you imagine anything more absurd? No, you cannot, but listen anyway." He began to read.

"The idea is not English. It is not consistent with that fair and honest equality, which our national character and temper have maintained, time out of mind, at our public places of amusement.

"What does he know about equality? My theater welcomes everyone!"

"Yes, sir. Did you want anything in particular, sir?"

"What? Oh, yes. I need you to take this list to the box office and tell Brandon to let in everyone on it. He's to disburse the people in various places around the house — boxes, galleries, pit. He'll know what to do."

Ned carried the paper to Mr. Brandon's office at the front of the theater. Mr. Brandon was a mild, inoffensive man — hardly the bullying demon that Mr. Clifford's supporters made him out to be.

"Mr. Kemble wants these people to get in for free," Ned said.

Mr. Brandon took the list. "Letting in more trouble, if you ask me."

"Sir?"

"Things are getting out of hand, and we don't have enough constables to make a blind bit of difference." He shook his head. "At least I've learned my lesson and won't be laying hands on any of them again."

"Do you think Mr. Kemble should give in?" Ned asked.

"I do, but you didn't hear me say it." Mr. Brandon waved Ned away. "Go on with you. I'd better see to getting the doors open."

Ned hurried along the corridor to the dressing rooms. In his pocket was the button given back to him by Grace. She told him that she'd been mistaken, that it was not a match for her mother's button. Ned would keep what he knew to himself. If Grace's mother had been one of those poor souls obliged to leave a part of herself at the Foundling Hospital, then he would not be the one to say anything more about it. The past was past, and it didn't do any good to dwell on it.

୧୬୫

The leaden November afternoon—a full two months since the start of the season and the riots—was fading as quickly as Grace's resolve. A raindrop splashed onto the letter she held in her hand, smudging part of the return address but leaving the direction untouched. She stepped into the post office closest to the theater before she could change her mind.

Since coming away from Aunt Augusta's house the previous Sunday, Grace had not been able to rid herself of the nagging suspicion that Aunt Augusta was not being truthful. Her explanation about another actress had been too quick, too glib. Was she trying to protect Grace's mother and by extension herself?

Only one person—apart from Aunt Augusta—was likely to know the truth.

After posting the letter, Grace ran across the street to the theater. Out in the Piazza, a misty sun was trying to break through the clouds and blur the edges of the frenetic activities of carts and hawkers and stamping horses heading to the market. As usual, Mr. Harrison was sitting in his chair, one swollen leg propped on his footstool.

"Ah, Miss Green! You are early today."

"I like to rehearse when the theater is still quiet."

"Which it so rarely is these days, more's the pity. You are on again as Juliet tonight? I heard good reports about the last time you played her."

"Thank you, Mr. Harrison. Perhaps I'll be lucky and the crowd will pay attention."

"These riots must stop soon," he said. "Last night I heard that several OPs staged a mock fight in the pit."

"I saw it from the wings. They also charged up and down the benches like a pack of hounds. These days, more action happens in the pit than on the stage."

"Mr. Kemble must give in eventually."

"I'm sure he will."

"And I hope for your sake that the riots end before you appear as Desdemona next week." Mr. Harrison's eyes crinkled with delight at the look on her face.

"Pardon me?"

"Oh yes, Mr. Kemble himself told me. Seems you're becoming quite the favorite, Miss Grace Green. Poor Louisa's nose is out of joint, and she'll likely give you a hard time, but I wouldn't let *that* bother you. She was a disaster when she played Desdemona last week. Did you hear?"

"No. What happened?" Grace had been away from the theater the night poor Louisa—finally taken back in desperation by Mr. Kemble—had gone on in *Othello* to face one of the worst crowds since the start of the riots.

"It was Louisa's bad luck that Mr. Clifford—he's a lawyer and a right troublemaker—brought an action against Brandon for false arrest a few hours before her performance. The OPs had a field day, which put poor Louisa right off her game. She barely gasped when Mr. Cooke strangled her."

Grace did not wish to benefit at Louisa's expense, but to play Desdemona! She'd never even dared to hope.

"Kemble will likely give you the news himself this evening," Mr. Harrison continued. "Are you pleased?"

"Yes! I've dreamed of playing Desdemona but never thought Mr. Kemble would pick me."

"Kemble's got an eye for talent." Mr. Harrison peered up at her. "You have the look of someone I used to know. Did I never tell you that?"

"No, Mr. Harrison."

"It's no matter. Off you go, then."

Grace wanted to laugh out loud as she stepped into the dark corridor. Desdemona! Instead of heading to the women's dressing room, Grace turned left and made her way around the side of the auditorium to the main lobby. Her fingers slid through the slit in her skirt to touch the note from Mr. Renfrew that she'd received the night before. He wanted to meet her! She could tell him now about Desdemona. He'd become so supportive of her acting in the past weeks, often bolstering her spirits with his praise. From the lobby, Grace mounted the large central staircase past a statue of Shakespeare set on a carved porphyry pedestal. At the top of the stairs, she turned toward the lobby reserved exclusively for the patrons of the two tiers of boxes, her heart hammering from the climb and from excitement. She should not have come, and yet how could this flutter of lightness, this anticipation that made her skin tingle, be wrong? She walked rapidly through the lobby and entered the box closest to the stage. A glimmer of light from a few candles in the auditorium was enough to let her see the box's luxurious interior—velvet curtains, gold tassels, thick pile rug, and chairs upholstered in light blue. She slipped her woolen scarf from her neck and shrugged off her cloak, letting it fall at her feet. What if Aunt Augusta's story about the poor actress was a warning? What if the same thing happened to her? Grace bent to pick up her cloak and then paused. Her fate could never be the same. She was a married woman—and on her way to becoming an acclaimed actress. She was not some helpless young female with no prospects and no protection.

"Old Kemble's not spared any expense up here, has he?"

Grace jumped at the sound of Renfrew's voice so close behind her. He must have come up the stairs from the Piazza entrance and waited in a dark corner of the box lobby. Instead of turning to greet him, she walked forward to the edge of the box and peered down at the stage far below. In a few hours, angry patrons would fill the auditorium, while onstage she'd try again to captivate them with her Juliet.

"No, indeed," Grace said without turning around. "I think we've always known that Mr. Kemble aspires to greatness both on and off the stage."

"That he does." Mr. Renfrew came to stand next to her. "But when all is said and done, Mr. Kemble is an actor. Only an actor. He will never be the equal of the men he tries to impress."

"Do you include yourself in that description?" His breath was warm on her bare neck and smelled faintly of rum.

"Perhaps. I am a younger brother, Miss Green, with few prospects. My family would rather I was idle than be associated with the theater, but I was born for the stage." He reached for her hand. "Like you were."

His palm was soft and dry against her palm. She placed her other hand on his arm. When she was with Percival, she waited and endured, ruthlessly keeping in check any twinges of fire in her belly. What would it feel like to give in willingly to a man?

He wrapped one arm around her waist and then with one swift movement drew her close. "All day I've existed in an agony of hope. I didn't know if you'd meet me or not. And now here you are."

"I . . ."

He kissed her—his lips hard against hers. She let herself melt into him, become a part of him. All her misgivings about meeting him dissolved.

He drew back. "We can't. Not here."

She made up her mind in an instant. "I know a place," she said.

Chapter Twenty-Seven

Of all base passions fear is most accurs'd.

Henry VI, Part 1 (5.2.18)

*G*race led Mr. Renfrew to the dressing room reserved for the exclusive use of Mrs. Siddons. Dust covered the dressing table, the costume rack was empty, and the sofa upon which Mrs. Siddons reclined between scenes was bare of pillows. Grace turned around to face Mr. Renfrew and in his earnest smile saw proof of his desire for her. He cared for her. Of course, he cared for her. It was enough.

Grace shivered in the cold room. She turned around again and leaned back into his arms. His lips parted against the bare skin of her neck. She was Juliet on her wedding night, Desdemona before the Moor accused her. Desire spread through her belly—new and forbidden and delicious.

His fingers stroked upward from her waist and stopped just short of the curve of her breasts. She exhaled the pleasure of promise in a long, low sigh.

"You are sure?" he whispered.

She nodded, not trusting herself to speak. She half turned her face to his, searching for a kiss, but he was not looking at her.

He removed his hand from her breasts and fumbled at the buttons of his breeches. On the dressing table in front of Grace, the script for *Macbeth* lay open, the words close enough to read. Mr. Renfrew bumped against her, pushing her forward, his fingers still scrabbling at his crotch. A dull panic bloomed in her chest. To distract herself, she peered at the words but could make no sense of them in the dim light.

What was he doing? This was not how it was supposed to be. She should be transported by desire, by tenderness — love even. He muttered a curse. Buttons popped and bounced across the wooden floor like dried peas. Something hard prodded her from behind, nudging at her like an overexcited dog. She had to say something, tell him to stop, that she'd changed her mind. This was not love. Whatever he was doing had nothing to do with her. Percival had never taken her like this, like she had no more feelings than a stick of wood. He was always at least gentle.

But before she could find words, Renfrew spun her around and hoisted her skirt. The wooden arm of the divan dug into her waist as he bent her back. He grunted, one hand moving up to her mouth, covering it so she could not cry out. She tried looking into his eyes, but they were closed, his mouth screwed with concentration.

He took her quickly — much more quickly than Percival had ever done. A groan, a sigh, a stepping away, and then all she had to do was rearrange her skirt, her eyes on the floor, looking anywhere but at him.

She heard Mr. Kemble calling for Ned out in the corridor. She crossed to the door and listened.

"Grace?" Renfrew's voice was soft now, contrite even.

She waited for Mr. Kemble to pass, and then, without a backward glance at Thomas, she slipped out of the room and ran down the corridor to the dressing room she shared with the other actresses.

ಬಂಛ

Ned rounded the corner into the corridor leading to Mrs. Siddons's dressing room. He was preoccupied with thinking about the scenes and machinery needed for the evening performances—*Romeo and Juliet* first, followed by a farce. Grace would act Juliet for the second time opposite Mr. Charles Kemble, and Olympia was set to take a turn in the farce. Even considering the riots, Ned was feeling good about the evening ahead. Alec would come around one of these days—it's not as if they hadn't had rows before. Ned's temper sometimes got the better of him, and as for Alec, his sharp tongue often put him on Ned's bad side.

Ned could have wished for an opportunity to talk with Olympia alone—find out the score with the general—but he was content to bide his time. He'd had plenty of practice being alone. A few more weeks or months wouldn't make much difference.

The door to Mrs. Siddons's dressing room opened. What was this? No one was supposed to go into the great lady's private space. When he'd spent one night there after having his forehead laid open by the rattle, Ned had hardly slept for worrying he'd be discovered. Mr. Kemble wouldn't take kindly to his sister's space being used without her knowing.

A tall figure, blonde hair swept up, skirt crumpled, emerged into the corridor and turned toward the women's dressing room. Ned flattened himself against the wall and waited, dreading to have his suspicions confirmed. Sure enough, moments later, Renfrew opened the door and stepped out.

೮೦೦೮

As usual, the dressing room crackled with nervous chatter. Grace looked around for Olympia but couldn't see her. She asked Louisa for a basin of water.

"Ned's not brought the water in yet."

"Where he is?"

"Not here." Louisa's lips were scrunched together, tiny lines already radiating outward, numbering the years she had left to shine onstage. "What's wrong with you? You're that flushed."

"I'm fine."

Grace found her costume on the rack and took it to a quiet corner of the room. She ripped at the ties of her soiled gown, dropped it to her feet, and stepped out. Her red velvet costume for the ballroom scene lay like a puddle of blood on the chair beside her. Where was Ned with the water? He always took care of them, made sure they had tea and soap and the right scripts for the right play. Ned was their support, their ally. They could not do without Ned.

She could not do without Ned. He was her one constant every night at the theater. It was Ned who always made sure that Grace got her cues and knew where to stand. It was Ned who soothed her nerves as night after night the riots put everyone on edge. Grace knew what Ned thought of Mr. Renfrew. She should have trusted his judgment since obviously she could not trust her own. How could she have been so blind?

Grace pulled the red gown up over trembling thighs and laced the bodice tightly over her breasts. She folded her hands across her belly and breathed deeply, pushing down the bitterness rising in her throat. In less than an hour, she would walk onstage, her head held high, her spine erect.

She could do it. She had to do it.

⁎⁎⁎

Ned closed one hand over Renfrew's mouth and with his other hand pushed him back into the dressing room. He slammed the door behind him with his heel. The room was pitch black with no candles lit, but Ned didn't need light to do what needed doing.

Renfrew squirmed like the rat he was.

"Call out and I'll snap yer neck." Ned tightened his hold. "Stay away from Grace and all of the girls, you hear me? Or I'll go to Kemble, and you'll be out on yer duff." He drew his hand from Renfrew's mouth and then drove his fist into his stomach. Renfrew's knees buckled, and his breath came out with a whoosh and a groan.

"Don't hit me," he gasped. "I've done nothing wrong."

Ned grabbed Renfrew by his collar and held him up so the toes of his boots just grazed the floor.

"She asked for it," he gasped. "They all ask for it. Whores, the lot of them." Ned shook him again. "Olympia too. She's a ripe one, she is."

In the darkness, Ned sensed Renfrew's leer. Goddamn, snot-nosed toffs. Where did they get off thinking they could do whatever they wanted? Men like Renfrew ruled the world and kept men like Ned working for them, slaving their lives away, and for what? The chance to lick their bleedin' boots?

Ned put every ounce of his strength into connecting his open palm with Renfrew's face. He would have liked to break the bastard's jaw, but that would be cutting off his nose to spite his face. He'd need to explain to Mr. Kemble, and that was the last thing Ned wanted to do. The whack of skin on skin was obscenely loud and supremely satisfying. Ned let go of Renfrew's collar, felt him glide like sand released from a ten-pound bag to the floor, heard his skull thud against the arm of Mrs. Siddons's sofa.

With any luck, Mr. Thomas Renfrew, rising star at the New Theatre Royal, Covent Garden, would need a full pot of paint to wipe away the mark of Ned's hand on his cheek

.

Chapter Twenty-Eight

Cry "Havoc!" and let slip the dogs of war . . .

Julius Caesar (3.1.273)

Several days after Grace's turn as Juliet, Olympia caught up with her just as she was entering the theater. It was another rainy November afternoon—the air a thick stew of coal smoke and damp. The weather matched Grace's mood. Her timing in *Romeo and Juliet* had been off, her lines mumbled, her gestures wooden. For once, she'd been grateful for the rioters who barely regarded the stage while they went through their nightly rituals—OP dances and chants and songs and shouts.

Both girls were to perform in the afterpiece that evening—a production of *Don Juan* that was scheduled to run for three more nights. Grace did not enjoy the piece, billed as a *tragical-pantomimical ballet*, but even with Louisa hired back on, the theater was short several actresses. Everyone had to pitch in.

"We are early," Olympia said when they reached the stage door. "Would you mind walking with me?"

"In this?"

"The rain does not signify." Olympia looked up at Grace. "Please. We can stay under the arcade."

The two girls walked out into the Piazza and crossed to the east side where an arcade stretched all the way to the Strand. The covered space was crowded with strolling ladies and gentlemen, and a few Cyprians just emerged from the brothels to start their evening's work. Even after almost two years in London, Grace was fascinated by the range and number of shops concentrated in this small area. They passed haberdashery shops and bookshops, dress shops and print shops, and of course several coffeehouses and taverns and tearooms.

"You are quiet, Olympia," Grace said after they'd walked for several minutes.

"As are you. We are not a lively pair today."

"Perhaps we are both just fatigued by the riots." Grace said. She knew that was not the reason for her own feeling of lassitude, but she was curious what was bothering Olympia. "Your mother is well?"

"My mother." Olympia sighed. "Oh, Grace, I don't know what to do!"

"Good heavens, Olympia. What is this?"

"You know that my mother lived quite openly with the general."

"I was aware, but that does not reflect on *you*, Olympia. You cannot be blamed for your mother's actions."

"My mother wishes to return to the general. Although he is not kind to her, she has grown accustomed to the luxuries that he provides and that I cannot with my pay from the theater. My only hope of keeping my mother away from the general is to marry a wealthy man."

"They are rather in short supply at the theater," Grace said drily.

"I was engaged to be married this past summer, you know, to a respectable-enough man, but he broke it off when he found out I'd been an actress. He all but called me a harlot. It's why I came back."

"Did you love him?"

"Good heavens, no!" Olympia laughed bitterly. "I was marrying him for my mother's sake. Love played no role in my acceptance."

Grace kept silent.

"Forgive me," Olympia said. "I should not burden you with my problems." She brightened her tone and skipped forward a few steps to the window of a shop selling sweetmeats. "See here, Grace. My favorite bonbons! We both deserve a treat."

Grace followed Olympia into the shop. She wanted to ask her about Ned but didn't dare. If Olympia's mother needed her to marry well, then Ned could have no role in Olympia's future.

By the time they returned to the theater, both girls were in better spirits and ready to take on another evening playing in dumb show to the angry crowd. Mr. Harrison was as usual seated in his chair when they crowded, laughing, through the stage door. He rose stiffly to his feet.

"Ned's taken off," he said bluntly.

"What do you mean?" Olympia asked. "Where would he go?"

"He came in an hour or so back. There was a letter for him brought by Alec—he used to work here? The direction looked like it was written by a woman."

"Who would write to Ned?"

"That's just the thing. He went all pale when he read it and then rushed out."

"Do you have the note?"

"What? No. I just got a glimpse of the writing on the envelope before Ned balled it up in his hand. I didn't see what he did with it. He just said he was gone to meet a woman and that he'd be back before the play went up." Mr. Harrison shook his head. "Mr. Kemble won't like Ned not being here to get everything organized backstage."

"It's probably nothing," Grace said. "You know Ned. He'd never abandon us. You can be certain he'll be back within the hour."

She couldn't exactly say why, but Ned's sudden absence from the theater made her uneasy. If the note was written by a woman, Grace couldn't help thinking it might have something to do with her Aunt Augusta.

ಖುಲ್ಠ

Even the driving rain could not squelch the stink rising from the river. Ned stopped to get his bearings. Rigging slapped masts that creaked in the wind. He had never ventured so far south and east of Covent Garden. The gaiety and lights of the Piazza might as well belong to another country. All around him loomed soot-blackened, tightly shuttered houses. The gloom suffocated his resolve, the river stench overpowering. How did people live here?

Ahead, a single torch lit a hanging sign. The crudely drawn anchor reassured Ned. At least he was in the right place. The play — a farce called *The Suspicious Husband* — was scheduled to start in three hours, which meant he had just enough time to meet the woman and then get back to the theater in time to get everyone to their places. Ned reached the door to the tavern and pushed it open. The person who wrote the note must want money. Why else would she contact him after so long? He knew he should stay well away, but he couldn't bring himself to pass up the chance to meet the woman who had borne him, even if she'd cast him off like he was no more use than a rotten apple ground into the soiled hay on the market floor. He could at least give her a few shillings and send her on her way.

He expected to find the tavern alive with light and noise. Instead, he walked into darkness. Something scuttled past his foot, and his throat closed around a mouthful of stale air. Panic gripped him—his old fear of the dark. He was ten years old again and trapped in a coal bin where he'd lain for hours before being found. His breath came in loud gasps. He had to get out! But before he had a chance to turn around, the door slammed hard against his back. Blackness pressed against his eyes like cold steel.

He held out his hands, clutched at air, gulped back another ragged breath, and then bit his tongue. He remembered how coal dust had coated every part of his body, how his eyes had stung with it. There was no coal dust here—only the reek of the river. And he was no longer a child.

Something hard smashed the back of his knees. His legs gave way and he slumped forward, banging his forehead against slimy floorboards. He just had time to realize that he'd been tricked, when a brush of fur whisked past his cheek, and he passed out.

ஂ௸

It was the clink of coins that woke Ned up. Someone was shifting them from one hand to the other.

"He's a big one. I'll need help."

"You'll manage fine on your own. He's out cold and his arms tied good and tight. Drag him by the legs. It ain't far."

"It's far enough." The second voice was higher than the first and sounded sulky, like the dragging of a body was an imposition.

"You've got your man, so stop your griping. It ain't my lookout that you didn't bring more muscle with you. The tide's high now. You'd best go while you can."

A hand closed around Ned's ankle and pulled. Ned kept his eyes shut. His head throbbed, and bright flashes pierced the darkness under his eyelids. He was facing upward, with his hands bound behind his back, the knuckles grinding into the floorboards.

"I can't drag him on me own." The voice rose higher. "You got to help me."

"I ain't got to do nothing."

To Ned's relief, the floor vibrated with the clumping of feet heading for the door. With the big one out of the way, he'd easily take the peevish-sounding one. Ned pulled against the ropes around his wrists. The knots held like bolts of frozen iron. He knew he had to use his legs.

"I'll pay extra. Another shilling if you'll help me drag him to the boat."

Ned held his breath. Feet shuffled, and the man closest to the door coughed and spat. "I gotta be somewhere else."

"It won't take long. You said yerself the dock's close by. If we both take a leg, we'll have him there in no time."

"You ever feel bad about it?"

"'Bout what?"

"This. You know, takin' men against their will, like?"

"Nah. The King's Navy needs 'em to fight this blasted war. Think of it as doin' your patriotic duty."

"Fair enough. Make it two shillings."

Ned gritted his teeth. If he didn't move now, he'd never get free. He opened his eyes. In the light from a guttering candle, he glimpsed a dark figure at the door and another close to his feet. With a grunt, he pulled back one leg and drove it upward, connecting foot to groin with every ounce of his strength. A scream ripped through the empty room. Ned slammed down both feet and heaved himself to his knees. His bound arms unbalanced him, but with an immense effort, he got first one foot and then the other under his body and stood up. He towered over both men. The man he'd kicked lay on the floor, his screams as shrill as a woman's. The other man lurched forward, both arms outstretched to grab Ned. He dodged out of the way and then kicked at the man's kneecap. Alec had always said to go for the kneecaps.

"They drop like a stone. Never fails."

The man staggered backward but did not go down. Ned drove his shoulder into the man's head, snapping his neck back. He was a free man, by God. The King's Navy could go hang.

The screams from the man on the floor subsided to gasping whimpers. "Bastard!" he gasped. "I'll make you pay for that."

Ned threw his whole body at the man at the door. "Out of my way!"

To his surprise, the man stepped aside. "Be my guest."

Ned kicked at the door, but it did not even shudder against the iron latch keeping it closed. He tried nudging at the latch with one shoulder, but he was too tall. The ropes binding his wrists ground through his flesh to the bone. The men he'd injured would kill him if he didn't get out. His body would be thrown into the Thames, another casualty of the war, regretted only because he'd died before being of use on the high seas.

"You can rest easy," the man called to the man still on the floor. "He'll not get out."

"Hurt him!"

"I intend to."

Ned had a second to wonder whether he'd die on the point of a knife or with his brains smashed across the thick walls, when the world went black again.

Chapter Twenty-Nine

But He that hath the steerage of my course
Direct my sail!

Romeo and Juliet (1.4.112–13)

*M*a'am?"
A short man wearing a torn jacket and with a half-healed cut slashed across a dirty cheek stepped in front of Grace as she was coming out of the theater at the end of the evening. Alarmed, she backed up against the stage door.

"What is it?"

"Name's Alec, ma'am. I used to work here? Friend of Ned's? We ain't never been properly introduced, like, but you stayed in my room?"

"Yes, of course," Grace said, relieved. "I should have thanked you long since. Do you know where Ned went? He didn't come into the theater tonight, and we are all worried."

"You and him are friends, right?"

"Yes, Ned has always been kind to me."

"Yeah, well, that's Ned, innit? But begging your pardon, ma'am, I don't know who else to tell. I can't go to Mr. Kemble. He don't approve of me, see. Thing is, I've done somethin' bad, ma'am, and now Ned's in trouble."

"What do you mean?"

"We had a falling out, him and me, and I got mad, you know? I went and took money from Mr. Renfrew to bring this note here for Mr. Harrison to give to Ned."

Grace wanted to reach out and shake the little man. "What does Mr. Renfrew have to do with anything?"

"He's got it in for Ned, you know?"

"No, I don't."

"He said Ned deserved what was comin' to him, see. And on account of me also bein' mad, I helped him."

"Please just tell me, Alec. You're not making any sense."

"Sorry, ma'am. Beggin' yer pardon, but the note what Ned got? He thinks it's come from *her*. I was watchin' when he came out of the theater. He threw the note away, but I picked it up. See?" He held up a crumpled ball of paper.

"What are you talking about, Alec? Who do you think wrote the note?"

"His mother, like."

"But that's impossible. Ned's mother is dead."

"You know about her?"

"Yes, I mean no." Grace took the balled-up paper from Alec but did not look at it. "Why are you coming to me?"

"I got to make things right with Ned, ma'am. Soon as he took off, I started to worry that he might be walkin' into a trap. That Mr. Renfrew's a right son of a bitch."

"But you took his money."

"I ain't proud of it. I followed Ned, see, down to the river, to a tavern, and I saw right away that he weren't meeting

315

no woman. They took him, ma'am. To the boats. A press-gang, right? Renfrew must have paid them. People do, you know—pay to have people taken? I couldn't do nothin' to stop them." Alec nodded at the note that Grace held in her hand. "Please, ma'am. Can you help?"

Grace smoothed the paper out. Carefully looped handwriting, as crafted and controlled as the hand that penned it, covered hot-pressed notepaper that smelled faintly of lavender. Grace leaned against the side of the building to steady herself.

"Ma'am! You're that pale."

ஐ

"I have an idea." Grace grasped her husband's arm. "You're about to take on your first starring role, Percival."

"This is not the time for riddles, my dear."

"We must get to the theater."

"It's the middle of the night!"

"Alec can get us in." She turned to Alec, who was standing, hat in hand, in the vestibule of Grace's home in Bedford Square. She'd run with Alec all the way from the theater through streets glistening with a recent rain. "You can do that, can't you, Alec?"

"I ain't got no key."

"Oh!" Grace's face fell.

"But that don't mean I ain't got my ways." Alec's gaze swiveled from Grace to Percival. "What's the theater got to do with anything? We should go to the magistrates."

"They turn a blind eye to this sort of thing," Percival said. "It is unfortunate, but impressment is used all too often to dispose of someone without actually killing them." His cheeks, normally pink with an excess of good wine, had drained, leaving him looking much older than five and twenty. He stared down at the note he still held in his hand.

Grace held her breath. At first, he'd laughed off the connection to his mother. Absurd notion. How could Grace think such a thing? Then, she'd held the paper to the light, made him stop and look until finally he saw the truth.

Percival crumpled the note into a ball and threw it toward the fire. "What do you have in mind, Grace?"

"We're going to raid the costumes at the theater," Grace said, masking her relief by pulling open the front door. "And we don't have much time."

"Let me send for a carriage."

But Grace wasn't listening. She descended the steps to the street and set off in the direction of the theater. Percival ran to catch up with her, Alec close behind. She did not speak until they reached the Bow Street entrance.

"You're sure you can get us in?" she asked Alec.

"Anything for a lady," Alec said as he drew a looped piece of wire from his pocket and bent over the padlock that secured the stage door.

"He's a criminal!" Percival whispered. "What have you gotten me into?"

"Alec knows where they took Ned."

Percival stepped away from the door. "I can't be a party to this."

A soft click stopped him. Alec pushed open the door and disappeared into the darkness.

"Please, Percival, you can't turn your back on Ned, not if there's a chance your mother wrote that note."

Before Percival could reply, Alec appeared at the door, holding aloft a lit candle.

"Where to, ma'am?"

"Mr. Kemble's dressing room."

"You can't go in there!"

"He'll never know." Grace pushed Alec forward. She'd already violated Mrs. Siddons's dressing room; she might as well make it a family affair. "Lead the way, please." She heard Percival muttering under his breath, but she ignored him. Alec led them down the dark corridor.

"Find something military," she said as soon as they entered the room. "A uniform of some sort, the more ribbons and braid the better. Thank goodness Percival is as tall as Mr. Kemble."

"Right you are." Alec set to work rummaging through the extensive collection of costumes hanging from the rack along the wall. As the public rightly suspected, no expense was spared to ensure that when Mr. Kemble did get onstage, he wore only the finest materials.

"What are you playing at, Grace?" Percival asked.

"Trust me." She felt all the resolve of a Lady Macbeth at that moment—strong, determined, capable.

"How 'bout this?" Alec held up a dark blue jacket complete with epaulets and naval insignia. "There's a hat that goes with it." He tossed the jacket at Percival's feet and then produced a fine admiral's hat dripping with gold braid.

"You cannot seriously believe . . .?"

"I can," Grace said. "And it's the least you can do."

"But . . ."

"You know I'm right, Percival. Ned would not be in this trouble if it weren't for your mother. He's done nothing to deserve it."

"Am I responsible for my mother's actions?"

"Would you have only Ned pay for them?"

"But why would she do this? It makes no sense."

"It apparently makes sense to your mother. You can be sure that I plan to visit her very soon, but in the meantime, we cannot waste time." Grace held Percival's gaze with as much composure as she could muster.

The quality of mercy is not strained.

"You can do this, Percival. You have a chance to help."

"So you think Ned is—?"

"I don't know, Percival, but obviously, your mother does. I am sorry, but I believe her capable even of this."

A spasm passed over Percival's face—the shadow of a pain he'd never shared with her. Grace's heart softened. Percival also could not be faulted for the sins of a parent.

"Ma'am?"

"Yes, Alec?"

Grace kept her eyes on Percival as he pulled off his coat and reached down for Mr. Kemble's jacket. His white linen shirt clung to a broad chest tapering to a lean waist. Grace turned away quickly to find Alec staring at her.

"We got to hurry."

"We're ready." Grace turned back to Percival, who was pulling on a pair of high leather boots to replace his buckled shoes. She reached up to adjust his collar and then impulsively kissed him on the mouth—the first time she'd ever done so voluntarily.

"Be careful," she whispered.

With a mocking curve of his full lips still wet from Grace's kiss, he stepped back and executed an exaggerated military salute.

"King's Navy at your service, ma'am."

৪০৫ঞ

The floor was moving, a soft rocking that made his rise to awareness a slow, gradual, calming journey. For several minutes, Ned drifted with the rhythm of the floor, the creaking timbers a comfort, like he was safe inside a swaying carriage taking him back to the theater where he'd watch Olympia onstage. He loved the way she played the comic roles and was only sorry the crowd was too preoccupied with the cursed riots to appreciate her.

The stink of sickness and urine and sour beer brought him to the truth. He kept his eyes closed rather than acknowledge it, but *the truth will out*. He remembered that line from *The Merchant of Venice*. He'd watched a rehearsal just that afternoon. The play was to go up on the eighth of December, if he remembered correctly—a good two weeks hence. Dates and plays and angry men swirled through his brain. Where was he? His fear of darkness wrapped around him, choking him. If he kept his eyes closed, he could pretend that light still existed. The floor lurched under him. He slit his eyes open, praying as he did that his suspicions were wrong.

They were not.

He was in the hold of a ship—an anchored ship that rose and fell with the flow of the river. His cheek rested against something prickly but yielding—a bale of hay by the smell of it. For the horses? Did the navy keep horses in the hold? Ned listened for the sound of hooves against wooden floorboards but heard only scraping wood and a whistling that must have been the wind. He felt it on his bare head and neck. The bastards had taken his scarf. Frozen air swirled down through an opening above him. Could he see the stars? No, it had been raining when he'd come to the river. There would be no stars and no moon—just the heavy wet skies of a dark November night.

How long had he been in the ship? He remembered the clink of coins and the smash of a fist against his jaw. That must have been not long after three in the afternoon, when he'd arrived at the tavern. But he thought that a great deal more time must have passed. Apart from the sounds of the ship and the wind, Ned heard only the deep silence of the dead hours after midnight when the world slept. He'd loved that silence ever since he'd started working at the theater. Every night when he locked the stage door behind him and walked down the empty street, he sensed everywhere around him, for miles in all directions, the thousands and thousands of souls in the great city of London joined in the oblivion of sleep.

"Sir!"

The voice came from the opening above him. Heavy boots pounded on the deck. Ned pulled at his wrists. They were still bound, and now his feet as well. He lay on his side but was still able to turn his head.

"Stand aside, man. I've orders from the admiral."

"What admiral? Say! You can't come on board without permission."

The flare of a torch washed across the opening, reddening the sky. Ned was surprised at how close he was to the deck—no more than ten feet. It was a small ship, not one of the navy's warships.

"Yer wantin' to take it up with the admiral?"

Ned knew the rough cockiness of that voice—had grown with it from child to boy to man. He would have smiled if he had not been so terrified.

Chapter Thirty

Men should be what they seem;
Or those that be not, would they might seem none!

Othello (3.3.130–31)

*T*he reedy voice of the guard up on deck sounded close
enough for Ned to strangle. "Who's this admiral
you're talking about? I ain't seen no admiral. They don't
come around at this time of night."

"This one does. See?"

Ned heard a quiet bump against the side of the ship,
waves slapping—another, smaller boat. What was Alec
doing?

"He's come straight from the Admiralty to sort out the
mistake."

"What mistake? What are you talking about, man? I can't
see nobody."

"Sir!" Alec's voice calling down to the water held just the
right touch of subservience. Ned had heard him speak like
that to Mr. Kemble while abusing him behind his back.

"What's going on, man?" The voice that shouted back sounded familiar, but Ned could not place it. He was definitely a nob with the entitled tone of someone accustomed to getting his own way. One of the actors? He couldn't imagine Alec convincing any of them to come on a rescue mission. Ned almost laughed at the thought of Mr. Kemble getting his white stockings dirty on London's East End docks.

"Sorry, sir. I ain't being allowed aboard."

"Ho! You there. Let my man on deck and do what he asks, or there will be hell to pay for you."

"I ain't got no orders."

To Ned, the guard sounded young and inexperienced. Very likely, he'd drawn the short straw to get saddled with graveyard duty. That he was alone on the deck was also a surprise, although Ned wasn't about to question Providence.

"There's been a mistake. You've taken on a man the government has an interest in."

"What interest?"

"None of your business, lad. I know the man I want is in the hold. I'll have him out in a jiffy, and we'll be on our way. The Admiralty will make sure you get commended."

Ned could almost hear the wheels turning in the young guard's brain. Footsteps clumped to the edge of the ship, the torch going with them, leaving behind a black expanse of sky.

"You can see his hat, man," Alec said. "Is that the uniform of a skivvy?"

There was a long silence while, presumably, the guard peered down at the boat bobbing on the river below. Ned could imagine Alec getting ready to fight the guard if he had to, but more than willing to talk himself out of trouble. He hoped Alec had armed himself with something more useful than a wooden stage sword.

"What's your name, sir?" the guard called down.

There was a slight pause, and then the deep voice rang out into the night. "Green. Admiral Green. Now fetch the man we've come for, and we'll be off. I've got to be back at the Admiralty by dawn."

Green? Ned strained to hear more.

"I ain't never heard of you." The boy might not get far in the world on brains, but he certainly didn't lack persistence.

"That's it, then. I'll have your name, lad," shouted the posh voice. "Come on, out with it."

"Hawkins, sir. Gerald Hawkins."

"Right, Hawkins. I'll let the Admiralty know that when faced with your duty, you shirked it. Alec? Come on down. I'll direct the constables to come around in the morning."

"What? No! Begging your pardon, sir. I didn't mean no disrespect."

The torch flared again across the top of the opening. Ned heaved himself to his knees.

"Ho! You there!" Alec called down. A rope ladder dropped into the hold and a minute later, Alec landed next to Ned, winked a greeting, and then cut the ropes binding his wrists.

"My ankles too."

"Got 'em." Alec leaned forward. "Sorry, mate. Shouldn't never have left you."

"Yer here now."

Ned climbed up the ladder to the deck. The young guard's face loomed out of the darkness. He grasped a heavy boat hook with shaking hands. Alec followed Ned onto the deck and then stepped around him to face the guard. "Yer can put that down, lad. I've got me man now."

The guard backed away, his hands still gripping the boat hook. "I shouldn't let you go." His voice cracked from low to high.

Alec motioned with one hand for Ned to get behind him to the side of the ship. "We'll be gone before yer know it. Put down the hook. There's a good lad."

Ned swung himself over the side and down a rope ladder to the small boat. He dropped the last few feet, landing in front of a tall man holding a torch—Grace's husband.

"Evening," the man said pleasantly. "Percival Knowlton at your service. We have met before through my wife." He talked as if the two men were sharing a cigar after dinner instead of struggling to keep their balance in a small boat bobbing on the river. Ned could just make out the outline of an overlarge hat—from Mr. Kemble's private stock, he realized with a start.

"Grace sent you?"

"I suppose you could put it that way, although I prefer to believe that I came of my own volition." Mr. Knowlton elegantly lowered himself onto a narrow seat in the stern of the boat. "I suggest we get going, or shove off I believe is the expression. We've been fortunate to find and liberate you while it is still dark."

The man was as cool as Mr. Kemble. What was it with the swells? Did they ever get riled? "We got to wait for Alec."

Percival raised his voice. "Are you coming, man? We've no time to waste."

A muffled cry from above was followed by the crash of something metal against the wooden railing. A wash of moonlight broke through the heavy clouds. The hull of the ship and two figures struggling on the deck jumped into view as if they were on the fully lit stage. Alec shouted at the young guard to let go of the hook and then lunged for him. He was a good head shorter than the guard, but Ned had no doubt Alec would get the better of him. He'd fought and won against many much larger opponents.

"What's he doing?" Percival asked. "I told him before that we must avoid violence at all costs. That was the purpose of this ridiculous getup."

"Hush!"

"I say! You needn't take that tone with . . ."

The boat hook— a wicked curve of sharpened steel set in a sturdy wooden handle—sailed over the edge of the deck. Ned lunged forward to catch it, was close enough to feel the rush of air across his hand. Then he heard a thud and a scream just as Alec dropped into the boat.

"Row, man!" Alec yelled.

Ned grabbed an oar, although never in his life had he used one. The small boat swung wildly back and forth, bumping against the hull of the ship, the oarlocks clattering.

"Wait! I'll take the other one. We got to pull together."

Alec fell next to Ned onto the board laid across the middle of the boat. "Got it?"

"Yeah."

"Right, then. Hold on while I turn her. We're going against the current, so it will be hard pulling."

"I'm ready." Ned was at least grateful that his arms and shoulders had not been injured by the brutes who took him. The image of Olympia sent warmth through his frozen limbs. His fingers curled around the oar, and on Alec's command, he pulled. His greater strength swung the boat again, but he knew enough now to ease off and match his rhythm with Alec's.

"Steady on, Ned. We've got to keep her straight."

"He's in a bad way," Ned said, cocking his head back to where Knowlton lay slumped in the stern.

"We got no choice but to row. It ain't far."

Ned leaned forward and then pulled back, forward and back, the strokes finally matching Alec's. Ned shut his eyes and grunted with the effort of rowing upriver against the current. How much longer? And when they got to the dock, could they get back through London's dark streets in time?

A moan whispered across the splash of oars on water. He still lived. Ned thought of Grace, her face shining with excitement when she came offstage. She'd sent her husband to find him. Why would she do that?

"We're close, man. A few more pulls."

The prow of the little boat ground against a low dock. Alec leaped out and tied the boat, while Ned scrambled on his hands and knees to the stern. In the darkness, Ned could not see any wound, but he smelled blood and heard Knowlton's shallow breathing.

"We got you, sir. Just a bit longer and you'll be home."

"Grace." The word slid across a breath that ended in a sob. Gone was the haughty tone, leaving behind a man like any man.

80CB

"Forgive me."

Grace laid her hand across Percival's and smiled down at him — perhaps the first genuine smile she'd ever favored him with. "Hush, Percival. Alec's gone to fetch the surgeon."

"Alec?" A wry smile brought back the old Percival. "Good man, that. And Ned too. Hadn't expected it." He winced and cried out. When the spasm of pain passed, he panted, his eyes wet with tears.

"You must stay quiet."

"I'll soon have more than enough quiet, my dear."

Another jolt of pain stiffened his limbs, and he grabbed for her hand. His fingers wrapped around hers, still with enough strength to hurt her, although he'd never yet raised his hand to her. Had it ever been in her power to hurt him?

"Grace!"

"Please, Percival, you must not exert yourself."

"I will be quiet soon, but please promise me something."

"Of course, anything."

"I have not been a good husband to you."

She did not reply. The lines of pain on her husband's face, the glittering of eyes staring at death shamed her. From now on, she must try to be a wife to Percival.

"You are right to stay silent. I deserve no more." He raised his hand a few inches, but the effort was too much. He dropped it back to the bed. "I want you to be happy, Grace."

"I am content enough."

"You do not need to lie, Grace. Accord me one last courtesy."

"I'm sorry."

"What for?" He gritted his teeth as another wave of pain shuddered through his body. "Blast it, Grace," he gasped. "The pain is severe."

Grace laid the back of her free hand on his brow. It was burning with fever. Her husband's handsome face slackened, his grip on her hand suddenly boneless.

"Percy!"

She laid her head against his chest. She would not let him die. The beating of his heart—if it did beat—was stifled by his thick coat still damp with rain. It was not right for him to die wearing Mr. Kemble's costume. With a frenzy of renewed energy, she seized the lapels of his coat and heaved. Grace tugged one arm of the coat, exposing a white shirt splashed with blood. She pulled at the sleeve of Percival's other arm. She would not let him die in his coat. It wasn't decent.

A hoarse whisper stopped her.

"Grace."

"Yes, Percival," she said, keeping her voice calm, the relief of hearing his voice again so powerful that it shocked her.

"See to it that Ned's taken care of."

"You can see to it yourself. You're not going to die. The wound is not so deep." She had no idea if that was true, but the fact that he'd regained consciousness was cause for hope. She peeled back his shirt. Alec had said something about a boat hook dropped from the deck of a ship. The hook appeared to have broken the soft skin of Percival's neck, by a fluke just missing an artery.

"Bring water and towels," she said without looking up.

"The surgeon will be here soon, ma'am." Betsy stood very close, her breath coming in short gasps.

"I can attend to my husband in the meantime. Go!"

Percival tried to smile and then winced. "You've never spoken of me so warmly."

"You've never been skewered by a boat hook before."

His chest trembled beneath her touch. "You are cruel to make me laugh."

"At least you still can." She dabbed at the blood. The injury was nasty, to be sure. Although the skin was punctured, it was a shallow, clean wound.

He would not die.

Chapter Thirty-One

Let grief
Convert to anger; blunt not the heart, enrage it.

Macbeth (4.3.228–29)

*T*he property room at the New Theatre was more of a cupboard than a room, but when Grace was not waiting in the wings for her cue, she sometimes went there to get away from the noise of the riots. She loved the jumbled variety of objects crammed into the small space.

For the fifth time since September, Grace was playing Lady Anne in *Richard III*. She was already becoming associated with the role, which suited her well enough, although she would much prefer having sole rights to Juliet or Desdemona. But once the riots ended — if they ever did — Grace might not be able to hold on to any of the roles she'd been given in the absence of Mrs. Siddons.

She put her hands on her hips and stretched her shoulders back as she gazed around the room. A dozen or so swords of varying lengths and hefts hung above a stack of muskets and next to three enormous ash cudgels. One shelf spilled over with purses containing counterfeit money and jewels for using at opportune times in various plays, particularly the farces. From the ceiling hung a guitar with two strings missing and a drum, its sticks protruding from one side. Other shelves contained untidy heaps of artificial flowers and fruit, several large goblets, a bunch of skeleton keys, a jumble of half-burned candles, two sets of dice, and an iron cauldron. Grace smiled as she remembered the poor girls who had played the witches on the first night of the riots. The cauldron had not been used since that production of *Macbeth*. She wondered when it would be again. Various small props were piled on a table—scissors, oversize quill pens, two daggers, three pairs of convict fetters, and two decks of playing cards.

The evening was the first on which she'd left Percival since his injury four days earlier. The surgeon had warned her that his recovery would be a long one, but that her husband was, so far as he could tell, out of danger.

"Grace? I thought I might find you here."

She didn't move. Her heart pounded at the sound of Renfrew's voice. It was the first time he'd spoken to her since they'd been together in Mrs. Siddons's room—and since Ned's abduction. She still didn't know exactly what part Mr. Renfrew had played or why. She kept her back to him. Perhaps if she didn't respond, he'd return to his dressing room and leave her alone. She had just one more scene to play before she'd be finished for the evening and free to get home to Percival. His forehead had been slightly hot before she'd left for the theater, and to her surprise, she felt anxious about him.

"Grace?" Renfrew snaked one arm around her waist and pulled her toward him. Thick, wet lips found her neck.

"Where have you been these past few days? I heard a rumor about Ned and a press-gang. Shame they didn't get him."

Grace tried to wrench herself away, but his grip on her tightened—his arm like a band of iron under her breasts, grinding her stays into her flesh.

"I don't like being ignored, Grace." He loosened his grip and pulled her around to face him. His breath stank like he'd been drinking gin for days. With one hand, he pushed the door to the property room closed. "You weren't so shy the other day."

She couldn't breathe. The room pulsed with the detritus of theatrical life—everything designed for illusion, as false as the man who held her. If she cried out, someone backstage might hear her. Perhaps Ned would walk by. Her cue wouldn't come for another twenty minutes. If she could loosen Renfrew's grip on her, she could grab hold of one of the cudgels and bang at the door.

"I said that I don't like being ignored," he said, his lips now grazing her cheek. She shuddered with revulsion, every muscle rigid.

"Let me go," she said. "My cue is coming up."

"As is mine, but we have many minutes yet, long enough, I'm thinking, to renew our friendship."

"My husband was injured trying to rescue Ned."

"Your *husband*? You weren't very concerned about him the last time we met."

"You're hurting me." Her voice sounded thin and frightened in the darkness. "I'm sorry if you think . . ."

"Think what, my dear? That you wanted it as much as I did? You pretend to be so high and mighty—no doubt believing you're destined to be the next Mrs. Siddons. *The Tragic Muse*. There's a laugh. You're nothing compared to her. Never will be." He tightened his hold, digging the fingers of one hand into her waist while with the other hand he stroked her cheek. "But I can talk with Mr. Kemble, convince him to give you more leading roles, even when these blasted riots are over. Old Kemble listens to me." He thrust his hips against her. "You won't be the first to use your charms to get to the top." He moved his hand down to fumble at the neckline of her black velvet costume. "You can stop pretending you're not wanting what I have to offer and help me get this damn dress off."

Grace tried to step away, but the edge of the table stopped her. She reached back and curled her fingers around the hilt of one of the daggers, feeling as filthy as Renfrew smelled. The dagger was made of wood and would not do much damage, but it was her only chance.

She expected to feel fear, but the only emotion gripping her was pure, cold rage. First her father, then that man in the street, and now Renfrew? With one swift movement, she brought the dagger up and plunged the blunt tip into the soft skin under Renfrew's chin. At the same time, she raised one foot and drove it into his shin, and then thrust her forehead forward and down to connect with his nose. A sharp crack sounded like thunder in the small room. She remembered overhearing two of Kemble's pugilists boasting about how to take down the rioters.

"The nose be the most sensitive part, don't ye know."

"Smash yer fist up."

"Or better yet, yer elbow."

"Now yer talkin'."

Grace felt something spray across her face. With a scream, Renfrew let go of her and scrabbled at his nose. She backed toward the door and pushed it open with her shoulder.

"If you touch me again, I'll go straight to Mr. Kemble," she said.

"He'll never believe you."

"Yes, Mr. Renfrew, he'll believe me." In the flickering light from the corridor, Grace saw thin streams of blood leaking between his fingers. "I can assure you that Mr. Kemble will be *very* interested in what I can tell him about you."

She stepped out into the corridor. The roars and catcalls and trumpets and rattles of the rioters competed as usual with the actors onstage. One of the callboys rushed past, carrying a metal fire box almost as big as he was. She smelled the pungent mixture of substances that were ignited in the box to produce the fire effect—a brilliant red light that bathed the stage in an eerie pink glow during the ghost scene. After the effect was completed, a callboy used a bucket of water to douse the flames and kill the noxious smell.

Grace followed the boy carrying the metal box to the wings and watched as he helped another boy hoist it seven feet high and then stood ready with a lighted taper for the cue. Fixing her attention on the boy and his task helped tamp down the shaking in her legs. Where was Ned? She had to look a right mess. With her wide sleeve, she scrubbed at the specks of Renfrew's blood that had sprayed across her face. It would have to do. Several minutes later, another callboy called her cue, and she trudged back onstage for her final scene with the sleeping Richard. On the other side of the stage, Mr. Renfrew, as the ghost of Lord Hastings, lurched on, his face still streaked with blood. Since his character was meant to be a ghost, no one in the audience was likely to notice the blood — or care if they did.

Grace had never felt more like a ghost herself as she delivered her final speech. The noise in the pit surged and receded — waves on a beach sucking the heart from the play. As soon as she came offstage, Grace fled down the corridor to the dressing room. She quickly discarded her costume, then pulled on her gown and took up her cloak. Never in her life had she wanted more to go home.

Mr. Harrison was snoozing in his chair by the stage door. Grace tiptoed past him and was almost to the door when he called to her.

"You are not hurt, my dear?"

She froze. How could he know? Had Mr. Renfrew already passed by Mr. Harrison and left the theater? What lies had he told about her?

"I am perfectly well, Mr. Harrison, thank you." She turned to face him.

To her surprise, he leaned forward and took her hand. "Take care, my dear," he said. "Young ladies such as yourself . . . let's just say that the theater can be a cruel place. Go home to your husband."

"Yes, sir, I will." She pulled her hand away. "Will you help me find a carriage?"

Mr. Harrison grimaced as he heaved himself to his feet. "Of course, my dear. Follow me."

80C3

"Damn the fellow!" exclaimed Mr. Kemble.

"Sir?"

"Renfrew. He's gone and left us in the lurch. He was to appear in *The Roman Father* tonight, and now I'll have to get Cooke to do it. It appears that Renfrew's high-and-mighty sister has decided that the theater's not respectable enough for him."

"What's happened?" Ned asked.

"He didn't even have the courtesy to tell me to my face." Mr. Kemble pointed to a note open on the table. "He sent that instead. Go on, you might as well read it."

The terse note consisted of just a few lines informing Mr. Kemble, respectfully, that Mr. Renfrew had decided to seek a life off the stage. Ned looked up. "Seek a life?"

"I don't know why I hired the fellow in the first place. Pretentious prig."

Ned held out the note, but Mr. Kemble waved it away. "Glad you're back, Ned. You're fully recovered, I take it?"

"Yes, sir."

"Bad business. Well, all's well that ends well, eh?" He laughed at his own joke, and Ned smiled obligingly. Thanks to Alec, Ned knew the part Renfrew had played to have him press-ganged, but he still didn't have any idea who'd written the note luring him to the docks. He wasn't so sure he wanted to know.

"I heard what the court done about Mr. Clifford," Ned said.

"Terrible business. Our poor box office keeper's been demonized. Imagine accusing him of laying hands on Clifford and falsely arresting him! Mr. Brandon's got to be sixty if he's a day. Absurd to think he could do any damage to a strapping big oaf like Clifford. Nonsense, all of it."

"What's going to happen, sir? About the disturbances? I heard people are calling for Mr. Brandon to be dismissed."

"Does loyalty mean nothing to these people? I'd sooner dismiss myself."

"Yes, sir. I'll go find Mr. Cooke."

"Here's hoping he's sober," said Mr. Kemble. "The company's glad to see you back, Ned." He paused. "*I'm* glad."

ഇ⃝ଔ

In the play that evening, Louisa took the female lead. She forgot a fair whack of her lines and mixed up the few words she did remember. The prompter in his small box close to the stage tried his best, but Louisa had no chance of hearing him. Ned might not have liked her much, but he did feel sorry for her. It was a rum go for the actors. If Mr. Kemble was not careful, he'd have a revolution on his hands. When the curtain finally descended and the theater cleared out, Ned was more relieved than usual to climb the stairs to his room.

Alec was still up. He'd moved back into their shared lodgings the day after he'd helped rescue Ned. Without saying a word, the two men knew they'd never talk about their time apart. Alec was lying on his bed, his hands linked behind his head.

"I thought you'd still be with Daisy," Ned said.

"Naw, I told you before that she's gone off somewheres. I don't know where. Miz Gellie won't tell me."

Ned slumped onto the bed and started taking off his boots. "Riots ain't letting up, and Mr. Kemble won't bend. At this rate, we won't have no peace by Christmas."

"I been thinking," Alec said.

Ned looked up sharply. "What?"

"That note from the woman sayin' she was your ma? What you want to do about it?"

"You think it was real?"

"Aye. Renfrew weren't working alone. That note were written by a woman."

"I ain't planning on doing nothin' about it," Ned said. "What good would it do?"

"Don't you want to know who she is?"

"No." He lay back on his bed.

"You got to find out."

"I don't."

"If it was me, I'd want to know."

"The woman could have got me killed. She's a devil."

"Miss Green and that husband of hers must know about her, else why'd they help you? Go see her. Find out the truth."

"What truth? That she threw me away when I was a babe and then arranged to have me pressed into the navy now I'm a man? I ain't having nothing to do with her."

"If it was me, I'd go," Alec said quietly.

Ned turned to stare at him. "You don't know that."

"Aye, I do, Ned." Alec kept staring at the ceiling. "I'd give anythin' to meet my ma, ask her why, like."

"You know why. It's the same story for all of them."

"I doubt they thought about it like that. For them, for *her*, it were the only story."

Ever since he could remember, Ned had carried an ache in his chest—quiet most of the time, but sometimes, like now, flaring up to remind him just how little he'd mattered to the woman who had given him life.

"Well you ain't me," Ned said. He leaned over and snuffed out the candle.

৪৩৫৩

Even the surgeon was surprised by how quickly Percival appeared to recover from his wound. Five days after the rescue, he was sitting up and taking soup. His ordeal softened him in Grace's eyes. He no longer appeared quite so haughty with his neck swathed in bandages. Betsy tended to him with quiet sullenness. As soon as Percival regained his strength, Grace would arrange to have Betsy sent back to the West Country. The poor girl didn't look happy in London, and she seemed to be developing an unhealthy regard for Percival, spending more time than necessary tidying his room and bringing him cool cloths.

Grace smoothed the cover across Percival's chest and was tempted to bend forward and kiss his forehead—the simple act of a fond wife. But no, it was a role she was not yet prepared to play.

"Mr. Kemble asked after you last night," she said.

"And what did you tell him?"

"That you are much improved."

"You played Lady Anne again, did you not? I trust you were pleased with your performance."

"It went well enough, considering the disturbances are still going on. Why do you ask?"

"Don't look so surprised, my dear," Percival said. "I realize I have rarely asked about your roles, but that does not mean I am not interested."

"Mr. Kemble has asked me to play Desdemona on the fourth of December."

"Desdemona, is it? You never told me."

"As you said yourself, you did not appear to be interested."

"Then I have been remiss." He reached for her hand. "I promise to pay more attention in the future."

Grace let her hand stay in his, the dry warmth of his palm an unfamiliar sensation against the smooth skin of her own palm. She curled her fingers around his. To her surprise, a jolt spread into her belly, like the yolk of a cracked egg sliding to the floor. The last time she'd been with a man . . . No, she wouldn't think about that. It was in the past. Maybe Percival would be in her future. She smiled down at him. "I'd like that."

"Good."

A relaxed silence stretched between them. Since her marriage, Grace had learned to turn away from the silences. If obliged to share a tête-à-tête dinner with Percival, she'd occupy her mind with learning lines rather than spend any energy on the kind of idle talk that filled the hours for happy couples. Could she love him? The question popped into Grace's head and stayed there, waiting for her to receive it with something other than her usual curt dismissal. Renfrew had been a mistake, and Percival had risked his life to save a man whom he must wish was never born.

Gently, she disengaged her hand. "I am going out this afternoon," she said.

"Oh?" He smiled up at her.

"Betsy will see to you if you need anything. I'll be back in a few hours."

"Yes, of course."

Was it her imagination, or did he look like he wanted her to stay?

Chapter Thirty-Two

. . . for truth is truth
To th' end of reck'ning.

Measure for Measure (5.1.45–46)

*W*hy did you not send for me sooner? He might have died."

Augusta's first words to Grace when she entered the small sitting room at the front of her aunt's house fortified Grace's resolve. What point was civility with a woman so determined on incivility?

"And if he had, Aunt, you would deserve all the blame."

"Good heavens, Grace, there's no call for you to take such a tone with me. Remember who I am." Augusta swept aside the train of a long gown too fussy for day wear and lowered herself onto a hard chair next to the window. Tea for one was laid out on a small table. She nodded toward another chair but did not ring the maid to bring a second cup.

"I'm well aware of who you are." Grace did not sit.

"You are hardly one to talk, Grace. When Mr. Renfrew came to me with his scheme to get rid of Ned, he told me about you."

Grace sank to the chair. "He lied."

"I doubt it." Augusta regarded Grace appraisingly. "You would not be the first to be infected by the loose morals of the theater."

"I was not aware that you knew Mr. Renfrew."

"Then you were misinformed. He is Mrs. Partridge's younger brother, and Mrs. Partridge is a particular friend. By chance, Mr. Renfrew and I discovered a mutual interest in your Ned. Mr. Renfrew's scheme had all the virtues of economy and expediency."

"What interest could you possibly have in Ned? He has done nothing to you."

With surprising agility, Augusta sprang to her feet and walked restlessly back and forth across the room. Her eyes—blue like Percival's—turned to ice chips as she gazed past Grace into memories. "You know nothing about it. Just like your mother. *She* said that I deserved everything I got."

"My mother?"

Augusta fixed her gaze on her joined hands. The fine lines webbed across fading cheeks could not disguise the ghost of a young girl in trouble. "You think you understand, Grace, but you do not. You cannot."

"Then tell me. Why did you want to harm Ned? He could have been killed."

"I doubt it. Men survive the navy all the time. And they should be glad to go. Britain cannot win this war without men." Augusta picked up a thin teacup, examined it as if looking for cracks, then put it down without taking a sip. "You may think me a monster, but what I did was for the best—for Percival and for you too, my dear, although you're too blind to realize it. The public does not quickly forgive scandal. If the truth about Ned's parentage ever came out—and such things always have a habit of coming out—you would be ruined. The theater will not protect you."

"What does my mother have to do with anything?"

"Charlotte and I had the misfortune of falling in love with the same man," Augusta said. "And to your mother's dismay, that man chose me."

"What are you talking about?"

"You have no idea about love, Grace. I've seen how you look at Percival. You don't deserve him." Augusta's face twisted in a sneer, the resemblance to Percival startling. "But I can see that I'm wasting my breath. You'll take your mother's side no matter what I say."

"My mother can hardly speak for herself."

"Then ask your father." Augusta regarded Grace coolly, as if trying to decide how next to wound her. "I've had enough of this interrogation." She resumed her seat.

"I wrote to my father last week."

Augusta threw back her head and laughed. "He won't believe anything you say. Why would he? You were not there."

"Then tell me."

"Your father believes your mother bore a child before her marriage—a child that she was forced to leave off at the Foundling Hospital."

"Why would he believe that?"

"Because that's what I wrote and told him."

"When?"

"Two years ago—not long before your poor mother died."

ଧ୦ଓ୪

Ned was working alone in the paint room when Olympia slipped in to stand next to him, watching as he moved out a new fly to examine it with the aid of a candle.

"We could never have predicted this," she said. "Fifty nights! We thought it would all be over in a week."

"Mr. Kemble's stubborn." Ned wished he could gather her in his arms, hold her close, and protect her from the jeers and the whistles, the stomping, and the bellowing of the rioters, who the night before had celebrated the jubilee of the riots like it was a royal event. Fifty nights of rioting— and they were proud of it.

"People say these riots are like a call to revolution, that the next step is bringing in troops."

"Mr. K. won't allow it," Ned said with more conviction than he felt. "So far as I can see, the riots are just an excuse for men to act out, like they got nothing better to do. I wonder how them puny clerks that come in every night would like it if I went round to their offices and waved rattles in their ears while they were trying to fill in their damn ledgers."

"You'd never do such a thing, Ned."

He grinned down at her. "Try me."

Unlike most of the rooms backstage, two large windows at the rear of the building brightened the paint room. A beam of sunlight cut through the dust and shone like a halo around Olympia. She was to play a peasant woman in the farce that evening and wore her hair in two braids wound tightly around her head. Ned swallowed hard and returned his attention to the fly he was examining. It was stretched upon a large frame and showed a mountain scene of rocks and ice below a sky of swirling storm clouds.

"It can't last much longer," he said. "Mr. K.'s got to bend."

"Do you believe that?" Olympia's voice caught. He saw tears in her eyes before she turned away from him.

Alarmed, he put down the candle and gently cupped one hand under her chin. She tensed for a moment and then softened into his touch. "What's troubling you, Olympia?" he asked. "It ain't just the riots, is it?"

She placed her hand over his. One tear slid down her cheek as she shook her head. "I'm sorry, Ned."

"What do *you* have to be sorry for? The riots ain't your fault, and neither is whatever's bothering you."

"You don't know that."

"But I know you, Olympia," he said, pulling her close. He was on dangerous ground now, but he no longer cared. His brush with death had given him a new appreciation for life. Maybe it was time he stopped being alone. For several blessed moments, she stayed close, not even flinching when he wrapped his other arm around her. For the first time, Ned dared to hope. He'd do the right thing by her if she'd have him.

He tilted her chin up and kissed her. She met his kiss with a gentle passion that promised the world. He tightened his hold and molded his body against hers. He'd never felt anything like this before—like he'd finally come home.

And then she placed her hands on his chest and pushed him back, breaking the connection so abruptly that Ned felt as if he'd severed a limb.

"I'm sorry, Ned. But we can't. *I* can't."

"Why not? I love you, Olympia. I can take care of you. Marry you."

"I can't marry you."

"What's stopping you? I ain't quality, I know that, but I won't let you down, Olympia. I can take care of you, if you let me."

But Olympia shook her head. "I'm sorry, Ned," she said again. Before he could stop her, she ran toward the door past a table piled high with charcoal sketches of ancient buildings. The door thudded open, and she disappeared into the maze of backstage corridors.

Ned smoothed his palm over the roughly painted rocks in the foreground of the fly. He'd been alone his whole life, with no one to care for him or about him. He should be used to it. So why did he feel like he'd just fallen through one of the trap doors onstage, crashing through to the cellar, shattering every bone in his body?

80C3

"Dreadful woman!" Olympia exclaimed. "Why would she do such a thing?"

"My aunt believes that Ned was her son. She wanted him out of the way to avoid scandal if the truth came out."

"I suppose we can be grateful that she didn't succeed." Olympia stared out the front window of Grace's house to iron palings slick with rain. She had come to help Grace prepare for Desdemona, but the play lay unopened on the table between them.

"You care a great deal about Ned," Grace said.

"I've never said."

347

"You don't need to. I've seen how you look at him and how he looks at you. He adores you, Olympia. I believe he'd do anything for you. And you do like him, don't you?"

"Of course I *like* him." Olympia smiled. "Please, Grace, let's not talk anymore about Ned and especially about the future. No matter how much he likes me—or I him—nothing can come of it."

"I don't understand why not."

"Let us turn the subject. Please. Have you told Percival why his mother tried to get rid of Ned?"

Grace shook her head. "Percival knows his mother wrote the note that lured Ned to the docks, and perhaps he even suspects why, but he doesn't know that Augusta wrote to my father. I don't want to tax Percival with the truth when he's still so weak."

Olympia picked up the copy of *Othello* and then laid it down again. "She wrote to tell your father that your mother had borne a child?"

"Yes. My aunt has admitted to deliberately lying to my father, although she wouldn't tell me why. My mother is innocent." Grace took a deep breath. "I've never told anyone this before, but the day my mother was killed . . ."

"Do not say if it distresses you."

"Please, I must. For almost two years, I've been convinced the accident was my fault. My father insisted it was. He changed so much after that morning, Olympia. Until now, I never understood why."

"What are you saying?"

"Just before the horse bolted, I heard a loud sound—a sort of crackle like the rattles the OPs swing."

"A branch?"

"No, nothing like that. I think it was someone deliberately making a noise to spook the mare."

"You suspect your father?"

Grace shrugged. "I'm sorry, Olympia, I've said too much. You came here to help me rehearse." She picked up the copy of *Othello* and handed it to Olympia. "I go on in two days, and my grasp of the last scene with Emilia is not yet as strong as I would like."

"You are sure?"

Grace nodded. "Please, would you read the part of Emilia? I must practice."

The two girls read the scene together. Grace got along very well until she faltered over Desdemona's last words before Othello entered her bedchamber to kill her.

"Why I should fear I know not
Since guiltiness I know not, but yet I feel I fear."

Chapter Thirty-Three

Time shall unfold what blighted cunning hides:
Who cover faults, at last shame them derides.

King Lear (1.1.280–81)

Grace arrived early to the theater on the afternoon of December 4. The women's dressing room was empty and quiet. A pale blue gown hung on a rack—her costume for the first of her scenes as Desdemona. She wondered if her mother had ever had the chance to play her. Poor Charlotte Johnson had died too soon—a victim, like Desdemona, of a lie she had no part in telling. Hatred for Augusta welled up, but Grace forced herself to close her mind to it. She had a role to play that night—her most demanding yet. She could not let herself be distracted. The day before, she'd rehearsed the violent ending to Desdemona's young life with Mr. Cooke, who was playing Othello. Her neck still felt bruised from the pressure of his fingers.

It is the cause, it is the cause, my soul.

Othello's line thrilled and terrified her. Why had Augusta lied? What cause? How could she have betrayed her sister so cruelly? She had deliberately written to Tobias to tell her that Charlotte had borne an illegitimate child. That knowledge must have led Tobias to seek revenge upon his wife. Grace could not help wondering if he'd intended to kill both his wife and his daughter on the cliff top that breezy April morning.

If so, it was little wonder he hated Grace for surviving.

Grace tried to imagine the feelings of Augusta—a young woman desperate and in trouble. She placed her hand on her own stomach. Bile churned up her throat. Surely not. She'd rather die.

"Grace?"

Ned knocked on the open door of the women's dressing room. "There's someone come to see you, Grace. He's at the stage door with Mr. Harrison."

"Who is it, Ned? I don't have time to receive visitors."

"It's your father."

ᔕᓚᘓ

Grace had not seen her father since the previous January—almost a year earlier. He seemed smaller than she remembered, his skin sagging from cheeks mottled red with drink and neglect. He gave the impression of a man who had given up on life.

"I stopped first at your home," he said. "Your maid directed me here. I can't believe your husband has continued allowing you to act. I misjudged Percival."

"Hello, Father. Will you stay to watch me tonight? Ned can find you a ticket—for a box, of course. You would not want to be jostled in the pit." Grace instinctively stepped backward to avoid his fists, although she knew he would not dare—not with Ned standing close to her and Mr. Harrison rising from his chair, his face ashen.

"Still impertinent," Tobias sneered. "Like your mother, until she learned obedience."

"She learned despair."

"How dare you!"

Grace stepped forward, emboldened by Ned's presence. She would not let her father hurt her again.

It is the cause.

"I am not afraid of you, Father," she said. "You destroyed my mother's life, and then you tried to destroy mine. My aunt told me what she wrote to you."

"Augusta did me a favor. I'd long suspected the truth about your mother's past."

"Augusta lied."

"Augusta?" Mr. Harrison was on his feet now, his gnarled hands clamped hard on his cane, his legs quivering. "What's this?"

"My aunt, Mr. Harrison," Grace said. "Augusta Knowlton, once Augusta Grant. She was an actress, like my mother."

"Your mother? What was her name?"

"I fail to see what my late wife can have to do with you, sir," Tobias said. "I'll concede that she once belonged to this obnoxious profession, but that was many years ago. She has paid for her sin."

"What sin, Father?" Grace cried. "My mother was innocent."

"She was a whore." Spittle flew from his mouth. "I was a deluded fool when I married her. I saw her onstage, and to my shame, I thought her the most wonderful creature in the world." Tears glazed his eyes. "Charlotte bewitched me, and I've regretted my weakness ever since."

"And me, Father? Am I part of your regret?"

"You! I can't even say for sure that you are mine. If your mother strayed once, who is to say she did not stray again?"

"Stop!" Mr. Harrison waved his cane, narrowly missing Tobias's shins. He turned to Grace. "Your mother was Charlotte? Charlotte Grant?"

"Yes. She and my aunt both acted at the Theatre Royal in Bath. It was in the early eighties, I believe."

"And you, sir, believe that your wife strayed?"

"More than strayed. She had a child and then abandoned it before marrying me. Wicked—rotten to the core. I've been cursed."

"I knew your wife, sir."

"What?"

"I knew her well, and I remember when she left the theater to marry you. I tried to dissuade her. Charlotte had so much to offer the stage. She was a true original—not unlike her daughter." He smiled at Grace. "I cannot think why I never saw the resemblance, my dear. My eyes are not what they were. You have her voice and I believe will surpass her as an actress." He turned to glare at Tobias. "As for you, sir, a simple recital of the facts should prove to you that your wife—although she had faults, to be sure—was innocent of what you accuse her of."

"Please, Mr. Harrison, tell us what you know," said Grace.

"I don't have time to stay here and listen to lies," sputtered Tobias.

Grace walked forward to stand directly in front of her father. He stank of unwashed linen and rotting teeth. She couldn't imagine that he'd once been capable of captivating a woman like Charlotte Grant. Then she remembered her own folly with Mr. Renfrew and knew she could not judge. "You will stay and hear what Mr. Harrison wishes to tell us, Father," Grace said calmly. She cocked her head toward the door. Ned took the hint and went to stand in front of it, his arms crossed.

Mr. Harrison lowered himself back into his chair and smiled approvingly at Grace. "Thank you, my dear. Twenty-seven years ago, I had the great good fortune to be engaged by the Theatre Royal in Bath. You may look as affronted as you wish Mr., ah . . ."

"Johnson," Grace supplied. Tobias merely scowled.

"Mr. Johnson. The theater in those days was perhaps not as respectable as it is becoming in our own more enlightened times, but it was also not altogether the den of iniquity it is so often considered. Mrs. Siddons herself got her start just a few years before the time of my story, and you can hardly consider her as anything less than respectable, for all the faults of her late husband."

"Get on with it, man," growled Tobias.

"Please, sir, I am an actor—or at least I was. I thrive on the dramatic." Mr. Harrison turned his head so only Grace could see his face, and winked. She could not help smiling, even as her heart flexed and squeezed with dread. What if her aunt had not lied after all?

"I fell in love with an angel," Mr. Harrison said. "And to my very great joy, she returned my love. We intended to marry—and would have if not for the interference of her sister."

"Augusta," Tobias said flatly. "No wonder my wife rarely spoke of her."

"No, sir," Mr. Harrison said. "Charlotte—your late wife—had the great misfortune to believe that I preferred *her* to Augusta. When I could not return her regard, she was, how you say, a woman scorned. To retaliate, she convinced me that Augusta did not love me. She told me that Augusta had left Bath to marry another man. I don't know what Charlotte said to Augusta to make her go, but I suspect she convinced her of my indifference." Mr. Harrison sighed. "I never knew that Augusta was with child. Our great Bard writes of intrigues and jealousies that we believe can only happen on the stage, but he merely takes from life. Charlotte—your mother, Grace—it pains me to say, was as treacherous as an Iago. She shortly after left the theater to marry and several years later bore you. She cannot be cleared of wrongdoing, but she is innocent of the sin you charge her with."

"Augusta wrote to me," Tobias said. "Why would she lie?"

"Augusta is in London?" Mr. Harrison asked. For a few moments, the lines of old age smoothed out, and he was again the handsome leading man, blue eyes flashing. He looked over at Ned, understanding dawning for the first time. Ned stepped forward and clasped the old man's hands.

"You are Augusta's son?" Mr. Harrison asked, his voice choking.

A shadow of sadness passed across Ned's face. He stayed very still for a minute and then finally, reluctantly, pulled back his hands. "No, sir," he said. "I wish I were, if it meant I'd be related to you. Augusta thought I was the child she gave birth to and then abandoned at the Foundling Hospital. I was born there too, but I am not her son."

Young Tommy skidded into the room, his eyes wide. "Ma'am? Miz Green? There's a message just come for you. Real important, like. You got to go home straightaway."

Chapter Thirty-Four

Look upon thy death.

Romeo and Juliet (1.1.65)

You must prepare yourself, madam," said the surgeon. Percival's eyes were closed and his breathing rapid. Jagged strokes of crimson marred his fashionably pale cheeks.

"How?" Grace asked. "He was awake and talking to me when I left this afternoon."

The surgeon shook his head. He was a young man with narrow fingers and a tiny red mouth like a blob of sealing wax. Grace did not trust him, but she had no choice. When Percival groaned, Grace took his hand and then almost dropped it.

"It's the fever, ma'am. He's burning up. I suggest cool cloths."

Another groan, this time with one word—mumbled over and over. Percival's head rolled from side to side. "Grace . . . Grace . . . Grace."

"I'm sorry, ma'am. There's nothing more I can do."

"But you must!" It wasn't right for Percival to die. "Please! Do something."

The surgeon rose from the bedside and busied himself with packing his bag. "I don't even dare bleed him now, ma'am. I'm sorry. The infection is of a putrid sort. I cannot help him."

"Don't tell me you're sorry!" Grace laid her hand on Percival's forehead, kept it there despite the terrible heat. "My husband cannot die."

"There is one thing you can do, ma'am," the surgeon said. A wispy black moustache tickled his sealing-wax mouth.

"What? Tell me!" Grace stumbled forward, knocking the surgeon's bag from his hand. It landed on the carpet, its contents spilling out. "Tell me!"

"You can pray, ma'am." He dropped to his knees and hastily gathered up items from his bag. Then, before Grace could go at him again, he ran from the room.

She slumped onto the chair next to the bed, all hope drained. This was what the lies had led to. In trying to protect one son from the shame of another, Augusta was soon to lose both.

Grace had cried many times onstage—wailed even—in an attempt to reach the pigeonholes at the theater.

But never had she felt as she did now—as if her heart was laid open on a slab of frozen steel.

୫୬

Grace stayed by her husband's side for most of the night. When finally Betsy persuaded her to give up her post, a cold dawn was breaking.

"Go downstairs, ma'am. Tea and food be laid out for you in the breakfast room. I'll sit with him until you get back. Don't you worry. He be quieter now."

Grace nodded without understanding, but instead of entering the breakfast room, she took her cloak from the peg by the front door and left the house into air pregnant with unshed moisture. She walked with blind purpose toward the river, desperate suddenly to see water, to find solace in its easy, constant movement. She reached a street that ended in black mud beyond which flowed the river at low tide — a wide, brown, swollen mass that bore as much resemblance to her beloved Bristol Channel as Iago to Othello.

Grace closed her eyes against the pain. The way ahead brimmed with darkness — as frigid as the river sweeping London's filth to the sea. Why had she turned her back on Percival? Now it was too late.

If you must marry, Grace, marry for love.

That's what her mother had told her to do that last morning of her life, and Grace had ignored her. She'd put her longing for fame above the demands of her heart. Counterfeiting emotion was so much easier than feeling it.

She picked her way across the mud toward the water, her boots sinking and squelching. The river did not smell fresh and wild like the sea. Even on a day so cold that curls of ice crested the black mud, the river stank of rancid flesh.

What if she kept walking? Was the current fast enough to carry her away? Would it pull her under before she had a chance to cry out, the cold killing her as swiftly as the choking water? Grace stepped forward, welcoming the numbness of frozen toes inside her thin leather boots. Black water lapped over her toes. It would be quick. Why *play* Ophelia when she could *be* Ophelia? With hair unpinned and eyes fixed on phantoms, Grace could join Percival. Perhaps in the next life, they'd have another chance. And even if that was not possible, she'd go to a place where nothing was required of her, where through death she'd become an object of pity for a few weeks and then forgotten. She'd have no need to forgive herself or anyone else then, no need to *feel* anything. And who would blame her? Into the wind, Grace recited lines drawn out from Macbeth when he was at the limit of his endurance and his sin:

"Life's but a walking shadow, a poor player
That struts and frets his hour upon the stage
And then is heard no more: it is a tale
Told by an idiot, full of sound and fury,
Signifying nothing."

Another step and the bottom of her skirt grew heavy. It would drag her under quickly, that and her thick woolen cloak. In the middle of the river, a dozen men, faces raw with wind and effort, rowed a large boat upstream. Her hand strayed to her belly. Could she love a child born of humiliation? Evil ran like dirty water in her father's veins. Was Grace also evil? Had the sins of her father, her mother, her aunt, stolen all chance of love?

She wanted out.

A wave splashed toward her. She stood very still and waited for another wave. Soon she'd no longer feel anything. Soon, she'd welcome darkness.

"To take arms against a sea of troubles and by opposing, end them."

What arms could she bear against her own sea of troubles? She could not save Percival or erase the memory of Renfrew's hands on her body or ignore her own mother's treachery and her father's hate. Nothing. No one. She had nothing to offer and no desire left to give.

A freezing patter of drops — sharp as cut glass — blew into her face. Without thinking, she gasped and jumped back. Foul water stung her eyes. She blinked rapidly. The water swirled over her boots as her heels sunk deeper into the mud, sticking there. Panic gripped her. With a cry, she tried turning around, but the mud held her fast. She pulled first one leg and then the other, heard finally the suck of mud releasing her. She staggered away from the river's edge, slipping across stone and debris, terrified by what she'd almost done.

"Oy! Miss! You best take care. The wind's come up and the tide's turning. It ain't safe here."

A boy smeared head to toe in black mud ran toward her. A bag slung over one skeletal shoulder bumped against his hip. His eyes — green as spring buds — were the only wholesome thing about him. Grace had heard of his kind. Called mudlarks, they were the lowest of the low. The whimsy of the name contrasted sharply with the reality of a young life coated in river slime, with little to eat and no future.

"Follow me, miss. I'll get you to the bank. You shouldn't be out here. The river's no place for a lady."

Her heart still pounding, Grace followed the boy across the mud to a set of wooden steps leading back up to the road.

He turned and held out his palm to show her a disk, a medal or a coin of some sort. In the fast-fading light, the profile of a man was just visible.

"See here, miss! I just found it. It's yours for a penny."

"May I look?"

The boy edged toward her, ready at a moment to run if she tried to take his treasure from him without paying. He held it up between two filthy fingers, flashing first the side showing the head of a man wearing a jester's cap. Grace leaned forward to peer at the words stamped in an arc above the head.

The boy drew back, alarmed.

"I won't take it from you," she said, "but please, let me look. I promise I'll pay for it."

The boy clearly didn't know whether to believe her, but he held the coin steady. In the dim light, Grace read the inscription.

OH MY HEAD AITCHES.

Grace stared at the medal for several seconds and then began to laugh, the sound harsh in the cold air. The head was a caricature of Mr. Kemble, and the inscription referred to his affected way of saying *aches*. The boy closed his fist over the coin and backed away.

"Please, miss, I don't want no trouble. I ain't doin' nothin' wrong bein' here. Why are you laughin'?"

The wind gusted across the stinking mud as Grace's laughter faded to a shiver. "I'm sorry if I frightened you."

"I ain't frightened. I'll take a ha'penny if you got it."

Grace pulled a small gold watch from a pocket sewn into her cloak. Her stiff fingers brushed across the inscription.

MY DEAR CHARLOTTE

GOD'S WILL BE DONE

TOBIAS

Grace's mother had always disliked the watch—had refused to wear it when her husband was away from home. She said it was too heavy for a lady, but Grace suspected that the inscription distressed her. Grace held the golden disk in her outstretched palm. The child's eyes widened. He'd probably never seen such a treasure in his short, brutal life.

"Will this be enough for you to give me the medal?" Grace asked.

"They'll think I stole it."

"But you didn't. Take it. I'm sure you'll find someone to give you money for it. Or keep it to remember the strange woman you met by the river."

The child snatched the watch, dropped the OP medal into the mud, and dashed back along the embankment. Grace hoped he'd eat a hot meal that night, although she doubted he'd see any benefit from his sudden windfall.

She stooped to pick up the medal and wiped it against her skirt to clean it. Straightening her spine against the biting cold, she picked up her sodden skirts and mounted the steps to the road.

Grace would face the worst and find her own way forward. She'd not be the first woman to do so.

Chapter Thirty-Five

How long a time lies in one little word!

Richard II (1.3.213)

A hundred times on his walk from Covent Garden to Grosvenor Square, Ned resolved to turn back. What did he hope to gain by meeting her? Nothing good could come of it. He found the house and walked along the side to the kitchen, half hoping that she was out. He rapped at the back door with the bare knuckles of one hand.

"We're not havin' any!" a young woman said as she opened the door. "Get on with you."

Just in time, Ned got his foot in the door. "I want to speak with your mistress."

"What for? She ain't going to talk with someone like you."

"Tell your mistress that Ned's here," he said. "She'll know."

"I won't. Mistress will have me skinned alive if I let you in."

"Aw, come now. Do I look like I'd hurt a fly?"

"You're a lot bigger than me, so yes. And how do I know you're not a thief?"

"Do I look like a thief?" Ned flashed his widest smile, what Alec called his charming smile, the one that made him look like a cat that just ate cream.

"Guess not. You look a bit too prosperous. I take it you're employed."

"I work at the theater. Covent Garden."

The girl's eyes widened. "You're not an actor, are you? I ain't never met one of them."

Ned laughed. "They wouldn't be letting me onto the stage. No, I take care of things behind the scenes. But I've been known to talk to the actors. And the actresses too." He winked at her.

"Are they wonderful?"

"Some of 'em. Have you ever been to the theater? I don't mean the circus or a revue. I mean the real theater."

"'Course I never been to no Covent Garden, nor Drury Lane neither. Do I look like a lady?"

"You're as good-looking as any of the ladies I see going into the theater."

"Go on with you."

"How about I arrange for you to watch a play from backstage, meet the actors and actresses?"

"You can do that?"

"Name the day. I'll even come fetch you and take you home."

"And how would your wife like that?"

"I don't got a wife." Ned grinned. "But if I did, I'm sure she'd trust me—even with a pretty girl such as yourself."

"You've got a tongue on you, and that's no mistake." She stepped aside and opened the door wide. "I think you'd best go in unannounced."

"That might be better," Ned agreed. "And what's your name?"

"Hannah." She flashed him a smile. "Mistress is in the sitting room."

Ned followed Hannah along a dark corridor to a narrow vestibule at the front of the house. To his right, an open door led to a brightly lit room, the warmth of it spilling into the drafty hall. He wondered at the stinginess of a woman who kept a fire blazing for her own comfort and kept her maid shivering.

Ned filled the doorway with his height. The room smelled hot and stale and sweet. The woman was sitting on an upholstered chair facing the fire.

"Mrs. Knowlton." He said the name flatly, without question, without the respect a man of his class should show to a woman of hers.

The woman swiveled her head to peer up at him. With a composure worthy of the actress she'd once been, she replaced a flicker of alarm with a slight curl of her upper lip.

"You."

He walked a few steps into the room, stood above her — loomed above her — for a moment letting himself enjoy the power. He could hurt her. The consequences might even be worth it to see her suffer for what she tried to have done to him.

If the woman was worried that he might harm her, she gave no sign. As cool as a queen, she rose from her chair and turned to face him. Tall like her niece, she drenched the space between them with her dried-out lavender smell.

Hard lines at the sides of her mouth deepened, and then, for a moment, bloodless lips twitched and softened. The smile was so fleeting that Ned would have missed it if he hadn't been watching and waiting. It's what he'd come for: proof, however slight, that this woman—no better, no worse than his own mother—still had some bits of a heart.

"What do you want?"

"I come to tell you somethin' that you won't want to hear."

The blue of her eyes was like a glittering winter sky on a clear day when the sun gave no warmth. Shiny silver threads wove through her gown. Above the mantel, an older man with prominent whiskers scowled from a framed painting. The artist had set him in a tropical place, a white house with columns in the distance, a dark figure in the foreground holding out a plate of fruit.

"Tell me."

Ned shuffled feet too large and too dirty for the fine carpet. "I ain't your son," he said.

"Of course you are not."

"No, ma'am, I mean that I'm really not your son. I know you think I am, else why would you have wanted to get rid of me? I heard your story from Mr. Harrison at the theater, and I don't blame you for bein' desperate, and all. At the hospital, I saw plenty of girls just like you were. The people what run the place didn't think I saw, but I snuck out at night, like, and watched lots of things happen that I weren't supposed to know about."

"What are you talking about?"

"I was born there, ma'am, just like the child you left off."

"You must despise me."

"For giving up a child? Not really, ma'am. You were young. Desperate. They all were."

"You know nothing about it."

"I don't blame you—leastways not for that."

"You shouldn't have come here. I'm sorry for what I did, if it's any comfort. But Mr. Renfrew's as much at fault. Handing you over to the press-gang was his idea."

"I ain't spending another minute thinking 'bout Mr. Renfrew. Last I heard, he's gone to a company up north. They can have him."

"I can't undo the past."

Years of not knowing—of hoping, of wanting so desperately to find her—fell away, and he was small again. He reached under his shirt and with a quick, satisfying wrench, broke the cord. The button dropped into his hand. For the last time, he ran his fingers over the roughened edges.

"You can take this, now," he said. "I don't need it." He dropped the button at her feet. "I took it off your baby not long after she was christened."

"She?"

"Yes, ma'am. A daughter. That's what you had. I weren't much more than six years old, and I had no business being anywhere near the nursery, but I snuck in and took the button that you'd pinned to her blanket. I guess I wanted something for myself. I hid it for years—until they let me out—and then I've hung on to it ever since. I don't know why exactly. Maybe I just liked to pretend it was from me own mother. The governors at the hospital—they kept the records about the mothers and their babies locked up, like, so we couldn't never get at them. We weren't even supposed to know about them."

"A touching story."

"Do you want to know about the girl?"

"I suppose I can't stop you telling me." The woman's jaw tightened, her lips pressed together so hard that her whole face was as rigid as one of the stone statues at the theater. But her body betrayed her. She stepped forward and clasped her hands in front of her to keep them from shaking.

"They christened her the day before she died."

"She died?" Augusta sank into her chair.

"Yes, ma'am. A lot of the babies did. I weren't meant to see them being taken away. Some of them were so small I could have carried them in one hand, even me being a lad and all."

"What did they name her?"

"Desdemona."

The face that had once commanded cheers and applause from scores of men in the pit crumpled. A line from *Othello* came back to Ned.

It is the cause . . .

He turned around and left the house and walked rapidly through the wet streets to the theater.

℘℃℥

Percival's fever broke in the afternoon of December 6. One moment he was glassy-eyed and burning up, and the next, as if a candle had been snuffed out, his eyes cleared, and he looked up at Grace as if he'd never left her.

"My dear?"

"I am here, Percival. You must not exert yourself." She smiled down at him.

"I doubt there is much risk of that." His voice strengthened. "Why do you look at me like that? Has something happened?"

"I am just fatigued." It was too soon to tell him how close to death he'd come. She took one of his hands in her own — it felt lighter now, as if his very flesh had burned out along with the fever. Percival's eyes flicked to the door as Betsy entered the room, carrying a tray of tea things. Her face was as white as the belly of a dead fish.

"Thank you, Betsy," Grace said. "Please ask Mrs. Granger to send up supper. I will dine with Mr. Knowlton tonight."

"Yes, ma'am." Betsy's eyes looked ready to pop from her head, making the resemblance to a fish even more acute, particularly since the girl had grown very round of late. Grace thought again of her resolve to send Betsy back to Somerset. She did not look happy in London.

Betsy stood back from the tea things but did not move toward the door.

"Betsy?"

Percival glanced up at the girl and then fixed his gaze on Grace. "You must get some rest, my dear. We can't have you knocked up. What is your next role? Now that I am on the mend, you must get back to it."

"Mr. Kemble is considering me for Ophelia on the nineteenth. But I have not yet given him an answer. I did not want to leave you."

"I have given you a great deal of trouble."

She squeezed his hand and was gratified to feel him weakly return the pressure. The darkness was behind them now. Percival would recover, and they'd start over. It wasn't too late. She stroked his cheek and bent forward to kiss his forehead — the simple action of a fond wife that she finally felt ready to do. He smiled up at her, and for the first time since her marriage, her heart expanded.

A shriek sliced the thick, hot air. Grace felt her shoulder gripped and pulled back, forcing her to let go of Percival's hand and almost throwing her to the floor.

Betsy tore off her cap and leaped forward.

"Liar!" she screamed. "You said you cared for me! Liar!" She threw herself onto the bed.

"Betsy!"

"Good heavens! Get her off me. The girl's gone mad."

Grace grabbed Betsy around the waist and managed to drag her away from Percival before realizing the truth. She almost let the struggling girl go, but if she had, Betsy's flailing fists might burst open Percival's wound.

"He said I was sweet," Betsy sobbed. "He said he'd take care of me!" She collapsed back against Grace, her heavy body almost toppling her. Grace stroked the girl's forehead to calm her as she pulled her backward to the door. Grace did not dare look at Percival. If she saw even a hint of a sneer, she'd be in danger of hanging for murder.

With the help of Mrs. Granger, Grace wrestled Betsy into a nightgown and tucked her into her small bed under the eaves on the top floor. Grace had never been up to the cramped area where Betsy spent her nights.

"Is there a fire?"

"No, ma'am."

"But it's freezing in here."

"Yes, ma'am. It's December and all."

The one filthy window was frosted over, giving a blue tinge to the room. Grace waited until Betsy dropped off to sleep and then followed Mrs. Granger down the stairs to the warmth of Percival's bedroom. Shame gripped her, the pain of her own neglect so acute that she wondered if she might faint. *She* had let Betsy fall prey to her husband's appetites. *She* had been too preoccupied with her own needs to watch out for the girl. *She* had cared more about throwing herself at a second-rate actor than tending to the comforts of the people living under her own roof.

"You have interfered with Betsy," she said flatly as soon as she entered Percival's room. "She is with child."

He raised one eyebrow. "Foolish girl."

"Is that all you have to say?"

"You can hardly expect me to remain virtually celibate in my own home. If the silly girl was willing—and believe me she was willing—then I cannot be blamed for the outcome."

Grace had never in her life wanted to hurt another human being—even her father. Now she needed every fiber of her resolve to keep her hands from his throat. "You are despicable."

"Oh please, Grace. She's not the first maid to get herself into trouble. I suggest we return her to the West Country. If her mother is still alive, she can take her in, and if not, I'm sure some other farmer's wife will be glad of an addition to the family for the right price. I am not averse to paying."

"How generous of you."

"As I've said before, my dear, sarcasm does not become you."

Grace turned and left the room without another word.

Chapter Thirty-Six

*Machinations, hollowness, treachery, and all
ruinous disorders, follow us disquietly to our
graves.*

King Lear (1.2.101–02)

*M*r. Kemble slipped into the coat Ned held out. "You'd best go with me, Ned," he said. "I may need your help."

"I'm happy to come, sir, but what help can I be?"

"You can stand by the door and be ready with my coat when I get up to leave, which I hope to do as soon as possible. Damn me, I wish I didn't have to go."

"But you set up the dinner, sir, with Mr. Clifford and all. It's the end, isn't it?"

"Yes, Ned. It is the end. Tonight, I'll be forced to eat enough of my own words to choke a horse. I wouldn't be surprised if the joint served at the Crown and Anchor *is* horse. *That* would be a fitting end to this mess." He picked up his walking stick. "We'd best be off, Ned. The sooner we get it over with, the better."

The Crown and Anchor Tavern, located in the Piazza a few steps from the New Theatre, was one of the favorite haunts of the men who had emerged as leaders during the Old Price riots. As a show of good faith, Mr. Kemble and the other managers had invited the OP leaders to a dinner put on with all due pomp and good cheer. Mr. Kemble promised to go onstage after the dinner to announce the terms of the peace—that he'd lower the prices for the pit and order a section of the private boxes removed.

At half-price time on Thursday, the fourteenth day of December, Mr. Kemble returned to the theater from the Crown and Anchor and wasted no time making good on his promise. Before the fourth act of the main piece—a farce called, fittingly enough, *The Provoked Husband*—Mr. Kemble walked onto the stage.

The crowd waited for once in silence as Mr. Kemble outlined the terms of the peace. He reduced the price of the pit from four shillings back to the old price of three shillings and sixpence, but kept the price for the boxes at seven shillings and the lower gallery at two shillings. He also promised that, at the end of the season, he would restore the annual boxes to public use.

There was a moment of silence when Mr. Kemble finished speaking, and then, as one voice, the audience burst into angry jeers, the noisemakers as vigorously wielded as if it were Day Two of the riots and not Day Sixty-five.

"What now?" asked Alec. Ned had arranged to have Alec hired on as a scene changer. Mr. Kemble was so pleased that Ned had survived impressment that he'd made no objection.

"They want Brandon dismissed and Mr. Kemble to apologize."

"Bleedin' insane," Alec snorted. "Why should Brandon be fired? He weren't doin' nothing more than his job, same as us."

Mr. Kemble stood for a few more minutes upon the stage. The bellowing for Mr. Brandon increased until finally Mr. Kemble bowed and withdrew. He swept past Ned, his face purple with fury. Minutes later, the door to his dressing room slammed shut. Mr. Brandon emerged from the shadows.

"No! Mr. Brandon, sir!" exclaimed Ned. "You can't go out there."

"Brandon out!"

"Dismiss Brandon!"

Mr. Brandon waited backstage for several more minutes. The yells turned to chants—a thousand voices raised in unified outrage.

"I must try talking to them," he said. "Mr. Kemble and the other managers deserve that much from me."

Ned watched helplessly as Mr. Brandon shuffled out onto the stage. He had served the theater for over thirty years, but now he might as well be a martyr thrown into the flames. The crowd screamed and hissed and booed. Each time Mr. Brandon called for their attention, the noise increased. A stick flew from the pit. He dodged it just in time, but another stick bounced off his leg. A rotten orange hit his shoulder and splatted onto the stage. Mr. Brandon turned and fled into the wings.

"Drop the curtain!" Ned yelled.

The crowd kept up the noise for several more minutes, but when the afterpiece did not begin, most of the audience lost their enthusiasm. Within half an hour, the theater was empty. After making sure that all the actors, including Mr. Kemble, had left, Ned checked that the theater was secure and let himself out into the wet night. He ached with the frustration of thwarted expectations. Would nothing satisfy the crowd? He felt as old as Mr. Harrison. Maybe that's how he'd end his days—peevish and always chilly, manning the stage door. At least Mr. H. had his glory days to relive. Ned had nothing.

୫୦୦୫

To Grace's surprise, Augusta listened in silence to her description of Percival's recovery and the fate of poor Betsy. They were in Grace's sitting room, drinking tea supplied by Mrs. Granger. Grace almost felt sympathy for her aunt. The shock of seeing her son so soon after his brush with death had worn away a layer or two of her armor. Augusta took a sip of the hot tea, gripping the handle of her cup with clawlike fingers. She set the cup down on the spindly side table with deliberate care.

"I'm afraid I feel myself obliged to add to your troubles."

"Aunt?" Grace took up her own cup and sipped.

"You must wonder why I wrote to your father. It was wrong of me, I freely acknowledge."

"My mother paid with her life."

"You don't know that for sure."

"It is true that I have no proof that my father had anything to do with her death, but I suspect him."

"Your father is not an amiable man."

"And you did a terrible thing, Aunt. So much of this heartache would have been prevented if you had kept silent."

"I am not inclined to make more than a partial apology. I had a reason for my interference."

"What could possibly justify telling my father that my mother had given birth to an illegitimate child when she had not?" Grace picked up her cup again and then set it down without taking a sip. She held her breath as a spasm of nausea rose and then subsided. The tea leaves must be stale. She would talk with Mrs. Granger about it after her aunt left.

"For one of the basest of reasons," Augusta said calmly. "Money, or more precisely, my lack of it. Let me explain."

"Please."

"What do you know of Percival's financial situation?"

"Pardon me?"

"You heard me. I suspect you know very little, which is hardly surprising. I also knew almost nothing about my husband's affairs until his death forced me to face the unpleasant truth. Mr. Knowlton was ill suited to manage the estate his father left him. You may not realize it, but my husband's father had made his fortune in the North—in trade. I am not ashamed of it, and considering the connections of your own father, I don't expect you to be either."

"No, ma'am. I'm well aware that my father made his money at sea. He had no pretensions to the gentry." Another spasm of nausea gripped her—this one so strong that she pressed her hand against her belly.

"Quite. When the death of Mr. Knowlton revealed to me the full extent of his poor decisions, I was forced to sell his estate in Jamaica."

"I was not aware that he had one."

"Percival knew about the sale, but he did not know its effect on his inheritance. I have maintained a generous allowance for him—and you have benefited. But I could not sustain it without help."

"And so you arranged to have me disinherited," Grace said. "No wonder you did not wish me to marry Percival."

"For that and other reasons," Augusta said. "He had his pick of so many young ladies—some with considerable fortunes. You brought nothing to the marriage."

"Considering Percival already had my father's estate, that is true. So, Aunt, I'm to believe that you wreaked all this havoc to secure your son's future. Congratulations. He has survived an injury that almost killed him, thanks to your actions, and now he's shamed himself—not to mention me—by interfering with the maid. Am I to thank you for that too?"

"You will suit yourself on that score. Have you decided what you plan to do?"

"I am fortunate, Aunt, that what I wish to do and what I must do are the same. I will work to secure my own fortune by continuing my career on the stage. I don't see I have any other choice."

"Whatever money you make will still belong to your husband."

"I am aware, but you can be sure I won't stand by, as you did, and allow my husband to squander it. I am not a fool."

"No, Grace, *that* was something I've never thought about you." Augusta rose from her chair and snapped open her fan. "Good day to you. Inform Percival that I will wait upon him again next week."

As soon as her aunt left the house, Grace bolted upstairs to find a chamber pot.

Chapter Thirty-Seven

Unthread the rude eye of rebellion,
And welcome home again discarded faith.

King John (5.4.11–12)

*O*n the evening of Friday, December 15, Ned and Alec watched from the wings as Mr. Kemble stepped once more onto the stage, his demeanor still as haughty as it was on the first day of the riots. He faced a packed house. All of London wanted to see if the great Mr. Kemble had been made to bend.

"Brandon's gone," Ned whispered.

"Bloody shame."

"Mr. Kemble's said he'll give him a pension."

"It's the least he could do."

Mr. Kemble began to speak, his deep voice unhurried as with little visible effort, he projected to the highest galleries.

"Ladies and Gentleman, having had the misfortune to incur your displeasure, Mr. Brandon has withdrawn from the office of box office keeper of the New Theatre."

"Poor bugger," Alec said.

"Shut it."

The crowd applauded, and after bowing, Mr. Kemble started to walk offstage. A renewal of boos and hisses stopped him.

"Now what?" asked Alec.

"They want him to apologize."

"Fat chance of that."

"I dunno. Listen."

Mr. Kemble paused and then pulled himself up to his full height and strode forward to the front of the stage. Below him the orchestra conductor looked up expectantly, one hand holding the baton in readiness for his cue.

"Ladies and Gentlemen," Mr. Kemble began. "In understanding that some notice ought to be taken of the introduction of improper persons into the theater, I have only to declare in my own name, and in that of the rest of the proprietors, that we lament the circumstance and shall consider it as our first duty to prevent its recurrence."

"What's he on about?" Alec asked.

"He's saying he's sorry for bringing in the boxers— Mendoza and Dutch Sam and their lot—back in October." Ned ran his fingers over his forehead, the scar still fresh. "A fine mess that was."

"So why didn't he bleedin' say so?"

"Fancy Mr. Kemble *lamenting the circumstance*." Ned grinned at the sound of the audience cheering with as much energy as they usually injected into their shouts and boos. "They're coming round!"

"About time."

Ned peered out at the pit, trusting to the darkness backstage to keep him hidden from the audience. "Look there!" he cried, pointing to the pit, where, amid much clapping and hallooing, several men were hoisting a huge banner. Ned read it out loud for Alec.

WE ARE SATISFIED.

"That's it then?" Alec asked.

"I guess so."

Mr. Kemble accepted the applause with a thin smile and curt bow. The noise continued for many more minutes until, exhausted, the crowd subsided into murmurs and coughs.

"Stand aside. Here he comes."

"Cue the actors, Ned," Mr. Kemble growled as he passed. "Let us get back to being a theater and not a circus for the amusement of ruffians with nothing better to do than threaten the livelihoods of honest players."

"He ain't really sorry, is he?" Alec asked as soon as Mr. Kemble was out of earshot.

Ned shook his head. "'Course not. But at least he's seen sense. Help me get the lads moving with the scenery. We got us a show to put on."

80CB

The applause rolled and crested—ocean waves crashing against the cliffs on a bright day. Grace stood alone in front of the audience, her hair still unbound from the mad scene, her sea-green gown luminous in the candlelight. The pit heaved with cheering, clapping men. Shouts of *Brava! Brava!* rose above the applause. Every person in the theater, every heart, and every pair of hands united in appreciation of Mr. Kemble's new star.

Grace curtsied again and again, her arms sweeping in elegant arcs, her eyes downcast. She had done it. Ophelia was hers. Mr. Kemble had to keep her on now. She had a future with the company and could bask in the adoration of strangers every night for decades. Percival couldn't stop her. No one could stop her.

"They love you!" Ned exclaimed when the audience finally let her leave the stage.

Grace nodded, her eyes blurred with tears. They should have been tears of joy, but her heart felt hollowed out, like an abandoned shell on the beach at Clevedon. She walked slowly away from the stage along the dark corridor leading to Mrs. Siddons's dressing room, allocated temporarily to her use. The nausea that had plagued her for several days had fortunately subsided, but her head ached, and she longed for silence.

"Grace?"

Percival stood at the open door to the dressing room. His arm was still in a sling, and he'd lost so much weight that his coat hung off his shoulders. Even the cravat at his chin sagged. The handsome breaker of hearts, the man Grace once thought she could love, bowed stiffly. "A splendid ovation, my dear."

"I had not expected you." She entered the room and stood aside to let him pass. He sank gratefully onto the sofa. Grace had paid to have it recovered.

"Thank you, my dear. I'm afraid my days of sitting on a hard bench in the pit are over."

"You should have found a seat in one of the boxes."

"I could not get one. You saw how packed the theater was this evening. Everyone wanted to see Mr. Kemble's new protégé perform Ophelia. You did me proud, my dear."

"I did not do it for you."

"We must find a way forward, Grace. I've said I'm sorry about Betsy. The girl will be taken care of. Can we not let the past go?"

"I don't know, Percival. Can we?" She joined him on the sofa, her after-performance weariness at war with the triumph of conquest.

"You must know that I've loved you since the first time I saw you onstage in Bath when you dropped the dagger."

"You've never said."

The same shadow of hurt that Grace had glimpsed only occasionally flashed across his face. She remembered him mixing water for her wine when she was exhausted and confused by the riots. He could be gentle. He could be kind. Could she forgive him? She had done the same as he had, although he'd never know.

"Why did you come with me to rescue Ned?" she asked. "And please, don't tell me that the answer is obvious. It is not to me."

"Because I knew that you wanted me to."

"I have never said I loved you."

"No, Grace, but that is not to say you never will." The old Percival was back—smooth and confident.

"I cannot give up the stage." She gazed down at her clasped hands.

"I will not ask you to."

The more I give to thee, the more I have, for both are infinite.

Another spasm of nausea made the decision for her. She held out her hand for him to take.

෮෨

Ned found Olympia in the costume room. She had her back
to him. Mrs. Beecham was kneeling at her feet, pinning and
fussing. Olympia was playing Rosalind again in *As You Like
It*. She wore a new costume for the start of the new year. The
first few days after the theater re-opened in January had
been rough—the crowds dismayed to find that the
promised renovations to the second tier of boxes had not
been completed. The riots began all over again, but
fortunately lasted only a few nights. Mr. Kemble appealed
to the OPs sense of fair play—they could not expect the
boxes to be removed so swiftly—and the crowd settled.

"Olympia."

When she glanced over her shoulder at Ned, his heart
squeezed. With her hair gathered under a wide-brimmed
boy's cap adorned with a white feather, she was all eyes and
mouth—indescribably sweet. The blue tunic that Mrs.
Beecham was pinning came to just below Olympia's knees,
revealing calves clad only in pale-colored stockings. The
deep-red sash wrapped around her waist emphasized
rather than hid her figure. Mrs. Beecham took one look at
Ned and hastily scrambled to her feet.

"I've got to go check on Mrs. Siddons," she said. "Now
that she's back, she wants no end of attention to her
costumes."

Ned waited in silence for her to leave.

"You're looking very serious, Ned," Olympia said. She
pulled off her cap. The pins holding her hair fell, pinging as
they hit the floor. Hair the color of the polished stage
boards—brown and gold in the candles—cascaded down
her narrow back. Ned swallowed hard and stepped
forward.

"I heard your mother's gone back to the general."

"How do you know?"

"I got me ways, seein' as I guess you could say I'm interested, like." He reached for her hand. "What's stopping you now, Olympia?"

She stood very still. From the pit, she'd look like a lad just stepping into life. But close up, she was a woman with rounded cheeks and the face of Ned's dreams.

஫ఴ

"She said yes? You sure she's right in the head?"

Ned grinned at his friend. "You're just jealous. We're to be married in February. You'll come, won't you?"

"'Course I'll come. Wouldn't miss it, though I never expected either of us to get tangled up with the law."

"Marriage ain't getting tangled with the law, Alec."

"Close enough. You'll be bound to her forever, Ned. You know that, don't you? No more freedom for you."

"If you're worried about finding someone to share the room with, I can ask around. One of the callboys might be interested, or maybe a utility. Places ain't easy to find these days."

"Nah, you needn't bother." It was Alec's turn to grin. "You ain't the only one lookin' to get respectable."

"Daisy?"

"I told you she's gone and all. No—it's Mrs. Beecham at the theater I got me eye on. She's a fine-looking woman and makes a good income. I can't ask fairer than that."

"Have you asked her?"

"I'm gettin' round to it. What's the hurry?"

Ned slapped Alec on the back and ordered another two mugs of beer. "We've landed on our feet after all. Old Mrs. King wouldn't have believed it."

"She'd have believed it of you, Ned," Alec said.

"Why'd you say that?"

"Didn't I never tell you about the time she had me into her office?"

Ned shook his head.

"She told me to stay away from you, that I was a bad influence, like, and that you was too kind for your own good and that I wasn't to go corrupting you. She was a right bitch."

"Ah, well, what did she know?" Ned downed his beer in one gulp. "I got to get back. Olympia's waiting for me at the theater."

"Already she's got you by the short hairs."

Ned grinned and waved him away. A new life lay before him—one he never dared hope for. He was a lucky man and all.

Chapter Thirty-Eight

November 1810

Where joy most revels, grief doth most lament;
Grief joys, joy grieves, on slender accident.

Hamlet (3.3.193–94)

*G*race pulled the blanket tightly around her son to shield him from a sudden gust of autumn wind, then pulled open the stage door. It was her first day back at the theater since his birth four months earlier. Olympia met her in Mr. Harrison's room. She had promised to look after the baby while Grace went on as Juliet with Mr. Charles Kemble as her Romeo.

Olympia's own daughter had not been in the world for more than a few weeks, and Olympia had no plans to return to the theater. She confessed herself blissfully happy with married life. Grace couldn't help feeling a touch of envy mixed with happiness for her friend.

"Dear me, Grace. You'll smother the poor child. Here, give him to me." Olympia held out plump arms. "Percival is well?"

"His wound still pains him," Grace said. "The surgeon tells him he's not to ride anymore, but Percival ignores him, and I've given up trying to stop him. He has little enough to occupy his time. My aunt keeps a tight rein on the money she gives him."

"Your father?"

"My father still lives despite his best efforts to drink himself to death. He's even given up on his causes, more's the pity. At least there was a time in his life when he did some good in the world."

"Did he ever admit to spooking the mare?"

"No."

"You are content to let the past stay in the past?"

"What choice do I have?"

"At least your husband must be grateful that you've returned to the stage."

"I know very well that independence is a long way off for me," Grace said, smiling. "But, yes, I believe Percival is learning to be grateful. I have made him promise to be a better manager of *my money* than his father was of *his*."

"I wish you luck with that."

"You are contented, Olympia?"

"The example set for me by the general with my poor mother did not prepare me for such happiness," Olympia said, her cheeks dimpling.

"Ned is a lucky man."

"And you? Are you sure you're ready to go back onstage? People might think it's too soon since the birth of your son."

"Plenty of actresses have returned sooner," Grace said. She loosened the blanket from around the baby's chin. Solemn, brown eyes regarded her. Grace sometimes fancied that the child was peering into a world very different from the one in which he found himself.

"He's like his father," Olympia said.

"Yes, very like."

Grace kissed the baby's forehead, nodded a greeting to Mr. Harrison, who half rose from his chair, and then walked along the corridor to a small dressing room. It was nowhere near as elegant as the one provided for Mrs. Siddons, but it had the advantage of being for her sole use.

Ned had seen to it.

Author's Note

Several years ago, I was cleaning out my office (always a dangerous thing to do) and came across an essay I'd written when I was a graduate student many years earlier in the Centre for Drama at the University of Toronto. The essay described the Old Price Riots at the Theatre Royal, Covent Garden, in 1809. At the time I unearthed the essay, I was just finishing my first novel, *The Towers of Tuscany*, about a fictional woman artist in fourteenth-century Italy and was working on my second novel, *A Woman of Note*, about a fictional woman composer in nineteenth-century Vienna. I decided to complete my trilogy with a story about another woman in the arts — an actress. *The Muse of Fire* was born.

When I read a work of historical fiction that is based on real events, I love discovering which bits of the novel are fiction and which bits are real. In *The Muse of Fire*, fact and fiction are inextricably linked. Ned and Grace, along with Alec, Olympia, Thomas Renfrew, Percival and Augusta Knowlton, Charlotte and Tobias Johnson, Betsy the maid, and Mr. Harrison, are fictional. So far as I know, the Theatre Royal, Covent Garden, did not employ a stage manager with Ned's responsibilities, and a Grace Green never acted in any of the performances described. However, most of the performances mentioned in the novel are real, with the exception of the production of *Romeo and Juliet* in Bath and *As You Like It* in London. I must make posthumous apologies to the actresses and actors who took the roles that I assigned to Grace, Thomas, and Olympia. For example, the role of Lady Anne that Grace plays with such spirit several times during the OP Riots was actually played by Miss

Norton. All other actors mentioned, such as Mr. Cooke, who played the doomed Richard III, and Mr. Charles Kemble, who played Romeo to Grace's Juliet in *Romeo and Juliet*, are real. All references to roles taken by Mr. John Philip Kemble and Mrs. Siddons are also real.

Mr. John Philip Kemble (1757–1823) plays an integral role in *The Muse of Fire*. He was a force to be reckoned with, and most of the actions ascribed to him really happened. His conversations with Ned are fictional; however, his stubbornness in the face of the ongoing theater riots is both real and legendary.

Here's a partial list of all the real people and events mentioned in *The Muse of Fire* in the order in which they occur in the novel.

- Mrs. Sarah Siddons (1755–1831) was considered the greatest tragic actress of her time. Her most famous role was Lady Macbeth. With her striking figure and expressive eyes, "The Siddons" was the rock star of her era. She was also the sister of John Philip Kemble and Charles Kemble. Mrs. Siddons did not play Lady Macbeth opposite Mr. Thomas Renfrew in Bath, and she didn't have an understudy named Grace Green at the Theatre Royal, Covent Garden. However, Mrs. Siddons did appear as Lady Macbeth opposite her brother Mr. John Philip Kemble, who played Macbeth, on the opening night of the New Theatre Royal on September 18, 1809, and she did sweep off the stage declaring that she would not return until the disturbances were resolved. Mrs. Siddons did not act again at Covent Garden until January 1810. Two years later, she retired from the stage at the age of fifty-seven.

- Peg Woffington (1720–60) was an Irish actress discovered when she was a child in Dublin. She achieved great acclaim on the London stage, particularly for her performances in breeches parts, and was known to have several lovers including David Garrick, the great eighteenth-century tragedian.
- Mrs. Dora Jordan (1761–1816) was a famous comic actress, who appeared frequently at London's two Theatre Royals—Drury Lane and Covent Garden. She was particularly popular in the role of Rosalind in *As You Like It*—a breeches part assigned to Olympia Adams in the novel. Mrs. Jordan was also the long-time mistress of William, Duke of Clarence, later King William IV (the uncle of Queen Victoria). Mrs. Jordan had ten illegitimate children with the Duke of Clarence, and all of them took the surname FitzClarence. Mrs. Jordan's life ended sadly. She and the Duke of Clarence separated in 1811, and she eventually lost custody of all her children. She died penniless in Paris five years later at the age of fifty-five.
- The events related to the fire that devastated the Theatre Royal, Covent Garden, on September 20, 1808, occurred as written in the novel and claimed the lives of twenty-two people, including several firemen. Was the fire that burned the Theatre Royal to the ground started by unextinguished pistol wadding? No one really knows, but it is a popular theory. We do know for sure that Thomas Renfrew did not hand the smoking pistol to Grace and that she did not throw the pistol onto a pile of scripts.
- Mr. Richard Brinsley Sheridan (1751–1816) was the owner of the Theatre Royal, Drury Lane, where both

Mrs. Siddons and Mr. Kemble acted before moving to the Theatre Royal, Covent Garden. Sheridan was also a renowned parliamentarian and a famous playwright. *The School for Scandal* and *The Rivals* are considered his best works, although he also adapted the version of *Pizarro*, an extremely popular play of the period, that is described in the novel.

- The King's Theatre at the Haymarket featured Mr. Kemble and Mrs. Siddons in a production of *Douglas* shortly after the fire destroyed the Theatre Royal at Covent Garden. The pompous speech delivered by Mr. Kemble in the novel is reproduced exactly as reported in the press at the time.
- The Duke of Northumberland forgave a loan of £10,000 to build the New Theatre because of his gratitude to Mr. Kemble for teaching the duke's son elocution. The letter forgiving the loan is reproduced verbatim in the novel.
- The stone-laying ceremony for the New Theatre Royal, Covent Garden, on December 31, 1808, occurred almost exactly as described. Both Mr. Kemble and Mrs. Siddons stood next to the Prince of Wales (later King George IV), and both refused to hold umbrellas.
- Astley's Amphitheatre across the Thames in Lambeth presented its productions in the summer months. I've taken an historical liberty by setting the scene with Olympia in the late winter and having an elephant make a cameo appearance. Elephants and other wild animals, particularly lions and tigers, were not featured at Astley's until after 1825, when Astley's was acquired by a new owner.
- The Theatre Royal at Drury Lane did indeed burn down in February of 1809, leaving London without its two

patent theaters until the New Theatre Royal at Covent Garden opened in September.

- The riots began as described in the novel on Monday, September 18, 1809, with a production of *Macbeth* starring John Philip Kemble and his sister Mrs. Sarah Siddons. All the events related to the riots—the reading of the Riot Act; the committee struck to investigate the theater's finances; the OP placards, dances, and medals; and the productions mentioned in the novel—are real.

- Angelica Catalani (1780–1849) was one of the most celebrated sopranos of the time, particularly famous for her three-octave range. Her exorbitantly high fees (she was known to receive 200 guineas for singing *God Save the King* and *Rule Britannia*) and her Italian origins attracted the ire of the Old Price rioters, who booed her with cries of *Cat* and *Nasty Pussy*.

- Mr. George Frederick Cooke (1756–1812) was one of the principal actors at the Theatre Royal. He is famous both for his legendary binge drinking and for initiating the romantic style in acting later made famous by Edmund Kean. The role of Richard III was one of his most famous.

- Mr. Kemble hired professional pugilists Dutch Sam and Dan Mendoza to battle the rioters in early October 1809. The OP rioters particularly objected to Kemble hiring the boxers and would not stop the riots until Kemble apologized.

- Mr. Harrison mentions being booed when he played Hamlet in place of Mr. Garrick in the 1770's. While this event is fictional, theater riots occurred at both Drury Lane and Covent Garden throughout the eighteenth century for a variety of reasons, including ticket price increases, one actor taking roles associated with another actor, and disapproval of a particular playwright or play.

- Mr. Brandon, the box office keeper, was charged with assaulting and falsely arresting Mr. Henry Clifford, a lawyer and one of the leaders of the OP riots.
- Mr. Clifford and his cronies dined with Mr. Kemble at the Crown and Anchor Tavern in Covent Garden on December 14, 1809, and the terms of the peace were established.
- The riots ended on Friday, December 15, 1809, when Mr. Kemble finally apologized for hiring the boxers, and the *We are satisfied* banner was hoisted from the pit.

Acknowledgments

I am extremely fortunate to have many wonderful people who have helped me bring *The Muse of Fire* into the world. Mary Vingoe, Ruby Cram, Alison Bate, Tom McKeown, Mariana Holbrook, Katharine Vingoe-Cram, Julia Simpson, Maggie Bolitho, Lisa Voisin, Lynn Crymble, and Jacqueline Reiter read various drafts and sections of the novel and provided invaluable advice. Stephanie Williams, my friend forever and an amazing proofreader, was a tremendous help during the final editing of the novel. John Dowler cheerfully and expertly designed the cover. Marc Baer, professor emeritus at Hope College and the author of the marvelous *Theatre and Disorder in Late Georgian London*, patiently answered my questions about the OP Riots and read both an early and a later draft of the novel. Terry Robinson, assistant professor of English and Drama at the University of Toronto (my old alma mater!), kindly read the novel and corrected historical errors. Anthony Vickery, assistant teaching professor in the Theatre Department at the University of Victoria, provided me with insights about early-nineteenth-century stagecraft. I am also indebted to the encouragement of the late Professor Lise-Lone Marker at the University of Toronto, who many years ago made me believe I had a knack for writing. If any errors still remain, they are 100 percent my fault.

I particularly wish to thank both Jodi Warshaw and Danielle Marshall at Lake Union Publishing for their enthusiastic support; Jessica Murphy, my wonderful developmental editor, who helped me whip *The Muse of Fire* into shape; Mariette Franken at Kindle Press for shepherding the novel through the publication process; and Paul D. Zablocki for his insightful and much-appreciated copy edit. I'm also very grateful for the hard work and dedication of all the team at Lake Union Publishing and Kindle Press. And finally, as always, I owe everything to my wonderful family—my beautiful daughter, Julia Simpson; my remarkable mom, Ruby Cram; and my partner of over thirty years and my daily support and love, Gregg Simpson.

Selected Bibliography

All quotations from Shakespeare's plays are taken from *The Alexander Text of William Shakespeare: The Complete Works*. London and Glasgow: Collins, 1975.

Following are some of the books I consulted while writing *The Muse of Fire*.

Ashton, John. *The Dawn of the XIXth Century in England, A Social Sketch of the Times*. London: T. Fisher Unwin, 1886.

Baer, Marc. *Theatre and Disorder in Late Georgian London*. Oxford: Clarendon Press, 1992.

Brooks, Helen M. *Actresses, Gender, and the Eighteenth-Century Stage: Playing Women*. Basingstoke: Palgrave Macmillan, 2015.

Davidge, William. *Footlight Flashes*. New York: American News. Co., 1866.

Dibdin, Thomas. *The Reminiscences of Thomas Dibdin*. London: Henry Colburn, 1827.

Fyvie, John. *Tragedy Queens of the Georgian Era*. London: Methuen & Co., 1908.

Hartnoll, Phyllis. *The Theatre: A Concise History*, 4th ed., World of Art. New York: Thames & Hudson, 2012.

Johnson, Claudia D., and Johnson, Vernon E., comp. *Nineteenth-Century Theatrical Memoirs*. London: Greenwood Press, 1982.

Moody, Jane. *Illegitimate Theatre in London, 1770–1840*. Cambridge: Cambridge University Press, 2000.

Ranger, Paul. *"Terror and Pity Reign in Every Breast": Gothic Drama in the London Patent Theatres, 1750–1820*. London:

The Society of Theatre Research, 1991.

Richards, Kenneth and Thomson, Peter, eds. *Essays on the Eighteenth-Century English Stage*. London: Methuen & Co. Ltd., 1972.

Robinson, Terry F. "National Theatre in Transition: The London Patent Theatre Fires of 1808–1809 and the Old Price Riots." *BRANCH: Britain, Representation and Nineteenth-Century History*. Edited by Dino Franco Felluga. Extension of *Romanticism and Victorianism on the Net*. Web. August 29, 2017.

Stockdale, John Joseph. *The Covent Garden Journal*. London: Stockdale, 1810.

White, R. J. *Life in Regency England*. London: B. T. Batsford Ltd., 1963.

Book Club Questions

1. What is the nature of Grace's journey to becoming an actress? Consider the choices she makes in the novel. How does she grow and change?
2. What motivates Ned—is he a nice guy, or does he have his own demons to battle? How does he grow and change? Why does he want to stay away from women until finally he falls in love with Olympia?
3. Is Percival a sympathetic character? Why or why not?
4. Why has Tobias Johnson never been a good father to Grace? Tobias has a negative influence on Grace, but what is his point of view?
5. Why is Grace prepared to give up everything for the theater? Or is she?
6. What role does Olympia play in Grace's growth as a woman and an actress?
7. Why does Olympia suddenly agree to marry Ned?
8. Mr. Kemble was a real person. Why do you think he refused to accede to the demands of the OP rioters for so long, and then finally capitulated?
9. What does the novel show about the position of actresses in the early nineteenth century?
10. What does the novel suggest about the value and function of the theater in a society?
11. What is the theme of *The Muse of Fire*?
12. Hundreds of women found fame on the stage in the eighteenth and nineteenth centuries. Several of the most famous names are mentioned in the novel. Research the stories of Sarah Siddons, Dora Jordan,

and Peg Woffington to identify their influences on the development of British theater and to determine the challenges they faced in seeking a career on the stage.

13. Several actors are also mentioned in the novel, including John Philip Kemble, Frederick Cooke, David Garrick, and Charles Kemble. Research their stories—why were they famous? What innovations did they bring to the theater?

14. Isaac Cruikshank, a well-known political cartoonist in the early nineteenth century, created a wonderful series of cartoons about the Old Price Riots. Do a search for Cruikshank's cartoons and enjoy viewing the riots through his sardonic eye.

About the Author

Carol M. Cram is the author of three novels of historical literary fiction. Her first novel, *The Towers of Tuscany* (Lake Union Publishing, 2014) and her second novel, *A Woman of Note* (Lake Union Publishing, 2015) were both designated Editor's Choice by the Historical Novel Society in the UK. *A Woman of Note* won First in Category for the Goethe award and *The Towers of Tuscany* won the Grand Prize Chaucer Award for best historical novel pre-1750 (Chanticleer Book Awards). *The Muse of Fire* completes Carol's themed trilogy about women in the arts. Carol is also the author of over fifty bestselling college textbooks in computer applications and communications for a major US publisher (Cengage Learning) and was on faculty at Capilano University in North Vancouver for two over decades. Carol holds an MA in Drama from the University of Toronto and an MBA from Heriot Watt University in Edinburgh. She lives with her husband, painter Gregg Simpson, on beautiful Bowen Island near Vancouver, BC, where she also teaches Nia, a dance/fitness practice.